United We Fall

By

Joseph A. Mourgos

From

The Planet Jexx Series

Volume #1

Dedication

This book is dedicated to my parents, James and Esther Mourgos, for fostering my love of Science Fiction.

Acknowledgments

"Ride, Captain, Ride," Blues Image, 1970

"Sounds of Silence," Simon and Garfunkel, 1964

"Only the Lonely," Roy Orbison, 1964

Special thanks to my friends Janell, Gloria, Sarah, Tuesday, and Heath, and to my brother James for reading and critiquing my work and providing much-needed confidence.

Cover Art: Sarah Maksim

Cover Design: Joseph Sampson

Thank you all.

ISBN-13: 978-0997323801 2nd Edition.

PART ONE: Divided We Stand

CHAPTER ONE: Path to Redemption

Marine Captain Derrick Folsom enjoys riding his classic Indian motorcycle through the countryside. He normally has a date screaming in his ear as he takes the tight curves through Upstate New York. He likes to go fast to get their blood pumping, scare 'em a little. He smiles to himself at the memory of the last woman he brought into these hills.

He sees a curve ahead and notices his speed is fifty miles per hour. *Safety first, Derrick.* He slows to take the curve. His bike moves beautifully despite the wet conditions of the road.

On this cold, rainy afternoon in October 2061, he is alone. The joy of the ride is replaced by the bitter memories of his fallen comrades and how they perished under his command. *That was five years ago, but it seems like last week.*

Derrick slows below the speed limit while riding under the canopy of trees that shields his face from the rain. He enjoys the respite for a moment, but once in the open again, he thinks of the battle that cost him his squad.

Derrick cannot shake his share of responsibility for the ill-fated mission in Somalia, though there was plenty of blame to go around. Ordered by his commanding officer (CO) at literally the last minute to rescue the leader of the new African government, his team went in without proper intelligence. Over time, the families came to understand what was at stake. The media stopped asking questions and left him to his life.

The world didn't blame Derrick or his team for the bloodshed in Africa that became known as the most expensive learning experience of this century. He alone blames himself, even today.

Derrick pulls over at a turnout to remove his helmet and wipe the sweat from his brow. *What the hell kind of Marine am I?* he wonders before putting the helmet back on and moving forward.

The captain had been in the corps for the last fifteen years. He signed up at the age of twenty-two after completing studies at Ashford University in California with a degree in sociology. He joined out of respect for his father, who had served as a boom operator in the Air Force, but Derrick had loftier goals. *The Marines had cooler uniforms, too.* He likes to help people and saw the service as a stepping-stone to something greater.

His mother had been a teacher, so he found a way to honor them both by finishing Officer Training School (OTS) at the age of twenty-four and getting his commission as second lieutenant and first command in the country of Venezuela. His "official" duties involved bringing the nations of the South American continent together, though he suspects much of what he did involved spying for the CIA.

He hangs on to the idea that it was his actions and leadership that eventually led to the formation of the South American Federation. It was a great day for the people of the entire continent, who suddenly became citizens of what is now one country and thus a part of a smaller community of nations on Earth that once numbered in the hundreds just a few decades ago.

The success of the South American Federation garnered Derrick a promotion to first lieutenant. He and his people were then sent to similar duty in Somalia, though this time they were occasionally called upon to battle rebels who fought against the joining of all the countries on the continent into one.

On the verge of completing his mission, he was granted a promotion to the rank of captain. Then things got complicated.

"Globalization means less opportunity!" Derrick remembers hearing from the captured warlord responsible for the massacre of his Marines. *"It is not meant to help those who are in power, but those who have none!"*

Who knows? The power-hungry dictator may have had a point—just before the Marine captain put a bullet in his skull. *The fault in the idea of uniting the world as one people lies within the human desire to control and dominate*. Derrick thought at the time. "Power is a dangerous thing in the hands of fools," Derrick remembers telling his squad when they first hit the ground in Merca.

The rain is getting heavier now. Derrick looks down at the speedometer that reads seventy. *How did that happen?* He eases back on the accelerator.

The last few years have seen an increase in the acceptance of the one-world government plan. President Dobson of the United States has led the way from the beginning but has recently stepped up his efforts. *Another power-hungry dictator in the making.*

Once the world is one, under one flag and one government, the greatest election in history will take place for the first time. There will be hundreds of candidates vying for the job of first premier of planet Earth. *There's no way it's going to work. If you bring two cultures together, they'll take the best of each other and move on. If you take seven cultures and do the same, there will be resentment and hate that will lead to conflict.* Derrick shakes his head as he discovers that he is doing seventy again.

There are currently eleven government entities in the world. The European Union and Asian Alliance are complete, for the most part, with only Iran and China left to resist. The South American Federation and African Union are working well, amazingly, leaving only Canada, the United States, and Mexico to work out the details of becoming one nation on the North American continent.

The Caribbean Islands, including Cuba, will fall in line soon, "whether they want to or not," it has been said. Australia, New Zealand, and most Pacific Island nations have come together under the "Aussie Pact."

Folsom became captain on the eve of African unification, when a peaceful transition of power was taking place. The kidnapping of Kamal Maw changed all that. Derrick's team was called in the dead of night to perform a rescue in the town of Merca, where rebels were holding the minister in a hotel.

With the unity of Africa at stake, Derrick took his veteran team—Sergeant David Gallow, Corporal Lance Barnes, Corporal Vanessa Hush, Lance Corporal Rebecca "Becky" Wells, and Lance Corporal Jason Flowers—into harm's way.

The intelligence was good as far as location—the town of Merca, a few miles south of Mogadishu. They knew what hotel the minister was being held in and where it was. The strength of their enemy was grossly underestimated, however, leading to the bloodbath that killed his Marines.

Derrick was lucky to have survived and has the scars to prove it. He even accepted the African Service Medal for his heroic act of saving the minister, which allowed the unification of the continent to move forward.

He takes a wide curve with care, mindful of the slick conditions of the highway. *I've got solitude out here—that's comforting.* Sarcasm aside, he pulls out of the curve and throttles up just a bit.

Derrick continues along Highway 95 near the town of Oakfield, where Lance Corporal Wells's father, who is a sculptor, erected a monument to the massacre in Merca. The old man designed and built the bronze statue depicting the battle from the Marines' point of view, showcasing their bravery under impossible odds.

At the time of its construction, Derrick questioned the placement of Wells's daughter, the first to die, against a wall with her comrades around her in a defensive pose. Corporal Hush was the medic who saw to Becky's wounds, which were too extensive for her to be of any use. The pain in her face is evidence of her feeling of futility.

She was his only child, after all. Derrick takes another curve, carefully.

Today, Derrick works from his home in New York City. He has an office in the Pentagon but rarely goes there except to show the uniform at various functions that require his presence. When given a choice, he resists the limelight and the inevitable questions that accompany that light. *Civilians want to know what battle is like but don't want the story told in great detail—which seems rather pointless.*

He is proud of the work he does that involves intelligence interpretation; his reports give commanders valuable information on how to deal with the people under their control in various parts of the world. *I'm still bringing the world together despite my personal feelings on globalization—that's ironic.* He smiles as he takes one more curve in the road. *Almost there.*

Captain Folsom's name had come up in the past year as being eligible for promotion to major and a possible move to the White House, but he turned it down immediately. He knew that such a promotion and transfer would jeopardize his happiness. The Marine Corps may question his actions in the future, but today they're content with a should-be major who likes to take rides into the countryside on a rebuilt motorcycle from a century ago to clear his head.

Over the last mile, Derrick feels the wind picking up as his bike effortlessly climbs the last of the hills. It's a good bike. *My baby.* His smile fades as he comes upon the cemetery and enters the meadow of the dead. He rides slowly, out of respect for those resting in peace for a half-mile on either side of him, until he comes upon the monument at the center of the meadow. The bronze statue sits on a small precipice to raise it above the grave markers of the soldiers surrounding it. There is a space reserved for Derrick when he leaves this Earth, though it is not something he pays attention to.

Derrick kills his engine with a turn of the ignition key. It feels ten degrees colder now as the peaceful sound of the rain taps his plastic uniform cap cover, replacing the quiet roar of his bike as he contemplates the lives of his people who died for a cause. *Not mine and not theirs*. He gets off the Indian and walks the last ten meters to the first grave marker, that of Sergeant David Gallow.

Derrick has dropped to a knee to say a quick prayer when he feels the presence of someone behind him. At least whoever it is has enough respect not to interrupt him until he rises. He turns to see two men standing before him, the older of whom he recognizes from five years past, his former commanding officer, William Childs. *What the hell?* Childs is now a general, and the star on his shoulder stands out even in this dim light.

"He was a good man," Childs says as he looks over the monument before finishing the thought. "They were all good Marines."

Captain Folsom looks his former commander in the eye. Standing next to the general is a lieutenant who holds an umbrella over his superior's head despite being a foot shorter. *We all have to start somewhere.* Derrick thinks of the poor soul on umbrella duty while addressing the general. "How would you know that, *sir*?" He finishes the last word with disdain in his voice. This man dares compliment the people he sent to die?

"I've read your reports," Childs shoots back.

The captain steps closer to Childs, realizing that all good commanders are aware of the necessity of sending soldiers into battle under difficult circumstances, knowing that they may not come home. A commander who is unable to face those difficult decisions won't be one for long.

Childs's career spans decades.

What took him so long to acknowledge his people's bravery? Derrick can't guess, but instead says, "When did you get promoted to general, *sir*?"

Childs smiles as he pretends to polish the star on his right shoulder. "Right after Africa became a country instead of a continent. I have you to thank for that, and for this."

Smug bastard.

Folsom slowly shakes his head in disbelief before kneeling in front of the next grave marker, that of Corporal Lance Barnes. He lowers his head to say a short and sincere prayer in his heart for the young man who was especially close to him. Always trying to please, volunteering for anything and everything to gain attention and respect and not caring about a little thing called risk. *Not outwardly, anyway.*

Derrick feels the rain stop. No, the general motioned for “umbrella boy” to hold the portable canopy over Derrick’s head. He continues his prayer in silence, using his Marine Corps discipline to hold his rising anger in check.

Childs’s laugh is more of a short chuckle before he speaks again. “Religion is meant to be private, captain, that’s why we closed the churches.”

Folsom stands, ignoring the general’s comment and moving to the next grave marker, that of Corporal Vanessa Hush, a strong woman in more ways than one. She had intelligence and bravery like most Marines, but she also had grace.

So much grace.

She would have taken a bullet for a comrade without a second thought. *Even this son of a bitch.*

Dropping to a knee and bowing his head, Derrick asks, “Why don’t you rewrite the constitution again, *sir*?”

Childs smiles. "Once the world is together as one, it will be. But first things first, captain. Our duty didn't end with Africa's unification."

Folsom stands, not missing a beat. "What countries are left that we haven't influenced to join the global community? Not everyone is keen on the idea, sir." He turns to the young lieutenant still holding the umbrella over his head. "I'm going over there," he says as he points to the next grave marker five feet away. "You best not follow."

The lieutenant is confused and looks to the general for guidance. His expression betraying his thoughts. *Why would someone want to get soaked? The rain is getting worse.* Childs motions for the young man to return to the staff car at the foot of the small hill. The kid moves quickly. He walks with dignity, but fast, and at least smart enough to say nothing.

"Captain—*Derrick*, I'm here under orders from the president to develop and train a team of intelligence people made up of military sources from all over the world who will act for the security of the planet," the general says.

Derrick stands from Becky Wells's grave, having prayed and adjusted the African Service Medal on his uniform. *We all got one; only mine was not posthumous.* "How does better security unite the world? We're just a few years away from becoming one government, general. Just whom are we securing the planet from? Ourselves? Is this to be the new control system of the world?" Derrick slaps the rubber-like device attached snugly to his forearm to drive his point home. "I hate my shackle."

"I wish you wouldn't use the slang term for the my-sat-com device, but even I have to wear one." Childs says as he raises his arm to prove it.

"Everyone over thirteen is required to wear it, that's why they're called shackles. It's how you tracked me here, no doubt."

The general leans closer, in case their shackles are "listening." "There are forces outside of our sphere of influence that may intend to do us harm."

Derrick holds back his laughter. "Aliens?" Is that what you're talking about?"

The general isn't laughing. "Possibly." His face is emotionless, just like it was five years ago in the headquarters bunker outside Mogadishu.

"I like my job, sir." The emphasis on the last word is gone. "Thanks anyway," Derrick says as he turns and kneels before the last grave marker, that of Lance Corporal Flowers, last in rank but not in integrity. He bows his head to say a prayer similar to the others, from his heart.

Each of them holds a special place there.

General Childs is glad the captain didn't have a squad of ten as he rolls his eyes and checks his shackle for the time. The sky is darkening, forcing the fifty-something officer to squint at the small hologram the shackle produces to deliver information. There is no screen to look at. The rain is getting colder too. Childs tightens the coat around his neck as he watches the rain run down his captain's dark-skinned face. *Or is that a tear?*

"I need a good team to start the world off on a sure footing. I want you leading it," he says.

Globalization is a joke, but this team made up of individuals from many countries is the punchline, Derrick thinks but doesn't say as he stands from the last grave and looks Childs in the eyes. "I've written papers and opinion pieces on the subject of globalization. Seven or eight governments representing the planet that work together for the betterment of mankind is a good thing, general. The president's goal of uniting the world under a single government is outrageous. There will always be people who will resist."

"Precisely why this team is needed. They will act for the planet, not for the government."

Derrick, standing toe to toe with his former superior, is about to be insubordinate but holds back. "That's been tried before, you know."

Childs continues the sales pitch, "The president told me as much himself."

"So we'll be hunting aliens." Derrick scoffs as he turns away, intent on getting back to his motorcycle.

"Among other duties. I will explain everything in due course. Report to my office at the Pentagon in a week to read up on the assignment and sign the appropriate documents. I'll talk to your CO about your transfer."

Derrick becomes livid, turning abruptly and charging the general. Childs doesn't flinch, even when the two men are nearly touching each other. "Now I don't have a choice? I thought I said NO!" Derrick steps back, pursing his lips. *Have I gone too far? This bastard hasn't seen anything yet. And to disrespect me in front of my squad is*…"Sir!"

Childs softens his tone, trying a different tack. "Derrick, you need this. You've been coming here every year since the mission in Merca. Your people are dead. It's time to move on. I'm giving you a golden opportunity here—take it."

"You've been watching me that long?"

"I've watched you beat yourself up. You're not responsible for their deaths, captain."

No, YOU are! Derrick doesn't say, though he wishes he could. Spent of adrenaline, he mutters, "They haunt me."

Childs puts his arm around the shoulders of his captain, whom he respects, and offers consolation, something new to him. "Of course they do. Let them go and the nightmares will go with them."

Derrick wonders if he has been wrong about the general; maybe this man does have feelings after all. "Are you speaking from experience, sir?"

"Just common sense." The general says the last with a smile as he walks back to his staff car, passing Derrick's motorcycle as he does so.

The young lieutenant must be watching, as the car's antigravity engines hum to life. *Perhaps the kid is not so worthless after all*. Childs chuckles at the sight of Derrick's bike. "The position includes an antigravity staff car. I'll spring for a decent cycle for you!"

In silence, Captain Derrick Folsom watches his former superior get into his staff car, the antigravity vehicle floating two feet off the ground, and waits for it to speed away.

Such vehicles are a wonder to behold. They are of a new technology, the source of which no one outside of government knows. The vehicles just appeared overnight, practically. They are available only to the super-rich and some powerful governments. They move in relative silence but for the hum of their generator.

"I could always resign," Derrick says, not to himself, but to those resting around him, seeking their counsel. He sits on the centerpiece of the monument and thinks as the intensity of the rain increases. It feels cold enough to be snowing.

Or is that just me?

CHAPTER TWO: The Plan

The Milky Way galaxy is made up of thousands of independent worlds, some advanced, some just on the verge of discovering fire; others still have been around since the beginning of known time and have formed the basis of government by which the galaxy is run.

The galaxy also consists of several great and powerful empires. The greatest of these are the Vorelisians. The Vorelisian Empire is a collection of hundreds of planets under one rule. The leadership is made up of representatives from each of these worlds, with a lord ruling over them all.

Worlds not represented in the Imperial Chamber of Vorelis include those that are colonies of one that *is* represented. Others are planets with primitive populations considered "untouchable" and "protected" by the laws of the Galactic Council, the supreme ruling power of the galaxy, much like the United Nations was on Earth a quarter of a century ago, before it was dissolved.

The laws of the Galactic Council are created under the collective will, and vote, of the members of the assembly. The process is democratic in scope and has existed for thousands of years. Resolutions put forth by the Galactic Council are enforced by the military arm of the Security Council, the Galestikons.

The Thimmi Empire is the main adversary of the Vorelisians. They have a 30 percent higher population and devote the majority of their economy to the deterrence of the more advanced Vorelisian military machine. It has been said that Thimmi military technology is made up of stolen Vorelisian technology from decades past.

A single leader, simply called "the great leader," leads the Thimmi government. This leader uses the military to maintain order on the planets he rules. A dynastic regime, the Thimmi Empire has annexed some worlds upon request, while others have been conquered or coerced into submission. The Thimms are also very good at terraforming and colonizing uninhabited planets in the creation of more colonies. Few worlds in Thimmi territory are "untouchable".

The Vorelisians and Thimms share a common border for a thousand light-years and have each won and lost battles over planets along that border. These battles have cost the lives of billions. As each society improves its civilization, war comes to be seen as an unacceptable alternative in the eyes of the people on both sides.

Therefore, in the case of the planet Jexx, the two sides agreed to petition the Galactic Assembly to make the decision for them as to which side should be the rightful owner. A vote was held within the Assembly of ten thousand, resulting in a tie.

The vote was taken five hundred years ago, and Jexx remains uninhabited.

The Vorelisians and Thimms have lived in relative peace since, with just this one splinter under their collective skins. The planet Jexx has a history, as most worlds do. This one involves a meteor that destroyed all life on the planet seven millennia ago, and it has just recently returned to habitability. Both the Vorelisians and Thimms have a legitimate claim to it, as the planet's parent star wobbles across the border due to the pull of the planet upon it as it orbits.

The vote in the Galactic Assembly is repeated every few decades, always with the same result.

Tie.

Every lord and great leader who followed has tried various schemes to win Jexx for his respective empire, and each scheme has failed every time. With another vote scheduled to be made approximately twelve years from now, the two sides have hatched new plans.

With polls and secret tallies being made by both sides, the Vorelisians took the first step in a plan to better their chances. A young lieutenant by the name of Xaix concocted the idea of sponsoring an unknown world into the galactic membership.

The inhabitants of the selected world would have to be united as one people to be eligible for membership into the assembly. It is expected that this new member would then reward their sponsor with a vote in their favor. The first vote of this newest member would then give Vorelis the planet Jexx. The technology level is irrelevant. Several possible candidate worlds were presented to the Vorelisian lord, and his decision was based on wormhole proximity to their empire. His choice would not dare be disputed.

Earth.

To accomplish the mission of bringing Earth together as a united people, the Vorelisians dispatched one man, Dr. Charles Lightner, from his home on the border planet of Paal to the planet Seara and through the wormhole that connects it to Earth.

The humans of Earth must cooperate.

The Thimms, upon becoming aware of the Vorelisian plan through their spy network, sent an agent of their own to Earth to introduce the people to a greater society and hopefully thwart the Vorelisian agent's influence.

The Thimmi agent's name is Captain Arno Pilas.

Lightner and Pilas are human in appearance, and roughly the same age, but with very different life experiences. Both are educated to a high level, Lightner is a scientist with a well-rounded resume in several disciplines, and Pilas is an officer in the Thimmi military with several battles under his belt, on land, sea and in space.

Humanoid beings are commonplace throughout the galaxy, with few exceptions. The differences between most peoples depend on the mass of their respective worlds and the environments where they have evolved.

A larger planet with high gravity would cause its people to have stronger bones and greater strength when compared to an average citizen on a planet with a lower gravity.

Pilas is from the Thimmi planet Opfinia, which lies as close to its parent star as Venus does to the sun. The hot environment and close proximity to the planet's star gives the Thimmi captain smaller eyes than an Earth human and a light-orange complexion.

Lightner's complexion is light red. It stands out in sharp contrast to his off-white hair. On Earth, he looks twenty years older than his young age of forty, and appears to have permanent sunburn.

Upon landing, both agents worked to limit their contacts with people to avoid questions as to their appearance. Both men were chosen for their ability to "fit in" on Earth, a relatively small planet by comparison to their home worlds.

For the last ten years or so, Lightner and Pilas have gone about trying to bring the world together as one people and recognize the need to speed up the process as the next vote nears.

As a scientist, Lightner is the gift giver, presenting the world with technologies that will, in a short period of time, end famine, drought, most sicknesses, and cancer. At the proper time, as the public becomes aware of him, he will introduce himself as a friend to the Earth.

Pilas, however, is going the political route. He has revealed himself to the current president of the United States and, since his arrival, has manipulated the man into completing diplomatic negotiations with several continents, thereby forming the basis for globalization. He does not, however, know of the formation of the Earth Defense Force, or EDF.

Ten years is a long time for a man to live away from home. Loneliness sets in, coupled with boredom and certain needs; the lives Lightner and Pilas lead outside of their mission objectives are subject to approval by their respective governments.

Eight years into his infiltration into scientific circles, Charles Lightner took a week to craft a request to be allowed to seek out a member of the opposite sex for companionship. Headquarters reluctantly agreed. Within a few months, he was fortunate to meet a woman who is a senator from Nevada and head of the Senate Committee on Scientific Progress. Her name is Madeline Verona.

CHAPTER THREE: The Power of the Sun

The small twenty-seater bus travels across the Nevada desert floor at two hundred miles per hour. Doctor Lightner is in the back, watching the sun set to his left as the antigravity vehicle speeds past the Bullfrog Mountains. *Almost there.*

Rising in the east, setting in the west, due to the rotation of the planet from west to east. He smiles at the simplicity of how Earthers teach their children the principle of *sunset*. He was learning the names of stars and measuring their distances when he was a child. Back home on Paal, they filled the sky like nowhere else in the galaxy because of the lack of nebula obstruction between his world and the galactic center.

Madeline Verona, committee chairman and senator from the Silver State, slowly approaches Charles, watching him stare out the window, seemingly in a trance as she sits next to him. The bus's engines hum quietly, allowing her to speak softly into his ear, unnoticed by the other members of congress, who don't know the status of their relationship. He's not sure he does, either.

"What are you thinking about?" she asks.

He looks into her green eyes, admiring her face and the bright blond hair that frames it perfectly. He hesitates for a moment, wondering how he was able to attract such a beautiful lady.

Madeline was conceived when genetic alterations were becoming all the rage. Two people could bring a child into the world who looks nothing like either of them if they so choose, a side effect of the scientific goal to weed out imperfections and defects. People no longer need glasses and no longer suffer from asthma or other cardiopulmonary ailments. On average, more people are taller than in the last generation and tend to live up to ninety-five rather comfortably.

"You," he says as he smiles and touches her hair. *Like silk.*

"If you're trying to win me over to advance your Soliquid agenda, you're succeeding," she says with a chuckle as she leans over to kiss him on the lips.

Soliquid is by far the most important gift he can give to humanity. After this, he will be able to reveal himself to the world, but by doing so, he could lose her.

She pulls back, catching his eyes scanning the bus. "What's the matter? We don't have to keep our relationship secret anymore. We've been together for two years. Frankly, I think the cat is already out of the bag."

He sees the Soliquid plant in the distance, the particle accelerator tubes taking up miles of desert land. "I know, I'm just a little nervous. I need this project to succeed." He came close to saying *for my government*, but he has never been one to commit a Freudian slip.

She runs a hand across his chest as she tries to read his face, wondering if he ever uses the creams she buys him for his sunburn. “You spend too much time outside.” She observes as the bus slows. “We’re here.”

The engine hum goes silent and the bus lowers itself onto small stands lowered from the vehicle itself that protect the spinning antigravity magnets from touching the ground.

The nine congressmen and women who have accompanied the senator and the doctor have gotten off the cool air-conditioned bus and into a hair dryer set on full. The evening air is hot even with the sun down. The high temperature feels good to Charles. It reminds him of home.

The Soliquid property is a forty-acre field of solar panels with particle accelerator tubes stretching out from the three-story plant into the desert for miles before circling back to its opposite side. A small car could fit inside these tubes.

Once Charles’s planned Soliquid plants start producing energy in mass quantities, there will no longer be a need for the humans of Earth to fight over resources. He will then make the announcement to the world: *"Peace is here, and the Vorelisians have brought it to you. Join us!"*

Madeline is concerned about Charles's aloofness. She takes his arm as he follows the others to the front gate. "Hey, can we talk about this?" Her grip is firm, but she does not seem alarmed. She has no fear.

Charles stops. He doesn't pull away. He loves this woman, and he loves his empire, but he cannot serve both. *I have a mission to accomplish. I cannot reveal myself to her, not yet.* He struggles within his mind about what to say. *Not now.*

As she has stated, they've been together for two years. She looked into his past, as anyone getting into a relationship should. She couldn't find anything prior to ten years ago and didn't think that was suspicious. Perhaps she was blinded by her attraction to him. She only knows that she loves him for who is now. She wrote it off, having told her friends that he's no longer "off the grid," a phrase that refers to someone without a shackle.

As of a year ago, not having a working shackle within five feet of its owner is punishable by eighteen months in a new prison-city somewhere in northern New Mexico. Charles has said that he received his shackle when he arrived in North America, and Madeline believed him, though he doesn't sound Scottish at all. His accent is more Boston-Irish.

She doesn't know that his Vorelisian device is disguised to only resemble a shackle. The rubberized unit fits snugly against his lower arm, between the wrist and elbow.

"We'll talk later," he says, convinced that he's making the right decision to tell her the truth about him. After all, he may need her support if the people react with fear instead of the trust he is hoping for when the time comes. *What of her fear?* he asks himself.

Madeline lets go of his arm and whispers, "Dinner tonight?"

"Of course." He finishes with a genuine smile that melts her heart, the way it had when she first met him at a Congressional hearing. Back then, he sold the idea of African unity with the use of desalination plants along the Atlantic and Indian Ocean borders; areas long abandoned by drought have come back to life and have been repopulated. The African Union leaders know him, as does a growing portion of the world, as the greatest genius the world has ever known.

Now he's selling the idea of Soliquid, a powerful new energy source of solar-power molecules mixed with various gases like nitrogen, hydrogen, or helium, depending on the level of power required. Vorelisian scientists have used other gases in centuries past, before the advent of ion weapons or gravimetric explosives, but the Earthers don't need to know about them—yet. This new power source will liberate nations from fossil fuels and usher in a new era of peace for the world.

Madeline follows Charles into the complex along with the rest of the group. She contemplates their relationship with a degree of insight. Now in her late thirties, Madeline has come to the conclusion that previously, she has attracted a certain kind of man—the *wrong* kind. But Charles Lightner is a different kind of man, a departure from the men she has dated in the past. She's never met anyone like him anywhere on Earth.

Nor will she.

CHAPTER FOUR: Captain Arno Pilas

The sixty-sixth president of the United States is Richard Dobson, a heavyset man in his fifties who is currently serving his third term in the White House. His greatest accomplishment, next to establishing shackles as the only legal means of electronic communication, is the abolition of term limits for those of his office. During his first term, he argued, *"The people must have the freedom to decide whom they want to lead them. Term limits quash*es *that freedom*!"

As a concession to Congress, the amendment to the Constitution he proposed did not include an establishment of term limits for those in the House and Senate.

Of course, while this distraction of government was happening, Dobson awarded the shackle-manufacturing contract to his cousin in Minnesota.

The man is ruthless. With an 80 percent approval rating among the people and the military supporting him, he can afford to be. Richard Dobson fears no one, with the possible exception of the man entering the Oval Office. He is Captain Arno Pilas of the Thimmi Empire, and while Madeline knows not where her love hails from, Dobson knows this man very well.

Pilas removes the trench coat, scarf, hat, and sunglasses that conceal his skin and eyes as he approaches the president's desk. He sits in one of the plush chairs in front of it, allowing himself to enjoy the feel of it for a moment before speaking. He speaks with a raspy voice, as if his throat is constricted. *Is the air on this planet causing that? What does he sound like on his home world?* Dobson wonders as the alien says, "Mister President, I am pleased, as always, to meet you in person."

Dobson stares at the orange-skinned man before him and turns away. *Damn, his eyes are tiny,* he thinks as he cautions himself against leering for too long. Not wanting to appear rude to his guest, he continues his motion toward the refreshments that lie on a small cart to his right. *Son of a bitch looks like a 50/50 ice cream bar.* "Can I offer you something, Captain Pilas?"

Pilas's breathing becomes labored for a moment as he looks over the choices available. He coughs and reaches into his inside breast pocket for a pill. The little red miracle is supposed to assist in breathing thin air by expanding lung capacity.

Dobson turns toward him while holding out a glass of California red wine. "I must apologize for the thin air of my planet. You told me it was twenty percent thinner than your home planet of… I forget the name. Should I order an oxygen tank for you?"

Pilas reads his face., *No, this man wouldn't forget a detail like that.* "Opfinia is my home world, and I wish to get back to it eventually." He takes the wine and continues, "I'm getting used to the air on this little planet. I'm fine."

Dobson returns to the seat behind his desk. He watches Pilas down the wine as if it was his first drink after hiking all day in Death Valley in July. "Do your people make wine?"

"My planet is too hot to grow grapes. We import most of our food, including this wine of yours, but this is usually reserved for the privileged."

"Does anything grow naturally there?"

"We have trees that produce a thin sap that is good for drinking. It is similar to milk." Pilas runs his hand over his short brown hair, looking as if he's ready for his first day in the Marine Corps.

An awkward silence follows. Dobson knows why Pilas is here: to get an update on globalization. Dobson quickly clears his desk of papers and pictures of his dog. Underneath is a built-in ultra-high-definition monitor. He turns it on with his shackle to reveal a map of the world. He speaks quickly, defensively, as a victim would before a mob boss. "You'll be happy to know that the formation of the United States of North America is complete. There are only minor hurdles to overcome before the entire planet can be joined under one flag."

Pilas stands to get a better look at the crisp, clear map that takes up most of the four-by-six foot desk. The image is not unlike old World War II battle maps that generals would routinely hover over as they planned their strategy for conquest. “Iran and China,” he mumbles as he looks upon those particular countries, colored in black with white lettering. They stand out like a sore thumb compared to the others that are color-coded by affiliation: the European Union is blue, the African Union is yellow, and so forth.

“What of them?” Pilas asks, his voice rising with a note of impatience.

Dobson is ready for that question, and he says with confidence, “Once the unions are complete, Iran and China will join the world peacefully. Just a few more years, I estimate. The political and economic pressures would simply—”

Pilas, leaning on the screen, looks closer at China as if able to see cities. The map is not a satellite image, but a simple graphic representation. He glances up to meet the president’s eyes. He’s less than a foot away. “I want you to think in terms of months, Mister President. Not years. My superiors will not be too happy with you if I report that you are—how do you say?—dragging your feet.”

“What can I do?” Dobson chuckles, the nervousness growing in his stuttering voice, “I can’t take their lands by force. Diplomacy takes time, captain!”

Pilas stands up straight, his patience wearing thin. "No, what takes time is the process of sponsoring Earth into the Galactic Community of Worlds. What takes time is the voting that will take place among the thousands of ambassadors in the assembly." Pilas gets nose to nose with the most powerful man on the face of the Earth and ends his speech. "The first vote you will take part in will award the planet Jexx to the Thimmi Empire. We've waited five hundred years, Mister President. We will not wait a second longer than necessary."

"I understand." Dobson watches Pilas walk to the cart to get another glass of wine for himself, then continues, "I wish there was a way I could—" He stops mid-sentence as Pilas sits back down, smiling in a way that unnerves Dobson further. *Why the hell is he smiling?*

Pilas's tone changes to one of eerie calmness. "You have a gift of leadership and a desire for power, Mister President, faculties I do not possess, though I do admire them. I have faith in you and your abilities to solve the problem of division plaguing your world and to unify it."

Not sure where the alien is going with this line of communication, Dobson answers, "Th—thank you." *I think*, he doesn't add.

Pilas laughs at the president's discomfort. "Allow me to offer you another incentive I think you'll understand." The smiling and respect gone from his tone, Pilas pulls a small computer from his coat. Powerful enough to control a spaceship's flight to Mars and back, though as small as a cell phone, he rests it on the president's desk so the content he shows will appear on it.

Pilas runs a video, seemingly real, showing a fleet of large spaceships, each as big as a city, using tractor beams to tow an asteroid into the path of a lush and beautiful green-and-blue planet. It's obviously not Earth, but Dobson gets the message pretty fast when he witnesses the asteroid smash into the planet, turning it into a yellow and black ball of fire.

The video ends. The most powerful man in the world has just been schooled on what real power is. He looks up at Pilas. The once cooperative and benevolent alien has a look of hatred that he hadn't seen in the ten years since they first met in this very office. Sweat beads on the president's forehead like drops of rain on the windshield of a parked car.

After another long silence, Pilas speaks at last. "They never knew what was coming until it was too late. We gave them enough warning to beg our forgiveness, but…" his voice trails off as he picks up his computer device and returns it to his pocket. He sits and begins anew, his attitude changed as quickly as light to dark when the switch is clicked. "Do not tell me what is impossible, Dobson. Tell me what *is* possible."

"I will put pressure on Iran and China," Dobson says. "You will have a united Earth very soon. I must win the election of first premier to complete the plan for you."

Pilas rolls his eyes, though it'd be difficult for anyone to notice. *This leader is like a child who's been promised his favorite candy bar.* "You will rule over this world until the day you die, just as we promised."

Pilas retrieves his coat, gloves, and hat. "It's late, sir. You really should get some sleep. You look tired."

Dobson cannot see the smirk of satisfaction behind the alien's scarf. "I'll do that," he says with little sincerity as the door closes behind Pilas. He waits a couple of minutes for his hands to stop shaking before using his shackle to contact General Childs.

A holographic image of the general appears in front of him a moment later. "Good evening, Mister President. What can I do for you, sir?"

Dobson wipes away the sweat that has formed around his mouth. *Compose yourself, dammit!* "Childs, I need to step up the timetable for that defense team we discussed last month."

“I’m on my way to India right now, sir. Minister Shabal promised me a candidate, and then I’m going to visit an old friend in China who owes me a favor.”

“Excellent.” His confidence returning, Dobson kills the connection and sits back in his chair. *I know I’m going to have to kill that alien bastard somehow, someday, soon. Patience, Dobson. Patience.*

***

The president of the United States retires to his residence in the White House alone. He is in his element when he walks the halls of an empty building, even one as large as this one. He has no wife or children. He has spent his entire life working to obtain more power. With every step up the ladder of politics, there has always been another rung. He didn’t think there’d be anything beyond the presidency of the United States until Pilas came along with the promise of ruling the world.

As Dobson lies in bed, contemplating the next step upward in his bid for world control, he thinks of Pilas. *I am using him to further my career, but he is also using me*. An idea pops into his mind, one that will make Iran and China sit up and take notice. He puts on his shackle that was lying on the nightstand to his left. No one, not even the leader of the free world, is exempt from being close to his device at all times, lest the National Security Agency (NSA) be summoned by it.

Diplomatic pressure hasn't worked in the past. I don't see it working now. It's time to bring in an operations specialist. He tells his shackle to contact someone who has no trouble sleeping in these situations, CIA Director Dennis McCarthy.

McCarthy comes on a moment later, looking tired at one in the morning. *He managed to straighten what few hairs he has left on his head at least.* Dobson reveals his plan to the director, careful not to mention the involvement or even the existence of the Thimmi Captain Pilas. Everyone under his command must be kept unaware of his dealings with an alien force, lest it create a panic, or worse, jeopardize his goal of becoming first premier.

McCarthy and Dobson discuss the plan until one forty-five. Afterward, the president wallows in his satisfaction. *This is going to be perfect.*

Who needs sleep to dream?

CHAPTER FIVE: The Lieutenants

The Rambili Mandal Naval Base lies on the east coast of India near the city of Vishakhapatnam. It is home to several dozen anti-aircraft, anti-submarine, and amphibious warships, as well as a small fleet of rescue ships. One such vessel, the *Karakorum*, is in port. The ship has been rotated in while the other four of its type remain on patrol in the Indian Ocean and beyond. It is the size of a destroyer but lightly armed.

The sailors of the *Karakorum* have scattered for their shore leave faster than a pack of mice in a warehouse that spot a hungry cat for the first time in their lives. The last group off the ship has just sped away in a crew bus, signing with joy and leaving the lone token security guard on the dock envious.

Thirty minutes later, First Lieutenant Shanti Dae steps off the ship and onto the dock proper. The short trip elevates her heart rate as she passes the gap between ship and dock. *I know better than to look down.* She is carrying several bags, appearing to be holding everything she owns while wearing most of her civilian wardrobe.

She makes her way across the dock, cursing herself for missing the bus. She has just been traded like a Babe Ruth rookie card. *If only I was as valuable to the government.* She carries her possessions with relative ease on her five-foot-seven frame.

Shanti doesn't feel that any of her shipmates will miss her much, at least not in the way she would want them to. She was popular with the men looking to hook up with her, but she had a man back home and could not live with herself if she betrayed him, so she never did.

Loyal to a fault is what her commanding officer put in her last evaluation. She's still not sure if that was put in as a compliment or not.

It wasn't until recently—the past week, in fact—that she'd gotten a letter from her boyfriend calling off their relationship. She had seen it coming and wasn't surprised. She wasn't really in love; at least she didn't think she was. *With this new assignment, I don't have to go home and face him, or Mother*, she reflects as she trips on a broken piece of concrete when the dock changes from wood.

Shanti can't remember the last time she had been in love. The heartbreak over losing her boyfriend, if one could call it that, lasted less than a day. She has always considered herself a solitary person, entrenched in her pursuit of greater heights within the Indian Navy. Now that's changing. *Maybe I should find love instead.*

She often received compliments on her looks, especially from her captain, who had made several sexual advances toward her. She refused him for the last time a few days ago and suspects that to be the reason he traded her to the American Space Agency, NASA.

She considers her pursuit of a career is what ended her relationship. She walks briskly down the access road to the dock gate while resisting the hot forty-knot gale blowing in from the sea. *I might be on to something with that assessment.*

There are few women in the Indian Navy, especially in the area of sub evac and rescue. Shanti trained for three years in saving submarine crews in distress, including those unable to surface. She finds the current situation ironic in that the only time she was called into service in a real-world rescue attempt was to save the crew of a grounded American sub. The sub never surfaced, but she managed to lead the rescue to a successful conclusion. The sub was scuttled after a US Navy SEAL team removed its nuclear fuel rods and weapons. That crew got a new sub and moved on, with the exception of the captain, who was demoted to janitor. Shanti got a medal and a promotion. Now she's going to work for the same American government that never thanked her for her assistance. *They're into the business of interfering in the affairs of the whole world but have trouble with words like "thanks."*

She continues to walk toward the airstrip just beyond the gate ahead. She glances up at the sun through dark sunglasses, taking in the heat of the day and feeling apprehensive about what her assignment with NASA is and why her superiors seem to know no details of it.

The guard at the gate probably watched her all the way from the ship to his shack without so much as a thought of helping her. She doesn't care about that. She has come to know, and expect, that men are chauvinists, at least every one she meets. She is not averse to meeting new people, *but why always the same type of people?*

The guard would probably rush to her aid if she were dressed in her uniform; *a short skirt and heels, that'll be the day.* At the moment, she may as well be wearing a potato sack with engine grease for makeup and diesel fuel for perfume. She walks up to the guard and drops a bag to produce her ID.

The son of a bitch actually has a look of surprise when he sees that she is an officer. "Thank you, lieutenant," is his response as he makes an attempt at coming to attention.

Sure, I'm not a fucking admiral, but how about a little respect? Shanti wonders as she picks her bag back up. She could give him a hard time, but what's the point? She'd just be making an enemy and be late for her meeting. With whom, she has yet to find out.

Mysteries. I hate mysteries.

"Thank you," she replies sarcastically as she strolls on toward the headquarters building not much farther away, although the fatigue in her legs would say otherwise if they could speak.

She can see the flag of India waving beneath the flag of the Asian Alliance on the same pole. *We're just a part of the whole*. She wonders how long it will be before she sees the blue standard representing the entire planet fly on that pole. *The other two may or may not be there with it*. The flag of a United Earth has yet to be made official, but the designs are commonplace. *There is time for that unveiling.*

She decides to take a shortcut through a hangar as conventional planes land in front of her. Her arms are getting sore. She shrugs it off.

I've felt worse pain.

***

The last place anyone would expect to see a poker game between the minister of the Asian Alliance and General Childs is here, at the headquarters bunker of the Rambili Mandal Naval Base. Three floors underground, the planning room is filled with local and world maps on the walls and large table. Old chalkboards dating back 150 years also line the walls. The only light is a single, naked bulb hovering over the table where the general has just taken his friend's last dime. William collects his winnings and regards Shabal's uniform as he contemplates the next hand. "That's a nice medal you're wearing," he says.

The minister looks up at his friend, who has a shit-eating grin on his gloating face. “Forget it. You’ve taken enough from me. This is payback, I assume, for all the games of one-on-one I’ve taken from you over the last twenty years, William.”

General Childs feigns being wounded in the heart as he replies sarcastically, “Oh, that hurts.” Under his breath, he mumbles, “I wish I never got you into basketball.”

The minister stands to stretch his arms and legs. He fades into the darkness as he strolls away from the dim light as he changes the subject back to the reason they’re both here. “I hope you understand the risks I took finding the right officer for your little project.”

The general, looking out the corner of his eye in response, doesn’t question his friend’s meaning. He’s getting an officer from the Indian Navy, *please*! He picks up the cards and chips as he responds. “Please don’t ask me to explain the purpose of the team I am putting together, Shabal. You know I can’t discuss it.”

Shabal returns to the table and sits. He looks considerably less friendly than just a moment ago. “My people are the best in the entire Asian Alliance.”

Only because China is not a member yet, Childs thinks as Shabal continues. "I have one on the way now but will not turn her over to you until I know more about this team."

The best? Her? A Woman? Childs's first thought is that the fifty-five-year-old minister of the most populous union on the planet must be going senile. He sits back in the rickety old wooden chair and speaks softly, forcing his friend to lean closer to hear him. "The president is working on a plan to unite the world—"

Shabal cuts him off, shouting with sarcastic surprise, "Really? So the last hundred years of wars, terrorism, catastrophes, conspiracies, and UFO sightings were just a warm-up for this?"

Childs continues, more serious but gentle, ignoring the minister's reaction. "There hasn't been a UFO sighting in ten years. My teams will be collecting intelligence and will watch for potential threats from outside Earth's sphere of influence."

Did he say "My teams*"?* Shabal thinks as he looks at Childs over the top of his gold-rimmed glasses. He is old school, though few people his age would go through the eye perfection procedure anyway. "Threats from another world? I didn't know we had made contact."

The general speaks in a whisper. He knows no one can hear through the thick concrete of the walls and ceiling, but any room can be wired. His shackle isn't even getting a signal. *Good thing I don't need a signal halfway around the world,* he thinks before stating, "Let's just say the formation of the teams is a precaution and leave it at that."

"And what happens if something is found by this team?"

"We will be training for that eventuality. I don't know the details of the president's plans, my friend, I only follow his orders. I suspect he's trying to build a strong case for first premier of Earth."

Shabal's smile returns as he shakes his head in disbelief. "Don't we all wish that?"

"Globalization started with the European Union and has spread to every corner of the world. It will culminate in the unionizing of the planet eventually. When it does, we will vote for a single leader to guide us to a new era of prosperity."

"While you hunt for aliens."

"Some believe that aliens already walk among us, influencing our affairs." Childs speaks like a man who knows more than he lets on. "My orders are to put a team together that is made up of the peoples of the world as a show of solidarity and defense against that influence, should it exist. That is our goal. You have my word."

Shabal returns to the darkness as he plays with his small beard. *What a rotten liar my friend is*, he thinks as Childs follows him. Over by the door, the Alliance leader picks up a phone and asks, "And after that?"

William replies, his expression serious, as if trying to sell something nobody wants. "After full unification, the Earth Defense Force will continue to serve the people as the planet's military, protecting us from all threats, internal and external."

Shabal smiles. *Yeah, and there's that bridge you want to sell.* "And you won't use it to further your own political goals, William?"

The general's grin returns. "I have ambitions, true. You could say I became a politician when I put this star on my shoulder."

The male voice that is barely audible on the other end of the ancient-looking phone greets Minister Shabal with name, rank, and position in the lobby. Shabal cuts him off before he starts detailing the names and marital status of his family members. "This is Minister Shabal, has Lieutenant Dae arrived yet?"

"She has just reported in, your Excellency," comes the quick response.

"Very good. We'll be up shortly." He hangs up, not waiting for the affirmative response. Shabal turns to the American general. "I am holding you to your word, my old friend. There are three loves in the world—the love of God, the love of country, and the love of self. I believe your team is destined for failure should you add a fourth."

General Childs straightens his coat, preparing to leave. "You left out family. That's where I put the human race, and God is on his way out." The general heads out the door as the minister follows.

We shall see. I have ambition as well.

***

In the headquarters lobby, Shabal and Childs approach Lieutenant Dae and her bivouac against a far corner.

Childs turns to his friend, stopping short of Lieutenant Dae's hearing. "You've got to be shitting me! She doesn't look like she could lead a homeless man to a good meal! You couldn't assign to me someone a little more…masculine? Or at least above a hundred pounds?"

The Indian doesn't meet William's gaze, but stares at the lieutenant, who has removed most of the layers of clothing she was wearing and stuffed them into a duffel bag that is already bursting at the seams. "She has scored most highly on every intelligence test we have. That is what you asked for, isn't it? Intelligence personnel?"

The minister pulls out his computer-phone and calls up a file while putting the general at ease. "Do not judge a book by its cover,

William. When you read her file, I'm sure you will be pleasantly surprised." The minister and general tap their gadgets together as a means of transferring Lieutenant Shanti Dae's personnel file, Shabal's phone to the general's shackle. Childs's device beeps to indicate a successful transfer. The government of the United States now also has a copy.

The two men continue toward the lieutenant. She stands at attention upon their approach and salutes the general. "First Lieutenant Shanti Dae reporting as ordered, sirs. I apologize for not meeting you in uniform, but—"

The minister speaks quickly with an air of formality in his voice and to shut her up. He has never enjoyed pleasantries or condoned suck-ups. "Lieutenant Dae, you are hereby assigned to the command of General Childs, under the jurisdiction of…" Turning to Childs, he asks, "What branch of the service is she being assigned, William?"

"NASA," comes Child's quick and calm reply that sounds forced.

Shabal waves his hand, motioning for her not to lift her bags. "You may leave your uniforms behind, lieutenant. The general has arranged an EDF uniform for you. It is most likely already at the plane. Your other possessions will be taken care of."

Childs watches Shanti's eyes dart from side to side, as if just remembering something important. He ignores it. "Uniformity breeds unity."

Lieutenant Dae's breathing picks up with the anticipation of what is to come. "I look forward to working with you, general. Thank you, sir."

The general and lieutenant walk away together, leaving the minister behind, standing there with the largest of her three duffel bags and a confused look on his face. *What the hell am I supposed to do with this?* After a moment of thought, he calls over the lobby clerk to assist him.

Outside the building, Shanti and the general walk toward the airstrip about a half-mile away. The sun is lower now and not so hard on her. It also helps that her new superior is helping her with her bags, carrying two of them. *Maybe not all men are assholes.* "May I ask where we are going, sir?"

Childs replies without a hint of emotion. "*I'm* going to China. I've got another deal to conclude. You will be taken to Groom Lake Base. I will meet you there in a day or so. You will begin training with the rest of the team immediately."

Puzzled, she inquires further. "I've never heard of Groom Lake. What kind of base is it, sir?"

The general smiles. “You probably know it best as Area Fifty-One. Don’t worry, there are no aliens there.” He finishes the next sentence under his breath. “Not anymore, anyway.” He pauses to let that little tidbit sink in as they walk along the tarmac toward his private plane. “You will be issued a government computer-phone like mine,” he says as he pulls back his uniform tunic to reveal the device against his arm.

“A shackle?”

Childs laughs. “We’re establishing this unit in secret, Lieutenant. Only the president and a select few know of its formation. Your shackle won’t have full tracking abilities. It’s special, just a link between your fellow teammates and an eye on the world.”

Shanti repeats the catchphrase of the shackle’s manufacturer, “*No one is unknown.*” Lieutenant Dae’s relief is short-lived. Walking toward the general’s aircraft that is parked at the flight terminal ahead like a bus waiting at the curb for her, she becomes nervous. Beads of sweat appear on her face as her hands begin to tremble.

The general notices. “Is something the matter, Lieutenant?”

She was hoping it wouldn’t happen. She had not flown or even been in an extremely high place in years. She thought she might have gotten over it, but the feelings have started to overwhelm her. *I'm not even on the damn plane yet and I'm shaking like a leaf in a hurricane.* She babbles an answer, "I'm s-sort of afraid of flying, sir. High places too, but more so the flying part. I don't like..." Her voice trails off.

Childs stops in his tracks at hearing her words and drops her bags. He can put up with having a scrawny female on his team. He can even put up with the tinny quality of her voice, which makes nails on a chalkboard sound like angels flapping their wings by comparison. But *this*?

He can see his aide approaching from the plane. Umbrella boy is now carrying a folding cart with which to carry luggage. Childs turns red. "How the hell did you ever get into the military, Lieutenant?" He asks.

"I'm Navy, sir," she mumbles in her own defense. "Always at sea level—or under it. I'm s-sorry."

The aide has loaded the bags on the cart and wheels it away, pretending not to hear the exchange. He'll let out the laugh building in this throat later.

Childs shakes his head in disgust. "Get aboard the plane, Lieutenant! You will learn to fear nothing when I'm through with you!"

"Yes, General, sir!" she replies quickly and turns toward the plane with her head lowered, in shame or panic, she couldn't say.

It's a small plane, like a corporate jet. When she left home for the Navy, she remembers her father telling her that big planes are safer than little ones. Maybe he only said that because she was about to board a large plane at the time. She hopes now that the reverse is true. Looking underneath the aircraft at the pancake-shaped antigravity device causes her some relief. *Antigravity planes can't crash. Can they?*

Where was her father when she needed him? He taught her so much, regretting not having a son but making the most of it. *He was a good dad*, her mind wanders. *Retired at home, he's probably building something or working in the garden with Mother. Must be nice to be retired at the age of fifty-two, but then, he deserved it. He is a hero, after all.* They should be getting notified of her change in duties soon.

Back to reality. She approaches the stairs leading into the plane, at the moment fearing the general's anger more than the aircraft. Although, the aircraft fear is gaining rapidly with each step as her heart beats faster and faster. She doesn't want to disappoint her new boss on her first day. *That boat has sailed.*

Reaching the top step, she walks into the plane, her mind racing with flight or fight as if she had just stepped into hell itself.

She makes her way through the empty cabin of the twenty-seater antigravity aircraft. It has red carpeting and white leather seats. *Impressive and luxurious*. She is alone. *Is that good or bad? No one to clutch on to when the turbulence starts, but also no one to save me when the plane crashes onto a deserted island in the Pacific—or the Aleutians, perhaps.*

Do antigravity planes get turbulence? She doesn't know. Should she know?

Her mind is racing again.

Shanti finds a seat over the left wing. Then she changes to another seat behind the wing. *Why do antigravity planes need wings? They do, that's all, in case the antigravity generators fail. Fail? Why would they fail?*

Focus. Focus. Focus. She knows that she is capable of overcoming this fear. *It's not rational. Millions fly every day.*

Her superiors back on the ship, and even at headquarters, never knew of her fears. They didn't *need* to know. She was Navy, on a ship, sometimes underwater. You can't get into less altitude than the ocean.

Except for space.

Why didn't I think of that? I'm going to be trained in space! I'm going to be working for freakin' NASA! All I had to do was sleep with my damn captain and I wouldn't be here, suffering this torture of having to fly.

There's a tough choice to make: fear in an assignment she doesn't want or sleep with a slobbering, old, fat captain. *Alert the judges, we have a tie,* she thinks as she locks her seat belt and pulls the restraining strap as tight as she can stand it.

Through the air at Mach 30 or in space makes no difference.

Shanti calms herself by counting the engines and going over what she knows of modern aircraft. *This one has four thrusters, two in front and two in back. Wait! It has smaller thrusters on top and bottom for ease of maneuverability. Too many parts! Too many things can go wrong!*

She closes her eyes as sweat washes her beneath her clothes. She hears music along with the hum of the engines as they come to life. *Concentrate on the old tune*. It's "Only the Lonely" by Roy Orbison. She contemplates the reason the worldwide radio station is playing that tune. *It must be a hundred years old; some kind of audio anniversary. Unless somehow the station knows I'm on this plane*, she thinks with a nervous chuckle.

"This is going to be a five-hour long flight, and the song is only worth three minutes at best," she mumbles to herself, her voice acting as a calming mechanism. "A hundred years ago, this flight would be fifteen hours. I should be thankful."

Relax.

Shanti looks out the small window at General Childs, who is now boarding another aircraft, one with Chinese markings. *Must be nice to not live in fear of things like this*, she figures as the lights in the cabin go off and the plane begins to taxi. She moves her eyes from her superior to the tower, picturing the controllers laughing at her misery.

The aircraft gets to the end of the runway, where it sits all alone until it gets clearance to take off a moment later. The small plane doesn't require a lot of runway, but the pilot takes his time. The plane takes flight.

I should've slept with the son of a bitch!

***

The car ride to the golf course of the elite from Beijing's Shehezhen Air Base north of the center of town takes less than an hour along the G6 Jingzang Expressway. The Chinese have worked antigravity technology into everything, from buses to skateboards, streaking ahead of their western counterparts, which are bogged down in bureaucracy.

General Childs's host, General Second Grade Chow Hui, doesn't care for such luxuries. Hui enjoys the feel of the road beneath him. "Riding the rubber," as it has come to be known. The three-star general of the Chinese Army also likes to drive himself on China's roads, which have become less congested over the last twenty years.

At the moment, however, Hui is content to sit in the back of the golf cart with his longtime friend as his aide and caddy, Captain Kong Jen, drives the two players to the ball somewhere in the bushes. The men are in civilian clothes. William is wearing a golf-themed Hawaiian shirt and a solid green baseball cap with a star on it. Hui is dressed in a casual style, a pullover shirt and shorts. Jen is dressed sharply in her green dress uniform.

Childs notices the captain's stoic face as she focuses on finding the ball, shot by Hui and lost somewhere near or in the bushes adjacent to the sand trap.

"It's getting late," Hui says in his broken English.

Childs takes a moment to process what the man said, *just keep the sentences short and slow, please*, as he nods in agreement.

The cart stops.

"I have found it, General," Captain Jen says with confidence and alarm, as if finding the damn ball were as important as spotting an incoming missile. Her command of the English language would impress the king of England. Her use of it is obviously for William's benefit.

Hui answers his subordinate in Mandarin, knowing the American won't understand him. By his tone and her reaction, however, Childs wonders if he just promoted her to major.

Childs shakes his head as the two men walk to the ball. It's on a patch of green, separated from the bushes by a few inches, enough for Hui to make a shot. He tests his balance and shuffles his feet to gain proper form. Childs, growing impatient, decides to return to the conversation they started at the airbase. "Hui, I need an answer. Have you found someone to be on my team?"

Hui takes a final practice swing before striking the ball. It flies straight for a moment before slicing to the left and away from the hole.

The captain watches the ball as it enters the trees. "Excellent shot, sir."

Childs is taken aback. *Is she kidding? That acting job should gain her an Academy Award!* He continues, "I'm sure you have had time to read up on the project the president is putting together to unite the world."

Hui hands his golf club to Jen and mutters something to her in Mandarin before taking the American general aside. "We are most interested in this team you are putting together, my old friend. You must understand my government's resistance to globalization."

It's good to have connections, but why does everyone refer to me as 'old friend'? Childs wonders before making his assurances, as any good politician would. "It is for the benefit of the entire world. This team will be focused on intelligence, though I'm looking for members able to fight when called to. We have no secrets. The teams will be diverse and work outside the control of any one government."

Hui laughs out loud, the booming kind of laugh that replaces the word *bullshit*. "No, no secrets, unlike your government secretly growing by three countries. Your leader has many secrets."

"I know nothing about that."

"I believe you, my old friend."

Hui doesn't refer to Childs as an "old friend" for nothing. The two men fought together in Taiwan and North Korea when China became paranoid about globalization and began absorbing nations as buffer states, the Chinese leaders expecting the inevitable invasion. America did not get involved directly, but William did. He fought as a diplomat most of the time, from within the ranks of China's new enemies, to support his friend. He and Hui have known each other since studying together in England.

The fear of war returns as Hui continues. "Your Navy has amassed several fleets in conjunction with the ships of the Asian Alliance near our border. So while my government does not cherish the idea of inclusion, I feel it necessary to oblige you."

"You're giving me someone from your agency?" Childs is surprised at this revelation. He was expecting to get a soldier from a Special Forces unit, not an agent from the Ministry for State Security (MSS). *I'm not sure about allowing someone like that access to sensitive information, but then, trust goes both ways*. "Whom did you have in mind?"

Hui gestures at Captain Jen, who smiles when Childs's eyes begin to roll. He puts a hand on his forehead, feeling a headache coming on. "Oh, not again," he mumbles before speaking up, not caring if he hurts the young captain's feelings. "Are there no military *men* in the world anymore?"

Hui barks in Mandarin again to the captain, who stands at the most rigid attention Childs has seen since he was at Parris Island.

She speaks up to defend her abilities and her commander's decision. "General, my task for the past two weeks was to study this team you are forming, and the selection of Captain Folsom is risky at best, if not unwise."

Hui mutters something else, chastising her for the insult, perhaps.

She continues in a more respectful tone, bowing her head slightly as she does so. "I mean no offense. I would be honored to serve you on this team, General."

Childs steps up to her, looking down into her bright brown eyes, wondering how she knows about Captain Folsom's selection so soon. "You will have to take a demotion in rank in order to fit in, Captain. Are you amenable to that?"

She swallows before answering. *Was that her pride going down her throat or just excess saliva?* he thinks as she says, "I do not mind, sir. I will follow your orders to the letter."

The American general smiles and steps back to regard Hui again. "So this is how you plan to watch us, eh?"

Hui smiles in return, as if in agreement, though he would never admit it. *So obvious.*

Childs turns back to the young "lieutenant" and finishes with his command. "You will be assigned to NASA under my command. You will be provided a uniform, so don't bother bringing any. I will see you on the plane in one hour, Lieutenant Kong. Dismissed!"

The American general has westernized her name, putting her surname last. She looks at General Second Grade Hui for confirmation of the order.

He speaks in English for the benefit of his guest and friend. "Don't look at me, Lieutenant. You are under his command now. You will follow his orders!"

She salutes General Childs before turning on her heel and marching quickly toward the clubhouse a half-mile away. The two men watch her go until she is lost in the trees.

Once she is out of sight, General Hui turns to his counterpart. "Shall we finish our hole before we lose daylight?"

Childs knows how this man thinks. He just got a spy onto his team, with his consent. Upon further reflection, however, she may be just what they need. "Let's do that, Hui." *Good luck finding your ball now*, he doesn't add.

CHAPTER SIX: Messages

Captain Pilas walks along the crowded streets of Washington, DC. He is returning to his apartment building north of downtown, near Meridian Hill Park. The seventy-story building he lives in is one of three in the city that is self-contained. A resident has the freedom to go anywhere, of course, but there is no need to. The skyscraper contains clothes shops, salons, a gym, theaters, convenience stores, doctors and dentist's offices, and even a bowling alley.

Pilas has been gone for fifteen hours in an effort to find information on the Vorelisian agent he knows is on the planet. It took him that long to travel to Prince William Forest Park near Quantico, where his one-man transport is hidden, and complete a survey of his intelligence satellites. He is glad to be returning in the dark of night, but the crowds are still plentiful, and people like to stare, to see what kind of person hides his face while walking down a well-lit sidewalk.

At the front door, Pilas eyes the black van parked across the street and dismisses it. *I know the president is having me watched, but the watchers don't know anything about me. They wouldn't know proper surveillance from a hole in the ground*, he thinks as he enters the building and gets to his home on the thirty-third floor. Upon entry, he activates the oxygen generator in the center of the room, takes off his coat, scarf, and hat, and breathes normally. The furnished apartment is small, about four hundred square feet, but it's comfortable.

Pilas goes to a drawer and pulls out a small box with a long antenna. He scans the room and deduces that no one has been in the apartment since he last left. He puts the box back in the drawer and opens one of the sofa's arms. Inside is a small receiver/transmitter with a blinking red light that tells him there is a message waiting.

After a retina scan, the machine identifies him, and the message opens as a hologram. The image hovering in front of him, over the coffee table, is that of his superior, Admiral Shan Tolomak.

"Well, well…you look pissed, sir," Pilas says out loud to the man who sent him here, knowing that, of course, Tolomak can't hear him. Pilas respects the rank and the position, but not the man. *He only smiles when people die or when planets explode. The two events typically go hand in hand.*

The admiral is dressed in his white service uniform. He is in his fifties, with white hair and black eyes. The area behind him is dark to make him stand out. "Captain Pilas, I am encouraged with your progress in bringing unity to the people of Earth," he says. "However, the current timeline you have established for Earth's entry into the Galactic Community does not leave much room before the vote for the planet Jexx. We have the time to bring the Earth into the community, but the Supreme Leader wants it done sooner to allow for any potential problems to be resolved."

Problems? There won't be any problems if you people just let me do my job and leave me alone! Pilas's mind screams as he stares intently at the image, as if wanting to burn a hole in it. He feels that he knows what's coming next and is just waiting impatiently for it.

Tolomak continues, "I am dispatching Ambassador Hoyth and his diplomatic team to assist you. Hoyth has hired an independent pilot. They have successfully penetrated the Vorelisian border and should be at Seara soon. Our diversionary plan is already in play."

WHAT? NO! Pilas jumps up and paces the room, releasing his anger with his movements. *This can't be! I am meeting my timetable. This is outrageous!* He gets face to face with Tolomak again to vent out loud. "This is my world, old man! I will not share credit with anyone for unifying an entire planet! This is something I've dreamed of, to make a mark in the history of a world! You can't take that from me!" He falls to his knees in front of the hologram and sobs, whispering "No. No. No."

The holographic mechanism, aware that Pilas is still in the room, continues playing the admiral's message. "For my part of the mission, I have assembled a hundred transport ships to move any Earthers who may wish to colonize another world. From your reports to me on their lives, I may have to get more." He ends with a chuckle, knowing full well that anyone transplanted to Jexx for colonization will die out after his or her planned sterilization. The few remaining Earthers will be killed, and Jexx will be owned solely by the Thimmi administration. "We've waited five hundred years for this planet, we don't want to wait any longer."

"Good plan, but I can handle the unity of Earth and colonization of Jexx without an ambassador to help me," Pilas retorts.

"Work closely with ambassador Hoyth, and together, you will rule Earth once their unity is complete and they've accepted our sponsorship into the community of worlds. Tolomak out."

The message ends. Pilas stands and steps back. Something inside him clicks. The angry fuse that was burning a moment ago has burned out. He begins asking himself questions and answering them. "Where is Hoyth now? Past the border, he said…probably near Seara."

Seara is a planet within Vorelisian territory. The wormhole there leads directly to the planet Earth. A simple voyage, provided they can elude any patrols in the area. *The plan is in play.*

"What if Hoyth gets caught by the Vorelisians? He won't get caught. The independent pilot probably owns a small cargo ship that Hoyth has made modifications to for this trip."

In the bathroom, Pilas continues the back and forth out loud to no one. He listens to his own voice trying to convince him that he cannot win while his mind devises a separate plan for his possible victory should Hoyth's plan fail. The two sides join somewhere in the middle of reality. "Of course, having a contingency plan is a good idea." *I have had this mission for ten years, and there is now light at the end of the tunnel*, he thinks as he puts a teeth-cleaning device in his mouth. As it scrubs the tartar and bits of food off of his teeth using sonic waves, he goes over the plan again and again. By the time he gets into the shower, he is content in the knowledge of what may transpire and what he must do to manipulate it.

For cleanliness, he chooses soothing, warm water over sound waves. He goes to bed no longer thinking of Hoyth or Tolomak, but of the Vorelisian agent he must also find.

***

Charles Lightner wakes up with the sun beaming into Madeline's bedroom window and her arm across his chest. He can't remember when he was this happy and sad at the same time. *How do I tell this woman I love that I'm from another planet? Certainly, I can trust her.* He stares at the ceiling of her apartment in

Washington, DC. *I don't want to lose her, but then, I may have to when this assignment is over. My government may not allow me to stay here.*

Self-doubt rears its ugly head. *I'm not the most handsome man on this world. What does she see in me?*

His eyes go wide when his computer pad inside his white lab coat begins to beep for his attention. The noise brings him back into focus. He moves Madeline's arm ever so gently, trying not to wake her but failing. She responds by pulling him closer. She hears the beeping too but is ignoring it. She doesn't want her time with him to end so soon.

He slides away from her, and she opens her eyes. He says, "It's morning, Maddy. I have to get to work."

She rises onto her elbows, "Yeah, me too." She turns to get up on her side of the bed and regards his coat. "You want me to get that for you?"

Charles moves quickly to the coat to silence the device inside, remembering where the switch is so he doesn't have to pull it out in her sight. "No!" He laughs at himself for his panicked reaction, noting the look of surprise on her face. "I mean, I got it."

She smiles and puts on her robe, covering her perfect, large breasts. "I'll make some eggs."

In these times, breakfast is one of the few meals people in this part of the world eat at home, because getting to a food station is too much of a hassle first thing in the morning. With preservatives outlawed, stores went out of business. Food stations are a faster and more efficient method of getting food from the farm or factory to the people.

Charles watches Madeline walk into the kitchen and responds with a semi cheery “OK.” With Madeline out of sight, he checks the message on the pad. The text from the Vorelisian satellite he put in orbit when he arrived on Earth ten years ago informs him of an intercepted Thimmi signal to Earth. *“This is bad,”* he mumbles.

Madeline calls from the kitchen, “You want sausages too, babe?”

He sticks his head into the kitchen. *This would be a good time to tell her. I may need her support sooner than I thought if the Thimms are making a move*. He chickens out as he watches her stir the eggs, causing her left breast to appear to fight its way out of the confinement of her robe. “Er, no. I have to skip breakfast, I’m afraid.” He returns to the bedroom to dress quickly.

She puts three small sausages into the frying pan, and they sizzle. She changes the subject, not knowing when she’ll see him again. “You know the planet is coming together. You’ve seen my reports, right?”

Charles responds loud enough to be heard, "Of course!"

Madeline takes a deep breath, summoning up the courage to announce, "When that happens, I'm going to run for first premier!"

Charles enters the kitchen and puts a hand on her shoulder. "That's great!"

She turns at his touch and sees him fully dressed. *That was quick.* "What's your rush?" she asks. "Can't the space station wait a few minutes?"

"I-I have other issues that require my immediate attention. I'm sorry. I will enjoy hearing more about your plans later."

Not hearing the apprehension in his voice, Madeline continues with the business of the day. "You *are* going to be at the committee meeting this afternoon, aren't you? You've won four votes. That's a good start, but the Oilers are circling the wagons against ideas like Soliquid."

That's another Earth vernacular Charles has yet to understand. He ignores the statement. "Is unification going to be a problem, you think?"

She pauses as she considers the question. *Why does he care about globalization more than his own project?* "No, most of the world is in agreement. We only have a few holdouts to get on board."

"I'm concerned for you." His thoughts drift to the Thimms' plans and their agent on this planet.

Madeline misunderstands. "I'll still have a job in the Senate if I lose the vote. Life won't change much unless I win."

You couldn't be more wrong, sweetheart. The Thimms are here. He should tell her. He wants to tell her *now*, but he needs to get more information. "I have to go." He kisses her cheek from behind as she stirs the eggs for the last time. "If I don't see you at the meeting, will you speak on my behalf?"

She chuckles softly, "Am I on your payroll now? OK."

He gives her shoulders a gentle squeeze just before exiting the apartment.

***

On the street, Charles hails a cab to take him to the airport. *It's a five-hour flight to Las Vegas. If only civilian aircraft had antigravity installed, it would take considerably less time*, he laments. Add the rental and two hours to drive to his spaceship hidden in the Mojave Desert. Seven hours total. "Damn," he whispers to himself as the car pulls up.

Across the street, a man dressed in a scarf and gloves, with a heavy coat and fedora, gets into a cab going in the opposite direction. Charles dismisses the man as odd, given the comfortable weather this morning. He has more pressing matters to attend to.

Plans are changing. The Thimms are upping the stakes. *They must be stopped.*

CHAPTER SEVEN: Groom Lake Base

Captain Derrick Folsom disembarks via the rear-loading ramp of the Air Force C-29 cargo plane dressed in his new NASA military uniform. It is black, similar to his Marine Corps uniform, but there are subtle differences.

I'm the only person on the planet wearing this costume, he feels as he glances at the crew still on the plane behind him. They snicker behind his back but stop when he calls to them, "Don't worry, you'll be getting a uniform like this pretty soon." *That shut them up.*

The four men wheeling his Indian motorcycle down the ramp to join him on the tarmac suddenly seem less happy. He knows that when the world becomes one, there will no longer be a need for the military in its current form. There will be a sharp increase in police within the cities; the Worldwide Security Company (WSC) coupled with the Earth Defense Force (EDF) will protect the citizenry. *Childs will continue to form units. He's currently on task to form an Air Force squadron,* he ponders while reading his orders again. He is to lead EDF-1 and is starting to look forward to it.

He soaks in the warmth of early November in the desert. He closes his eyes, allowing the gentle breeze to siphon away his stress.

I have arrived. This is the beginning of a new chapter, and I will make the best of it.

Air Force regulations prohibit any vehicle traveling by air to contain fuel or oil. Derrick walks his bike to a nearby aerospace ground equipment (AGE) station, where he is surprised to find someone else dressed in an EDF uniform, though it is of the fatigue variety. Derrick removes his sunglasses as he approaches the young man, who is staring at a computerized clipboard. “Excuse me, Sergeant.”

Sergeant Alfonzo Furtado stops humming the tune “Ride, Captain, Ride” and snaps to attention, surprised as Derrick is at seeing another person wearing the same type of uniform. He salutes. “Good morning, sir,” he says with a genuine smile, atypical of most troops who meet officers.

Apart from the style of uniform, another difference is the placement of the rank insignia. For both officers and enlisted, the rank is displayed on the shoulders (dress) or lapels (fatigues). The sleeves are for patches, and Alfonzo’s patch denotes his assignment to EDF-2. On the left breast is stitched Furtado’s name. Dress uniforms have awards and ribbons displayed on the right side, of which Derrick has thirteen.

Derrick returns the salute and smiles. “Where did the general find you?” he asks as the two men shake hands. Alfonzo is about a foot shorter than the captain, and with his stocky build and mirrored sunglasses, he reminds Derrick of the Central American dictators of a century ago. He studied the history of the region before taking his first assignment in Venezuela.

The sergeant's accent is slight to the captain's ear. "Sir, my name is Alfonzo Furtado. I was recruited from the European Air Force."

Still trying to place his accent, Folsom asks, "Portuguese?"

Furtado smiles with pride. "Yes, sir. You need gas, sir? That's a beautiful ride."

I like this guy already. Folsom lets go of the bars as the sergeant takes them. *It's like allowing a stranger to hold your own child's hand while crossing a busy street.*

Furtado lowers the kickstand and stops the bike next to the gas pump a few yards away. He reaches for the manual switch to turn on the flow of fuel as the captain continues.

"I see you're assigned to Unit Two."

"EDF-2, yes, sir. You know, I've got some oil in the hangar. It's fifteen-fifty weight. I'll get some."

Volunteering his service, eager to please. Remind you of anyone? Derrick asks himself as he lifts his shackle to make a call. "Not for long, Sergeant."

After a few minutes of debating with the general the merits of having Furtado on *his* team, Folsom closes the call by the time his bike is ready to ride. He then asks where the bachelor officer's quarters (BOQ) is located.

Alfonzo points in the direction of a few small buildings next to a giant radar dish. "It's right next to that big black saucer, sir. The dish, I mean."

"What *is* that? Radar that powerful would pick up gnats coming from the moon," Folsom wonders aloud as he gets on his Indian and starts the engine. It rumbles like a tame dog.

"It's an energy receiver of some kind, I think, sir. The International Space Station fires beams at the dish from orbit. It's some new power source from space. The energy is stored in the silver-colored building next to it."

Right next to the BOQ? "Does the station ever miss?" Folsom asks tongue in cheek, though Furtado responds seriously. "Not to my knowledge, sir. They've only had two firings since I got here three days ago."

Folsom smiles as he puts his shades back on and swaps his uniform cover for his black helmet. “See you soon, Sergeant. We’ll be at Hangar Twelve in the morning.”

Furtado comes to attention, his smile returning as he hears the familiar tone on his shackle informing him of news. As his new superior rides away, he checks it to confirm the change in orders. He is now part of EDF-1. He returns to humming his favorite tune.

***

Upon his arrival and check-in at the BOQ, Captain Folsom is assigned to room 398. He has the desk clerk program his shackle to be a room key. As Derrick returns to his bike, he notes that it is parked next to a wooden hitch railing, similar to how a cowboy would hitch his horse in old Western films. *Yep, there’s a new sheriff in town*, he chuckles to himself while retrieving his bag and walking along the concrete sidewalk around the BOQ building. His feeling of the old West is turning into memories of staying at a run-down motel in Detroit a few years back.

He finds his room. It looks comfortable for the most part. The paint isn’t peeling off the walls and he doesn’t smell mold; remnant memories of another assignment he’d like to forget about. The moment he sits on the bed, he gets a call on his shackle from the EDF-2 commander, Captain Amanda Blassi. Reluctantly, he answers the call, and a hologram of the captain appears before him. The hologram contains text on the bottom of the image identifying the caller by rank and position.

Pretty girl, but the yellow hair with red highlights makes her look as if her face is on fire, Derrick judges before saying, “Hello, Captain.”

Her smile of welcome lasts but a moment as she gets down to business. “Captain Folsom, I’ve just been informed of the transfer of Sergeant Furtado from my unit to yours.”

He lies down, shifting the hologram projection to the ceiling. *I miss regular phones*. He is tired and impatient after his journey so far, and with more administrative work ahead of him, he doesn’t have time for complaints. “So what? It’s day one, Captain. You’ll have time to replace him.”

“No need to get defensive, Captain, I’m merely acknowledging the transfer.”

“Our shackles did that ten minutes ago. What do you *really* want?”

What’s up this guy’s ass? Blassi wonders as she asks, “Did I catch you at a bad time?”

“I just flew in from DC. I’m tired.”

“Tired from a thirty-minute flight? You must be older than your record shows.”

Frustrated, he reaches over to touch the shackle. “I’m closing the call now, Captain Blassi. Have a nice day.”

“Hold it! I just wanted to advise you to read Furtado’s record carefully.”

“I plan to study all of my people. I’m a thorough person.”

Just then, a warning siren blares outside Derrick’s window, loud enough to scare the bejesus out of him. He bolts upright, shifting the hologram from the ceiling back to the wall. “What the hell is that?”

The hologram image follows him to the window, and Blassi speaks loudly enough to be heard over the siren. “It’s nothing to worry about, just another magnetic energy burst from the International Space Station.”

Derrick looks out at the giant radar dish he spoke with Furtado about earlier. It is pointed at the horizon and is moving slowly, as if tracking something in space that he cannot see in the daylight.

Just then, a burst of energy, a bright white laser light lasting four seconds, strikes the collector inside the dish, causing Derrick to shield his eyes. Blassi continues, “Cool, isn’t it? Blinding, but cool.”

Derrick walks back to the bed. “What were you telling me about Furtado’s record?”

The hologram returns to the ceiling just as a yellow warning light flashes on it. “I’m sorry,” she says, “I have another call. Furtado is an expert marksman. You might want to exploit that.”

The hologram switches off before Derrick can thank Fire Hair for the information. He attempts to call her back but finds that she is on a priority call with General Childs. *Watching our every move, are you, general?*

He shakes his head as a call comes in from the front desk. He answers it reluctantly. “This is Captain Derrick Folsom, Earth Defense Force Unit One.”

CHAPTER EIGHT: Arrivals and Departures

The day cannot come to an end fast enough for Derrick. He is on his bike and speeding off the base after learning that a member of his team is arriving soon at McCarran Airport in Las Vegas and will need pickup. There are people Derrick can call to handle a simple thing like this, but on day one, he feels the need to greet each member in person.

"Time!" he shouts, unnecessarily for the shackle to hear. It picks up voices extremely well and is not affected by the noises of the wind or even his engine. In his ears, the shackle responds in a pleasant female voice into his helmet, "It is four p.m."

His shackle continues to speak to him, broadcasting the record and life of Lieutenant Shanti Dae. During the two-hour trip, it will tell him everything he needs to know and some things he doesn't. It's late in the afternoon, and the sun is falling toward the horizon to his right as he hits the highway southbound.

A pothole jolts him. *Didn't see that one, I should've requisitioned a car,* Derrick thinks between yawns. He has yet to ride in an antigravity vehicle.

***

First Lieutenant Shanti Dae listens to the engines go silent and opens her eyes to the fact that the flight has come to an end in a positive way, much different than the pictures that have formed in her mind over the past five hours of the disabled plane landing in the Pacific Ocean. It would eventually sink, making her food for sharks. She could also survive a crash into a volcano just before it erupts. *No, we're safely on the ground at last!*

She loosens her grip on the armrests and hastily makes for the hatch. The pilot is standing by the open door, waiting for her with a smile on his face. She pictures him slamming the door shut, jumping into the cockpit, and taking off again just for the sport of it.

STOP! she tells herself as her rational mind takes over, subduing the random thoughts of death and destruction.

The pilot is a tall, tanned man who looks as though he spends a lot of time at the beach as well as the gym. She looks him over for the third time as she slows down her pace toward him. "Are you okay, miss?" he asks with genuine concern in his light but strong voice.

"Yes. I'm fine. It's good to finally be on the ground."

He nods in understanding. "The hills surrounding this area always make for rough turbulence. Welcome to Las Vegas."

Shanti is at the doorway now, looking out at the sprawling city before her. Skyscrapers, strange-shaped hotels, the setting sun, and a blast of hot wind feel like home but with less humidity. *If it's a hundred degrees here in November, what is it like in June?* she wonders silently before turning her attention to the pilot once again. "I thought we were going to Groom Lake."

The pilot is a major, so she dares not speak too sharply, just enough to show her irritation. He gets the message and explains. "They're on alert right now, part of an exercise of some kind. Captain Folsom is on his way to the terminal to pick you up. I will transport your personal items when I get clearance to land at the base, unless you'd rather wait a few hours and I can fly you there."

She responds quickly, with a tinge of fear still evident in her voice after her mind starts screaming, *No!* "I don't mind being picked up. I'm used to desert environments. Is it far?"

"Groom Lake is approximately a hundred and sixty miles north of here."

Shanti smiles at the misunderstanding. She would have chuckled if she thought he'd take it as a compliment. "I meant the terminal."

"Ah, the terminal is right over there." He says as he points the way toward a brightly lit, flat building about a quarter mile away.

Exiting the plane, she sees a crewman put her duffel bag on the tarmac. *More walking. More carrying. Whatever happened to technology? An antigravity wheelbarrow, perhaps. I'm going to have a pair of strong legs before this assignment is over*. She picks up her white Indian Navy duffel bag and holds out a hand to stop the crewman from unloading the rest. “Just this one. You can fly the rest up later. Thank you.”

The airman nods and smiles. She feels his eyes on her as she walks away in her black EDF dress uniform. For a short woman, her legs appear long. She doesn’t like the idea of hoofing it to the terminal in heels, so she takes them off. The ground is warm and comforting; the sun hasn’t been heating it for a while now.

***

With her duffel bag at her feet, Lieutenant Shanti Dae sits on a concrete slab, leaning against the mirrored wall at her back. She is at the main terminal, waiting for a ride from her new superior and listening to the planes take off and land. The sun has gone down, leaving only the light of dusk. The streetlight illumination is beginning to take effect.

She expected this airport to be packed with tourists from all over the world. She has read much on the subject of “Sin City” and wonders what makes today special enough for the street population to be sparse. The gates down at the other end of the terminal seem busier, but just barely. Peering through the glass behind her, she sees mostly businesspeople. Straightening up, she dismisses the aberration and consults her shackle for something to do. *A game. A book.*

The 2060 census is still being tallied, but indications are that Las Vegas will top ten million. As a solitaire hologram hovers in front of her, Shanti catches sight of three men watching her from the gate to her left. *Must be the uniform,* she thinks as she dismisses their interest.

After ten minutes and three games of solitaire and two of chess, the eyes on her are starting to become a problem. *Where is Captain Folsom?* She tries to make out the mumbling and snickers between the men watching her but they're too far away. She glances behind her at the people inside, wondering if there is a police officer nearby. There is not.

As she stands to move to another bench at a gate farther from the three men, one of them follows her, moving quickly to get to her side. "Hey, little honey, you work here?"

She is momentarily taken aback by the question, but she shrugs it off as ignorance. He's obviously never seen the EDF uniform before. *Very few have*. "I'm Lieutenant Shanti Dae of the Indian Navy. I'm here on an assignment," she says as she sits back down.

With the large, muscular man standing on her right side, she fails to notice the other two approaching from her left until one of them startles her when he speaks. This guy is in his twenties, the youngest among them. “Indian Navy? Where’s your dot?”

She corrects herself. “Actually, I’m part of the Earth Defense Force. I’m waiting for a ride.” *“Lieutenant Dae of the Earth Defense Force”—that’s going to take some getting used to.*

The big man sits on her right, close enough to smell, though at the moment, she wouldn’t mind losing that sense right about now. “I can give you a ride,” he says as he drools. He wipes his mouth as the other men start laughing with him, his belly shaking like a bowl of jelly on a washing machine.

The second man, who has been quiet for the most part, sits on her left side and speaks clearly and with surprisingly good diction. *An educated man.* “I wasn’t aware of an Earth Defense Force.”

Feeling uncomfortable, Shanti tries to make herself smaller by pulling in her arms. It is not until now that she notices that these men have no shackles. *Not a one between them.* “It’s part of NASA, at least as far as I know. Today is my first day.”

The big man leans down to read the name on her duffel bag. “NASA has a military?” he asks, his voice low.

“Yes. Please, I wish to be alone.”

The young man stands in front of her, close enough that his leg is touching her knee. "Why? We're just getting to know you. That's the way it is in Vegas, isn't it? What do I know? We're from Chicago."

The chuckling begins anew, making her wish she were in her battle dress uniform. The black camouflage would make an effective deterrent. *Maybe a pistol or machete for good measure.*

The second man picks up the younger man's line. "No need to be rude, darlin', we just want a little fun."

The big man picks up a small device and says "Okay" into it.

The second man tries to make her feel at ease. "I like the sound of your voice."

The young man, whose breathing has become more rapid, huffs, "The only sound I want to hear is moaning."

The big man puts away the device he spoke into as he stands, joining his friends in the laughter. "Let's go."

He grabs her arm and pulls her to her feet. *What did I do to deserve this?* she asks herself. Shanti has read about Vegas's sex crime wave; girls are taken off the street, raped, and murdered. Things have improved with the advent of shackles, but implementation takes time. She shouts, “I am not a prostitute! Let go of me!”

The big man shoots back. “Well, it’s not like we were going to *pay* for anything!”

The second man affirms the plan as he watches a van come from around the corner behind him. “She’ll make good sport, eh?”

Shanti raises her shackle to call for help, but the big man covers her mouth and the young man pulls her shackle arm back. “No shackles, bitch! Let’s go, we’ve got a ride to take!”

“Don’t let her take it off, it will call the cops!”

The van stops at the curb in front of them. The driver is hopping in his seat with anticipation and cackling up a storm. “Get her in! Get her in!”

Shanti is being dragged toward the van’s sliding door, which the young man has opened. She tries to scream, but the big man’s hand is covering her mouth, muffling her cries. There is no one around to help her.

She thinks of her training, not so much from the Navy, but from her father when she was a teenager. *Not so long ago.* For a moment, she relaxes, and she is glad she put her heels back on. With her right foot, she kicks the young man in the groin. She breaks free using her left elbow to the big man and roundhouse kicks the second man in the head. He goes down hard, losing a tooth or two, courtesy of the concrete.

The boy is still down, *unthreatening for a while,* she guesses. The fourth man has left the van and is approaching with a knife, holding it high.

She has only a second, not knowing whether he knows how to wield the blade or not. All indications point to “no,” as he is holding it wrong. Most people back up when confronted with a knife; Shanti surprises her attacker by going on the offensive. As quick as she is, she clocks him in the eyes with two swift punches before he can lower the blade. He stumbles backward, blinded, albeit temporarily.

The big man, now to her left, pulls a gun from the small of his back—*a bad place to keep a gun in close quarter combat.* She grabs the man’s gun elbow with one hand and her finger is on the trigger with the other in order to guide the barrel of the .22 caliber weapon into position under his chin, pointing it upward.

The man with the knife wisely backs off, retreating into the van, while her current prisoner falls to his knees and begs, “Okay, okay!”

Shanti smiles. Fortunately for him, she is not a killer. The fourth man is in the driver's seat and revving up the van for a quick getaway. It's an old van, and easily identifiable by the rust pattern and colored tires, *a fad of the times.*

"Let go of the gun!" she commands the fat man, who has started to sob.

He obeys without question or hesitation, trembling as he does so.

She pushes the barrel of the pistol into the man's crotch. "One of the things my father taught me was how to defend myself. How am I doing? Is this good sport?"

"Please, no!" he cries, sweat now pouring off his balding head.

Lieutenant Dae activates the safety and pockets the pistol before delivering a few more choice punches to the man's face, followed by another roundhouse kick to the quiet one, who is charging in once again. He loses another tooth. The young one is still on the ground, sobbing over his crushed testicle, if she knows her business.

The fight is over. Her attackers are sufficiently disabled and the van is gone. So, naturally, this is the time the police arrive. An officer who looks more at home in a doughnut shop or bowling alley is “running” toward them from a far-off gate, barking commands into his shackle that Shanti cannot hear.

What she does hear is the roar of a motorcycle. She turns, wondering what fresh hell this is, and reaches for the pistol in her pocket. She stops when she sees that the man pulling up is wearing an EDF uniform.

Captain Folsom kills the engine and pulls off his helmet. “Lieutenant Dae, I assume,” he says as he looks down at the three men who are obviously at her mercy. *Well done, lieutenant.*

“Yes, sir. Lieutenant Dae reporting for duty.”

“I would offer to help, but I see you don’t need it.”

“Yes, sir,” she says proudly. “You must be Captain Folsom.”

He nods as the policeman arrives, huffing from the fifty-yard dash. The scream of authority in the form of a police siren is getting louder. *The cavalry is coming*, appreciated despite their tardiness.

An ambulance was called by her shackle when it detected a spike in her vital signs indicating distress. The men took precautions against her using her voice, but the shackle’s operations are far more complicated.

The cop takes her statement in between summoning underlings to get water for him, *and a hot dog*. The fact that the men who attacked her didn't have shackles will get them jail time in one of America's sparkling new prisons. Add that to their actions against her, and they'll be locked up for a long time.

Shanti grabs her duffel bag as the big man is being handcuffed. He barks at her, "Fucking Indian bitch!"

Derrick gets off his bike slowly and into his face, out of earshot of his lieutenant, and says "You best not be talking about my bike, sir!"

The man cannot win, nor should be try. He turns to the officer holding him and asks quietly, "Please take me away."

The cop reads from a small business card. "I hereby invoke my authority to jail you, sir. Let's go."

After Shanti finishes her statement, the police leave. She climbs on the back of the motorcycle tentatively, carefully, as if handling the captain's newborn child. She puts her arms around his waist as he starts the engine.

He feels her hands on him and makes a supposition. "I hope you're not afraid of bikes. I just landed a few hours ago and needed to take her out for a while."

Needed? She laughs as she gets comfortable. "Not really. I had a scooter when I was young."

"Good," he says as he revs the engine and moves away from the curb, slowly at first.

"I'm only afraid of flying," she says over the noise of the engine.

Folsom laughs loudly for a moment as his bike picks up speed. "Sorry, lieutenant, you only get to make one first impression!"

***

Speeding north along Highway 95, the 160 miles pass by in just under two hours. Lieutenant Dae observes the landscape from the highway, then from smaller roads as the sky continues to darken. She begins to see the stars that she has always taken for granted out on the sea. Still too early to see the Milky Way, she thinks of the assignment again, hopeful that she can succeed.

The captain is a delicate driver, probably for her benefit as a passenger. She relaxes her grip on his waist until he hits a bump in the road, followed by brief laughter. *He could've avoided that bump, probably.*

The bumps increase dramatically as they turn off the paved access road to one of dirt. "Antigravity would work great here," she comments.

She cannot see Derrick smile.

The weather is mild, though the desert wind is picking up. The bike approaches the main gate, which is lit like a beacon in a blanket of darkness. There, a lone figure walks out of his little security shack and onto the road to block their path.

With the bike moving slowly, Derrick can be heard without yelling. “We’re here.”

Shanti replies, “I’ve never seen this base, not even in pictures.”

“Welcome to NASA, lieutenant, the sixth armed service of the United States. This base was once a top-secret laboratory. It closed thirty years ago. Today it is open again for us to train.”

“A lot of room for one unit.”

“There are three units formed and present here already. I expect there to be many more in the coming months.”

“How many personnel are on our team, sir?”

“A plane should be arriving shortly with our last member. I will be leading four of you. We’ll cover everything in the morning,” Folsom says as he sticks his arm out for the shackle to be scanned. The young corporal confirms the captain’s identity and that of the

Indian lieutenant. He comes to attention and salutes. Folsom nods and continues onto the base.

Shanti is impressed with her captain's leadership so far but cannot shake the feeling that she has heard his name before. *Something on a news story from a few years ago involving a massacre in Africa.*

A light descending from the sky indicates a new arrival. As the plane touches down on the dry lake bed doubling as a runway, Shanti sees that it is a Chinese military transport, slightly longer than the old Y-20. She imagines a platoon in battle gear waiting in their seats, preparing to invade.

She mumbles, "That plane can hold a hundred troops at least."

Captain Folsom checks the time and rides to the motor pool that is adjacent to the terminal. "A lot of plane for one passenger. She's earlier than I thought she would be."

Shanti, keeping her eyes on the plane, witnesses a white cloud of dust trailing the aircraft as it touches down, as if a ghost was chasing it, illuminated by the runway lights.

Derrick parks his bike, kills the engine, and removes his helmet. "Let's requisition a car. I can't fit you both on my Indian."

"Yes, sir," she says, in full agreement. The ride was pleasant, ending the day on a more positive note and leaving her hopeful as to what tomorrow will bring.

***

The following morning, the team is assembled in the briefing room on the second level of Hangar 12. Captain Folsom, Lieutenants Dae and Kong, and Sergeant Furtado are each dressed in their crisp, shiny, black uniforms. They're standing at attention as their general looks them over.

General Childs inspects them one by one while finishing his semi long welcome speech with, "Today begins a new chapter in military history. Let's get to work. Fall out!"

Furtado laments on the show they just put on for no one. "All dressed up and now we have to change back to fatigues to train." He shakes his head.

Lieutenant Kong turns to the sergeant to make a point. "Military ceremony is important for the morale of the troops, Sergeant. We don't parade on the streets every day."

Don't they parade in the streets all the time in China? he asks himself. Judging by her tone, he elects not to answer aloud until the captain passes him. "Sir, can you tell us what our first mission is going to be?"

"No, I can't," he pauses for a moment before concluding, "because we don't have one yet." We're strictly in training mode, Sergeant."

Derrick watches his team disperse. *My team, EDF-1.*

CHAPTER NINE: Commanders

The drive from the McCarran Airport in Las Vegas to the Mojave Desert in Southern California takes less than two hours. Doctor Lightner has rented a solar-powered SUV to blend in with the most popular vehicles on the road.

After ensuring that no one is following him, he arrives at the national park and registers at a campsite. He pays in cash at the automated kiosk, one of the last vestiges in the country where it is still accepted. Paper money is still made for use at government facilities, but most people prefer to pay with their shackle accounts. The weather is mild, yet he feels a chill coming on this late in the day. *Or is that my nerves playing havoc with my mind?*

Using his Vorelisian-issued device that is disguised to look like a shackle, Charles makes his way to the rocks about a mile beyond the popular volcanic caves pockmarking the landscape. It is here that he finds his spaceship, a small three-person shuttle built for stealth and invisibility. This type of craft is best for short-distance travel, such as between planets in the same system, around the moons of a world, or in his case, a short excursion through a wormhole after being dropped off by a Vorelisian battle carrier.

It is not until he is within ten feet of his spacecraft that Charles can distinguish its surface from the rocks surrounding it. His device opens the door for him, which is a good thing in that he has trouble remembering the sixteen-digit combination.

Once inside the egg-shaped craft, the temperature drop is considerable. *Thank the stars.* The cold breeze provided by the air filtration system reminds him of the cold winds of his native planet, Paal. After a brief moment of deep breathing and wishful contemplation of his eventual return home, he resets the mechanism to a warmer temperature. *I've been coming here for years to escape my assignment on this planet, wondering when I will return home. It is time to come to the realization that I* am *home.* A feeling of dread passes over him quickly as his systems come to life.

As the computers are powered up and working on decrypting the Vorelisian message his satellite received, Lightner decides to program the electronic eye at the entrance for the next time he enters.

The computers take only a few minutes. They are the best the Vorelisian Empire has to offer; they've spared no expense in getting the opportunity to bring Earth into the galactic community, with the ultimate goal of obtaining the planet Jexx.

One could run a planetary war from the computers in this small ship. The number of screens alone looks like a television studio control room. The only screen Charles is interested in at the moment is communications. The message is complete and waiting for him.

First Colonel Ander Xaix, commander of the Seventh Fleet, childhood friend and fellow Paaliaq citizen, appears on the screen. Lightner's smile of recognition fades quickly at the sight of his friend's look of anguish and the destruction on the monitor behind him. A city is burning.

As if on cue, the image speaks. "Charles, I'm afraid I have distressing news. The Thimms have attacked our home planet."

Charles nearly falls to the deck, shaking his head in disbelief. "No," he whispers to no one. The image on the screen pauses until he puts his eyes back to it.

"Your family is alive and recovering. I spoke to your mother. She is glad you didn't have to witness the rain of fire onto the city. She will send a message when she can. She understands the constraints put upon personal communications. We believe this to be a diversionary tactic to tie up the fleet here, most likely to prevent us from assisting you. The Thimms are moving in ways that are unclear to us at the present time."

"They're diverting you from patrolling Seara! Dammit!" Charles shouts.

Frustrated by the fact that his friend cannot hear him, the doctor begins a recording of his own. He looks into a different kind of eye scanner, one that doubles as a mind reader, and orders the computer to upload the Thimmi message he intercepted earlier as well as the information from his mind, a mission update of sorts.

A record light comes on and he speaks. “Ander, I’ve intercepted a Thimmi transmission from a relay station within this system. You can listen to it for yourself. I am sure you will come to the same conclusion I did. The Thimms are using the attack on Paal to divert your fleet from your normal patrol near the planet Seara to commit an incursion into the Searan wormhole. They’re sending a diplomatic team to assist their agent here.”

He pauses for a moment, thinking of his parents in their later years, toiling in the garden of their palatial home in the hills outside the capital city, having to watch the rain of fire fall from the sky. The preferred method of attack by Thimmi ships is to launch small pellets of toxic chemicals in a missile or missiles over a target, depending on its size. At a specified altitude, the missile breaks up, sending the pellets down over a wide area, coming into contact with the atmosphere on the way down and forming small fireballs. Upon hitting the ground, the chemical is released. *No warning. No mercy. Few survive.*

Charles takes a breath and continues, “They’re bringing in colony ships to move a sizeable population from here to Jexx. If you can bring your fleet here to head them off, I can make an announcement to the people, telling them of our intentions.”

The computer beeps to indicate that another message is being received. Charles sends the one he just finished and opens the second.

Andier Xaix is lit differently; he is swathed in red light, speaking from the bridge of his battle carrier. The ship is obviously on alert. Not so urgent, apparently, or he wouldn’t be taking the time to compose a message to Charles. “Headquarters has instructed me to lead an assault on one of their planets as a proportional response to this attack. Our lord is preparing to address the Galactic Council himself. I’m afraid I won’t be seeing you as soon as I had hoped. Do what you must to bring Earth to us, but remember that you’re going to be on your own.”

That’s it, Charles laments to himself, *I’m on my own. Where we have the technology, the Thimms have the manpower and ships to spread over half the galaxy.*

His altered shackle beeps for his attention. It is a call from Colonel Edward Nealand, who is commanding the International Space Station. Charles slaps his forehead, remembering the scheduled firing of the field energy converter today. He stares at the device for a moment. It beeps again.

"Answer," Charles says into the device, his energy drained from his speech. A hologram of the Air Force colonel in his NASA space suit sans helmet hovers in front of the image of Xaix.

There's no good way out of this one, he thinks as he addresses the smiling apparition while feigning happiness. "Yes, colonel. I'm sorry, I forgot the test was today." *My mind is preoccupied*, he doesn't say.

Nealand smiles as he sits back in his chair, revealing the three scientists standing behind him. "We can start without you. These gentlemen seem to know what they're doing," he says, tongue-in-cheek.

The Magnetic Energy Project is a revolution in power production that the Earthers have invented themselves. It is in conflict with Lightner's Soliquid proposals but well worth the effort to explore. Energy is created by the magnetic field of the Earth being excited by the mass of an object, like the space station. This energy is converted into power that is streamed to the surface at one of seven collector dishes around the globe.

Small in scope, the lessons learned in these experiments will one day be used to power stations orbiting the planet and moons of Jupiter.

Charles finishes his conversation with the commander and closes the call. He feels the familiar chill going down his spine, though this time not related to the temperature of night outside his ship. He sends a distress call to Xaix and leaves to return to Las Vegas.

The trip back to Washington, DC will take the same amount of time as the trip here, though it will seem longer in his mind, as he will be spending the journey thinking of how best to reveal to the people of the Earth that they are not alone in the galaxy, a fact that some governments have known for centuries. *It's time to wake up the people.*

***

Commissioned in the latter half of the twenty-first century, the current International Space Station (ISS) is the third facility to be built in the mode of the first, which served as a giant laboratory until it was decommissioned and allowed to crash harmlessly into the Pacific Ocean in 2025.

Since Lightner gave up the secret of antigravity, under the guise of inventing it, the governments of the world have become proficient in the construction of this most recent station. Today's model took only four years to build, as opposed to the first one that was practically a work in progress up to its last orbit. This station is expected to last a hundred years.

The advent of antigravity, in addition to new alloys and construction techniques, has allowed this station to be manned by a larger crew of scientists, astronauts, and tourists. More experiments, especially those that benefit from zero gravity, have led to breakthroughs in medical and weapons technology. Doctor Lightner's assistance in the current project has advanced it considerably.

Colonel Nealand, a forty-five year-old Ohio native, got his current assignment as commander of the ISS after a long career that began as a diplomat's aide when he was a young, fresh, and naïve lieutenant stationed in Tehran, Iran, twenty years ago.

The people's revolt changed everything. During an uprising, a mass of freedom fighters, formed by several political parties, stormed the parliament building when it was in session. Nealand escaped with his life, though many of his friends were killed. During the subsequent crackdown by the military over the next few weeks, he was ordered not to conduct business in international affairs until an investigation into the possible involvement of the United States was completed.

During this time, Edward encountered a young boy, about nine, whom he caught picking his pocket. The boy was arrested and put in prison as an accomplice of his parents, who were proved to have sided with the Democratic People's Revolt. They were killed while trying to escape the prison, despite never leaving their cells.

Upon learning of their deaths from a friend in the government, Nealand became concerned for the boy's safety, and the guilt he felt at having him arrested inspired him to take action.

At the conclusion of the investigation, the Iranian government ordered the American diplomats and their staff to leave the country. With the help and bribing of a prison official, Edward managed to save the boy as well.

Nealand moved on by joining the NASA program to further the human exploration of space. A decade later, the new station was built and needed a commander. As a colonel and head of the project, he basically gave himself the position.

The Iranian boy, Behrouz Jafari, was forced into foster care during the time Edward was in training for NASA and moving from base to base for the last eight years. This year, Behrouz is turning eighteen, and Edward has lived up to his promise of being there for him. To be the father he always intended to be, though the world sometimes—often—got in the way.

Partnered with his friend, Russian counterpart Alexei Gregorivich Garov, Nealand is in communication with the lead scientist on the latest experiment that has hit a snag. He repeats his question, “Shall we go ahead with the test, Doctor Lightner, or wait for you?”

Looking tired and in a strange-looking room, Lightner responds, “Give me a day to get back to my lab. I would prefer to have my regular equipment with me when we run the test again.”

Nealand smiles at the hologram of the doctor and nods. “Understood, we’ll try again tomorrow at this time.” Edward closes the channel manually before turning to the disheartened scientists around him. “You heard him. Looks like we’ve got the day off.”

As they file out of the communications module, Garov takes the seat next to Nealand and waits for the inevitable venting from this man he has served with for over a year and knows so well.

“Do you believe this guy?” Nealand asks rhetorically, though Alexei answers with a shake of his head, in full agreement with his friend’s demeanor.

Edward continues, “He’s hiding something.”

Garov’s left eyebrow rises. “Who?”

"The doctor. He's acting most…suspicious. I cannot put my finger on what it is, though."

In his heavy Russian accent, Garov says in a boisterous tone, "It is good, yes? We will be prepared for tomorrow. Tonight, we watch baseball."

Nealand laughs as he activates a satellite feed to a live baseball game. Over the past twenty years, the sport has expanded around the world. Even the Russian League puts up good teams. Today, a World Series is just that. Nealand pauses to think of the effects of globalization on his favorite sport and the realignment that is sure to come from it. *As long as progress doesn't interfere with my fantasy league.*

Garov retreats to get a drink from the galley nearby as Nealand watches the managers exchange lineup cards in front of the mechanized umpires. Alexei returns a moment later and hands Edward a bag of beer.

Nealand comments as he takes the beer, "It is always a good day for baseball, my friend."

Garov gets as comfortable as one can in zero gravity. "Yes. Who is playing?"

"Alaska at Vegas. Who do you like?"

"Alaska," the burly Russian states proudly.

Nealand laughs, "Why, because it's close to Russia?"

Garov replies smugly, "Of course."

You guys sold it to us, you know, Nealand doesn't say.

The robot umpire says "Play ball!" in a mechanized but stern voice, and the game begins.

Garov watches Nealand insert a one-way straw into the bag and drink. "Good, eh? It's Canadian beer, eh."

Edward is careful not to let the liquid spill when he laughs at Garov's imitation of a Canadian accent. Getting beer into the circuits wouldn't be a good idea. "It's fine. This beats working any day."

***

The sun rises over Groom Lake Base. EDF-1 Captain Derrick Folsom, Lieutenants Kong and Dae, and Sergeant Furtado run at a steady pace along the dry lake bed that was once an emergency landing strip for the old space shuttle program.

Furtado chants the military cadence as he leads the pack. The team is together, dressed in their battle fatigue uniforms, with their rifles slung across their backs. The weapons resemble the Israeli Uzi of a century ago, but with longer barrels. The drill song hasn't changed much in that time, either: “I don’t know, but I’ve been told…on the moon is a pot of gold!”

Folsom shakes his head and smiles. The early-morning sun is warming the desert quickly as he and his team reach three miles. He has to remind himself that his people are not seasoned veterans, but rookies. They belt out the cadence proudly, repeating after Furtado as they jog in step.

The sergeant continues, “I don’t know, but it’s been said…the core of the Earth is molten lead.”

Folsom sees the strained faces of his people and considers slowing down. *I have to push them hard every day, to get them into shape for a mission that does not exist.* “Another two miles!” he shouts.

The team consists of a leader, a fighter, a spy, and a mechanic, who doubles as a marksman. They were obtained through their expertise and availability. On day one, Derrick envisioned a group of Navy SEALS under his command, but as he looks over this group, *his team*, at this very moment, he wouldn’t trust any mission, or even his life, to anyone else.

***

EDF-1 returns to the hangar area, where an obstacle course has been set up for them. EDF Team 2, under the command of Captain Blassi, is leaving the area for the shooting range.

Sergeant Furtado joins his captain to comment on an idea that he forms while watching his former team jog to the range. "Sir, we should get their scores. It would be good competition to see which team is better."

Folsom smiles as he looks over the area. It looks tame compared to what he went through. "Hit the course, Sergeant. I'll talk to Captain Blassi about your suggestion."

"Yes, sir!" Furtado replies happily as he charges into the course. His teammates follow close behind as they take it in tandem. They climb over walls, crawl under barbed wire, through holes and swing along bars over muddy puddles of water. Shanti misses the rope meant for her to swing across a shallow pool with. Undeterred, she tries again, with success coming on the third try.

Then comes the rope.

Lieutenant Shanti Dae pulls up at the rope tower, a fifty-foot pole with a rope attached for climbing and a ladder on the opposite side for descending. She cannot face her fear of climbing the rope. To be fifty feet in the air might be considered fun for some people and 'just part of the job' for others, but for the young lieutenant, the very thought of gaining altitude without something more tangible to support her than the small ledge at the top is unthinkable and frightening to the point of faking a pulled muscle.

The team knows better but says nothing. Jen and Alfonzo just learned something crucial about their teammate. Jen turns to Alfonzo and mumbles, “We’re only as strong as our weakest member.”

He nods and replies in an equally subdued tone as Shanti comes to within earshot, “Get her to tell you what happened at the Vegas airport when she arrived.”

Folsom, watching the episode play out in front of him, lets it slide—for now.

CHAPTER TEN: Straightforward Politics

Standing at the United States Capitol Building, looking out at the millions gathered between him and the Washington Monument, Dobson stands with the leaders of Canada and Mexico. They have just formally and officially dissolved their three respective countries to form the United States of North America.

The president has also demoted himself to governor to make himself equal to his counterparts around the world. Referring to the new country he now rules over, he speaks to the throng of people before him. "Our new land is now ninety-five states united as one nation, indivisible. We can be proud of our achievement and the new era of prosperity that is coming!"

The crowd cheers.

He continues, relishing the happiness of the people, diverse and obedient as they are. "Order and security have come to our continent! Our lives are going to change dramatically! Change takes time, but I believe in you! This is your land. Are you with me?"

The crowd cheers again, with much more excitement this time. The people expect this new nation-building exercise will result in lower prices, as it did in Europe and Africa. The people expect a strengthened economy despite the ballooning of government and the addition of poor Central American countries. More representation and a new constitution are considered necessary evils.

Dobson continues, addressing the threats of some groups who have promised revolution. “Only together can we move forward!”

Madeline, listening to the president speak from behind him, glances at her ninety-four colleagues seated with her, most with blank looks on their faces. The new constitution requires only one senator per state or province. They’re comprised mostly of newbies from the annexed countries to the north and south. She is not surprised when Dobson ends his speech with another rousing promise.

“Our new nation will lead the rest of the world in time as one united planet and one people! With your help, I will lead you, my people, for many years to come. Our petty disagreements will dissolve soon. I promise you!”

The government of *the people has just become a government* and *its people*. Madeline purses her lips, not sure if her dream of becoming first premier and leading the world is actually going to be good for the world or not.

The crowd’s enthusiasm hits its peak. The cheering is almost deafening to Madeline. She suddenly feels ill, whether from the noise or the sudden infusion of bullshit fed to her by Dobson's speech, she isn't sure. She knows the petty disagreement line is politics-speak for China and Iran not wanting any part of globalization. *They will soon have no choice*. She doesn't know what Dobson has in mind to confront that little problem in order to unite the whole planet as one people. She only knows her own ambitions and how she will eventually work *for* the people.

After the former Canadian and Mexican leaders finish their speeches, Madeline walks to a waiting antigravity staff car, one of the perks of Congress, and gets in. Her secretary and driver, Trisha, is listening to a radio pundit over her shackle discussing the sudden acquiescence of the Cuban government to freely attach itself to this new country as a state. The words "conspiracy" and "CIA coup" are bandied about before she shuts it off when she notices the senator getting into the car.

Trisha is a young and genetically modified beauty who speaks in a perfect voice as she looks at her boss via the rearview mirror. "That was a good speech the president made. I thought it was inspiring."

Trisha's voice is soothing and pleasant to hear. She could announce that a theater was on fire, and the audience would applaud. *Her mother must have wanted her to be a singer*, Madeline wonders silently. Genetic modification is done to cure family genetic abnormalities and to enhance a person's looks, including the structure of vocal cords—things that don't necessarily influence a person's will. *Pity*.

Madeline puts a hand on Trisha's shoulder, forcing her to face her employer at her touch. The young woman sees the sweat forming on Madeline's forehead as she commands in a weak voice, "Take me to the North Side Clinic right away."

Trisha says nothing at first, though the shock on her face speaks volumes. The senator looks as though she is about to collapse. "We're on our way." Trisha says comfortingly as she powers up the thrusters.

***

Dobson walks off the dais and into his own antigravity staff car. Inside is Dennis McCarthy, director of the CIA, a small organization of intelligence and secret operatives that, in recent decades, has gone back to its roots as a clandestine group of assassins, despite public policy to the contrary.

Dobson looks him in the eyes, his smile fading as quickly as a hologram on a dead shackle. "You couldn't call me in my office, McCarthy? We shouldn't be seen together."

McCarthy is a man of personal connection, a face-to-face director who leaves no ambiguity in his discussions or dealings with others. He has served the last two presidents in much the same way. When a terrorist group assassinated President McAllister back in the fifties, he sought out the group's leaders and their families by order of Vice President Larkin before she took office.

Media backlash against his operatives for their non-conventional interrogations and subsequent murders was swift and hard. He survived because of his recordings of conversations made with the new president. Larkin survived as well, but only by standing firm in her support of McCarthy.

His shackle is recording now. "I have selected a town in the Shaanxi Province for our demonstration, Mister President."

Dobson sighs, "Where is it?"

"The mountains of central China. It is in an area not susceptible to tornadoes. They have never had one."

The antigravity engines begin to hum louder as the vehicle picks up speed. It's a short trip back to the White House. Dobson's smile returns, albeit briefly, as he checks his shackle for his next appointment. "It's governor now, McCarthy."

The CIA director dismisses the correction as Dobson continues, "You have done very well. I will arrange for the Chinese ambassador to be present when this town is wiped off the face of the Earth. Is the weapon ready?"

"I've checked it this morning. It will do the job. Remember that it only has enough fuel for two shots. I would like to save the remaining fuel in an attempt to duplicate it."

"Understood. We'll attack tomorrow at noon."

The weapon in question is a weather-control device in orbit of the planet that has the ability to alter weather patterns anywhere in the world by firing an alien element unknown to Earth science into the atmosphere. The plan is to create a tornado in a place they don't normally occur to motivate the Chinese into joining the rest of the world into becoming one nation. The small town of Xiangbaimanzuxiang will be the perfect target for the ambassador of China to witness disappear and report back to his government that Dobson, the leading candidate for first premier of the Earth, means business.

They'll fold. Dobson is confident of that.

The car pulls up to the White House a few seconds later, floating up to the front door and parking on rubberized feet that extend from the undercarriage. McCarthy remains in the vehicle as Dobson exits.

The governor turns back to the spy with the door still open to add, "I only need one shot. If you can replicate that element, we may need to persuade Iran. Remember, tomorrow at noon," he reiterates.

Dobson shuts the door, not seeing McCarthy shake his head or hear his comment of "fool." It's bad enough to have to wipe out a small town's population of two thousand, but it bothers him that this task is interfering with his other main duty, assembling assassins on behalf of General Childs.

His shackle has stopped recording.

***

Dobson enters the Oval Office to find Captain Pilas, dressed in a green military-type uniform of a kind he's never seen. The alien stands as the governor approaches *his* desk. Pilas is in *his* chair. His overcoat, scarf, hat, and sunglasses are strewn across the end of the desk.

Dobson objects calmly, "You are in my chair, sir."

Pilas ignores the complaint and gestures for Dobson to sit in the opposite chair. "Sit down. We have much to discuss."

Dobson reluctantly obeys. The plan is moving forward promptly and efficiently. To prove this, the governor goes into an update on what he has accomplished in just the last few days. He has put the military on high alert. The Navy is moving into seas close to China and Iran in an intimidation move. Troops are being assembled, divisions readied. The Air Force is filling nearby bases with attack and support aircraft.

Pilas raises his hand to silence him. “I have no need for your updates, Mister President.”

Dobson thinks for a New York minute of correcting the alien with regard to his new title but reconsiders just as quickly. He could go into the new political structure forming in the world, *but that would be pointless.*

The Thimmi captain continues, “I’ve come here today to update you.”

Dobson’s right eyebrow goes up as his interest is piqued.

“There is a transport on the way here from my empire. It is carrying Ambassador Hoyth and his diplomatic crew of twenty advisors. They will spread throughout the world to work out agreements between all the leaders of your planet.”

What did he say? Dobson blinks a few times, trying to clear the cobwebs in his head. He stands quickly to question out loud what his mind is repeating a hundred times a second. “What did you say? Our arrangement is for me to unite the world for your empire, and you will leave it under my control once we’ve given you the planet Jexx! What is this you’re telling me now?”

“My superiors are not happy with either of us. Through no fault of our own, we are forced to speed up the timetable to satisfy them; therefore, I am changing the plan.”

Dobson looks around the room, thinking of calling the Secret Service agents just behind the door and wishing he had a gun in this office. If he did, it would probably be in the desk the alien from the Thimmi Empire is occupying. "What plan do you have now?"

"You will begin a war with China."

Dobson stands and backs away, his cowardice coming to the fore. "I can't do that! I'll be run out of town." *I can't mention the attack that I have planned for tomorrow that may precipitate a war in any case*. "War is a risky business. If they were to respond to a declaration of war with nuclear weapons…"

Pilas smiles. "Let them! My people are coming. The articles of the Galactic Council regarding crisis of lives will allow my people to rescue the Earth from itself."

"Crisis of lives? What does that mean?"

"Any survivors of a disaster on a planetary scale can be relocated to any uninhabited world, thus making that world yours. It falls under the refugee relocation resolution of the Galactic Council. All perfectly legal."

"You will help us populate Jexx and we will give it over to you when Earth has recovered from the disaster," Dobson finishes the thought like a fifth grader learning how to construct a sentence.

"Under our sponsorship and guidance, of course. I knew you would understand," Pilas gloats.

Dobson shakes his head, trying to comprehend this new plan. "This is unacceptable! Am I going to be left with a small population here to rule over?"

Pilas stands from behind the president's desk and walks slowly around it. Dobson keeps his distance, walking around the opposite side. "That's another change to the plan I should mention. I've decided it would be in the best interest of my people, and yours, if I were to rule this little planet. You'll lead the Earth people sent to Jexx until you die."

"You're mad."

"Dobson, I'm not changing our arrangement, my superiors are. We must all do as we are commanded," Pilas states without a tinge of reluctance in his voice. Dobson suspects this was his plan all along.

The agreement between the two men has taken a wrong turn. *There is no time to waste*. Dobson has just found himself in a battle for his political life. And more—he just doesn't know it yet. "My people will never go along with starting a war. Provocation is one thing. I have a plan in the works that should—"

Pilas is gathering his clothing as if preparing to leave. The president continues, “The Chinese and Iranians will never attack first, but if we are the instigators of a nuclear exchange, the whole world would rise up against us! It just can’t be done!”

The captain rolls his eyes, an action that is difficult to see due to their small size. “If the world rose against you, the world would be united. Mission accomplished.”

“But I—what about me?”

“I don’t care how you do it, Dobson, just get it done. Make it happen! War is a means to an end, remember that. If you can reach the end another way, fine.”

“I’m not sure I understand.”

“You don’t have to. Just do as you are instructed.”

Dobson lies unconvincingly. “Of course.” He considers telling the captain about the weather weapon he plans to use against the Chinese, but he’d also have to explain how the United States of North America came to be in possession of that technology. *I may need it later against this man.*

Pilas dons his extraneous clothing and walks to the door, unhappy with the plan forming in his mind. He has come to like Earth and her people. He wants nothing more than to rule it himself, but certain things stand in his way; an ambassador from the planet Ti, the Thimmi capital planet, for one.

He will do what is necessary to achieve the goal of obtaining Jexx for his empire, lest he be punished for failing. As he opens the door to leave, he turns back and says, "We must all do what we are called upon to do." He exits.

Dobson sits in his chair, as if for the first time, and leans back, attempting to relax but not able to get comfortable. *Now what the hell am I supposed to do?* he asks himself.

***

Thousands of satellites orbit the Earth. Most are peaceful in nature, owned by various governments for the purpose of monitoring weather patterns and studying the climate; others are links for television and telescopes pointed at the stars, still attempting to find habitable worlds for the humans of Earth to eventually populate when their home planet is no longer capable of sustaining the growing population.

Then there are satellites owned by the CIA, either for use as platforms for future laser weaponry to be aimed at the homes of the enemies of freedom or, as in this scenario, a special weather satellite with its emitters aimed at the skies over Xiangbaimanzuxiang, Shaanxi Province, China.

Controlling the satellite from a bunker thirty stories below the Pentagon building, CIA director McCarthy sits behind a computer console like a kid playing a video game. He takes his task much more seriously than simply blowing up an enemy. *China is not an enemy*, he has to remind himself. *Not yet, anyway.*

McCarthy checks his shackle on this early afternoon. He knows that the ambassador to China is watching from the Oval Office right now, sitting with a smug governor who is so bent on bringing China and Iran into globalization that he'd risk war with the two outcast countries. *Who needs them?* McCarthy wonders as he plots the coordinates of the small Chinese town located high in the mountains, population two thousand.

He reclines in his high-backed secretarial chair and charges the weapon. He's not completely sure how it works, but then, he's not a scientist. All he knows is that the gas that the unit converts to the energy required to function properly is not found on Earth, nor can it be replicated. He doesn't even know what the scientist who studied it named it, if he even gave it a name. "Moynihanigen," he chuckles.

Killed him too soon, I guess. He contemplates the death without regret nor apology.

The unit has completed the charging sequence.

He presses the firing button without hesitation and strolls to another computer that is monitoring the surface of the planet with greater signal clarity. With it, he observes the tornado form slowly as it moves across the plateau, gaining strength as it engulfs the town. He mumbles quietly to himself in a matter-of-fact tone, without emotion, “There it goes.”

By the time McCarthy leaves the Pentagon building, the Chinese ambassador is also leaving the White House to spread the news of the North American attack on his homeland to his government, expecting a reprisal.

Dobson is expecting China to play ball. McCarthy has a different theory of what will happen next.

***

The Vorelisian Seventh Fleet is made up of twelve cigar-shaped vessels of varying sizes. These mighty ships consist of six destroyers with the primary mission of protecting the three larger cruisers and the main battle carrier that houses a crew of one thousand and three squadrons of fighters.

The support ships include a troop carrier loaded with an assault force of five hundred men and a supply ship on which crews of the entire fleet are assigned R&R on long missions. It houses entertainment centers and clubs, necessary for the morale and well being of the fleet's personnel. Some say its very presence is essential.

The Mighty Seventh, as Xaix's group of ships has come to be known, is currently in orbit of the planet Seara, awaiting orders, having arrived in preparation for a possible incursion into Thimmi space in response to the recent attack on the Vorelisian planet Paal.

The bridge of the battle carrier is dimly lit, reflecting the lateness of the hour in which the crew is working. Most of the light in the room is coming from various video screens that are positioned above an equal number of control consoles manned by a crew of five, not including aides and support staff.

There is also the light from the yellow star in the center of this system of ten planets. Most are gas giants. Seara, fourth from the star, is the only planet in this system currently supporting life. First Colonel Xaix looks out the main window and sees the large, rocky third planet. When and if the order comes, that planet's wormhole will be their destination.

Among the dayshift crew are Executive Lieutenant Len Quell, a young man compared to most in his position as second officer. At only twenty-eight years old, he has aspirations of gaining command of this great ship. As second-in-command, he is well on his way. He was allowed an exception to the regulations regarding time in service requirements as a favor to his father, a friend of First

Colonel Xaix. Quell may very well be the lowest-ranking captain of any ship in the fleet when his time comes.

Under-Lieutenant Alice Lett sits at her communications console, monitoring radio stations on the relatively primitive planet below while conjuring up a name for a character in her latest novel. Quell often checks her work for security reasons, due to her sensitive position on the bridge, but deep down she suspects he likes her stories.

First Captain Jay Sonan is the ship's tactical officer and has been for the last twelve years. He is responsible for the security of the ship as well as monitoring its sensors. He outranks everyone on the ship but for First Colonel Andier Xaix and Flight Commander (Colonel) Tor Mens.

Position, however, takes precedence over rank, which is why a young executive lieutenant like Quell outranks Sonan on board the ship. The first captain's other responsibility is to relay commands from the carrier to the rest of the fleet, to coordinate battle strategies and orders given by the captain. Xaix is the most knowledgeable and trusted tactical leader in the empire.

Most people do not envy the job of "tack-o", as it is commonly known. Those in his position usually move on to second officer or captain, but Sonan's dream is to become commander of flight operations when Mens retires, and his current position is perfect for when that promotion comes.

He is a very patient man.

Flight commander isn't as glamorous a title as captain, though Tor Mens gets an equal amount of respect. He likes to be around the war machines on the flight deck located beneath the bridge when he is not commanding a squadron of his own. He enjoys flying more than anything in the universe. He is always prepared to fight, silencing his pacifist nature.

Last but not least—and that's not just his opinion—is the well-liked navigator and morale officer, Second Captain Karm Bowen. He sits between Sonan and Lett at the front of the bridge, with First Colonel Xaix behind them. The executive officer's position is behind the commander to protect him against any incursion onto the bridge by a potential enemy.

The commander of this ship is also the fleet commander. First Colonel Andier Xaix paces around the bridge, looking over the shoulders of his crew, making them slightly uncomfortable as he awaits his next order from headquarters.

Preliminary targets include a mining planet deep in Thimmi territory. It is called Tanli. Once operations there are disrupted, it is assumed, the resulting backlash will cripple the Thimmi economy, at least temporarily.

Under-Lieutenant Lett announces an incoming message from Dr. Lightner but is unable to discern it through the static interference caused by a solar flare.

"Can you get a fix on the message? It could be vital," Xaix asks. *I have to put the mission ahead of my friend. I hate being powerless*, he laments to himself.

Second Captain Bowen pipes up with information that is often unnecessary or obnoxious. "We are close to the wake of the planet's motion, sir. Perhaps we should move away from the planet."

"Thank you, Two-Cap," Xaix replies, slightly annoyed at the man stating the obvious. Wormholes only cause interference when a ship is inside it, not orbiting past it.

As they come around the blue and green planet again, Alice points out an anomaly. The star in this system has recently begun a phase of some kind. The solar flares have increased in intensity over the last twenty years, and may be a cause for concern. She makes a note of it in the log.

Executive Lieutenant Quell moves to Alice's console to assist her and perhaps inhale the scent of her hair. He hopes to learn more about the interference and knows that they are only two minutes away from Earth through the wormhole. *Two lousy minutes that may as well be two hundred years!*

Xaix presses, "Do we know if Lightner got *my* message?"

"No, sir. I'm s…" Quell's voice fades away. Apologies won't be of any help at this point.

Xaix shoots him a look and smiles. *He is a professional and always level-headed, but he is still a young man with feelings. I sometimes lose mine*. It is surprising, then, that when Quell announces another message coming in, this one from headquarters, there is some alarm in his voice. "We have the order to proceed to Tanli and attack, sir."

Xaix lowers his head. He is prepared for battle, as is the rest of the fleet under his command, but no soldier enjoys war. They prefer maintaining the peace. It's safer. But orders are orders, so Xaix gives the order to bring the fleet away from the orbit of Seara and prepare for travel into the wormhole located at the fourth planet, which will lead them to the edge of their territory. From there, the incursion through normal space at high speed will take the better part of a decade, as there are no other wormholes to navigate through.

Xaix will announce to the crews under his command what their orders are and what he expects of them. He will address the concern of those crewmembers from Paal who expect them to return and fight off the invaders. The ground troops left behind, in addition to the armed populace, will have to fend off the enemy on their own for the time being.

My friend on Earth will also have to fend for himself, he thinks as he envisions the trouble Charles must be going through. The unintelligible message from Lightner goes unheard. Andier knows they'll be stopping periodically during the voyage; perhaps by the first stop, Under-Lieutenant Lett will have the message cleaned up for him.

As the last ship in the fleet enters the wormhole of the fourth planet, a small transport approaches the Searan wormhole. If only Xaix could hear the message warning him of its arrival.

CHAPTER ELEVEN: Battles

The power of the USNA Navy is its eight aircraft carrier fleets. They are symbols of military might as they patrol the seas where they operate. The Navy, as part of the globalization of the planet, has joined with naval fleets of the European and Asian Alliances to show solidarity against the Chinese military buildup over the past week, since the town of Xiangbaimanzuxiang disappeared.

Indian and Japanese cruisers and destroyers are currently sailing with the aircraft carrier USS *McAllister* and her escorts in the South China Sea off the coast of Hong Kong, where a German carrier and her Korean escorts are already stationed.

In keeping with the tradition of naming such massive ships after respected and famous leaders, the *McAllister* is named after the sixty-third president of the former United States.

A group of revolutionaries, who were seeing their country slip away, fought to hold on to the principles the US Constitution stood for by planning and executing the assassination of the president. A lone madman managed to fly his private jet into Air Force One before he could be intercepted. His last words broadcast to the plane were; “Death to globalization! Death to the traitor!”

Unlike past assassinations, the conspiracy theorists were correct in connecting the killing to a newly formed political party.

Their efforts to bring the country back from its socialist policies and guarantee liberty for the people failed.

The group was hunted down by McAllister's successor, Betty Larkin, under the direction of the CIA, and quietly dissolved. They were labeled terrorists, but some have come to see them as patriots. Their actions had the reverse effect of their goal in that the United States increased its military presence in Africa to speed the unification of that continent.

Ten years later, the African Union was formed thanks to the heroic efforts of Captain Folsom and the then Colonel William Childs.

Today, the Chinese government is seeing those same efforts coming to the fore in uniting all of Asia under one flag through the military presence of American troops along its land border and by the navies at sea.

The government of China also resists the acceptance of corporate icons that influence and manipulate the people. China does not recognize the Asian Alliance under the leadership of Minister Shabal and has put strict limits on trade with its partners.

China has vowed to resist the New Order. To that end, the Chinese nuclear attack submarine PLA *Changzheng* is shadowing the USNA-led allied fleet on patrol.

Undetected so far.

While the sub is running in "silent" mode, sonar officer Han Ling is expecting to hear the familiar sound of a USNA attack submarine that typically accompanies their fleets. He is instead surprised to hear the sound of a much larger submerged vessel that takes his computer only three seconds to identify due to the noise its twin propellers, or screws, is making.

He quickly but calmly calls up to the control room to report the contact of a USNA nuclear ballistic missile sub (SSBN) known by the USNA Navy slang term "boomer", a Texas Class submarine capable of launching twenty nuclear missiles at his homeland. Each missile carries ten warheads within multiple independent re-entry vehicles, or MIRVS, which could wipe out most of the population along the east coast of China. *There could be only one reason why this vessel is here*, he surmises.

The captain of the *Changzheng*, Fain Gin, has recently received orders to sink any and all foreign vessels that stray past the internationally agreed-upon ocean border that stretches out from the coast by twelve miles.

The American boomer is quite close to that border, and Gin, a veteran of several battles won and lost, interprets his orders to destroy "without warning or mercy" carefully. He commands his attack sub to lie in wait as the larger vessel passes by. He breathes a sigh of relief when Ling reports that the American war machine is turning away from the coast in a leisurely maneuver. “They may not be aware of us,” Gin says to no one in particular.

A moment later, in a complete surprise to the Chinese crew, the SSBN begins to ascend rapidly from its current depth of eight hundred feet to five hundred and continues upward.

Gin turns to his second-in-command (XO) and speaks in a slightly alarmed tone. “They may be preparing to launch an attack. If they get to one hundred and fifty feet, we will have no choice but to destroy them.” There are many reasons for a sub to surface. They can’t fire their nukes until the launch doors are open, but any excuse available to the captain to avenge the deliberate destruction of a Chinese town, he will take.

Gin considers his options. Can he get away with destroying an American sub? Technically, no, but the signs are growing in his favor. He cannot allow the Americans to open their launch doors; one missile could kill hundreds of millions. Is protecting them worth the possibility of being wrong? *They are still rising, with no indication why.*

The XO orders the torpedo tubes to be flooded despite the sound such an event generates. “Bring us about!” he commands, followed by a mumble under his breath, “Get us behind the globalists.”

Gin considers giving away their position to the Americans as a warning and to gauge their response, which should be to retreat despite the well-known stubbornness of American sub captains.

SSBNs typically don't engage attack subs due to their slow maneuverability and lack of quiet speed. They usually have an attack sub escort of their own.

But where is it? Ling wonders before reporting, "The American boomer is still rising, sir! Passing three hundred!"

The weapons officer adds, "I have a targeting solution on the intruder, sir. Range, two thousand yards. Speed, slow and steady. Ready to fire at your command." His voice is calm and professional. Another day at the office.

"They're not intruders yet. Remain steady at your post," Gin fires back.

"Yes, captain." The young officer responds humbly.

"Stand by," comes the familiar command from the XO.

The captain doesn't want to make an error at this point. His mistake could precipitate a full-scale nuclear exchange. His lack of action could result in the same. *What should I do?*

The XO stands next to his captain, trying to read him. "We don't need to wait for them to cross the border, captain. They are close enough to launch their missiles and are within range of our torpedoes. We can argue semantics later. We must hurry if we are going to act. They're almost at launch depth."

Gin wonders silently if his XO actually hears himself when he speaks. "They should be aware of us. Their sonar is better than ours. They should have heard the tubes flooding. Why do they not run?" To Ling, he adds, "Speed of target?"

Ling responds into a comm box at his station, "Moving away from the coast at ten knots, Captain. Distance, one thousand five hundred yards."

"What could they be doing?"

The answer to the captain's question comes in the form of a ping generated from another direction—behind them!

"Another sub!" the XO shouts. "We're under attack!"

"Close on the American missile sub! Attack speed!" Gin orders quickly.

The *Changzheng* begins to accelerate. *Why doesn't the American boomer dive?*

Ling, with a bit more panic in his voice caused by the sudden appearance of the USNA attack sub, turns his attention away from the SSBN to locate the new threat and does so by using the

American's ping, or active sonar, as a source. "American New Orleans Class attack submarine bearing one-eight-nine. Range, two thousand yards and closing. Speed, twenty knots."

"What's *our* speed?"

"Eighteen knots and increasing, sir!" comes the reply from the XO, who is starting to sweat as he reads the gauges above the diving officer's head.

The tension mounts tenfold in the command center. Gin must remain focused. If the American attack sub were planning to destroy them, it would have fired by now. They're just trying to scare him and his men. And are succeeding. *Or perhaps it's a provocation.*

"Where is the missile sub? Don't lose him!" Gin says.

The XO confirms, "Enemy SSBN directly ahead, still rising."

The weapons officer adds, "Recalculating targeting solution. I need three seconds."

Ling turns his sonar listening device back to the coordinates where he last heard the giant submerged boat. He hears the unmistakable sound of rushing water—the missile tube doors must be opening. It's difficult to tell the difference between that and his own sub's propellers on full power. There are too many other noises in the water competing for his ears. He tries to isolate the sound he wants to hear as his voice cracks in his report, “Launch doors opening, captain! I think.”

Every officer on the bridge turns to the young sonar operator, simultaneously thinking what only the captain articulates. “You *think*?”

The XO, moving to the weapons station, shoves the weapons officer aside. “We must fire now!”

Ling quickly corrects himself and clears his throat. “Cavitations! they’re increasing speed.”

The XO is not easily convinced. “Are they running? Or simply getting out of the way for their attack sub to destroy us? Give me the order to fire *now*, captain!”

If the XO is the little devil on your shoulder, who on this boat is the angel? Gin wonders. He is pressed for time and, knowing the nuclear missile sub needs to be at a depth of 150 feet to launch, rushes to Officer Ling’s side and grabs his headphones to listen to the sounds himself. *I have time, right?* “What’s their depth?”

“One sixty, sir, and rising! They are still accelerating.”

Do they need to stop motion in order to fire? he doesn’t ask.

Gin listens hard to the headphones, calling on his experience and training for an answer to a situation like this. His past experience has all been in simulators, however. *Those battles were much simpler than this.* He hears the sound of rushing water and recognizes it as something in addition to propeller noise. He mumbles to himself, "Could they be masking the opening of their missile doors with their propellers?" He listens more intently, straining to hear each bit of noise. He hears what sounds like a door squeak, but the noise of his ship as well as the SSBN's propellers is dominating the ocean. *I have zero time for analysis.*

"They're at launch depth, captain, and slowing," the XO reports.

The American attack sub is closing in, their active sonar being used again to target the *Changzheng. Ping!*

Gin reacts to the blast of sound striking the hull and the sensitive equipment attached to it, blowing out one of his eardrums. "OW!"

The XO, frozen with fear resulting from the sound waves of the ping slamming into the hull, misinterprets what he hears from the captain, mistaking the Mandarin word for "ouch" for the word for "shoot." "Firing tube one!" he shouts as he presses the launch button before the weapons officer can stop him.

"NO!" the weapons officer cries out as he pushes the XO away from his controls.

The Chinese torpedo is ejected from the *Changzheng* and targets the SSBN immediately. Its speed gets to sixty knots in less than ten seconds.

Ling, sweat pouring off his brow, takes back the headphones. "Our torpedo is in the water, sir, On course. The attack sub is flooding its tubes. The SSBN is fleeing, sir. Countermeasures are in the water, and the sub appears to be surfacing."

"Dive! Dive! Dive! Flank speed! Get us out of here! Set course for the coast!" the captain commands.

The orders are relayed and obeyed quickly. The crew performs flawlessly.

Gin grabs his XO by the scruff of the neck as the sub banks hard to the left. "I heard their planes, not the missile tube doors. They were about to surface, you fool!"

"Two American torpedoes in the water, Captain, headed straight for us. Speed, sixty-five knots," Ling interjects.

Gin throws the shorter man aside and says, "They knew we were here all along."

"But how?" the XO asks.

"Detonate our torpedo now!"

The XO returns to the weapons station, where the weapons officer is way ahead of him in connecting the computer to their torpedo. “Ready to detonate, XO,” he says.

The XO stops, confused. “If we’re going to die, why not take them with us?”

Ling, more sedate than ever, knowing that this is probably the end, says, “The two American torpedoes are approaching fast. Range, five hundred yards.”

The weapons officer nudges the XO, snapping him out of his apparent daydream.

The XO reluctantly presses the “destruct” button. The sound of a quiet and muffled boom adds to the noise of the engines at full power and the ping sounds of the American weapons approaching at almost seventy knots now. *They’ve got minds of their own*, the XO thinks before confirming, “Our torpedo is destroyed, captain.”

The *Changzheng* responds to perfection as it reaches thirty knots and a thousand feet deep faster than their American counterpart, though the American torpedoes are chasing them independently with higher speed and superior targeting.

After a moment passes, Captain Gin begins to wonder why the American captain doesn’t reciprocate his actions by detonating his own torpedoes. “Left full rudder. Release countermeasures,” he orders.

Ling listens and reacts with little emotion. *We've lost.* “Here they come!”

“Bring us about!” the XO screams.

Ling continues with considerably less enthusiasm. “Target SSBN boomer is moving out to sea and remains surfaced. Two American torpedoes incoming. Impact in ten, nine, eight…”

The American torpedoes' active sonar increases in volume as they decrease in distance. *Ping! Ping! PING!*

One of the *Changzheng* countermeasure noisemakers draws one of the torpedoes toward it and away from the sub.

Ling becomes hopeful. “One torpedo veered away by our countermeasures, sir. Second torpedo closing. Four hundred yards!”

The XO walks away from the command center, hoping that their sacrifice will persuade the Americans not to retaliate further. It's not every day a man finds himself responsible for the deaths of billions of people. He stops to pray for a quick end to his life—in secret, of course.

Ling continues the countdown to impact. “Five, four…”

"Shut up, Ling!" the captain commands. "Right full rudder. Launch two more countermeasures!"

The sub banks again like a thousand-ton roller coaster car.

Two more noisemakers are launched from the *Changzheng*, but they are launched too far away from the lone American torpedo to be effective.

The torpedo slams into the Chinese attack sub amidships. The resulting explosion rips it apart. It folds in on itself from the pressure of the ocean collapsing its hull. The entire crew of one hundred perishes in an instant; their sub sinks to the bottom, —dead.

***

Word of the attack on the American ballistic missile submarine spreads like wildfire via news bulletins worldwide. The Navy, however, provides only their version of the attack to the media. Fragments of the torpedo are shown to the public to provide a solid self-defense argument. The SSBN was last reported in Tokyo harbor with extensive damage, though no pictures or video of any damage was made available.

Citizens of North America, expecting the worst, begin evacuating the cities in droves. Several politicians attempt to appease the public by reminding them of space-based defenses and the diplomatic channels in play that will resolve the tensions between the two powers.

The fact that the majority of Congress members have left Washington, DC for an underground shelter in Ohio is not widely broadcast.

Governor Dobson, whether through bravery or foolishness in the eyes of the people, has decided to remain in the White House, challenging the Chinese leaders to “do their worst,” all the while proclaiming the destruction of the Chinese sub as an act of self-defense, affirming the Navy’s story. He is ready to leave at a moments notice, expecting the attack on the Chinese sub to lead to war despite the assurances of the secretary of state that a diplomatic solution is in the works.

Dobson watches the news reports on three feeds showing on his desktop screen. He is surprised and perplexed by the fact that the Chinese have not gone public about the destruction of the town in Shaanxi Province and are disturbingly quiet about the destruction of their sub beyond their initial complaint. *They’re not even challenging the story we are putting out. Why?*

We should be at war already. What do I have to do, nuke the bastards? Dobson thinks as a harrier-type aircraft lands outside his window. The ultrasonic plane is there to whisk him to safety at a moments notice.

***

Captain Pilas sits in his armed transport, a small spacecraft parked among the frozen mountains of Alaska. He waits for news of Chinese retaliation.

***

Thanksgiving is put off this year in North America, as it no longer applies to a country that doesn't exist. Politicians from around the world, in addition to the American public, who prefer to stand with their traditions, hope to make the fourth Thursday in November a day for the entire world to celebrate the election of the world's first planetary leader. At present, however, the people are waiting for something to give—the unification of the entire planet into one people and one government, or World War III.

***

It's another day of training on this cold late-November morning in the Nevada desert. EDF-1 has completed its daily five-mile run and breakfast among the rocks has never felt so good to any of them. *The team is coming together. They are jelling well*, in Captain Folsom's estimation.

With the morning meal complete, the team marches at an easy pace to the obstacle course a mile away. It is near their base hangar. Lieutenant Shanti Dae falls back deliberately when Folsom gives the order to hit the obstacles. Her goal is to be last so as to tackle the fifty-foot pole alone. The pole is symbolic of her fears, and to climb it is to conquer them.

Once there, she watches the others ascend the rope and climb down the ladder on the opposite side of the pole. *Ladder, hah!* She has seen better rungs on submarines on the sea floor. Fear has frozen her legs and caused her heart to race. *Damn.*

Captain Folsom, in a change of routine, does not move to the end of the course to wait for the team to reassemble. Instead, he stands at the pole and waits for Lieutenant Dae to climb the rope. "I want you up that pole, lieutenant," he says. "We're all going to wait here until you do it, even if it takes all day."

Furtado returns from the end of the course, which is a short run to the finish after the pole. The pole is the final obstacle. He cheers on his teammate while being sensitive to her fear of heights. After three weeks of training, there are few secrets left between them.

Lieutenant Kong, however, has one secret. She watches for a moment as Shanti grabs the rope and pulls herself up two feet off the ground. *Hopefully the captain doesn't literally intend to wait all day,* she thinks as a pickup truck pulls up behind her.

The maintenance worker rolls down the window, inches from Kong's back, and says, "Warm today."

Jen turns to reply to the old man, "Warm yesterday. Teeth-chattering weather we're having."

With the recognition code complete, she takes a good look at her contact, a fellow agent of the MSS planted at the base a week ago. "I have nothing to report at present. We have no mission assigned to us," she reports.

"Strange," he replies before elaborating on recent events. She is surprised by the destruction of Xiangbaimanzuxiang fifteen days ago and the story behind the lost submarine, but even more surprising is the acquiescence of her government.

She takes note of the man's advanced age and requests details of his credentials and rank.

He refuses to answer. "I have no information I am allowed to share," he says with a smile.

Jen does not react outwardly, but understands the old man's meaning and respects him for it. "Do you have instructions for me?" she asks.

“Find the satellite that fired the weather weapon upon our homeland. We need proof to bring to the world court. They will not accept the ambassador’s testimony alone.”

Confused, Jen inquires about the apparent softness of their leaders back home. “Are they planning retaliation for the people? What of the crew of the sub that was sunk? Are they not going to avenge their deaths?”

“I have no knowledge of our government’s plans. I only follow their instructions. Your captain is approaching. I must go now.” The maintenance worker starts up the engine of the old pickup, a truck with tires, and drives toward the next hangar, as if actually working.

Captain Folsom walks up to Jen, who just now sees that the team is gone. “Are you going to join us, lieutenant, or do you plan to bullshit with the maintenance crew some more?”

She comes to attention to apologize. “Forgive me, sir. I was enthralled by the conversation I was having in my native tongue.”

Folsom responds sternly, “You’re one of us, lieutenant. You’re a part of a team that supports the world, no one country.”

Kong nods in agreement, though she isn’t sure if her captain believes what he has just said. She wonders if he isn’t setting himself up for another failure. *Who do we answer to?* She slings her rifle over her shoulder and asks, “Sir, do you speak Mandarin?”

He gives her a hard look and commands, “Move it!” He took her question as a commentary on globalization and remembers a short time ago when he didn’t agree with it at all. Lately, however, he finds himself warming up to the idea. He expects the diversity of language to disappear along with many cultures. In a few hundred years, even the separate races will be gone, replaced by a combination of all of them.

Almost the entire planet has accepted English as the main language, followed by Mandarin, Spanish, Russian, and French.

Folsom follows his young lieutenant at a slower pace. There is more training ahead; the shooting range and simulated hand-to-hand combat, followed by classes that indoctrinate them into things like teamwork and patriotism, the love of the planet and the people that inhabit her.

Jen runs back to the hangar while accessing her shackle to determine where her teammates are and how best she can infiltrate the secured building nearby. *I have a lot of work to do.*

EDF Unit Two enters the obstacle course. Captain Amanda Blassi shares with Derrick the scores of their last trip to the firing range. “You spend a lot of time there,” he says, stating the obvious.

Amanda smiles while trying to subtly reveal what she shouldn't. "I think the general wants my team to be made up of only snipers."

"That explains why Furtado is so good. The general obviously knew what he was doing."

"I've replaced him. Do you have an assignment yet?"

"No," is Derrick's reply, followed quickly by the one-word question, "you?"

"Moment's notice, they tell me."

The two captains leave each other with more questions about their new careers and their use by the leaders they supposedly don't work for.

***

Inside the hangar, Jen gets to her cot and sits, facing Lieutenant Dae, who is lying on her back on her own cot, staring at the catwalk above her. She isn't sulking or upset, but looks angry.

"Couldn't get up the pole?" Jen asks.

"No."

Lieutenant Kong thinks twice about offering assistance to any member of the team, having concluded that it may go against her mission of infiltration and espionage to get friendly with anyone here. Her original impulse of compassion, however, wins out. "I will help you."

Shanti sits up. She is somewhat surprised that her fellow teammate is coming out of the shell she has appeared to enjoy being in for the few weeks they've been together. Shanti has never met anyone so introverted. It is refreshing to make a new friend.

Friend, there's a word Shanti would bet the desert's supply of silver Jen doesn't hear often when someone refers to her. "Thanks," is all she says in reply to the offer with genuine gratitude in her voice, and for a moment, Shanti thinks she may have caught the hint of a smile.

CHAPTER TWELVE: Life and Lives

Madeline sits in the examination room of Dr. Randall Yates on a follow-up visit to find out what has been making her feel ill this past month. She has undergone numerous tests, including a full-body scan that makes an MRI feel like a gentle massage, while blood and cell samples are taken by means of small pricks to her skin. She is happy to have been given sedatives and mood relievers, through eye drops and nasal sprays respectively, but she's been sitting for over thirty minutes now, and her patience is wearing thin. *Maybe they're waiting for the drugs to wear off*, she wonders.

Dr. Yates enters, reading from a hologram projected in front of him by his shackle that reflects patient information and test results. He speaks with an air of happiness. "Congratulations, senator. You're pregnant with what I expect to become a baby." He pauses to gauge her response to his attempt at humor.

When it doesn't come, he continues carefully, "I'm guessing a girl, based on these results, but it's too soon to tell for sure. I'm usually right fifty percent of the time." He snorts as he holds back from laughing at his own joke.

Madeline is a rock, as still as El Capitan in Yosemite National Park. She is motionless until she tries to stand and crumples to the floor. The doctor sets her on a stool and holds his shackle in front of her chest to scan for her vital signs. Her heart is racing and her blood pressure is high. He helps her onto the exam table and lays her down. “I’m sorry. I shouldn’t have told you the sex of the child. I figured you’d find out soon enough when I transferred your results to your shackle.”

Madeline’s response takes a 180-degree turn from what he expected from an expectant mother—anger. “How dare you tell me I’m pregnant!”

Confused by her statement, he tries to ease her emotions with humor. “It’s not a tumor growing inside you, senator. I don’t understand.”

This is not the time to start a family, she panics silently as she responds, “I’m about to start my campaign for first premier. I can’t be pregnant.”

“Surely the government can help you with raising a child while you’re in office.” *As if you have a chance of winning*, he doesn’t add.

“Both responsibilities are mine, doctor. I wouldn’t pass off either of them.”

That’s the response he expects a mother to have. “My point is that you’re not alone. You have support, people willing to help you without being asked. You’re luckier than most mothers in the world.”

The Chinese situation is about to explode and she is to have her attention driven by a growing baby inside her. *What of Charles?* Her thoughts turn to the man she loves more than herself, and as a result, her blood pressure reaches 150/110. She wants their relationship to be based on the love she feels is mutual despite his reservations. *He is holding something back. There's something he is afraid of telling me. This will only complicate things.*

Dr. Yates reaches into a drawer for an eyedropper. "This will help you relax." He puts two drops of a strong sedative into each eye before Madeline can stop him.

"I need to make a call!" she shouts.

"It can wait, senator. The life inside you is more important right now."

She is already feeling woozy as the doctor puts a pillow under her head and calls for a nurse to reserve a room for her. Madeline is able to mutter commands into her shackle in order to send a modern-type text message: *"Need to talk. Where are you?"* She falls asleep before she can tell her shackle to send it.

"You'll awaken in about an hour, Madeline. You just relax," Dr. Yates says as he watches her vital signs drop to more acceptable numbers.

The nurse enters with an attendant pushing a gurney in front of him. They transfer Madeline to it for the short ride upstairs.

Dr. Yates alerts the Medical Authorities of America (MAA) to the senator's condition so they do not send the FBI to investigate.

***

Upon arriving at his laboratory in New York City, Dr. Lightner finds himself at a podium in front of a slew of cameras. His hastily called press conference is expected to be an announcement of some new scientific discovery, as has been the case in the past. There are tens of reporters gathered in the small conference room, some appearing as holograms.

He nervously clears his throat at the podium and sips some water, trying to clear whatever is in his throat that is preventing him from speaking. *That's all in your head, Charlie. Let's get on with it and let the stars shine where they shine.*

He taps the mic once to get the attention of everyone in the room and to silence their conversations. The time is 2:15 on a Friday afternoon, December 16, 2061. He marks the date in his mind before beginning his speech.

"Good people of the planet Earth." He pauses, his voice cracking a little. He again sips from his water bottle and continues. "The tensions between the eight governments of this planet are troubling. I have therefore found it necessary to speed up my government's plans to make this announcement." He looks out at the confused faces before him. *Good, that got their attention.*

The doctor hopes that China and Iran are watching as he starts again. "War is never the answer. You will not achieve peace and security by killing yourselves. You are one people!" He wipes his mouth, biting his forefinger and pulling it away to give him a sensation, any sensation besides the fear that is gripping him. *How will these people respond?* "I have been working from within the scientific community to bring about peaceful unification of the Earth through technological gifts, but my timetable has been altered due to…" *Stop! I cannot mention the Thimmi agent unless I can identify him.*

Charles clears his throat and shakes his head, as if that action will erase the memory from everyone's mind of what they just heard. "Now is the time to announce my true intentions for your world."

Someone in the back of the room shouts, "What the hell are you talking about, Doc?"

The rest laugh. It's a nervous laugh, an impatient laugh, the kind that spells fear. He must allay their fears lest they panic. "I mean you no harm. My mission is one of peace. My people wish nothing more than to sponsor your planet into the Galactic Community of Worlds." He speaks over the murmuring as he continues, "In order to be allowed membership, the one prerequisite is for this planet to be united as one people."

He looks out at the confused faces in the room. Some people are laughing, speaking aloud what they're thinking, that the good doctor has lost his mind. He decides to go for broke. "I am from the planet Paal. I have come as a representative of the Vorelisian Empire. I am not of your world."

The room falls silent. *Now*, they're polarized: *He's a nut* versus *He's a what?*

Reality sinks into their minds. This is no joke. Their response is quick and deliberate as those assembled in the room charge the podium to ask questions, as reporters do. "I will give details tomorrow!" Charles shouts as he retreats to his lab and locks the soundproof door behind him. He is not alone for two minutes before his shackle informs him of an incoming call from China.

***

Every mass in the universe, star or planet, exists on its own space/time/gravity plane. Each plane is multidimensional and is what the mass "rides" on as it travels through space, whether in orbit around a star or the galaxy itself. As it moves, it creates turbulence on its plane, much like the wake of a ship on the ocean. Just like a seafaring vessel, the greater the mass of an object, the greater the flux of space/time left behind it.

This flux creates wormholes, or rips in the plane, that spaceships can use to traverse thousands of light-years in minutes. Wormhole connections within subspace are common, and permanent as long as the mass exists to sustain them.

The size of the mass, coupled with its speed on its plane, indicates how long or short its wormhole will be. Wormhole connections exist for every star and planet known in the galaxy, and most likely beyond, though no scientist has, of yet, explored other galaxies to prove this theory. Current technology does not allow for the transportation of spacecraft through the wormholes of stars due to the great speed the ship would achieve. Its exit close to a star would cause its destruction.

Conversely, small planets like Mercury and Mars do not have sufficient mass to create wormhole trails beyond their own planetary neighbors, and gas giants are troublesome for navigation purposes as well. Similar to stars, they have their own set of problems.

The wormhole system was discovered a thousand years ago by a race of beings known as the Gightians. They're humanoid in appearance, but due to the light gravity of their planet, are taller than Earth people and have less bone mass.

A hybrid of the alien race 'The Greys' and Humans from other worlds, the Gightians are known as the scientists of the galaxy. They pride themselves on their intelligence and knowledge of the known universe.

Their education system is limited to their own people and their star system neighbors, the Galestikons, with whom they have a symbiotic relationship. The two planets orbit the same star, trade their respective goods, and assist each other in matters of intergalactic importance. Where the Gightians are the brains, the Galestikons are the brawn. The Galactic Council relies on both heavily when dealing with conflicts among members and finding solutions to those conflicts.

The Gightians are a peaceful people save for the experiments conducted on abducted individuals. Only recently, within the last fifty years, has the Galactic Council decided to put a stop to abductions from any planet in the galaxy, regardless of membership status. This was seen as a humanitarian move, ironically, orchestrated by the Greys themselves, who have been responsible for hundreds of thousands of abductions galaxy-wide in their recorded history. Their change of heart and policy on scientific experimentation has never been explained.

The population of Gight is small, about five hundred million. There are strict controls in place to maintain that number.

After witnessing the Vorelisian fleet leave the Searan system, a Gightian science vessel enters the area to study the Searan star that has exhibited some unusual wave patterns recently, suggesting that it is getting close to the end of its life. The Gightians are present to learn just how close the five planets in this system are to disaster, including the billion inhabitants of Seara itself.

Upon entering orbit, the Gightian crew observes a transport, identified through their transponder upon contact as a Thimmi vessel, entering the system from deep space. The ship makes one orbit of the planet, zipping past the Gightian ship in the process, and disappears into the Searan wormhole without any response to hails.

The Gightian expedition leader, Captain Kein Monroe, decides against contacting the Vorelisian authorities about the Thimmi incursion into their space given that the destination of the wormhole, Earth, is not a member of the Galactic Community nor a part of the Vorelisian Empire.

The study of the Searan star continues.

***

The Thimmi transport left its home port months ago near the Messier Star Cluster and has been jumping through wormholes within friendly territory in a clandestine manner to avoid being detected by Vorelisian spies, basically taking the "long way" to Earth and moving between available wormhole systems via conventional travel at near light-speed.

The last leg of the journey took the longest. The ship waited near the planet Seara for three days, motionless and powered down so as not to be noticed by the Vorelisian fleet that passed them on their way to the fourth planet's wormhole.

Ambassador Dahman Hoyth did nothing. He couldn't sound the alarm to headquarters, as his transmissions would've been detected. He couldn't make his presence known, because that would jeopardize his mission to Earth. He doesn't know what the Vorelisians are planning to do within his territory or what target they plan to attack, if any. He is confident, however, that his people will stop them. He is responsible for his role in obtaining the planet Jexx for his empire, and nothing will keep him from that duty.

The transport he and his diplomatic corps are riding in is old, but its defenses are modern thanks to an independent deal between the owner/pilot and a Galestikon weapons depot.

With the way now clear of Vorelisian warships and only a Gightian science vessel to concern them, Hoyth orders the pilot to ignore the galactic scientists and move into the Searan wormhole.

Two minutes later, the Thimmi transport is in orbit of the planet Earth.

Ambassador Hoyth looks out at the bright blue ocean, half bathed in sunlight. The Pacific gives way to landmasses of green and brown. Clouds of white are mixed in perfectly. Earth is truly a sight to behold. *What a beautiful world.*

The brightness in the transport cockpit dims slightly due to the eclipse of the Earth's moon occurring on the starboard side. Ambassador Hoyth would be a man in his seventies on Earth. He chuckles at this fact as the computer sets itself to Earth time, quickly reading the planet's size and speed of rotation to determine what time it is relative to the galactic clock.

Hoyth turns to the pilot and proclaims, "I've gained thirty years of age in this system!"

The pilot is neither impressed nor amused. He doesn't care for travel to new worlds. He's a man distrusting of most people, alien or not. He was hired to bring a team of twenty diplomats to Earth because his was the oldest ship his government could find, one that Vorelisian spies would have no record of. He ignores the ambassador's excitement to announce, "We're set to land at the preselected coordinates provided by your Captain Pilas. Shall we contact him now?"

"There is time. Let me enjoy this view for an orbit or two. I'm not getting any younger, you know," Hoyth says with another laugh.

“It’s your money and your time, Mr. *Ambassador*,” the pilot says as he activates the controls for an easy descent into the atmosphere, then continues, “but I’m on a schedule provided by our Titian leaders.”

Ti (pronounced Tea) refers to the capital planet of the Thimmi Empire.

With the pilot’s attention on the controls, Hoyth spots the International Space Station approaching at a high rate of closing speed. “Look out!” he screams, but before the pilot can turn his head, Hoyth has already leaped into a mad dash toward the hatch at the rear of the bridge—no easy task for a man of his age and size.

The inertial compensators are impaired due to the sudden burst of speed the pilot uses to escape the imminent collision, forcing the ambassador against the hatch he is trying to get to. He slams into it, breaking several ribs in the process. He opens the hatch while screaming in pain, the only sound aside from the protest of the engines at full power.

The pilot, in a panic of his own, shouts “Shut up!” as he attempts to stop the emergency maneuver in progress.

A newer transport would have a proximity alarm for occurrences like these.

A newer transport would have a faster computer that would know when it is safe to stop and allow control to return to the pilot.

A newer transport wouldn't have its braking thrusters frozen because older ship owners sometimes cut corners on expenses for little things like maintenance.

A newer transport would be able to read the mass in front of it as Earth's moon and not just empty space.

The dark side of the moon is rapidly getting bigger. It appears as a hole in the star field behind it.

Two seconds can be an eternity in certain situations.

Ambassador Hoyth gets through the hatch. He looks back as the braking thrusters come to life. "Finally!" the pilot exclaims, though the ambassador can see the darkness of Earth's moon filling the viewport, He realizes he has but the blink of an eye to live as he continues to an escape pod.

He blinks.

The transport does not slow down fast enough to keep it from skipping on the lunar surface like a rock on a pond.

After three such "skips", the ship has lost most of its underside, and air is escaping rapidly from most areas.

Ambassador Hoyth manages to get into the escape pod. No time to alert his fellow diplomats. *It's over for them, but I may yet survive,* he thinks as the ship slides across the soft lunar surface and stops at the edge of a large, deep crater.

Dahman can see only the ground upon which the pod is resting. He is therefore unable to fire the pod, as the crater's edge is blocking the pod's ejection route. "Just my luck," he mumbles to himself as he activates the distress beacon and hopes Pilas gets to him before his air runs out.

After inspecting the canisters of oxygen and determining there to be about ten days' worth, he breathes a bit easier and with renewed hope, though he wonders how much time his body will last given the extensive internal damage it has sustained.

CHAPTER THIRTEEN: What Goes Up…

Colonels Nealand and Garov didn't just see the alien craft zip past their position at an incredible speed, they *felt* it. Garov's heart rate is still at 180 beats per minute, though slowing. The ISS is equipped with many cameras, one of which no doubt caught the craft make a hasty retreat toward the moon in a flash of light.

Edward has regained his composure and reaches for his friend to help him off the deck, "Alexei, are you all right?"

"Yes…yes…Did you see that light? It looked like…" He pauses to search for the right word.

"Thrusters," Nealand says for him while scooting to the communications console in the command module with Alexei close behind. He activates the high-definition radio and punches in a code: 11659.

Alexei watches from literally over his shoulder, floating above the commander in the command module's microgravity. "Unidentified flying object signal. I will check the hard drives for any saved images," Alexei says.

Nealand agrees with a nod as his friend exits toward the nose of the station, one ladder rung at a time, while mumbling something about the current state of space travel to himself.

Mission Control in Houston is quick to come on the line, given the top-secret channel that is alerting them. The channel is secure, and the professional-sounding male voice is patient and calm. “ISS Thirteen, good evening. What is the nature of the craft you’ve spotted?

Edward doesn’t know whether to be creeped out or confident by the tone of the voice. He tries to match the confidence of the controller at the other end of the radio while getting his pulse under control. “Unknown. Colonel Garov and I only saw lights and thrusters moving away from us at high speed after a near collision.”

“Destination? Trajectory?”

“It sped toward the moon. We lost sight of it at that time.”

“Does Colonel Garov corroborate this event?”

“He is checking for any images our cameras may have captured,” Nealand states, becoming uneasy at the thought of what the next step in NASA’s investigation will be. The public won’t be told, of course. He is secure in the knowledge that events such as this have happened before, given the need for a secure channel in the station’s communications system entitled “UFO signal.”

“Roger that, ISS Thirteen. Anything else to report while the event is fresh in your mind?”

"We felt some kind of gravitational pull. I will now check our orbit and speed."

"We show you stable and on course, ISS Thirteen. We will alert the Russian representative. Continue your investigation and we will—" There is a short buzz over the speakers, followed by silence. Nealand looks out a porthole and sees another light, this one smaller and moving comparatively slower than the previous UFO that almost hit them. The single light becomes two as it draws near. Edward finds it curious that, despite how close this craft is to his station, he cannot make out a body, but only lights.

He jumps back when a light flashes toward him. *A laser blast!* "What the hell is going on?" he questions loudly to no one. *Is this the anticipated retribution that we expected from the Chinese?* he wonders as he checks the location of the Chinese station under construction a few thousand miles away and in a higher orbit.

Another laser blast slams into one of the larger solar panels, causing it to overcharge and explode. Garov is hurrying into the module, his face ashen with terror. "We're under attack!"

The station lists toward the planet Earth as the power dies. The strange lights outside the station are now firing with greater frequency, as if the first shots were tentative or practice. The real attack is only now beginning. The second main solar panel is destroyed easily.

They are descending, slowly for now; their momentum will keep them aloft for a few minutes. *Hopefully enough time to evacuate*. Nealand thinks as he switches to battery power and calls over the intercom system that is running on batteries, “All personnel evacuate the station! All personnel evacuate the station! Abandon ship! Abandon ship!”

Garov doesn’t run. He steels himself against the act of self-preservation for his friend’s sake. “What do we do?”

“Did you get any pictures?” Nealand asks as he makes his way out of the command module, intent on getting to the escape pods at the center of the station. “Our new friend out there ain’t Chinese!”

“I have the hard drive in my pocket. Our cameras have hundreds of pictures of the first ship. I do not know about this one.”

Nealand stops to look out another porthole to assess their situation. There’s a lot less space outside than just a moment ago. “We’re losing altitude fast. We have to hurry.”

“We have two pods: one for the scientists, one for the crew.”

“We have to see to their safety first!”

The two NASA officers move faster than even they thought possible in a zero-gravity environment as they travel half the length of the station in under a minute. The station is heating up, thanks to the friction of the upper atmosphere. This also causes a faster descent and an increase in gravity as the Earth gains the upper hand in getting this space-faring object to the ground.

By the time the two men get to the pods, they are in full gravity. Two of the station's seven scientists arrive from the opposite direction—Drs. Steven and Anne Trachsel. They've been working together in space for fifteen years, married for eleven of them. He is an astronomer, and she an astrobiologist. They found each other as adults in their early thirties when they joined the NASA station program. Anne speaks first despite being nearly out of breath. "Our colleagues have left in Pod One with the rest of the crew. We're the last."

Steven, also fighting for oxygen due to the rising heat in the area, checks the alert on his shackle. "One of my scopes found something!"

Nealand opens the pod's outer hatch. "This one is ours, then. Let's go!"

Garov opens the pod's inner hatch, which is heavier than it should be. "I'm feeling heavier. We're running out of time."

Steven takes off in the direction he came from, to the surprise of all. "Wait for me! I'll be just a minute!" he calls.

"Where the hell are you going?" Anne objects.

Steven doesn't answer as he turns a corner and disappears from sight.

Edward shakes his head in bewilderment. "We're about to burn up. We don't have time for this!" He grabs Garov's arm and gestures for him to get into the pod. "Get in!" Garov complies, climbing into the pod quickly, but when Nealand grabs for Anne's arm, she pulls away. "I'm not leaving without my husband!"

Garov activates the controls, powering up the batteries inside the pod. "He's got thirty seconds before we leave. After that, you choose!"

Nealand gets into the pod, for a moment giving the impression that they will leave without the crazy scientist—and his wife. Anne stares at them both in disbelief until he says, "He now has twenty seconds."

***

Steven Trachsel gets to his lab to find his prized telescope gone, burned away minutes ago. He burns his hands retrieving a data card from the master computer. What takes only a moment feels like an eternity, as the blue sky outside is clearly visible. He is surprised the hull has stood up as long as it has.

With the data card pocketed, he runs, falling three times from the turbulence rocking the station. When he shows up at the escape pod, he is comforted to see his wife waiting for him with a relieved smile on her face. Her smile disguises her true feelings, as evidenced by the way she pushes him into the pod and asks, “What the fuck was that all about?”

With the hatch closed behind him, the titanium pod becomes quieter, as if finding peace in the midst of chaos. “I think I have found a habitable planet in the Carina Constellation!” Steven says.

Garov looks at him wryly as Nealand readies the pod for flight. “Was your telescope pointed down at the time, doctor?” The Russian asks.

Steven ignores the colonel’s comment as he straps himself in and takes his wife’s hand. The violent shaking is becoming worse.

After making sure everyone is strapped into their seats and the hatch is properly sealed, Nealand fires the explosive bolts that eject the pod away from the station at nine g’s, or nine times the Earth’s normal gravity.

The heat of the outer shell causes the interior temperature to rise considerably as the occupants try to get a view of their former home through a small porthole. Garov, closest to the porthole, reports what he sees. “The station is breaking up.” *At least it won’t harm anyone,* he thinks as it plummets into the Pacific Ocean.

At the optimum altitude of ten thousand feet, Colonel Nealand fires the braking thrusters and activates the parachutes. There’s a moment’s hesitation as they unfold. A minute later, the two-thousand-pound pod slams into the Bering Sea about three hundred miles north of Tanaga Island.

Anne cranes her neck in an effort to see but gives up. “Did you see the other pod, colonel?”

“No,” Garov replies quietly.

Edward attempts to be positive. “They ejected long before we did. They could’ve landed in Australia, for all we know.”

Steven unstraps his harness as the pod rocks gently and inquires, “So what do we do now?”

Colonel Nealand replies positively. “Our distress signal is functioning. We sit tight until the Navy picks us up.”

Garov stares at the astronomer, feeling his anger rising. “And when they do, I am going to punch you in the face, doctor.”

***

Captain Pilas lands his small spaceship amid the snow-covered mountains of Alaska, away from the national parks and cities. The only life around him is the polar bears. He shuts down the power of his twin engines and laser weapons and watches the International Space Station fall from the sky like a giant, flaming meteor. "That's done," he mutters to himself, content and pleased. No one will suspect him of shooting it down, not even the imbecile governor he has wrapped around his little finger.

Satisfied that his ship is well camouflaged from satellite cameras, he gets into a primitive-looking but operational jeep that he used to get this deep into the wilderness. *Just need some hydrogen fuel and back to Washington to inform Dobson who is responsible for this outrage.*

The Chinese.

Once that's leaked, the public will demand revenge in the form of all-out war. *My plan is working perfectly.* He will add his voice to theirs when he announces his presence to the world as the ally of peace. "Just do as I say and no one gets hurt," he says to himself with a laugh as he practices his speech to the people.

His happiness is cut short with the discovery of a weak but identifiable signal he hears over his "special" car radio, the same type of signal used by Admiral Tolomak but in a more urgent tone.

It is a Thimmi distress call from the moon. “The moon?” It doesn’t take long for Pilas to figure out the meaning of it. *Ambassador Hoyth’s ship has crashed on the moon,* coupled with the incorrect reason, “the Vorelisian agent did this!”

I must find that agent and kill him. If I need help from the Earthers, I will force it from them.

***

Landline phones still exist at military installations and in the offices of some government buildings, where they can be secured to a greater degree than shackle communications. Governor Dobson ends the call from Pilas on the old red phone in the Oval Office. He has made his closest advisors aware of the existence of the Thimmi captain, but not of their plan to unite Earth for his benefit.

Director McCarthy and General Childs have just begun a report on the destruction of the International Space Station and are awaiting their leader’s decision on how to proceed.

Dobson sits back in his plush leather chair at his desk and tells his two friends about the short conversation he just completed. “Captain Pilas tells me the Chinese are responsible for the attack and downing of the station.”

"Can we trust him?" Childs asks, feeling the question is moot under current circumstances. *It is obvious the governor and this alien being are working together.*

McCarthy takes a more aggressive approach, "This means war, sir," he says matter-of-factly, with little emotion and even less genuine care for the lives that have been affected and will be destroyed by whatever action comes next.

Childs speaks as he sits. He's not a young man anymore, and his back is killing him. "Mr. Governor, we don't know for certain who is responsible for the destruction of the station, despite your friend's assertions. This could be a setup."

Dobson regards his general a moment before speaking. *Always unafraid to speak his mind.* "What about that UFO the station encountered?"

"Perhaps," Childs speculates before he is contradicted immediately by McCarthy, "Commander Nealand witnessed the alien craft fly to the moon *after* the near collision. He was not attacked by it. The answer is obvious."

The governor drifts off as he considers Pilas's advice that reads in his mind like commands. The more he thinks of the possibility of war—an all-out nuclear exchange—the more his humanity resists the idea. The promises of power and glory are lost in the decision-making process. *At the end of the day, I do not believe him. I am being deceived and will be left out in the cold by his promises and actions*. He looks up at Childs, who had just said something. "What?"

Childs repeats himself. "Shall we upgrade our defense to DEFCON Two, sir?"

Perhaps the very preparation for war will frighten the Chinese enough to bring about the unification Dobson so desires. "Do it," he says with a quick nod.

McCarthy's shackle interrupts him as he is about to voice his opinion on the idea. He reads a text on the hologram in front of him and states, "Sir, the Iranians have aligned themselves with the Asian Alliance."

The general throws in his two cents. "Looks like they've decided which side to be on."

Dobson leans forward on his desk, resting his head on his hands. He is content in the events he sees forthcoming. "Indeed. They know the space station is gone. They monitor it as well as we do." To the CIA Director he asks, "Any response from the Chinese?"

"No, sir. DEFCON Two won't shake them into joining the Asian Alliance." McCarthy turns to Childs, adding, "With all due respect, general."

Childs blinks slowly, understanding the man's intentions.

Dobson stands, causing Childs to get back on his feet as well as his superior addresses him. "Continue the upgrade to DEFCON Two. I want you to talk to the commanders and scientists of the ISS right away."

Childs turns to leave but is stopped by the governor's hand on his arm. Dobson says in a low voice, "Will, I want to know exactly what they saw before we take any further steps."

Childs smiles, glad to have a leader with a clear mind. *If only he knew*. "Yes, Mr. Governor."

McCarthy walks with Childs toward the door. The governor follows them. "McCarthy, I want you to find Dr. Lightner. He tells the world he is an alien and then disappears? What the hell is that? I would like to talk to him as well. Doesn't he wear a shackle? Can we track him?"

"He is off the grid. Technically, he is not required to wear a shackle. He is not a citizen of this country," the director says.

Childs finishes the thought, "Or the planet, for that matter. Our social laws don't apply to extraterrestrials." With that, he is out the door.

McCarthy has his hand on the door but turns back with a query. “Sir, have we given much thought to the Asian Alliance becoming so powerful with the addition of Iran and possibly China that they will control much of the world’s wealth?”

Dobson dismisses the question. There are more urgent things to worry about. “We’ve got two aliens on this planet, both wanting to sponsor us into the Galactic Community. I frankly don’t give a damn how powerful Asia is becoming. We’re all in this together.”

McCarthy responds with a halfhearted, “Yes, sir.”

The door closes behind him, leaving the governor alone. He returns to his desk to update the color codes on the digital map there. They all appear to be right: six continents and China, *the odd one out*. “One more,” he says.

He picks up the phone to call for an antigravity plane to be dispatched to Alaska right away.

CHAPTER FOURTEEN: Dragon Fire

Dr. Lightner has never been to China before today. He has only assisted in the planning of two Soliquid plants with a team of fellow scientists from China and Japan whom he met in Tokyo.

That was three years ago. Surely their plants have been built by now. The antigravity car he rides in is a limousine, typically reserved for transporting heads of state, but Charles is an exception. The car enters the Zhongnanhai complex, the central headquarters for the Communist Party of China and the State Council. There are soldiers adorned in green dress uniforms complete with large caps and rifles slung over their shoulders.

"An imposing sight," Charles observes to his chaperone sitting in the seat across from him.

Wu Jianyu, whose first name coincidentally means "universe builder," smiles and responds in a steady and polite tone, his voice sharp yet broken, as his English isn't perfect. *Why should it be?* Charles thinks as he listens. "We want to show you we are a strong nation, doctor. This presentation is not meant to intimidate. We only wish friendship with…" His voice trails off as he tries to think of the name. "Your people."

Charles is flattered by Wu's attempt at remembering Charles home planet. "My people are the Paalians. Paal is a member planet of the Vorelisian Empire. I am here to represent the empire in unifying your planet peacefully."

The car stops. The driver, a young woman also in uniform, runs to the passenger-side door to open it for the doctor and Mr. Wu, after which she stands at attention until they enter the main building, that is built like a palace.

Charles regards the dark clouds above as a precursor of possible things to come in his mission. *Is the ownership of a vacant world with only strategic military value worth putting this one at risk?* "To be friends with me is to be friends with your enemies on this planet."

Jianyu smiles in understanding, yet is not sure if he does.

The main lobby and connecting corridor are lined with tapestries and paintings of past leaders and other prominent figures in China's proud history. The marble floor is darker than a night sky found anywhere on Earth, with white streaks traversing it that remind Charles of the heavy space traffic around Vorelis, the capital of the empire. *This is no time to get homesick.* The two men walk the corridor in silence.

Charles breaks the silence as they approach the end. "Let me remind you, Jianyu, that your world is only as strong as your weakest nation. This is the foundation for a united planet. Only together can you move forward. There is no room in the Galactic Community for strong worlds, only strong people."

The two men stop at a large door that is marked with several symbols embossed on the outside in marble. Jianyu pauses to consider Charles's words before opening the door for him. "I don't know what they'll say in here to that," he says, gesturing to the men in the room, who stand at the opening of the door. "You and I have our work ahead of us to stand behind globalization for the good of the Earth."

Charles smiles and bows his head, allowing Jianyu to enter first. *All or nothing*, he doesn't say.

The large room is decorated with golden statues and more tapestries on the walls that go from floor to ceiling. The table contains place settings of fine china and sparkling silverware. The seven uniformed men remain standing until Charles finds his seat.

Jianyu walks to a podium to introduce the doctor to everyone present. Each of them, in turn, smiles and bows to him in greeting. They sit together, the oak wood chairs surprisingly comfortable.

I hope they're still smiling when I'm finished talking to them.

***

Captain Amanda Blassi's family didn't expect her to live past the age of twenty. She was a girl who lived on the edge, hung out with dangerous and desperate people, and did drugs like they were going out of style.

But something happened to her on her twenty-first birthday that changed her forever. She herself could never say what it was exactly; perhaps someone she admired had died, perhaps God spoke to her in her sleep, or maybe she had just had enough of the life she was living and wanted a change.

Whatever that 'something' was, it led to her going to college in Indiana, where she was born and raised, and graduating in the field of business administration.

When she couldn't find work for a year, she joined the Air Force. She enjoyed basic training so much that her fellow recruits thought she was nuts. She received a marksmanship ribbon for her affinity with weapons. After working for a while in the Consolidated Base Personnel Office (CBPO), she went to OTS. Her inner rebel told her to start giving orders instead of taking them.

As a young lieutenant, Amanda seriously considered joining Air Force Special Forces Pararescue, which has the chief responsibility of going behind enemy lines to save downed pilots. She didn't feel she was capable at the time and let the desire for adventure pass.

It was not until she was promoted to captain seven years later that she became bored with being a paper pusher. When General Childs put the word out that he was forming an independent unit of marksmen, she signed up. Her scores with handguns and rifles impressed him into putting her in the lead role of commander of a special unit of snipers.

Soliquid plants are considered a unifying project because the open technology and construction of them worldwide are what Dr. Lightner envisioned as being the catalyst that unites the planet. It is no surprise, then, that those who do not support globalization, specifically an Internet group who call themselves Isolationists, would attack a Soliquid plant in the Mexican state of Monterrey before it went online. Once in operation, that one plant would have powered the entire province of Mexico. The attack spurred the government into action.

After months of training with her team and turning them into top-notch shooters and fighters, Amanda is shocked to receive word that their first assignment is going to be protection duty.

She sits with her hands clasped in front of her mouth to conceal her anger, but her superior, General Childs, sees through the attempt. He is communicating with his shackle via hologram from his plane somewhere over the Pacific. “Don’t argue with me, captain. There are no unimportant assignments,” he says.

"But doesn't the Nevada plant already have security?" Amanda asks.

"Of course, but those rent-a-cops wouldn't last five minutes against the Isolationists. They're a very well-armed group."

"Why not send us after them, then? We can combine EDF-One and Two and maybe a light armor and air squadron to take them out once and for all."

Childs sits back in his seat, and his shackle's camera follows him. "That would be a good idea if we could find them. We have just united all of North America into one country, and we're still putting resources together to feed everyone."

"Not to mention putting a shackle on the arm of everyone thirteen and over," Amanda mumbles as she puts her hands down.

Childs ignores the comment. "You have your orders. Your team will guard the Soliquid plant in Nevada. Bear in mind that I expect these terrorists to come to you. Do not take this assignment lightly."

Amanda, looking sharp in her black dress uniform, sits up straight and affirms, "Yes, general."

As he reaches for the cutoff switch, he makes a comment of his own, "And color your hair, will you?"

The connection is cut off just as the four men in her team behind the hologram start laughing. They stop the moment she looks at them. She has heard the snickers behind her back, the nicknames—"Fireface," "Glowhair"—but she likes her look; it gives her distinction and connects her with her past, a past she does not want to forget lest she repeat it.

The hangar she and her team occupy is dark and quiet again after the holographic glow fades. "Well, you heard him. We're on guard duty. Saddle up!" Amanda orders.

Her radioman, Corporal Jack Morten, approaches her slowly while she speaks into her shackle. "Contact Captain Folsom."

The shackle beeps as the corporal says, "Ma'am, we'll need transportation."

A hologram of Derrick appears as Amanda whispers to her subordinate, "Requisition a Humvee with the appropriate weapons and radio." When the main hangar door opens behind her, the sunlight entering the area lights up Jack's face. She addresses his nervous look. "We'll be fine. We all have to start somewhere."

Jack cracks a smile while nodding, "Yes, ma'am."

Meanwhile, Derrick is becoming impatient. "Did you call me to watch you give orders, captain?"

Amanda cocks her head playfully as she responds, “Maybe I did.” She turns serious. “I have an assignment starting now. My team and I won’t be able to engage yours in that shooting competition idea of Sergeant Furtado’s.”

“What is it?”

“I’m not supposed to talk about it. You know how it is,” she says.

“At least you’ve got something. We’re still in training and waiting mode.”

“I don’t know how long it will be.”

“Be safe. I know the world looks bad right now.”

“No worries there.” She says before putting her hand over her mouth in a light manner, as if to stop herself from revealing a secret. “Bye.” She signs off with a smile.

***

Madeline wakes to the vision of Dr. Yates standing over her. “How long was I out?” she asks as her nervousness returns.

He replies without looking up from his instruments. “Two days.”

"How am I?" she asks, sitting up and reaching for a cup of what she expects to be water.

"Still pregnant."

"Please stop trying to be funny. You're not very good at it."

Yates smiles while shaking his head in disagreement over his sense of humor. Madeline looks at her shackle on the nightstand to her left and asks, "Any messages?" She sips the fluid, which turns out to be a protein drink that looks like water. It is also odorless and colorless like water but has the thick texture of maple syrup.

"You mean from Doctor Lightner?" he asks, the humor gone from his voice. "The National Security Department already went through your shackle and found nothing."

"Why would they do that? I'm allowed to have relationships if I choose."

"Is he the father?"

"Yes," she answers quietly, as if embarrassed. She sits up further, wondering why she just felt that way.

"You didn't know, did you?" Yates asks.

"Know what?"

"That he's an alien."

Madeline's blank stare answers that and a host of other questions the doctor doesn't bother to ask. He continues, "We'll have to keep an eye on you, but I'm releasing you today."

Madeline's eyes dart around the room. She's not looking for anything tangible, but her mind is racing. *Why didn't he tell me?*

CHAPTER FIFTEEN: Team Seven

The conventional passenger jet, which resembles a merging of the SR-71 and Concorde planes of a century ago, touches down and speeds to the end of the runway at the Kazakhstan spaceport. Its black frame glows a light yellow from the friction of the air in flight at Mach 17. A braking parachute unfurls from its tail, slowing the aircraft quickly as it rolls along the dry lake bed on its nitrogen-filled tires.

Several vehicles meet the NASA plane after it comes to a stop, including fire trucks, an ambulance, a bobtail tow vehicle hauling the stairs that its driver is hurrying to push up to the hatch, and a Lincoln Town Car. The Lincoln, Colonel Nealand's personal staff car, is the latest solar-powered antigravity model. NASA gave it to him as a perk of his position. There are only seven like it in the world. Hydrogen or nuclear generators power other antigravity vehicles, and most of them are self-driving. This one isn't.

The driver of the car is Behrouz Jafari. He is dressed in a black suit with matching fedora and a silver tie worn around his neck. He looks sharp and relaxed as he gets out of the Lincoln and leans against the front fender with his arms crossed in the cold and constant wind.

The pressure he puts on the car causes it to dip and compensate for the added weight. He listens to the hum of the solar converter that is currently keeping the car on idle. This is to keep the vehicle at a continuous hover two feet off the ground and to keep the interior at a comfortable sixty-five degrees.

Out here in the open landscape, the temperature must be close to thirty. He asks his shackle for the temperature and finds himself off by one degree. There's no ice out here in the desert, though it's cold enough. *The problem is the wind!* He braves the conditions as he waits for the plane's passengers to get off.

Behrouz Jafari came to the United States under the guardianship of Colonel Edward Nealand. Due to investigations into alleged kidnapping charges and Nealand's upward rise in rank and prestige, the boy found himself living in a foster home in Detroit with people who were known simply as "The Family."

'The Family' was a gang of criminals who used the foster care system to cover the drug and prostitution rings they ran, which the children under their care were forced to partake in one way or another.

It took a few weeks of indoctrination and training before the leaders finally determined the best role for the boy to fill. He couldn't shoot, he was a terrible liar, and he couldn't fight other kids his size, but he could drive, and he was clever.

So clever was Behrouz that he was able to start a shackle scam on the side when they first became mandatory. The scam allowed those who resented government intrusion into people's lives to hack into the system. He saw the shackles as an intrusion into people's privacy. If the government was going to allow that, then why did he care if identities were stolen as long as he got a piece of the pie? Behrouz slept fine at night.

Aside from driving, and because of his age, his job was to act as lookout when the Feds came snooping around. Although he was trained in the art of violence, he was never put into a position to experience any. *Besides the fact he wasn't good at it.* The only action he saw was driving the getaway car from robberies.

"This kid can drive," they would say.

As shackle laws and punishments took hold and began to be enforced, Behrouz's opportunities fell like a stone along with the overall crime rate. At eighteen, he was awarded citizenship in his new country and subsequently was given his own shackle to help him run his life.

His newfound respect for the United States grew until one day he alerted the FBI about who he was and who he was working for. Agents dissolved The Family, and Behrouz was a free man in spirit as well as status.

The Family's leaders were imprisoned for violating the One Society Act of 2050, which proclaims gangs to be terrorist groups and strips privacy rights from the people. There was little evidence to prosecute them for the numerous crimes they'd long been associated with but, in Behrouz's eyes, something was better than nothing.

The Family has vowed revenge.

Behrouz smiles as he pulls his coat tight. He waves excitedly at Colonel Nealand, who is descending the stairs. Edward spots him and waves back.

Colonel Garov emerges from the plane a moment later and embraces the air. "Ah, a good northern breeze. There's nothing like Russian air!" He is relieved to be on solid ground, not realizing that the wind is coming from the south, though no one within earshot of him would ruin his happiness by pointing that out.

Nealand and Jafari embrace at the car for a long moment before engaging each other in Behrouz's native language of Farsi. "It has been too long, my young friend," Edward stutters, trying to recall the last time he spoke Farsi. Or even the last time he saw his adopted son.

Behrouz is happy that his father is making the attempt at speaking his old language, as poor as it is, but like most considerate immigrants, he answers in English, “It is good to see you, Father. I’m glad your accident wasn’t too bad.”

Behrouz hears a throat clearing and moves to open the rear passenger-side door for Colonel Garov before running to the front seat. Nealand takes the front passenger seat.

Garov gets in slowly, a bit apprehensive. “Edward, perhaps you should drive. We don’t have much time. Your general is waiting for us.”

Nealand puts a hand on Behrouz’s shoulder as the young man starts to turn to the Russian over the seat, ready with words of anger and resentment. He knows all too well about the young man’s short temper.

“Behrouz is a very capable driver, Alexei,” Nealand says. “I trust your seat belt is fastened securely.” Then to Behrouz, he adds in Farsi, “Show him.” The twenty-year-old grins like a Cheshire cat as he puts the antigravity car in reverse to pull away from the front of the aircraft. The Lincoln accelerates up to thirty miles per hour in three seconds before a spin-shift-glide maneuver puts it into forward motion with no break in acceleration. From outside the vehicle, it would appear to be on fire, with the thrusters firing on all sides at just the right times as it flips through the air and rolls over to reorient itself with the ground, a metallic ballet of sorts that Behrouz performs perfectly, causing some alarm from Garov.

The trick over, Behrouz checks his mirror to gauge Garov's reaction and gets what he expected: alarm. The Lincoln accelerates up to fifty flawlessly, the rear rockets firing a short burst to push it to seventy, and all the while, Behrouz is shouting at the Russian officer in Farsi, "How do you like my driving now, you Russian bastard!" Nealand laughs just like a proud father should.

The car exits the flight line and onto the main access road, toward the admin buildings only a few miles away. Behrouz lowers the speed down to thirty-five. He brings the car to within one inch of the ground without any assistance from the vehicle's computer.

Not knowing what the young Iranian man said, Garov looks to Nealand for a translation but gets more ribbing, "All manual control, Alexei!"

Garov sits back and shakes his head, knowing that he probably wouldn't like the translation of what he heard. He mumbles into Behrouz's ear, "I will never doubt you again."

***

The Lincoln staff car glides up to the curb at the headquarters building on the military side of the spaceport. Behrouz expertly deploys the wheels, which touch the cold, hard ground and slide to the curb with a slight bump. He leaves the engine at idle for warmth inside and on the hood, where he likes to sit and play games against the windshield.

Fluid motions, like an art. He looks at Nealand and Garov with a smug expression of pride and accomplishment. Nealand pats his shoulder, “Okay, okay. Don’t let it go to your head.”

Nealand opens the door and looks up the stairs of the five-story building, surprised to see General Childs descending to meet them. “First-rate service,” he says to Garov as he exits the car.

General Childs wonders who the expert driver is who handled the antigravity vehicle like a pro and is surprised to see such a young man getting out of it.

The colonels salute the general upon greeting him at the foot of the staircase. Garov’s salute is slightly subdued due to the fact that Childs is not part of *his* military. *This man has a hand in almost everything involving NASA and spaceflight. Too bad he has never been up there.*

***

Ten minutes later, in the large headquarters conference room, General Childs delivers the good news. “The world is coming together behind Dr. Charles Lightner, who has successfully brought China into the world collective. Not many people understand who the Vorelisians are or what getting involved in galactic affairs will mean for us as a race, but people all over the world are embracing the idea."

Garov takes a skeptic approach. "Sure, the alternative means world war. It's easy to get people to do things with the specter of death hanging over them."

Nealand expresses his reservations. "Do you think the Aztecs realized what was going to happen to them when Hernando Cortés arrived in their land?"

Garov nods in understanding, "They were welcomed as gods, were they not?"

Childs, unfamiliar with Mexican history, shakes his head. "So?"

Edward explains by making the connection, "We're the Aztecs."

The general positions himself behind a podium and attaches his shackle to an old projector through a beam of light from his device to the inputs available. *The technology in this part of the world has to be over fifty years old.* He begins to show images, the first of which is an alien ship. It is somewhat round but with a flat bottom, much like the one the colonels witnessed nearly colliding with the space station. "I appreciate your cautious attitude, gentlemen. You're not alone in your concerns. We are developing plans and tactics to protect ourselves in the event we encounter new enemies."

Garov stares at the image on the wall. "That ship is similar to the one that nearly hit us."

Nealand nods in agreement, then adds, "Smaller, though."

The general continues, "This ship arrived ten years ago." He switches to another image. "This one was photographed in the skies over Alaska at roughly the same time."

Garov and Nealand study the differences between the two ships. The small craft resembles an egg in shape and is silver colored, with small protuberances that could be stubby wings or antennas.

Nealand considers the shape as he stands to peer at it closely. A spaceship wouldn't need wings unless it was intended for atmospheric travel as well.

Garov notes the size. "Another one-man craft?"

Nealand contradicts his friend, "Big enough for seven. It's a funky angle."

Garov turns his head to change his viewpoint and agrees. "Ah."

Nealand looks at the general and states the obvious. “So we’ve got two alien ships.”

“Two ships, two aliens among us from two different races,” the general says before adding, “The governor has been in communication with one side. Lightner is on the other. And he’s got the Chinese behind him, with the rest of the world falling in line. I am in the process of forming Earth defense teams from all the world’s militaries in case one or both of these aliens become hostile.”

Garov speaks up. “So Lightner is one; who is the other?”

Childs taps the podium to mark time before answering, “His name is Pilas. I cannot tell you more at this time.”

Garov asks, “Which side are we on?”

Nealand doesn’t miss a beat. “The stronger one, of course.”

Garov shoots back, “Or the one more likely to conquer us. Friends don’t attack friends.”

Childs taps the podium again, harder this time, to get the colonels’ attention. His shackle’s metal attachment clangs against the metal top of the podium. The colonels look at him in silence. “We have scientists developing new advances based on alien technology.”

"Which alien's technology?" Edward asks.

"Neither of these two," he says as he waves away the images. He shuts down the projector and continues as the room lights brighten, "I would like you two to lead our advancement in the field of teleportation."

Nealand and Garov stare at Childs in disbelief for a moment before the Russian stands and proudly proclaims, "I'm with you, general. If we don't work to defend our home, who will?"

Nealand isn't as eager as his friend and balks at the idea. He goes to the window and looks down at the young man he has come to cherish as his own son. "I only have one concern before we can proceed, sir."

Childs joins him at the window. "The boy outside?"

Garov chimes in to assist his friend. "They have a history, general."

Childs raises a hand to silence Garov as he nods in understanding. "I'm aware, colonel." To Nealand, he says in a matter-of-fact tone, "I could use an expert driver like him, you know."

Edward continues to stare out the window at Behrouz. He is sitting on the hood of the car and playing a video game, using the windshield as a screen. The idling engine provides warmth. Edward lets his body language do the talking for him.

Childs whispers into the colonel's ear, "Consider it done, Ed."

The general turns to leave. He speaks to both men as he walks toward the door at a brisk pace. "I'll be right back with your contracts, gentlemen. Welcome to EDF Team Seven."

Garov joins his friend at the window and looks down on Behrouz from three floors up. "Why doesn't he get inside the car?"

Nealand ignores the comment and quietly inquires, "Do you really think we'd have a chance against two alien races if it came to that?"

Garov thinks for a moment before responding, "Welcome to Mexico."

CHAPTER SIXTEEN: Climate Change

Captain Pilas enters the Oval Office dressed in his usual garb and sunglasses to hide his features from the small gathering of leaders from around the world who are being served champagne for an imminent toast. Surprised and confused don't begin to describe his state of mind.

The Chinese ambassador is the honoree at the moment. He represents the Chinese leadership and their proclamation of allowing the full unification of the planet, with the caveat of joining Doctor Lightner and allowing the Vorelisian Empire to sponsor Earth into the Galactic Community.

The leaders present are all probable candidates in the upcoming election of first premier of Earth: Ministers Shabal and Maw from Asia and Africa, respectively; the Swedish woman from the European Union, whose name is too difficult for Pilas to pronounce, though he has seen her a few times, and her long blonde hair that reaches her waist is hard to forget; and Director McCarthy and General Childs, who round out the government officials Pilas knows by reputation or acquaintance. The other leaders he doesn't know at all, except for Governor Dobson, whom he spots last and makes a beeline toward.

Dobson is hosting this celebration of the Earth becoming united virtually overnight. The tensions that warned of war are giving way to peace. He senses the proverbial light at the end of the tunnel in regard to Earth's future and the upcoming election and the power that comes with the office he aspires to. *That power will be mine. I will remake the world, and the people will love me.* When the North American continent was united as one country, he felt that taking the position of governor was a demotion. He was happy to share power with the other three major leaders in the region, knowing this day would come. He expected it to take longer than a month. *What did Lightner say to the Chinese?* Whatever it was, he's getting to the Promised Land faster than with Pilas's plans, and more safely.

Speak of the devil. Dobson sees Pilas approaching from across the room and immediately feels like a teenager getting caught going through his father's wallet. He shouts to the alien captain to draw attention, just in case. "Happy New Year!"

Though it's a few weeks until that day, the sentiment seems appropriate given that, by the look of hatred in Pilas's beady little eyes, Dobson may not see the new year.

Defusing the situation isn't going to work. Dobson pulls the general away from a quiet conversation with his secretary, Sheila Harris, another child of the genetic alterations age. Her light-brown skin and round features are all natural, as are her blonde hair and green eyes, but if one were to inquire as to her ethnicity, her response would be "all of the above." It's less common at this time to find anyone in the former United States who is not a mix of at least two ethnicities.

Chances are that someone who looks like Sheila would never be born naturally, but advances in genetics caused her parents to come up with the idea of creating a unique-looking child, though they didn't consider that millions of other couples all over the country would have the same idea. Her appearance, therefore, is relatively common among those in her age group. The fad more or less died out in the 2050s.

Childs hired Sheila mostly because of her beauty but has never pursued her romantically or sexually. He is a healthy man with normal urges, however, who wouldn't pass up a chance at taking her to his bed at least once. Filled with liquid courage, he has her relatively alone and is speaking quietly to her. She is half-drunk herself and enjoying his company when Dobson intervenes.

The general is not pleased by the disruption, preferring to flirt with his young twenty-something secretary than meet with the heavily clothed man waiting by another door than the one he came in from. As they gather at the door, Dobson says nothing as he motions for McCarthy to join them. They all exit together. Dobson can see Pilas's anger rising. Judging by the expression on his mostly covered face, it's not difficult to make that assessment.

Once they're in another room nearby, the door isn't fully closed before Pilas tears into the fool he promised the world to. "May I remind you that no world has survived long after reneging on a deal with the Thimmi Empire, Dobson?"

The governor stands with his military and intelligence leaders, secure in their support. He speaks freely, without fear. "The Chinese wouldn't come on board with globalization unless we aligned ourselves with the Vorelisians. I figured it wouldn't make a difference to me, as I'll become first premier sooner this way, and without the bloodshed of war."

Pilas steps closer, until he is almost nose to nose with Dobson. "Oh, there will be bloodshed. You've just signed your planet's death warrant."

Dobson continues, unfazed, confident in the promise of Vorelisian protection offered by Lightner. "I don't need your help to become first premier, my Thimmi friend. In fact, this may be a good time for you to leave us."

McCarthy and Childs stand firm, momentarily proud of their leader showing courage, misguided though he may be in assuming the election is his for the taking.

Pilas folds the sunglasses he's been carrying since he entered the White House and drops them on a table. He opens his eyes wide and reaches into his inside coat pocket as if for a weapon. His hand is motionless as he speaks in a low, threatening tone. "You don't know what the Vorelisians are capable of, Dobson. You are sentencing the people of this world to death with this mistake."

Childs and McCarthy take a defensive posture, ready to pounce if a weapon is produced. Pilas's hand remains hidden.

Dobson, as smug and confident as he has ever been, smiles, unafraid. "There's an alien ship that has crashed on our moon. Could that be the diplomatic team you told me of?"

Pilas's blank stare answers his question. Dobson continues, "They're most likely dead. Your plan is finished. *You* are finished. Lightner has offered Vorelisian support and protection. It's about time you left."

Pilas shakes his head slowly, a mannerism he apparently picked up from living among Earth's people for so long. "You're a fool to trust the Vorelisians with your lives, let alone your planet."

McCarthy reaches for his pistol inside his own coat pocket. "You might want to remove your hand slowly, sir."

Pilas innocently pulls his hand from his overcoat as instructed. A sheepish grin appears on his face as he keeps his hands outstretched as a sign of surrender. "I mean you no harm. I would, however, request your assistance in investigating the crashed vessel on your moon."

Childs, anxious to end this worthless discussion in favor of a more intimate one, says, "You have a ship of your own with which to investigate, don't you?"

"I am only one man, general. I need personnel."

Dobson reaches out his hand, hoping to quell the anger he still feels coming from the alien, who is being surprisingly acquiescent all of a sudden. *I know better than to burn the bridge built between us completely.* "We have a team ready to assist you, captain. I would hate to see you leave us as an enemy." *Though I do want you to leave.*

Pilas takes the governor's hand and squeezes it gently. By the time he finishes whispering in Dobson's ear, the grip is like that of a vice. "You will come back to us, governor. You will swear your allegiance to the Thimmi Empire and me. You will soon have no choice." He releases his grip before the others can step in when Dobson tries to pull back. Pilas ends at a greater volume and with good cheer, "I appreciate your help, Dobson. You have my thanks."

McCarthy gets in the Thimmi captain's face. "We know you destroyed our space station. You've misled us long enough."

Childs joins in, crowding the alien as Dobson backs off, shaking his hand in obvious pain. “We’ll give you a team to investigate the crash. Hell, I’ll even let you be in command, but our relationship ends there. Understood, captain?”

Pilas recognizes that the tone the general is using is much like his own when he gives an ultimatum. He smiles in admiration. “It would seem I am at your mercy, general.”

***

Lieutenant Kong wakes up early on this December morning. It is still dark and colder than Himalayan ice. She quietly slides out of her bunk to avoid waking her bunkmate, Shanti Dae. She takes her coat from the locker she left open and goes into the open area of the hangar. Here, there are partitions set up for detention and interrogation purposes. *Whose idea was this?* she wonders as she creeps past the sleeping quarters of Sergeant Furtado and the newly acquired Private Behrouz Jafari.

Furtado stirs as Jen passes by the open door of the men’s quarters on her way to the hangar’s exit, a small door attached to the main doors. Opening the big doors would wake the dead. She steps through the doorway after checking behind her for anyone following. She is into the darkness and gone like the wind, which is howling fiercely in the Nevada desert. Furtado grabs his shirt, boots, and coat. He follows Jen out of the hangar while dressing. The team members are learning about each other as they progress through their training. He can't help but wonder what the MSS spy may be up to at this hour of the morning, though he doesn't wake the new addition to their team. *I'll let the kid sleep.*

Alfonzo has no plan to confront her, but simply to find out why she is out of the hangar at this early hour. He takes a moment to notice the galaxy of stars above as he tails the lieutenant to the base communications building.

There stands a solitary marine. He is alert and on guard, as marines tend to be. Kong approaches him openly and is granted access after she scans her shackle on the building's security pad.

Furtado waits a few minutes before entering the building with the same access.

The main communications room is filled with darkness, empty cubicles, and dozens of servers. Alfonzo finds a solitary light illuminating a cubicle in the back of the room. He sneaks up to her but she is so engrossed in what she is doing that she doesn't notice him. He watches her access lists of satellites located in a file that is seven levels above top secret. He decides to challenge her with a jolt. "Couldn't sleep, lieutenant?"

Jen jumps to her feet in a second, her weapon produced in a flash and pointed at the space between the sergeant's big brown eyes. Upon realizing who he is, she lowers it just as quickly. "If you want to be dead, just scare me like that again."

"What?"

It takes her a moment to realize that she just yelled at him in Mandarin. She tucks her pistol into the small of her back and continues in English. "You scared me. Don't do it again."

Furtado smiles, not fazed in the slightest—*OK*, mayb*e a little*. "I'm sorry. What are you doing here, Jen?"

"You don't need to know, *sergeant*." She uses his rank title to maintain her superiority and keep the fraternization to a minimum. She wonders for a lightning second if she could've killed him, even with good cause.

She returns to her seat, careful to close the file she was reviewing. *I'll have to try again tomorrow*.

He pulls up a squeaky-wheeled chair and waits for her to look at him before asking, "Did you find what you were looking for? You're trying to get info on that town destroyed in China, aren't you?"

Though they've been together for a short time, the team has bonded well. Jen has come to feel that she can trust these people.

How far? She decides this is the best moment to find out. “Yes. Now I suppose you’ll want to report me.”

Furtado’s laugh is short as he shakes his head. When he sees Jen’s stoic and patient expression, he quiets himself. “I don’t have to. Your shackle recorded your entry into the building. The government knows you’re here and what you’re doing. If they have a problem, they’ll know who caused it.”

She lets him laugh for a few more seconds before dropping a small bomb on him. “I disabled mine. The scan I used was fake. I’m actually surprised that it worked.”

He scowls in response, “Oh, wait a minute, that’s not fair, J— lieutenant!”

“You’re the only one who knows I’m here. I’d like to keep it that way.”

“You don’t have to worry about me.”

Unseen by the two, Captain Folsom appears behind them. “Now ask me.”

Jen jumps again, this time not reaching for her pistol. “You guys have to stop *doing* that! How did you know I was here, sir?”

Folsom taps Furtado's shackle, as if giving him up. "I didn't know *you* were here, Kong. I thought only *he* was here. What *are* we doing here, lieutenant?"

In defense of Lieutenant Kong, Alfonzo turns off the computer. "Nothing, sir. We were just following a lead in the Lightner case. We heard a rumor that he might be coming here to hide out."

Derrick has never been a farmer but knows manure when he smells it. "Don't make me check the computer's records for searches, sergeant. Report back to the hangar at once. We have a mission to support."

Kong and Furtado's eyes go wide. Can it be true? Finally! They both respond with an enthusiastic "Yes, sir!" as they file out, Furtado leading the way.

Folsom stops Jen with a heavy hand upon her shoulder. "Whatever orders you were given are irrelevant now. We're all on the same side—literally. The world is one."

Jen looks into his eyes. In them, she sees honesty and patience. Truth. Sincerity. She knows at this moment that with the turmoil in the world surrounding the formation of a new government and order, military units worldwide are being transformed into EDF teams. *There will soon be hundreds of them.* “You don’t sound very pleased at the idea of a one-world government, captain.”

“It’s no secret that I’ve never truly supported globalization,” Folsom says.

“Your record would indicate otherwise—Africa, South America.”

“We all have our duties to perform. Your comfort level in the world is measured by how well you understand your place in it. Do you know yours?” he asks, still wondering where her allegiance lies.

With all the training, the classes, the togetherness, and now with her captain’s understanding and compassion, Jen feels as if she has found her new home. She answers his question with a smile and a recitation of the Oath of the Planet that she took when she signed up—*volunteered.* “I am no longer a citizen of a country or alliance, but of the planet itself. The planet Earth is my home, and by the will of her people, I will serve and defend her with my life.”

Derrick nods, a smile spreading across his face. Is that pride? They leave together, in more ways than one.

CHAPTER SEVENTEEN: To the Moon

After a filling breakfast and plenty of hydrating fluids, EDF-1 gathers on the tarmac of the base to await the arrival of an alien officer whose people have crashed on the moon.

Captain Folsom stands two steps forward of his team, who are unarmed and dressed in their black fatigue uniforms; Lieutenants Kong and Dae and Sergeant Furtado stand at attention as the small Thimmi craft arrives and circles their position.

From behind them, from the hangar, Private Jafari runs to join them. He is dressed and equipped correctly but for the rifle he is carrying. He gets in line next to the sergeant, breathing heavily.

Folsom, appreciative of the young man's efforts to please, shakes his head as he moves to face him. He stares into the young man's eyes for a few seconds before saying, "Where do you think you're going, private?"

Jafari responds between breaths. "I'm…going…to…the…moon…sir."

Furtado begins humming "Ride, Captain, Ride" to cover his nervousness as the spaceship lands right in front of them. *We are meeting aliens, and no one is freaking out*…It's about the size of a small school bus. Its engines give out a loud hum, but the sound is no worse than an airplane on idle. The team remains at attention despite the dust cloud blowing on them as the ship settles and the engines are cut off.

Folsom watches the craft come to a stop before turning his focus back to the young man in front of him. "No, son."

"But—"

"You just got here a week ago. You're not trained for space travel."

Shanti glances over at Folsom's words, ever so slightly; *none of us are trained for space travel.* Her fears mount as the hatch on the alien ship opens. She hides it well.

Folsom continues. "You will stay behind and train with Team Three. I've already arranged for you to bunk with them for the next few days. Secure your weapon and report to them now. Dismissed."

Dejected, the young private turns to the hangar behind him. He looks back to witness the general who recruited him disembark from the alien craft. He stops when he sees Colonel Nealand get off the ship right behind him.

The general is introducing Nealand to Captain Folsom when Behrouz interrupts them, speaking to Nealand in Farsi. "Father, it is good to see you. They will not allow me to join you on the moon."

Nealand takes his son aside, his emotions mixed. “What the fuck are you doing?” he says in English, not caring at the moment about the level of embarrassment he is causing the young man. “You can’t just interrupt us in the middle of a conversation!”

Jafari’s humiliation is compounded tenfold. *But father!* he shouts in his mind. *Why are you doing this to me?* His eyes begin to water before the colonel, so involved in the upcoming mission, finally sees what he is doing and continues in a calmer tone, in Farsi.

“Go to your duties. I will return soon, and we will talk.” He finishes in English, for the benefit of his teammates and, more important, for his captain to hear, “I am very proud of you.”

Jafari walks away, taking the route to the hangar that best avoids the stares of his teammates, but none of them look in his direction. They continue standing at attention, facing the alien ship.

General Childs continues with the details of the mission in an attempt to inform Captain Folsom of how he will lead his team despite the presence of a superior officer. Colonel Nealand is accompanying the team only as a consultant to Captain Pilas, the alien officer just now exiting the spacecraft.

Nealand falls in line with Captain Folsom and his team, with the general assuming the position of team leader on the tarmac, two steps ahead of the right-most person in the rank when viewed from behind. Captain Pilas approaches and greets Captain Folsom for the first time.

Derrick notes the alien captain's heavy clothing and labored breathing. *It's a warm day out here in the Nevada desert, but in winter, easily breathable. His planet must have a richer oxygen level in its atmosphere.*

Furtado, behind his captain, wonders how Pilas can be a threat to the planet if he can't even breathe the air.

Pilas looks into Folsom's eyes for a full ten seconds before saying anything. "Greetings, captain. I trust we'll both learn something today. You may put your team aboard my ship now."

"It's a privilege to meet an officer from another world," Derrick says as the two men shake hands. *Cold hands are sometimes just cold hands.*

"Thank you," Pilas replies with all the sincerity of an apologizing politician. He turns and retreats to his ship quickly so as to breathe the cleaner and richer air inside.

Folsom leads his team up the ramp, following the alien into the craft, which he finds is smaller on the inside than it appears from the outside. *Dark too*, he adds to his list of first impressions. Behind him are Colonel Nealand, Sergeant Furtado, Lieutenant Kong, and…

Jen turns back to her friend Shanti, who is standing with her hands clasped around the entryway of the ship as if hanging on for dear life. *Oh shit*, she thinks as she rushes to Shanti's aid. Looking into her friend's large brown eyes, she says softly, "You can do this, Shanti. Remember the calming exercises I taught you?"

Furtado, also cognizant of the lieutenant's fears, returns to the hatch quickly and adds, "There are no windows in the back. Just think of it as a Humvee ride."

Lieutenant Dae forces her breathing to a slower cadence as she gets into the spacecraft, her knees shaking as she enters and looks to the rear. She avoids eye contact with her captain, who is seated at the front window next to the alien officer, who is just now closing the hatch electronically from his pilot's chair.

Folsom shakes his head as he watches his lieutenant pass by, his impatience growing over his people's hang-ups and irrational fears that he cannot fully appreciate. *A fear of arachnids—now, that's a legitimate fear,* he opines to himself.

The crew straps themselves into their seats at the rear of the craft. *It's just like riding in a Humvee,* Shanti keeps telling herself as the engines come to life and the ship rises, slowly at first. The initial burst of acceleration presses her against her seat. It is a momentary discomfort that passes the moment the ship compensates for it.

After a few seconds, it no longer feels as though they are rising. They feel nothing. They hear nothing but the low hum of the engines beneath them and everyone's deliberate breathing. It is surprisingly quiet.

The ship cruises to the moon—a short twenty-minute ride that is actually becoming enjoyable in Shanti's mind. *As long as I keep my eyes closed, I do not need to fear. The next thing I will see is the lunar surface. Solid ground*, Shanti imagines as she keeps control of her breathing.

Her thoughts drift to her parents, who still don't know what she is doing, only that she is assigned to NASA as an intelligence officer, an advisor of sorts. She pictures them sitting together in their home, watching television. Those pleasant thoughts are interrupted by Captains Pilas and Folsom, who appear before her and her teammates holding some kind of rubberized suits. Pilas speaks as Folsom distributes them.

"You will wear these during the mission. They are solar-powered space suits. They're fully charged, of course, with an hour's supply of oxygen."

Furtado takes his and examines it carefully. "Are we going canyoneering?" *These are too tight to wear our shackles underneath them.*

Pilas ignores the question and continues speaking while passing out the belts that go with the suits. "The utility belt is key. It contains your power pack, health monitors, and tools you will use on this mission. Once you are properly outfitted, I will pass out your helmets and go over your individual assignments with you." He walks away, back to the front of the ship.

Shanti makes the mistake of following him with her eyes. A mistake because behind the skinny alien is the main window. The moon is dead ahead and closing fast. "Oh shit!" she exclaims as she diverts her attention back to her space suit and begins to undress. They all strip down to their underwear to make the tight-fitting suit comfortable.

Furtado looks over his female counterparts and winks in Folsom's direction. "I knew I was going to like our missions."

Derrick smiles but does not respond, his attention on the task at hand.

Lieutenant Kong shoots Alfonzo a look of disapproval that erases his smugness, though in her mind she feels as lucky as he does.

After a moment of admiring the Asian lieutenant's legs, Furtado returns his attention to dressing himself. *The belt can't attach itself*, he thinks as he fumbles with it.

In addition to the utility belt, each member of the crew has a bag with a handle that is worn over the shoulders to hold their shackles and computer pads. Shanti is perplexed by the necessity of carrying the shackles at all, but orders are orders.

The rest of the trip to the moon is quick and easy on Lieutenant Dae. It helps to avoid looking out the rear window and seeing the Earth recede, albeit not at a great distance in astronomical terms. It still seems very far away. She silently wishes Pilas would keep his eyes focused on the moon instead of the controls.

A moment passes as the craft travels over the lunar surface at an altitude of five hundred feet. Shanti notices Sergeant Furtado humming "Ride, Captain, Ride" again. She speaks over the firing of the rockets that rumble through the fuselage as she attempts to occupy herself with the hundred-year-old tune. "You really like that song, don't you?"

He perks up. "Excuse me, I didn't realize I was so loud."

"I will have to listen to the original recording if we ever get back."

"If?"

She stops herself with a hand over her mouth before laughing nervously. "Did I say if? I'm still a little nervous, I guess."

"I'd be happy to loan you mine," he says with a smile. He raises his shackle but stops when Lieutenant Kong interrupts them with all the seriousness of a heart attack. "We're landing. Brace yourselves."

Furtado looks at her and smiles. "Yes, ma'am." *I'll melt that iceberg yet.*

The ship begins to circle, leaving Shanti wondering about Jen's timing. *Or is it something else?* A red field of light encompasses each of them in their seats.

"Landing dampeners on, captain," is the report from Captain Folsom, acting as Pilas's copilot in the front seat of the spacecraft.

The landing is smooth as the tripod landing gear is extended and the ship drops the last ten feet onto the lunar surface with a slight bump, cushioned by the legs that bend slightly from the fitted high-tech alien shock absorbers combined with the relatively soft ground. The rocks in the landing area leave no space for the craft to land flat on the surface, hence the need for the long tripod legs.

Folsom, a good student and fast learner, feels comfortable with the simple controls after this short trip. He is confident that, if necessary, he could fly it alone. He switches off the inertial dampening field when Pilas instructs him to. The red field of light surrounding each crew member goes off. "Dampeners disengaged, captain."

Colonel Nealand is the first to stand, eager to begin the mission of salvage and rescue of the downed alien ship nearby. "Let's go, people. Prepare to disembark."

The ship is dead quiet now, making each step Pilas makes toward the team that much louder. He checks each of them for proper wear of their suits. "We are at the main body of the ship. Our mission is to investigate the cause of the crash, salvage technology, and time permitting, bury the dead."

Pilas completes his orientation with assignments to the individual team members, each one nodding in agreement with his commands but thinking of the orders they've received from their own superiors earlier in the day.

Pilas depressurizes the cabin, paying close attention to the Earthers for signs of oxygen leaking from their face masks. He then opens the hatches. What tiny amount of air remaining in the ship escapes with a short-lived hiss. He observes the team a few seconds longer. They seem at ease—even Lieutenant Dae, to his surprise.

Pilas kills the internal lights as the gray light of the sun reflecting off the lunar surface fills the ship, in addition to the bluish light reflecting off the Earth. Earthshine, as it is known, creates an extra shadow.

The right-side hatch is closest to Shanti, who looks out at the alien ship wreckage and jumps the short ten feet to the ground. The light gravity ensures a soft landing. She makes her way to the beaten and broken spacecraft to begin her assignment: get inside, look for bodies, identify and tag them with the little scanner Captain Pilas provided each of them as one of the many things that justify a utility belt.

The readout on her suit informs her of the time remaining for oxygen conversion: fifty-eight minutes. *Plenty of time,* she thinks, *depending on how hard it is to find the entire crew of twenty-two.* She feels strangely comfortable here on the surface, breathing oxygen from the small, lightweight tank attached to her belt at the small of her back. No different than being underwater in diving gear except that the weight of the air tank is dispersed around her waist, as opposed to tanks that ride the back. She can't hear the hum of the conversion mechanism but can feel it vibrating gently at her waist. *Soothing.*

Shanti feels right at home after walking a few yards. *Maybe getting this assignment wasn't such a bad thing after all.* She thinks back to the American submarine she helped rescue when her Navy career began. She never saw any dead bodies, but as she hangs on entering this large alien transport, she knows she will. There are a lot of breeches in the hull, and she takes a deep breath before entering the largest one without fear.

Sergeant Furtado is the next team member to jump to the surface. Everyone hears him shout “Geronimo!” in a mocking tone inside their headsets. They don’t respond, not wanting to encourage his adolescent behavior. On the surface, he looks back at the almost-full Earth near the horizon. He smiles and gets serious about his task to accomplish in the ship’s engineering section.

Lieutenant Kong takes a moment to reflect on how much of American culture she has picked up in the short couple of months she has been with this team. She has even caught herself humming “Ride, Captain, Ride,” but so far, no one has noticed. She is happy to have found a friend in Lieutenant Dae and is becoming comfortable in the company of her male teammates as well. *They’re growing on me*, she thinks as she makes her way to a hull breech forward of where she saw Shanti enter the ship. She has to get to the bridge.

Furtado gives her a wave as he goes in the opposite direction to get to the rear of the ship, where Captain Pilas has ordered him to check on the condition of the solar generator and engines.

While gazing up at the broken transport, Alfonzo is humbled in his knowledge of engines and mechanics in general. *This thing is a total loss. What the hell does he expect of me? I don’t know their technology. What am I doing here?* He shrugs and enters the ship through a hull breech.

Captain Pilas descends via an antigravity beam located behind the center hatch the others didn't see. He surveys the wreck before entering the front of the ship, near where Lieutenant Kong went inside. The bridge of the antiquated vessel seemed intact from the outside, which may bode well for any survivors there, but not so well for the plan forming in his mind.

Colonel Nealand exits the shuttle after the Thimmi captain, with Captain Folsom right behind him. Nealand's task for Pilas is to find any signs of an attack, such as laser burns or impacts that don't match up with the layout of the ship in its current state.

***

Captain Folsom jumps out of the portside hatch. All the hatches then close behind him. He walks to the rear of the crashed vessel, looking down into the crater, the edge of which the ship is balanced against. *That's got to be a fifty-foot drop at least*, he estimates as he jumps to the nearest rock, then to the next and the next, continuing down into the crater, searching for bits and pieces and identifying them with his scanner.

He could feel totally alone on the entire moon with not a care in the world if he chose to let his mind wander. *I'm a creature of habit, a leader of soldiers. I don't have an off switch so I can enjoy things like these.* He is proud of himself and his coalescing team. He feels a bond he hadn't known since his time in the Marine Corps, surrounded by men and women he would die for, and they for him.

After examining bits of wreckage in the crater, he hops back up, rock by rock, until he emerges from it.

Among the small rocks of the lunar surface, yards from the edge of the crater he just climbed out of, Folsom notices a stone that is unlike the others. It resembles a tennis ball-size emerald. *An emerald on the moon?* He picks it up to examine it closely and finds that it is not green; it is black, but emitting a green glow. He scans the rock with his device and is shocked when it responds with a burst of light into his eyes before going black permanently.

Black as coal but shines like a diamond, he observes. A wave of dizziness passes over him. He blames the flash in his eyes, wondering what that was and becoming concerned for his health. *What the hell just happened?* he asks himself silently as he activates his communicator to call for assistance. "This is Captain Fol—" Disoriented and confused, he collapses into unconsciousness before he can say anything else.

He lies on the surface of the moon, the sun beating down on him. His eyes are half open, the whites of them replaced with a greenish glow.

***

Sergeant Furtado, now in the engine room, moves the three orange-skinned Thimms in green uniforms to the wall just to get them out of the way. The room is the size of a small airplane hangar, and it is a mess. Wires, in the form of fiber-optic threads as thin as a human hair, protrude from every console. Furtado, following the alien captain's instructions, opens a locker marked with a strange-looking letter *B* that in the Thimmi language probably means something else.

He pulls out several cones that, if rounded, would look like disco balls with their shiny sequins. He also finds several cables that are yards long. Using his shackle's holographic instructions, he finds the solar generator control system and clears it of debris. "It's a type of emergency power system," Pilas told him. At the console, Furtado waves his hands over different controls, and to his surprise, it comes to life with power. "Well, I'll be shit on a cracker!" he exclaims. *No way the fiber optics are intact to carry power throughout the ship*, which leads him to the answer to the question of the disco balls and cables. *This is going to be cool if it works*. His job is not to question why: he just wants to finish his portion of the mission and get back to Earth as quickly as possible. He checks his O2 gauge: *fifty-five minutes of air left*.

He makes his way with the cones and cables to the nearest hull breech to exit the ship and carry out his next task: set up the cones, which will absorb energy from the sun, and plug them into the ship using the cables.

"No way this is going to work," he mumbles as he hits the surface of the moon with a bump. He is slightly surprised at his ability to keep his feet. *Light gravity, gotta love it!*

***

Colonel Nealand completes his walk around the ship and, finding no evidence of any kind of attack, concludes that the pilot did not recover from his emergency maneuver in time to avoid crashing onto the moon. He takes his last photo using the scanner, then some more with his own shackle, before noticing Sergeant Furtado struggling with a mess of cables nearby. He joins him, activating his headset to transmit a message. "Need help, sergeant?"

Alfonzo looks up from his work, gathering the cables in the light gravity, and smiles. "Thank you, sir," he replies without hesitation and hands Nealand a cable to carry to the ship. "I should've done this one at a time, but there's a connection for this one somewhere forward. These cables plug into certain plates of the hull used to power the ship with solar."

"Somewhere? Should you not have located the plugs before setting up?"

Furtado holds up his right arm, revealing the holographic diagram on Pilas's scanner that he enlarges against the hull for better viewing. "Just following the captain's orders, sir."

Nealand regards the alien's orders with an unseen smirk inside his helmet and shrugs. He takes a cable and strings it along the lunar surface from the cones to the ship. He finds a connecting plug a moment later and attaches the cable to it.

To their surprise, the lights within the hull breeches come to life, albeit dimly. The sun is low on the horizon, providing less power than it normally would. Nealand responds quietly, "Well, how about that?"

***

With power restored to the bridge, Captain Pilas speaks into the mic within his helmet. "Those of you inside the ship, I remind you not to touch the hull near the areas of hull breeches, where insulation may be diminished. You may be electrocuted. Sergeant Furtado has restored power."

Lieutenant Kong, standing next to him and hearing the warning, wonders how power transfer is possible with all the broken wires around her. She realizes the ship itself is now acting as a conduit. *Good thing the deck is made of rubbery material. It also explains the construction of their space suits.*

She stops when the captain turns to her with a hand on the console next to them. “Your scanner has a diagram of this console. You’ll find tools in the compartment beneath it. Your task is to repair what you can. This console controls communications and the dish on the hull. I’m going up there to check on it.”

Jen doesn’t take orders lightly without full understanding, which leads her to ask, “Why do you need communications if you have a working radio on your shuttle?”

Pilas pauses to carefully craft his next statement. “It has other functions that might prove useful. Follow your orders, lieutenant, and don’t get too curious. I’ll be monitoring your actions and progress.”

Jen gets to work examining the tools in the small compartment. *How did he know these tools were here? Must be a common practice*. She waits for him to leave before getting started, but he has stopped at a dead body.

Pilas has found the pilot at the front of the bridge, bent and broken from the force of the crash. He moves the body to a more honorable position before passing across the bridge to the rear hatch. Once through, he hears the familiar voice of Lieutenant Dae in his headset. “Captain Pilas, I have successfully identified twenty of the crew after examining every compartment I could find. I am proceeding to the bridge.”

“Only one here.” He stops at the escape pod next to the ladder leading to the top hatch of the ship. It is still intact. He looks through the pod’s porthole at Ambassador Hoyth, who is struggling to breathe. The ten days’ worth of oxygen, taken from a series of open canisters strewn about the pod’s interior, is nearly gone.

What good fortune! Hoyth is exuberant at the sight of someone looking in at him. Pilas stares into the ambassador’s eyes, looking into the face of relief that he is about to be saved.

The absence of atmosphere on the ship causes Ambassador Hoyth’s screams to go unheard as Pilas opens the hatch and asphyxiates the old diplomat. He dies slowly, gasping for air like a fish on the deck of a boat.

Pilas waits a moment before looking into the dead man’s eyes, the look of shock still frozen in his face. He speaks in a soft whisper, “Sorry, Mr. Ambassador, but I’m not quite finished with this planet yet. Your loss has been accepted by headquarters, just as my report of your failure will be.” Activating his helmet comm. he calls to Lieutenant Dae. “I’ve found the ambassador dead in the escape pod. He apparently ran out of oxygen. All passengers and crew are accounted for. Get up here.”

“Roger that, sir.”

Lieutenant Kong, watching the murder of the ambassador from a safe distance, retreats back into the bridge, forgetting the question she was going to ask Pilas face to face. She returns to the task of repairing the console that Pilas is so secretive about, wondering what he has in mind. She is an expert in computers, but the problem isn't programming. She takes a moment to scan the interior of the console with her shackle. Her other specialty is information gathering, and she does it well. She looks forward to getting back to base and sifting through everything the team is learning today.

***

With the hour of oxygen almost used up, the team meets back at the shuttle, ready to return home after burying the dead in shallow graves dug into the lunar surface. They are now waiting for Captains Folsom and Pilas.

Lieutenant Kong is the first to question her captain's whereabouts. "Folsom isn't answering his comm. Fan out!" she orders.

Colonel Nealand isn't the slightest bit taken aback by receiving such a command from a lowly lieutenant, but instead follows the order. The team leader is missing. Without him, there is no team, and formalities over rank are irrelevant.

***

As the crew searches for Folsom around the wrecked ship, Pilas returns to its bridge to begin the process of bringing the people of Earth to his side. *Unification will be forced upon these people. They will follow me or die trying.* Pilas remembers the last message received from headquarters, informing him of the upcoming transplant of the Earth humans to Jexx with the promise of peace and prosperity for them on an uninhabited planet.

That directive was based on Ambassador Hoyth bringing the nations of Earth together diplomatically. The problem is that the Vorelisian agent, Lightner, wherever he is, is so connected to the people right now that they'll reject any Thimmi plan brought to them. The people have to *want* to leave the Earth, and that is the crux of Pilas's plan. *They can't be given any other choice for survival.*

The Thimmi captain sets up the defenses of the ship to repel any approaching ships or weapons that come into its range. *Only I will be allowed to disable these defenses.* A rare grin appears on his face. *The empire will get Jexx, and I'll have Earth.*

That task complete, all that is left for him to do is turn on the antigravity generator he took from the engine room, which is connected to the communications dish that Kong helped him repair. *What a useful group of fools,* he chuckles as he applies negative energy to the generator, creating a magnetic pulse wave that will adversely affect the magnetic field of the Earth.

The sudden weakening of the magnetic field will cause the people to be susceptible to the sun's harmful rays. Millions will die in a short time.

Once I appear as their savior, they will hail me as their god and will happily join the Galactic Community under Thimmi sponsorship. They will get us Jexx in the council and love me as their leader for the rest of my life.

CHAPTER EIGHTEEN: Rishal

Captain Folsom is standing in a green meadow with strong rivers running through it. A city of great height and prominence fills the horizon on this bright day. The skyline is of a city he doesn't recognize. *Where am I?* he wonders as he walks, now dressed in his old Marine Corps dress uniform.

He comes to a lone tree in the meadow, a tall American elm. *I must be dreaming, but I shouldn't be. There was a flash of light; the rock. I feel like I should know this place, but I've never seen a city skyline like that before. The buildings must be over two hundred stories.*

Just then, Private Barnes, the eager, young soldier from his old squad, falls out of the tree, landing on his feet in front of his captain, not having aged. "Hello, Captain Folsom" he says with glee and the sharpest of salutes.

Surprised by the appearance of the man and the realness of him, Folsom steps back. "OK, now I know this is a dream."

"No dream, sir. I am here to ask for your help." His smile fades as his tone turns serious. "I found this person in your mind with which to communicate with you. I trust the familiarity is satisfactory. I'd rather not take over your mind. I wish to be friends with you and your people."

"You chose a young man who was close to me to make an appearance?" Folsom purses his lips in anger as he imagines the general's secretary, Sheila. *A better choice. I would definitely listen to her.*

Barnes continues. "You have a strong connection to this person. This connection is like no other I have found in your mind. You feel responsible for my—for *his* death," he corrects himself.

"You said you needed my help. Who are you? I know you're not Private Barnes. What help can I provide?"

"Call me Rishal. Until very recently, I was a slave to the Thimmi Empire. The Thimms use my people to help control their navigation systems. We must comply lest we be destroyed. I have been in their servitude for twenty years."

Derrick sits at the base of the tree trunk and looks out at the skyline, still expecting to wake up at any moment. "I am only one man. What can I do?"

"My people, the Zetans, need your help to be freed from Thimmi oppression. If you can get to the capital planet of the galaxy, Galactico, and submit to a brain scan before the Security Council, my message will be conveyed."

"I can make no promises. We humans are still in our infancy regarding space travel, and we're not part of the Galactic Community." *Not yet, anyway*, he doesn't add.

"It may surprise you to learn that humans make up ninety percent of the galactic population. I have no doubt that you will find your place within the community of worlds. Will you assist me?"

"Right now, nothing is certain, but I will try. Let's see what happens next."

"One step at a time. I couldn't expect more. Thank you," Barnes says as he disappears. The last thing Derrick sees is that disarming, innocent smile of his.

***

Colonel Nealand, surrounded by the rest of the team, is gently shaking the captain to bring him around. "Come on, captain. Sleep time is over."

I'm back on the shuttle, Folsom acknowledges in his mind as he sits up. No one, including himself, is wearing their helmet. He is breathing normally now, getting more oxygen than he needs in the heavily O2-saturated alien ship. Pilas glances back as he pilots the shuttle alone, relieved to not have lost a man.

The Earth's horizon stretches from one side of the wide front window to the other. They're heading home. Folsom pulls Colonel Nealand close to him to whisper, "I have to report, colonel. I…" He stops himself and gestures with his eyes in Pilas's direction.

Nealand nods and whispers back, "Understood. We'll talk later."

Derrick stands to join the rest of his team in the rear of the ship. Lieutenant Kong greets him with a nod. "Sir, we have collected some interesting artifacts and technology."

"Very good."

"I have that rock that you were holding onto when we found you."

"Good," he says as he rubs his left temple. "I might need it."

As she turns to walk away, he stops her by raising his voice. "And lieutenant." She turns to face him as he continues in a softer tone. "Thank you."

She smiles as she turns to take her seat.

CHAPTER NINETEEN: The End of the World

The Earth journey's around the sun is an endless trip through space that has lasted billions of years. In a small portion of that time, the Earth's inhabitants were planted and grew into separate tribes, or nations, until eventually reaching the zenith of civilization.

The fruit they bore has the capability of nourishing the entire galaxy.

The journey around the sun for the past two months, however, has been anything but fruitful. It is now February 2062, and Madeline's pregnancy is starting to show. She has gone about her duties as senator of the State of Nevada as if unification with the rest of the world never happened.

The one-planet idea within the scope of humanity's growth as a civilization was thought of in the 1900s when those with the money to control power began spending it in frightful ways. Their plans have come to a head as the election of the world's first first premier is only a year away.

But something is wrong. People all over the world, in every walk of life, are suffering from conditions consistent with overexposure to the sun's UV radiation. The reported cases of cataracts has increased ten thousand-fold all over the planet in addition to the massive increases in melanoma and non-melanoma skin cancers.

By this time, medical science has advanced far enough to prevent several forms of cancer, though the methods used are not universal. Most scientists admit their frustration in finding the right combinations of medicine and technology to combat every case. Genetics have taken a prominent role in weeding disease out of family histories. For these reasons, it is perplexing that so many new cases have propped up with no explanation of why.

As she sits at her desk in Washington, DC, Madeline continues to look for answers to give to her constituents, who are flooding her office with questions and fears.

One possible answer is about to come from Dr. Steven Trachsel, the astronomer best known for having escaped the crash of the International Space Station a couple of months earlier.

Madeline's secretary, Trisha, has called her shackle to inform her of the doctor's arrival, but she was hoping for a call from Charles, who has been "missing" for months now. *The CIA knows where he is; they just won't tell me, despite the fact that he is the father of my child.*

The door opens as Madeline's frustration comes to a head and she slams her fist on the table. Doctor Trachsel enters the room, sees the pained expression on the senator's face, and takes a step back. "I'm sorry, senator, is this a bad time?"

She stands to welcome the man and holds out her hand to him. "It's a bad time for all of us. Why should I be any different?"

They shake hands, and he sits down, "I could come back later," he offers.

She sits and composes herself. "I'm sorry. I'm having a bit of a personal crisis," she says as she subconsciously rubs her baby bump.

With two kids of his own, the doctor understands immediately. At least, he thinks he does. He reflects for a quick second on his wife, Anne, and how they dealt with the birth of their first child. *This isn't the time, and I'm not a psychiatrist.* He uses his shackle to pull up a hologram of data charts, revealing what the world already suspects and what the government already knows. "As you can see, people all over the world are dying by the thousands every day. This is unheard of."

"Yes, doctor. The question isn't 'What?' It's 'Why?'"

He pauses before answering. "The magnetic field of the planet is disappearing, fading away. Slowly at present, but the process is accelerating. Soon, it will cease to exist."

Madeline sits forward in her seat, as if getting six inches closer will help her understand the situation any better. Feeling almost too alarmed to ask, she whispers, "How?"

Steven changes the data images on his shackle in favor of a video of Earth rotating in real time. He transfers the video feed to Madeline's desk screen, similar to the one Governor Dobson uses. He makes changes to the video, adding effects and visual aides as he explains.

She stands to view the planet like a general hovering over a battlefield, planning strategy.

After a few clicks on his shackle's control screen, Steven finds the image of the beautiful blue-and-brown planet Earth resting on a sea of black with a blanket of stars behind it. It changes to include a bright yellow energy field encircling it.

He explains, "This is Earth with a fully developed magnetic field. It is normally invisible, of course. The only visible evidence of the field's existence is the aurora borealis, or northern lights, when the sun's rays charge the particles in the atmosphere. In the southern hemisphere, the phenomenon is known as the aurora australis."

Madeline rolls her eyes up to his, as if to say *Duh*, though she refrains.

He lightens the yellow field, giving the impression of a weak power level.

"I'm rambling," the good doctor says apologetically, noticing the look. "I'm just a little nervous, I guess." The portion of yellow in front of the planet becomes less opaque, enough that more of the Earth's surface is seen. "This is the condition of the magnetic field today."

"There's hardly any yellow left."

"Precisely. We're running out of time."

"How much time?" she asks while massaging her belly again, this time thinking of the hardship to come. *How will my daughter live on a planet without a magnetic field? She won't! No one will.*

"We can take action to slow the death rate by informing the public," Steven says. "They'll have to accept some drastic changes in their habits. We have maybe fifteen, twenty years at the current rate of decay."

"We can't have mass panic, doctor."

"We may have to live underground until we are able to move the population to a new world."

She sits back, stifling a laugh. "And what planet did you have in mind? There are none in our system that can support life."

Trachsel smiles and presses several icons on his shackle to change the image on Madeline's desk from the Earth to that of a fuzzy blue dot in a sea of blackness. "I have a candidate in mind. I found it in the constellation of Carina. It is about seven thousand, five hundred light-years away."

She looks up, raising her eyebrows. "You couldn't find a planet in the Andromeda galaxy?" she says sarcastically.

"What about Doctor Lightner? He said he was from another world. Perhaps his people could help us."

Madeline stands and faces the window to avoid the doctor's gaze. "Charles Lightner has disappeared. I don't know where he is. I will have to brief the governor."

Trachsel stands while turning off his presentation. "Whatever we're going to do, we better do it soon. We need to move the populations away from the equator, where the field is weakest, first."

"And second?"

"Start building new cities underground, no matter the hardship such construction may cause. Many can survive in the subways of the cities while we expand them. We need to warn the people not to be in the sun at all if they can help it. Pass out sunblock and protective clothing." Steven stops talking. He lowers his head and gently bites the first knuckle of his right hand as if doing calculations in his head.

Madeline returns to her seat and asks, “What is it?”

He looks up at her with wide eyes and says, “I may have to reevaluate my time estimate.”

“Why?”

“The plants and wildlife will die off long before we do.”

Madeline slaps her shackle.

Trisha responds on the other end, “Yes?”

“Get me the governor. I need to speak with him right now!”

***

Trans-African Airlines Flight 352 is a traditional engine-powered aircraft with a cruising speed of six hundred miles per hour at thirty thousand feet. Three hours into the trip, the pilot, Captain Yaseen, and his copilot, Andrews, are alerted to a problem.

The plane, a Boeing 797-R model, on autopilot, has begun to circle as if it has just gotten lost.

Yaseen turns off the autopilot and takes the controls. He straightens the aircraft into a single direction and asks the navigator behind him, “What is our heading?”

“Course three-four-zero,” is the response.

Andrews objects. “That can’t be right! The sun is on our right. It is four o’clock in the afternoon; it should be on our left. We are traveling north.”

The navigator grows confused as the magnetic compass spins slowly to a new heading. He slaps the side of the console where the compass dial is. “I know we’re not turning again, but our heading is now forty degrees.”

Yaseen looks out the window at the terrain and checks his GPS instruments. “The satellites are in working order. We’ll follow them.”

Andrews becomes more nervous. “We cannot fly without a compass.” His lack of experience is clearly evident. But then, no one has experienced a pocket of emptiness within their flight path. The magnetic field is weakest at their current location.

The navigator concurs with Andrews, but without the nervousness in his voice. “Yes, we must turn back.”

The captain glances at both of his crew and returns his gaze to the horizon. "You would think I'd never flown blind before." He pauses before conceding to their fears. "Contact Nairobi. Inform them our compass is out and we are returning."

The navigator compensates for a malfunctioning compass by looking out the window. He recognizes Mount Kilimanjaro on the horizon and points. "That way."

"You're one hell of a navigator," Yaseen mumbles sarcastically as he turns the three-hundred-passenger load they're ferrying in the direction of the mountain. Louder, he assures them, "I know the way."

CHAPTER TWENTY: Falling in Line

Repeated attempts to contact Governor Dobson have been met with silence despite his secretary's assurances that he is in the Oval Office. After knocking for the fifth time, Madeline and Dr. Trachsel enter to find Captain Pilas, in a green uniform, without his sunglasses and outer clothing, holding Dobson's head back in his chair and forcing his eyes open with one hand while positioning some kind of scanner over them with the other. Director McCarthy is lying face down on the floor, seemingly dead.

Seeing the two incapacitated men like this shocks Madeline to the point of screaming, but she is unable to. Her mouth opens, her mind fully intending to make a sound, any sound, but it doesn't come. She has never seen an alien before, Lightner notwithstanding. Whereas Pilas is human enough, his orange complexion and beady little eyes frighten her to her soul in a way nothing in her life ever has.

Trachsel, however, is less afraid. "What the hell is going on here?"

Pilas looks up at them and responds by putting down the scanner and pulling up a funny-looking pistol. He fires twice and misses. The Earthers flee before he can fire again.

In the outer office, Madeline regains her composure and shouts commands at Dobson's secretary. "Call the police! The Secret Service! The Marines!" He complies without question.

***

A few minutes later, Dobson is awake and sitting at his desk. McCarthy and Pilas are seated on either side of him. They are conversing with the images of the five other governors of the world shown on the desk screen.

The men are shocked to their feet when two Secret Service agents burst into the room with their weapons trained on the floor. Three Marines follow, pointing their large and intimidating M-77 rifles at them.

Dobson is the first to speak. "What is this?"

One of the agents, Cameron Mueller, responds while putting away his weapon. "Apologies, governor. We got word you were being assaulted."

McCarthy and Pilas look at each other while Dobson pretends to stifle a laugh. "Who told you that?"

Madeline and Dr. Trachsel step forward from behind the armed men. *It's an easy thing to be brave when Marines accompany you with their big guns.* She speaks up with conviction. "I did!"

Dr. Trachsel looks around the room, especially at the walls behind him, expecting to see the evidence of laser fire he witnessed earlier.

Dobson lets his laugh out. “There is no emergency. I’m fine. Right now we are in a conference with the leadership of the world, so if you will excuse us.” He changes his tone from levity to annoyance as he continues. “And do not return unless I call you.”

The troops leave after apologizing again and shooting the senator and astronomer dirty looks.

Madeline and Trachsel remain after the door is closed behind them.

Pilas, back to wearing his shades and gloves but still in his green uniform, hasn’t taken his eyes off them during the whole exchange. “You may leave as well,” he says, sounding like a command.

Madeline steps closer. *Something is going on here*. She will not let it go as easily as the agents did. *It’s just the doctor and me now*. Her courage is wavering a bit without firepower to back her up. She looks straight at the alien standing behind the governor. “You shot at me with a laser!”

Before Pilas can deny the accusation, Trachsel points to a burn mark on the doorframe. He looks at Pilas over his steel-rimmed glasses. “How did these marks get here?”

Madeline doesn’t wait for an answer. She continues forward, knowing the alien has a weapon and is not afraid to use it. Her heart is pounding. “Sir, this alien was holding some kind of device over you not ten minutes ago. It was shining a light into your eyes. You were unconscious.”

Her confusion is compounded by Dobson’s explanation, not denial. “Were I under duress, don’t you think MAA would have been summoned?”

He’s got a point there, Madeline realizes as Dobson stands and continues, “This is Captain Pilas of the Thimmi Empire. He is here to assist us in our crisis. He was scanning our minds for information on the whereabouts of Doctor Lightner. I wanted to assure him that we didn’t know his location, so I allowed the scan.”

McCarthy steps closer to the doctor to block him from getting closer to Pilas. “The scanner gathers information from the memory center of the brain. Everything a person sees or hears is recorded. The scanner records the answers to questions taken from the mind.” The Thimmi captain states.

The doctor is intrigued and more than a little concerned. "Sounds like a Gestapo tactic."

Dobson shakes his head and chuckles, "Rest assured, we volunteered, doctor."

Madeline, still confused, looks Dobson in the eyes, trying to read him as she asks, "Why must you be unconscious?"

Pilas has moved to her side so quickly she doesn't see him until he's there. She steps back as he answers her question. "The scanning process is an intrusion into the mind that is very painful. A conscious person wouldn't be able to handle it."

Pilas turns away, leaving Madeline with a cold chill running up her spine that she could swear on a stack of Bibles scared the unborn child growing inside of her. She asks the obvious question: "Wouldn't the pain wake you?"

Pilas ignores the question and returns to standing behind Dobson to speak to the five images on the desk. "The Thimmi Empire is the most advanced race in the galaxy, but we are not perfect in the area of medicine. We are, however, very proficient at restoring magnetic fields. Doing so will take many years. In that time, we have other options for your people."

Dobson continues for the smiling alien who knows he has the Earthers right where he wants them. "Captain Pilas and I were just going over his terms for rejuvenating our magnetic field before it collapses completely."

Trachsel and Madeline speak simultaneously, with the same level of shock in their voices. "Terms?"

Madeline gets into the desk camera's view so the other leaders can see her. She directs her words at the leader of the Asian Alliance. "Minister Shabal, we are currently in talks to join the Galactic Community under sponsorship of the Vorelisians."

Shabal, looking like a man beyond his years, and as if he is preparing to jump out of a fully functional aircraft, says, "Doctor Lightner's message indicated that to be true, but we have since not been able to contact him."

"Surely he must be in Asia. The Chinese should be able to—"

Shabal interrupts her. "We are siding with the Thimmi Empire for the time being. The Chinese are negotiating with Australia and the Pacific Islands for a Vorelisian proposal but if Lightner remains hidden," his voice trails off.

It is surprising that man can stand upright while missing a spine. "Doctor Lightner will show up. We just have to be patient," Madeline begs.

Dobson looks her square in the eyes and speaks for the world, or so he thinks. "How many people must die while we wait, senator?"

She shifts her gaze back to Shabal. "What flight did Lightner take off the continent?"

"He has no shackle with which to track his movements, and the Chinese aren't helping. Please, I will answer no more questions."

She continues, appealing to the other leaders. "We have a deal in place with Doctor Lightner and the Vorelisians, governors! Are we going to forsake our agreements?"

Half of the so-called leaders shake their heads; the rest simply lower them.

If only the Vorelisians were here! her mind screams.

If only Charles were here! her heart cries.

Dobson rises. "We are forming a new agreement with the Thimmi Empire in exchange for their help in restoring the magnetic field. Unless you can tell us where Lightner is so that we may talk to him, the Vorelisian agreement is null and void."

Madeline's response is the most honest and truthful statement of fact that anyone with ears can hear. It mixes genuine concern with sadness. “I do not know where he is,” she says as she heads for the door. *I don’t know where he is—but I should!*

Doctor Trachsel remains at Dobson’s desk to inquire, “What does the Thimmi Empire want in return for our salvation?”

Captain Pilas smiles. “What is your life worth, doctor?”

Dobson elaborates. “We have handed over control of the world to Captain Pilas until such time as his government can be mobilized into action. They will evacuate as many of our people as possible while rejuvenation of the field is underway.”

Madeline, at the door, turns back. “I hope you have a plan for getting control back!”

Pilas looks up at her, his anger growing and subsiding in a breath. He addresses the doctor. “As an astronomer, I’m sure you realize that conventional space travel from the Messier Star Cluster would take no less than a decade.”

Trachsel laughs. “Conventional for you, you mean. It would take us several lifetimes. The Messier Star Cluster is about twenty-two thousand light-years away.”

Pilas nods in agreement. “Or you may perish as a race,” he says with all the calmness of a cougar about to pounce on an unsuspecting deer. “Your choice.”

The doctor doesn't answer, because there is nothing left to say. *Did we unite as a world and as a people just to hand over our lives to an alien race?* He considers saying that out loud to induce guilt in the leaders in the room, but he leaves the thought in his mind. He follows Madeline out of the room, leaving them to surrender the planet behind closed doors.

The leaders' vote for Thimmi control is unanimous but for the Australian leaders' abstention. Dobson makes the vote official. "You are in command now, captain. What are your instructions?"

Pilas stares at the former leader of the North American continent until the fool gets the unspoken message to vacate the seat he is in. Dobson moves away from the chair slowly, reluctantly. *How plans can change in a heartbeat.*

Pilas relaxes in the plush leather for a moment before leaning forward so those on the desk screen can see him. "Dr. Charles Lightner is, from this point forward, a fugitive from justice and must be captured. I believe he is responsible for the collapse of your magnetic field. He is considered an enemy of the Thimmi Empire. I want him found!"

The looks he gets from some on the screen betray their objection to surrendering the doctor, but he knows they have no choice but to obey him. Pilas leans back, satisfied that the world is now his.

Dobson, reserved and defeated, responds. “It is so ordered.”

***

Dr. Lightner drives his rented SUV off road from Vegas through the Mojave Desert in the darkness until he reaches his shuttle. Once behind the rocks and out of sight of the road, he gets into his small craft and activates the communications system. In moments, he is able to track news outlets from all over the world. He is shocked to learn of the collapse of the magnetic field and the coincidental offer of the Thimms to assist. Captain Pilas has taken full advantage of his absence.

Among the news reports: peoples from the equatorial regions of the planet are being relocated to the North American continent due to the weakening of the magnetic field; five million people have died so far in this crisis, which shows no signs of leveling off; and Pilas has formally taken full control of the Earth in exchange for his people’s help in resolving the crisis.

WHAT?

Lastly, he learns of the pregnancy of a certain Nevada senator. *For the love of sand!* He rushes back to his SUV for the trip back to Vegas. *I didn’t know! I must go to her!*

Charles takes note of his emotions, feeling a strong sense of duty…not for the plight of the world or his mission to unite Earth under the leadership and protection of the Vorelisian Empire, but for the love of Madeline and their unborn child.

I'm a scientist, not a soldier or politician. I may have failed my people, but I won't fail her. If I can't get these people to see the tragic consequences that will befall them for allowing the Thimms control over them, I will, at the very least, get my new family off this planet.

He finds his communication recorder and low-powered laser pistol and pockets them. Back at the hydrogen-powered vehicle, he contemplates the future of the Earth people and his mission. *Is what I'm doing worth it?*

He speeds back in the direction from which he came.

CHAPTER TWENTY-ONE: Roundup

The McCarran Airport missed Dr. Lightner's arrival because security is lax in this age of globalization. Terrorism was eliminated years ago. Remaining are protest organizations that are allowed to practice their hatred for government and its plans openly, thus resulting in little violence, as it would be nearly impossible to organize anything more than a simple march. Any more than that would result in their arrest before they could act. Governments all over the world watch these groups closely.

When the alert for Dr. Lightner's arrest came to the attention of all air and sea ports worldwide, he was on the ground in the Mojave Desert learning of his upcoming parenthood and the plight of the world under an adversarial Thimmi captain.

Getting on a plane will prove to be a challenge. Lightner walks into the terminal while forming a plan. *If I know the Thimms, Captain Pilas will have Earth's police and military forces on the lookout for me*. He ponders flying his own shuttle to Washington, DC, but knows he wouldn't get there safely. *I'd be likely shot down before reaching the North American governor, Dobson—or Madeline*.

He drove around the terminal three times before deciding on a course of action. Now inside, wearing his lab coat and carrying a concealed pistol, he walks through the place like he belongs there.

He removes the coat, fearing it makes him conspicuous, and drapes it over his arm, hoping his white shirt and black pants underneath will help him resemble a pilot enough so that no one challenges his presence.

"Excuse me, sir."

So much for that idea, Charles thinks as he fingers the trigger of the pistol inside his coat pocket. He turns to face the female voice that called to him. "Yes?"

The middle-aged woman, dressed in the uniform of the airline he is trying to pretend he is working for and appearing to be in a position of authority by her demeanor, moves in front of him. "Are you Captain Crimmins?"

Lightner fumbles with his make-believe shackle. In reality, it is a device of his own design that he quickly manipulates into reading the woman's shackle and getting Crimmins's information. In a moment, the pilot's ID is copied. Lightner stalls for time by speaking as if worried about something. "Excuse me, my wife is having a baby." *Hey, it's only a partial lie, like two-thirds of one.*

The supervisor cannot see that he is programming the device to forge the captain's ID. His plan would have worked were it not for the man who stops to say, "Pardon me, I'm Captain Crimmins. Can you direct me to the gate where flight three-nine-eight is waiting? I'm their pilot."

The woman looks up at the real Crimmins, standing behind Lightner, who is a foot taller, then back to Lightner himself, his "shackle" now claiming to be Crimmins's as she scans it. "What the…?"

Lightner runs while pulling out his pistol. *I didn't have time to formulate a plan 'B'!*

The airline supervisor quickly uses her shackle to alert everyone in the airport: security, airline employees, and even passengers. *This imposter will have to avoid nearly everyone to escape*. Later, she'll ponder how someone was able to fake a shackle ID so quickly and easily.

Charles runs out of the terminal on the flight-line side and toward a maintenance hangar where some aircraft are being worked on. He dons the coat as he runs, as its special abilities may become useful. It lacks cloaking technology but has other functions that may assist in his escape. He looks back to see three security guards running after him, and gaining.

"Halt!" he hears as he brandishes his laser pistol, hoping to frighten them enough to stop their pursuit.

The three men are not so easily scared; they pull out their own weapons, .45 Glocks. One stops to take aim at the fleeing doctor, not knowing or caring who he is; it's enough to know he is a trespasser and ID forger, both serious crimes. He fires a shot from a hundred feet away that he feels should have hit the running man but somehow ricochets off the hangar the suspect just ran into. He sprints to catch up to his comrades.

Lightner turns a corner and hangs his lab coat inside a paint locker. He is careful to make sure the edge of the coat is visible on the outside as he closes the door on it. He then hides behind the wheel of a small government aircraft opposite the locker.

The three guards enter.

The leader spots the coat in the locker's door and points to it. His comrades cover him as he opens the locker to find…paint! Before he can curse himself for falling for the oldest trick in the book, Lightner is behind them with his weapon drawn.

"Please do not move. It is not my intention to harm you," he says calmly in between breaths. *I haven't run this hard in a long time.* The three men lower their weapons to the floor.

"Don't shoot," the leader begs, barely retaining his dignity and the respect of his men. He summons his courage as Lightner steps back. "What do you want?"

Charles gestures at the government plane behind him. Based on its markings, it's from the state of New Jersey, *obviously here for maintenance*. The thrusters tell him it is an antigravity plane, and that spells speed; *excellent*. He reaches up to a release lever near the hatch that lowers the stairs. He looks inside at the controls in the cockpit a few feet away and makes a decision. *I can fly this thing alone*, he plots as he returns his attention to the three men in front of him, who are now on their knees with their heads lowered and their hands clasped behind them. "I need transportation, so I'm taking this aircraft—"

The leader, the coward, in an effort to redeem himself, drops to retrieve his weapon on the ground nearby. While rolling to his feet to fire, he slips on a grease spot. Instead of shooting Lightner, he accidentally shoots one of his men in the leg.

Charles, surprised by the act, fires at the leader before he can bring his weapon to bear on him. The shot sets the man's sleeve on fire. "Don't move!"

The leader is screaming in agony as he puts out the flames burning his skin with his other arm. The guard who was shot in the leg is also writhing as Lightner kicks their guns away and motions for them all to move away from the locker so he can get his lab coat back.

While putting the coat on, he sees an antigravity security vehicle, about the size of an open-air Humvee, floating toward the hangar at high speed from the terminal with four men aboard. "Damn!" he shouts as he gets into the antigravity plane and closes the hatch behind him.

Charles starts the engines just as the new security team arrives. They open fire on the cockpit, putting holes in the windows and fuselage as the plane moves out onto the tarmac.

Once outside the hangar, it's then a simple maneuver to set the antigravity generators to full. Like a helicopter taking off straight up, Charles is out of range of their weapons and at ten thousand feet in a matter of seconds.

At altitude now, he waits for the blood to return to his brain before setting course for Washington, DC. *Only an hour away.*

***

Word of a man stealing an aircraft from McCarran Airport who matches Lightner's description reaches Captain Pilas, who orders the Earth Defense Force mobilized with the instructions to capture or kill him, "whichever is safer," he says to General Childs.

***

EDF-1, now training indoors due to the high danger of the sun, gets the message a short ten minutes later. Lacking aircraft and pilots with which to capture Lightner, Captain Folsom is ordered to take custody of the Vorelisian fugitive once other mobilized teams apprehend him. EDF-1 will be responsible for holding him at Groom Lake Base until Pilas himself can interrogate him.

EDF-5, an Air Force squadron of seven planes under the command of Major Ken Roberts, attacks Lightner's plane over the Utah desert and severs its left wing using smart bullets. The bullets are capable of discerning which part of the target to hit and hitting *only* that part. They are best described as mini-cruise missiles, each with advanced maneuverability and computer guidance.

Despite the fact that the media will likely blow the operation out of proportion, Roberts takes into account its simplicity. Lightner's plane is not only unarmed, but low on power. The thrusters are in need of an overhaul, the reason the aircraft was in for maintenance in the first place. It is pretty easy to catch up to a plane going three hundred fifty miles per hour when yours cruises at fifteen hundred.

On the ground, despite a rough landing, Lightner is able to free himself from the wreck and avoid capture despite the efforts of the sheriff of Kane County and his ten deputies.

***

Back at Groom Lake, Folsom breaks the news to his team, who is loading up the antigravity Humvee with weapons and equipment. “Take your time. The suspect got away. We’re going to DC on a surveillance mission.”

Furtado relaxes a bit and hums his favorite tune. *Should be as simple as water in a glass*, he thinks as he inquires, “Captain, why is it we are supposed to arrest Dr. Lightner? Isn’t he the one responsible for advancing technology all over the world?”

Folsom thinks back on the inventions of the last decade and wonders how many the doctor is actually responsible for. He takes the question to heart, knowing the sensitivity of the subject. He pulls the team together to explain their position—or, at least, his understanding of it. “Our duty is to follow the orders of our leaders. It is rumored that Dr. Lightner is responsible for the destruction of the Space Station as well as the collapse of the magnetic field.”

Lieutenant Kong raises her voice with conviction, knowing in her heart that her people were never involved in the destruction of the station. “It makes sense. The evidence is clear that Lightner was conducting power tests from the station. Was he planning to take over the world, or at least blackmail us to obey him?”

Standing by her friend’s side, Lieutenant Dae agrees. “It makes me wonder what all those Soliquid plants are really for. I mean, we have enough solar energy to power half the planet already, don't we?"

Furtado is not convinced. "Those plants are under our control, not his. I think you're just being paranoid, Jen."

She shoots him a look, still not comfortable being on a first-name basis with a noncommissioned officer, no matter how attractive he may be.

"Lieutenant," he corrects himself.

She looks away as she mumbles, "I am not paranoid." Louder, she addresses his comment on control as she loads a satellite kit into the vehicle. "For how long would we retain control against an alien race? When you supply a world with technology, is it not easy to hold the use of that technology over the heads of the people? Without his guidance, we'd be lost. That could be his intent, to put us in need of him."

"To what end?" Furtado asks, thinking for a moment that the beautiful Asian officer is getting her aliens mixed up.

She continues to explain, feeling confident that she is right about this. "I believe the Soliquid plants' use is what has affected the magnetic field of the planet. Only though the leadership and assistance of this other alien…" She pauses, having forgotten the name, until Shanti reminds her.

"Pilas."

Kong finishes after nodding appreciatively to her friend. "Right, Pilas. Only he can help us through this crisis that Lightner has caused."

She climbs into the Humvee to continue loading the supplies the team will need for the trip and to assist Shanti, who is loading advanced surveillance equipment.

Furtado turns back to his captain, who is polishing the chrome on his Indian motorcycle. It will take the two of them to load the bike into the rear of the Humvee. "Sir, what happens if we're wrong?"

"The evidence is as plain as day, sergeant. Lightner is to be arrested as an enemy of the Earth. It is the duty for which this team, and ninety others so far, were formed throughout the world to accomplish: the defense of our home planet."

Alfonzo pauses, thinking about how wrong he feels his teammates must be, but says instead, "I'll load the body armor."

Further debate over the issue is broken by the arrival of Private Jafari, who shows up wearing the same battle fatigue uniform as the others but with the addition of racing gloves and slick high boots on his feet, seemingly ready for a NASCAR race.

Regulation wear, but this kid is having way too much fun, Folsom opines to himself as he looks over the new recruit. “Taking your driving responsibilities seriously, are we?”

Jafari’s joy in the upcoming mission is broken for a moment as he considers his captain’s words and his teammates’ chuckles. “Sir, I was just looking forward to the adventure, sir,” he says with a sheepish grin.

Folsom’s smile fades before he turns serious. “You have a long career of adventures ahead of you, private. Don’t be so eager to embrace them. It can be diverting, and diversion of your attention to the task at hand can be detrimental. Carry on.”

Jafari’s smile returns as he moves to the driver’s side of the Humvee. “Yes, sir!”

A few minutes later, word comes that the search for the alien doctor is being called off in Utah. Searchers found no body near the aircraft and no trace of him in nearby towns. Authorities suspect he will try to get to Washington, DC by other means.

“Saddle up!” Folsom commands, knowing their plan is to get to DC to keep an eye on Senator Madeline Verona’s apartment there, suspecting that Lightner will attempt to contact her.

The Humvee, under the superior driving abilities of Private Jafari, sets out on their mission at 250 miles per hour.

***

A short thirteen hours later, with breaks and a meal stop in Tennessee, the EDF-1 team arrives in Washington, DC, and begins their surveillance of Senator Verona's apartment. It is a cold February night in the sprawling metropolis, but the sky is clear.

Warm in their cramped vehicle, Lieutenant Kong takes the role of leader when she assigns the order in which the team may sleep. Surprisingly, she gives Jafari first crack at monitoring the computers for signs of anyone leaving or entering the senator's apartment, due to the fact that he is the most amped up from having driven them here. *He'll get uninterrupted sleep when he's done in two hours.*

Shanti volunteers to get coffee, but only Jafari accepts. She exits with Captain Folsom, who unloads his motorcycle from the Humvee and rides to the White House to meet with General Childs and Governor Dobson.

When Derrick enters the Oval Office a short time later, he is surprised to be joined by Captain Pilas, who recognizes him from the moon mission right away and shakes his hand. "It is good to have you working for me, captain," Pilas says.

For him? he thinks as a fake smile slowly emerges on his face. "Yes, sir. Any word on Dr. Lightner's whereabouts?"

Childs answers for the alien captain. “As you know, antigravity vehicles are rare. If Lightner is fool enough to come to Washington, it should take him a day or two to get here by conventional means but probably won’t use public transportation.”

He’ll hitchhike or steal a car, Folsom surmises.

Dobson continues. “Every person’s shackle from here to the West Coast is being monitored for signs of contact with the doctor. We should have no trouble catching him,” he says smugly.

Folsom wonders about the constitutionality of using ordinary citizens’ personal devices to hunt for an alien fugitive without their knowledge before wondering further what constitution, if any, this once-great land is being administrated under.

Pilas interrupts his train of thought as he objects. “The Vorelisians are not to be underestimated, gentlemen. He has technology on his side, and he may be getting desperate. There is no telling the depths this man will sink to. He has already set your world on the road to extinction.”

The alien life form occupying an infinitesimal portion of Folsom’s brain causes his left eye to twitch, as if shouting out for attention. Derrick can’t communicate with Rishal while he is awake, but gets the idea that Pilas is saying something that should not be believed. He shrugs it off as a nagging suspicion. He directs his attention instead to his former CO, General Childs, a man who appears to be distrusting of this alien as well by the look of him. "What is our next move, sir?"

William, appreciative of the diversion, answers with a nod to the Thimmi officer, "We need to capture Lightner. That is all you should concern yourself with, if not for the security of the planet, then to discover his motives."

Pilas objects again, "His motives are clear!" He calms himself before taking a different tack; "I estimate it will take a decade for my people to get here and begin evacuating the planet, assuming we cannot repair the magnetic field."

Dobson interjects his own knowledge of the situation. "Our scientists believe that, by that time, the Earth will be so saturated by radiation, the planet may be dead anyway."

Pilas simply nods, covering his inner joy that one day, soon, he will be king of this world.

Folsom doesn't speak. He wipes his face of the sweat caused by the stress of the moment. *The future spells doom for the human race no matter how you slice it*. "What can we do?" he asks.

Pilas directs them to the Governor's desk to show the plan he has devised for the safety and security of the people. "We have little time to implement my plan. We need to gather up the people into fifty cities worldwide."

"Why?" Folsom asks, already knowing the answer.

"Control, captain. As the sun affects the people of the Earth, they will register to live in these select cities that, within two years, if we're fortunate, will have domes built over them to protect the inhabitants from the sun's radiation."

"How?"

Pilas laughs for a moment. "I will not divulge my people's technological prowess, captain. Rest assured, there will be room for three hundred million people to live in these cities until help arrives."

Folsom looks at Dobson and Childs and is surprised to see absolutely no emotion on either man's face. "We are a world of ten billion! Are you seriously going to allow nearly that many people to perish?"

"Your planet does not have sufficient material to build the domes to the correct specifications to house that many. Three hundred million is a good estimate of what you are capable of," Pilas replies.

Dobson adds, not at all reluctantly enough to suit the EDF captain, “Some may have to be sacrificed in order to save the rest.”

Folsom is not aware that his voice is rising and cracking. Almost feeling the lives of those who will have to die, the little voice in his head is vehemently nagging him again, causing him to speak up. “And who is to decide who is going to live and who is going to die?” he asks while casting an accusing eye toward Pilas.

The Thimmi captain attempts to quell Folsom’s apparent fear. “Our forces, the EDF teams, will, of course, have first priority in any survival mission or evacuation.”

“This is our planet, captain! We should be the ones who decide the fate of its people!”

Pilas’s anger is growing. “And I am in command, *captain!”*

Seeing that he isn’t going to get any support from the other *so-called* humans in the room, Folsom lowers his head in defeat and to hide the biting of his lip. “That’s fine. I understand.”

The EDF oath reverberates through the ex-Marine captain’s mind: “I am no longer a citizen of a country or alliance, but of the planet itself. The planet Earth is my home, and by the will of her people, I will serve and defend her with my life.”

Pilas continues. "EDF teams will be responsible for the security of the people as they're moved to the protected cities. I trust your team, captain, so I have decided to split them up to supervise the security of this continent as the domes are being built. They will reassemble here to protect Washington afterward."

Derrick's voice begins to fail him as he thinks of the tremendous responsibility this alien is placing on his green team. *They're just kids, really.* "Where are the people coming from who will inhabit the cities? I mean, have specific places been designated for specific people?"

Pilas waves off the question as unimportant. "It doesn't matter." He leaves the room to return to his apartment. He is to contact Admiral Tolomak immediately to inform him of the change in plans. *I will enjoy ruling this planet, unless I have to kill it.*

Captain Folsom spends the night going over Pilas's evacuation and relocation plan with the two puppets he once respected as leaders.

CHAPTER TWENTY-TWO: To Catch an Alien

The following morning, the Thimmi captain joins Captain Folsom and the rest of EDF-1 at Senator Madeline Verona's apartment.

Captain Pilas, decked out like a private eye from fifties film noirs to cover most of his skin, has left his face visible under a gray fedora. He uses a scanner attached wirelessly to his "shackle" to determine the interior layout beyond the locked door.

Captain Folsom looks over the alien's shoulder. He's got four inches on the orange-skinned man from the Imperial planet of Opfinia. "Anyone home?"

The captain's reply is short and direct, as if trying to think of his opponent's next move. "Small life form detected, probably a cat. I doubt he knows we're here."

Did he mean the cat or the doctor? Shanti muses as she listens to the conversation between the two captains. She is dressed in her black fatigues and armed with a pistol, a snub-nosed .38.

The captain pulls out another device to unlock the apartment door.

Folsom objects quietly but forcefully. "The senator would probably insist on us having a warrant to enter her home."

Pilas ignores him until he hears a satisfying *click* and opens the door. "Doesn't apply to us. Let's go."

Derrick pauses, trusting that his actions won't come back to bite him in the ass. This is, after all, the apartment of a senator and candidate for first premier. He enters reluctantly behind Pilas and is followed by Shanti, who immediately spots the chubby kitty on the living room sofa and moves to pet him. *Or her?*

She loves cats, having had two while growing up. The cat responds by meowing. Shanti speaks to the animal in a soothing tone. "You poor little thing. Are you hungry?"

The rest of the team—Lieutenant Kong and Sergeant Furtado—joins Shanti.

Dae speaks first, to Folsom. "What are we looking for, sir?"

"Evidence that Dr. Lightner is here or was here. Kong, you're the computer expert. Find any devices and scan them for information."

Kong nods and begins her search.

The team spreads out to all the rooms of the large apartment.

Lieutenant Dae, alone in the living room now, looks out the window while continuing to pet the cat, who is purring softly. The apartment is on the fiftieth floor. Looking down at the ants on the street below makes Shanti feel sick to her stomach. She sits straight on the sofa to catch her breath. After a few moments, she goes to the window to look down again. *I have got to overcome this fear!* She uses her zoom glasses (high-powered binoculars attached to her face like normal spectacles) to see the people on the street as if she were fifteen feet above them.

There! She witnesses a man matching Dr. Lightner's description get out of a cab and enter the building. The cab driver's shackle is probably sending a report to headquarters. She removes the glasses and turns to warn the others, tripping over the end of the sofa in the process and shouting on the way down. "Captain!"

THUD!

Shanti hits the floor just as the two captains are entering from the main bedroom.

Startled, the cat zips past the alien captain, giving him an idea. "We should scan the cat for information."

Folsom is taken aback. "What?"

"It's a simple procedure to get data from a subject. Questions are asked of the scanner, and it probes the subject's mind for the answers. A general recording of a specific time frame is also possible in a case like this."

"I guess a cat's answers wouldn't be of much use, eh?" Furtado remarks as he passes, mocking a cat's meowing as if answering a question. He stops when he sees the expression of annoyance on Pilas's face and moves to the rear of the apartment to join Kong in her search for electronic devices.

Pilas continues under his breath, "Recordings of that sort are time consuming, and the animal would likely end up dead."

Folsom spots Shanti on the floor and rushes to her aid. He takes a moment to reflect on Pilas's personality. *Pilas saw Shanti on the floor before I did and did nothing.* The EDF-1 captain helps his lieutenant to her feet as she reports her sighting in a frantic tone. *She'll never last if she scares this easily*, he thinks as he listens.

She continues. "Should we hide? What if he's armed?"

Folsom, betraying his concern for the success of the mission and the doubts he has about it, shoots back, "what do you think we're carrying, water pistols?"

Captain Pilas orders their weapons holstered. He pulls out a laser pistol and adjusts the power setting to low so as not to kill his prey. There is a noise at the door just before it opens.

The scan card is in the lock. *Beep.*

Pilas stands in direct line with the door as Captain Folsom guides Lieutenant Dae to a spot against the wall, out of sight. *But close enough to pounce, if necessary. No time to alert Kong and Furtado in the back of the apartment,* Folsom concludes. *It's alien versus alien now.*

Dr. Lightner enters and, upon seeing Pilas, recognizes the orange complexion of the man as that of his adversary. "Who are you?" he asks.

Pilas smiles. He's won. He motions for Folsom to cuff the doctor. "You're finished, Vorelisian! You're under arrest."

"You have no authority to arrest me on a neutral planet, you fool!"

Pilas is almost giddy. "You would be right if these Earthers hadn't given me full authority and control."

Folsom comes up behind Charles with cuffs in hand as the doctor turns to him and whispers, "You're making a mistake, sir."

Folsom attaches one cuff to the doctor's left hand. "I'm just following orders, *doctor*. Don't give us any trouble, and you'll stay alive."

Dr. Lightner turns to look Folsom dead in the eyes, preventing the human captain from attaching the second handcuff. "I was under the impression that this was *your* planet."

Derrick's hesitation annoys him. The little voice in his head is telling him something, but he ignores it. "It is. Now turn around!"

Derrick grabs Lightner's shoulders and physically turns him so he can attach the second cuff. As he turns, Charles sees a sparkle of green light in the captain's eyes and asks, "Have you been on a Thimmi ship lately?"

"Why?"

Lightner drops the subject, intent on the more important task of freeing himself. "So you take orders from an alien being with delusions of grandeur. Is that it?"

Derrick ignores the question.

Pilas sits on the couch, holding his pistol steady on his lap. He is enjoying watching the Vorelisian squirm as they argue back and forth. *The Earther isn't fool enough to believe Lightner's lies.*

The little voice in Folsom's head is claiming the opposite, trying to convince its host that this evil alien isn't what he appears to be. Derrick hesitates again in attaching the second cuff.

Lightner manages to not only plant the possibility of deception into the captain's mind, but he also distracts him long enough to use the leverage necessary to push Folsom closer to Pilas.

Pilas stands and fires, hitting Captain Folsom.

The captain goes down, stunned and in pain, as Charles runs from the apartment with one handcuff attached. Lieutenant Dae gives chase, as Pilas is momentarily delayed. He has to make sure he doesn't trip over Folsom as he makes for the door after the doctor and lieutenant.

The rest of the team rushes into the room at the sound of the laser blast, moving quickly to their captain's aid.

In his eagerness to chase Lightner, Pilas falls to the floor, cursing the planet. *I'll never get used to this light gravity!* He eventually gets to the doorway in time to see Lightner at the end of the corridor with the lieutenant holding on to his lab coat, trying to prevent him from jumping out the open window. *I could shoot him if the stupid bitch wasn't blocking my shot!* Pilas thinks for a moment before taking careful aim, waiting for Lightner to break free of the smaller and weaker Earthling.

He does.

"Now I've got you, you Vorelisian pig!" Pilas shouts with glee and fires.

The other team members are still assisting their leader, who is writhing in pain on the floor of the apartment. A sleeping leg that reawakens when fresh blood flows into it is nothing compared to the sleep and reawakening of a man's entire left side from a laser blast, even at low power.

Lieutenant Dae is out of her mind and unable to function from the overwhelming fear that is consuming her. *Is this fool trying to kill himself by jumping out the window?* She makes one last attempt to pull the doctor to the floor, but he fights her off.

ZAP! ZAP! The laser bolts make the sound of high-pitched electricity shooting arcs across terminals on a power pole as they strike and burn the window frame.

Shanti looks back at Pilas in shock and disbelief. "What the fu—?"

She tries a headlock to stop the Vorelisian from going out the window, but she fails. He takes her with him. *Fifty floors.* Two more laser blasts whiz past them as they fall, Pilas doesn't care if a shot hits the Earther grasping Lightner as she holds on for dear life.

Shanti could've stopped him if she had a little more time. She's an expert fighter, but is powerless against the enemy of fear that grips her mind the way she is now gripping the alien falling with her.

Her fear has caused her failure.

Lieutenant Dae screams all the way to the street below. Her shriek is as deafening as the whine of jet engine powering up.

Pilas doesn't know that Charles broke his hand when he first arrived on Earth and had it repaired with one of the many advances in science he has gifted to the people of this planet. Due to the rubbery-bone replacement of his left wrist, he is able to easily slip the handcuff off of his hand.

With that problem solved and only fifteen more floors to fall, he deals with the human screaming in his ear by pulling his lab coat around them both as best he can. He positions himself to take the brunt of the fall, with the antigravity fabric facing the sidewalk.

Shanti can't feel or see the change in velocity with her eyes closed, but they are slowing enough to survive. As her panic causes her to push away from Lightner and certain death, she changes the position of the coat—and herself.

"NO!" he shouts. "I'm trying to save us both! Don't—"

The slowing was contingent on the placement of the coat to absorb the gravity waves pulling them down. Now that it's gone, they speed up again for the last two floors. Shanti takes the brunt of the fall, though not at full velocity.

CRACK!

Shanti lies on the sidewalk, conscious but unable to move or speak.

Lightner, who had landed and rolled away from her, returns to check her pulse. “I’m sorry. You should’ve let me hit the ground first. My body can handle it.”

Shanti, broken in many places, looks up at him. She is delirious and weak. “Cannot fail,” she mutters.

Lightner’s admiration for the Earthers has just increased tenfold. “You’re a fragile people,” he says with genuine care in his voice. He hears a siren in the distance and, reluctantly, decides to run away. “You’ll be OK,” he assures her before sprinting down the street. No one in the gathering crowd makes any effort to stop him.

***

Folsom, with movement returning, staggers into the hallway as Pilas rushes back from the window at the end of the corridor. He is heading for the elevator. “He’s wearing an antigravity coat. Let’s go!”

Sergeant Furtado is at his captain’s side, knowing where his loyalty lies. “With your permission, sir.”

Folsom nods. "Shanti gave chase. Assist! Help her! Call Jafari!"

Pilas is at the elevator, clicking the call button wildly as if that will make the machine move faster. He stops to shout back at the team, especially Kong who is still at the window. "He's getting away! Let's go!"

Kong returns to report to Folsom. "It looks like she is alive."

Derrick smiles, visibly relieved at that news. "Go with Pilas. MAA is on the way." Jen runs to the elevator. The doors close, leaving him alone in the hallway with his thoughts. "'A simple arrest,' he said. 'You won't need your guns,' he said. Son of a bitch." His shackle begins to glow yellow, the color indicating that an injury has been detected and a message has been sent to the Medical Authorities of America (MAA), hence the saying "If you need help, your MAA is always watching out for you."

***

Pilas, now inside the elevator, holds the doors so the Earthers can get inside. "The Vorelisian is getting away! Your mission is his arrest, not to save your stupid lieutenant! She should've gotten out of my line of fire!"

Furtado is about to say something in Shanti's defense but waits as the Thimmi captain continues, "She could've disabled him on the way down! She was armed, wasn't she? You people are worthless!"

The elevator is descending rapidly, though not fast enough for the Thimmi captain. He is still fuming. "You Earthers don't know much about following orders, do you?"

Lieutenant Kong answers the rhetorical question. "We know about honor, captain."

"Would you sacrifice your world for the life of one person? Is *that* honorable?"

She doesn't hesitate. "The world is better off dead without us to protect it."

Furtado is taken aback by her cold statement, though he suspects she has now gained the alien's respect, judging from the look on his face and subsequent nod.

On the street, the crowd has grown at the side of the building where Lieutenant Shanti Dae lies motionless but conscious.

Jen rushes to her side. *To hell with Lightner*. She takes her friend's hand and asks the most rhetorical of questions given the situation. "Shanti, are you all right?"

Pilas, standing behind Kong, looks down on the broken lieutenant. "Where's Lightner?" Not getting an answer fast enough, he turns to the crowd. "There was a man who fell from above. Which way did he go?"

Someone points in the direction down the avenue.

Pilas grabs Furtado to force his obedience. "Follow me!"

The sergeant reluctantly complies, shooting an apologetic glance at Jen, who nods in understanding.

"I'll tend to her," she assures him. Kong, staying with Lieutenant Dae, accesses her shackle as she chastises the crowd. "I don't suppose any of you bothered to call for help!"

The people gathered, in unison, look at her and at each other, as if thinking, *Who? Me?*

A bystander points to Lieutenant Dae's shackle. "It's broken, but I'm sure MAA knows about it."

Shanti, becoming more aware of what is happening, raises her left hand. *At least that still works. Everything else seems broken.* Jen looks into her friend's eyes and sees fear in them. "Jen, the doctor tried not to let me hit the ground. He tried to take the brunt of—"

"Shhh. Relax. Don't try to move."

"I was stupid. I guess I should be lucky to be alive. I get the feeling that we might be wrong about him."

The siren Lightner heard earlier pierces the quiet evening, breaking up the ambient street noise, getting louder, closer—not fast enough.

Lieutenant Kong gently puts her free hand over Shanti's mouth. "Don't speak. Save your strength."

She pulls back when Shanti speaks again. "At least I was breathing correctly on the way down, just like you taught me, my friend." She smiles and winces at the pain inflicted by her attempt to laugh. She begins to feel dizzy and weaker than a newborn kitten. She is falling into unconsciousness.

Kong replies with surprise and a little pride. "Really?"

Just before passing out, Shanti whispers, "No."

"Stay with me, Shanti! Help is here," Jen says.

She looks up at the antigravity ambulance turning the corner ahead of them, flying over traffic like a white angel coming to save her friend.

***

Sergeant Furtado and Captain Pilas run two blocks, inquiring of pedestrians and drivers alike if they've seen a man in a white lab coat running through the area. Their search amounts to nothing but an angrier Thimmi captain.

"We'll track the senator. He's bound to make contact with her again," Pilas says. "When I catch that Vorelisian, I will slap a *real* shackle on his arm!"

Furtado's reply is a subdued "Sounds like fun." After a moment of thought, he remembers the order to contact Jafari. *The kid has the Humvee at the front of the building. Surely he is monitoring our chatter.*

There is no answer to his repeated calls. *All he has to do is tell his shackle to answer the call. Something is wrong.*

***

In the Humvee, Jafari pays no attention to the beeping of his shackle. He is too busy chasing the car Dr. Lightner got into and is currently speeding down Constitution Avenue at seventy miles per hour.

He thinks hard about how best to proceed. *What would Captain Folsom do?* The antigravity of the Humvee allows Jafari to fly over cars in other lanes. He can cut off his prey easily that way but is afraid of taking on a possibly armed alien without backup.

The car ahead rolls on, taking a curve and speeding up to eighty. Behrouz can see the doctor looking back through the rear window.

Antigravity vehicles do not have inertial dampeners. When Jafari takes the curve, his inertia pushes him off his controls for a second, briefly enough to avoid an accident, but long enough to lose a little ground.

The young man thinks back to his days as a driver for The Family. *This is like one of my getaways, except now I'm doing the chasing.*

***

Accessing shackle reports, Pilas learns of the pursuit through the streets of Washington, DC, and commandeers a cab to join in the chase. Assuming they can catch up to Lightner and Jafari at all, he ponders the abilities of Earthers as he and Furtado get into the wheeled vehicle.

"Your Humvee driver is in pursuit, let's go!"

Sergeant Furtado follows, hoping to be of assistance to his friend.

***

In a vehicle burdened with wheels like most cars, Lightner's driver turns another corner, bent on getting the alien to the White House. The kid recognized the doctor when he asked for help on the street, and the young man couldn't refuse. His parents will later try to defend his actions as those of an unstable mind racked with dreams of heroism derived from playing too many video games that, in these times, are so close to reality, it is easy to fall into their trance. He makes a left onto Pennsylvania Avenue with his final destination in sight.

Lightner can see the White House ahead and wonders about the fuel consumption of an antigravity Humvee. *Soliquid hasn't been incorporated into automobile engines yet. How ironic would that be?*

***

Private Jafari, fully aware of the weapons at his disposal—specifically the missile rack on the left side of the vehicle and the machine-gun turret on top—wishes for a quick second that someone was here to help him use them, though with all the people around, there would be many injuries. He thinks of the conversation he had earlier with Captain Folsom about his desire for adventure. He shakes his head at the memory. *Be careful what you wish for.*

***

Lightner's escape vehicle reaches the gates of the White House, where another EDF team is waiting. The driver slows, hoping to just drop off the alien and keep going, but Jafari's Humvee rear-ends his car, causing it to spin and stop.

Charles knows he doesn't have a chance. *If only I can appeal to them before Pilas shows up.*

The kid bolts from the driver's side but is immediately stopped by an armed guard.

Troops arrive to drag Lightner from the backseat; others have their guns trained on him to prevent his escape. Charles watches Madeline, Dr. Trachsel, General Childs, and Governor Dobson emerge from the White House. His first thoughts are not about saving the planet, but about the woman approaching him.

General Childs's strong hand stops Madeline. "Charles!" she cries out.

The sergeant in charge throws Lightner to the ground and is applying handcuffs—tighter this time, under orders given by Pilas over his shackle a moment earlier.

The cab pulls up to the scene. Pilas and Furtado survey the area before walking slowly toward Lightner, well covered by ten armed troops. Pilas is obviously enjoying this. Furtado begins to wonder how well these two men know each other. He ponders how much Pilas is enjoying the arrest of Earth's greatest scientific benefactor.

As they get closer, Furtado listens to Lightner's accusations about the Thimms' plot to destroy Earth and relocate millions of people to a planet called Jexx. *Outrageous*.

Madeline breaks from Childs's grip and gets to the Humvee that Charles is being loaded into as if he is any other piece of equipment. She is two feet away from him when she begins to cry, "Charles, why didn't you tell me?"

Sitting in the middle row of the Humvee with his head lowered in shame, the doctor finally glances up at the teary-eyed woman he loves. She is just outside the open window, though she may as well be in another galaxy. He glances around at Pilas and the others, who are momentarily preoccupied.

"He's not going anywhere now," someone says with a chuckle as Charles motions Madeline closer.

He speaks softly so the guards nearby don't hear him. "Take the scanner from my coat. It's also a communications device connected to an orbiting satellite. I left it in the car. Contact First Colonel Xaix. All is lost without his help."

"I love you," she says as she pulls away.

"I hope so," he whispers as he leans back, defeated.

Madeline steps away.

Jafari and Pilas get into the front bench seat of the Humvee. Pilas glances behind him at Dr. Lightner, who looks up after a moment of feeling someone's eyes on him.

Pilas smiles, "I've got you, Vorelisian," he says matter-of-factly.

"How is the Earth losing its magnetic field, *captain*? An amazing coincidence that this crisis coincides with your recent trip to the moon, don't you think?" Lightner says.

Pilas turns back to face the windshield, losing his smile in the process, "I may ask you the same question when I scan your brain."

Defiant, Charles tries to sit up straight. "I look forward to it."

Jafari, while adjusting the thrusters and antigravity generators for travel, listens to this exchange and is puzzled by the doctor's reaction to having his brain scanned. *Why would he give in to having his brain scanned? He must want us to know something.*

Pilas, growing impatient watching Jafari stare into space, shouts, "Drive, private! What are you waiting for?"

Behrouz snaps back to reality and adjusts himself in his seat while glancing at the Vorelisian doctor. Lightner smiles and winks at him. *Is that a message?* he wonders as he responds to the command from Pilas. “Yes, sir.”

A moment later, the wheels retract as the antigravity generators come to life, and the thrusters power the vehicle away at a leisurely pace.

***

Madeline approaches the car Lightner used and reaches for the coat in the rear passenger seat.

General Childs stops questioning the young driver when he sees Madeline picking up the coat and walks up to her quickly. “Senator! May I ask what you’re doing?”

Unseen by the general, she reaches into the left coat pocket to retrieve the scanner. It’s about the size of a deck of cards. She manages to tuck it into her inside breast pocket, hidden from the general’s view, before turning to face him. “Excuse me?” she says innocently.

“That coat is evidence. I’m going to need you to step away from it, please.”

Madeline releases the coat as if she had just made a mistake in choosing something from a store rack. “It’s a nice coat. I just thought I would…” She pauses a moment before pretending to abandon the thought. “It probably wouldn’t go with anything I own.”

Childs laughs as he takes the coat and studies it, taking out the low-powered laser pistol in the process. “I’ll forget about it this time.”

Finishing up the charade, she asks, “Is that a gun?”

Childs stuffs the small yet bulky weapon into his pocket. “It merits further study, that I can say.”

Madeline walks toward Dr. Trachsel, who is conversing with Dobson at the front door of the White House. *About what?* she wonders. *Should I ask for their help? No, Dobson is on the Thimms' side now. I'll just ask Steven for a ride home.*

***

The antigravity ambulance skirts the downtown Washington, DC corners at twenty feet of altitude to safely get its two EDF passengers to the nearest hospital for treatment. The trip takes only ten minutes.

During the ride, the paramedics treated Captain Folsom for third-degree burns at the point of laser impact. Derrick has had a hell of a time trying to explain the burn on his left shoulder and subsequent numbing of his entire left side. *Most of the details of energy weapons and their levels of power use would go over the young paramedic's head anyway.* He doesn't think the subject merits comparison to the latest sci-fi action movie. He thanks the heavens that Pilas had set the power level to low. *He obviously wanted Lightner alive.*

Lieutenant Dae, however, will have to spend a day or two in the bone-mending machine before she can return to duty, thanks again to Dr. Lightner's generosity. The minerals added to her bones will give them some degree of elasticity. She smiles at the thought of becoming Rubber Woman. *Someone is going to have to remind me again how this man is responsible for the world's ills when he has provided so much,* she thinks as they arrive at the emergency room.

CHAPTER TWENTY-THREE: Contact

Madeline returns to her apartment, sneaking into the building like a burglar. She enters her home quietly. The silence is interrupted by the hungry meows of her cat, Fizzy. Fizzy is a four-year-old, long-haired, white Persian who hasn't been fed for a day and a half.

Fizzy's meows go from pleading to demanding until Madeline acknowledges her. "I know, I know," she mumbles as she drapes her coat on a chair. She tries to walk to the kitchen without stepping on her four-legged friend, playing her own variant of the Filipino dance tinikling, using her legs as the clapping bamboo sticks, which the cat avoids like a pro.

Once in the kitchen, the food is poured, and Fizzy is instantly content, eating and purring. "Oh, to be a housecat. Not a care in the world," Madeline says. *Provided cats have good owners and the sun isn't destroying the planet*, she thinks as Fizzy pauses from chowing down to look up at her caregiver, as if to say *thanks* while licking her chops.

And then it's back to the food.

In the living room, Madeline takes Dr. Lightner's scanner/communicator from her coat on the chair and studies its controls. Finding only two buttons, she presses one, and it plays back the last part of the message from First Colonel Xaix. "Headquarters has instructed me to lead an assault on one of their planets as a proportional response to this attack. Our lord is preparing to address the Galactic Council on this issue as well. I'm afraid I won't be seeing you for a long time. Do what you feel you must to bring Earth to us, but remember that you're going to be on your own."

Madeline presses the second button and the message repeats. Frustrated, she screams at the machine. "I don't want to replay the fucking message. I want to *send* one!" She is surprised and more than a little relieved at the sight of the "record" light in the lower right corner of the holographic image of First Colonel Xaix, who is suspended in the air in front of her, as big as life. So realistic is the image that she feels she can surely touch him.

"Voice commands. Of course." She begins after taking a couple of deep breaths. "First Colonel Xaix, you don't know me. My name is Madeline Verona of the North American Senate, planet Earth. I am a"—she pauses, thinking of the right word to describe her relationship with the Vorelisian agent on her planet—"close friend of Dr. Charles Lightner. He has just been arrested by Thimmi Captain Pilas, who has taken control of the leadership of this planet. We need your help. If you can assist us, we will allow your sponsorship into the Galactic Community, provided I can regain control. Please respond. Thank you."

Satisfied with the sent message, Madeline thinks about First Colonel Xaix's words. *They're not going to come. He said Charles was on his own. I can't rely on them.*

Madeline takes another breath and sits back on the couch just before Fizzy hops onto her lap, still purring, and making herself comfortable. "Sweetheart, you may have time to relax, but I don't." She moves her cat off of her so she can get up.

In her bedroom closet, she gathers denim clothing and a gym bag. She puts a .38 caliber pistol in the bag and begins to undress. Fizzy follows her into the room, intent on finding a warm body.

"Don't worry, Fizz. Someone will look out for you this time," she says.

Fizzy jumps on the bed to watch Madeline dress and pack before rolling up into a ball of fur against the pillows with no worries.

***

March has come, and so the heat will rise higher with the sun in the Nevada desert at the Groom Lake Base. Outdoor training is limited to the early morning, before the sun breaks the horizon, for obvious reasons. Sunrise is an hour away.

As more and more EDF teams crowd into the training facility, a secret test is happening in the open desert far from prying eyes and curious foreigners.

Colonel Nealand, in his dress uniform, leads a team of ten men in battle fatigues, together making up EDF-7. Seven is the only team in General Childs's worldwide army dedicated to the production, testing, and use of the technology surrounding teleportation. Today, they're about to complete the first test of the devices used in the transport of a human between two locations, using the Internet as a conduit.

Corporal Lewis Brandt is the first man to volunteer. He's a young man of twenty, with an eagerness that reminds Edward of his son, Behrouz. Lewis approaches Nealand from the ranks and takes an orb from him. It is about the size of a baseball. "How does this thing work, sir?"

Nealand looks the corporal in the eyes and says, "First, you put it on the ground in front of you."

Lewis complies as his teammates laugh at him for not figuring that out on his own. In theory, the orb creates a holographic door that the subject passes through before being digitized and sent to another orb with similar destination settings. *If you're going to walk through it, you can't be carrying it.*

Nealand continues, raising his voice slightly so all of them will listen. The time for levity is over. Colonel Alexei Garov is in Moscow with a similar device with identical settings. Previous test subjects, plants and animals, surround him. “This will be the first attempt at sending a human being over the Internet.” His comments are for the entire team but directed at Lewis, just to be certain that he understands the risks involved and that he is volunteering freely.

Nealand walks up to the young corporal and speaks softly but sternly. “You’re *sure* you want to go through with this?”

Lewis stands proudly, his chin up, and speaks loud enough for all of his teammates to hear. “Yes, colonel. I am ready.” Softer, he jokes to hide his nervousness, “If an insect goes through the door with me, will I be able to fly when I come out?”

Edward smiles briefly but otherwise ignores the joke as he contacts Colonel Garov on his shackle. “Alexei, we’re all set. Are you ready to receive?”

Garov, appearing as a hologram, shows the location of the orb on his side of the world. Nealand makes the hologram life-size so the team can see the room Garov is in. His orb is lying on the floor. Alexei activates it. “Ready when you are, my friend.”

Corporal Brandt stares at the orb in front of him until it opens a seven-foot holographic door. Lewis looks through it to see the room on the other side and the smiling Russian welcoming him. “Today, I make history,” he mumbles as he walks through the door.

And disappears.

Nealand waits a few moments before asking the obvious question. The other soldiers have already reacted, some lowering their heads in sadness, others dropping to a knee in prayer. “Did you get him, Alexei?” he asks hopefully.

“I saw him walk through your side. He did not appear here,” Garov says. “It should be virtually instantaneous.”

Edward shakes his head. *All the tests were perfect. I don’t get it.* “Very well. I’ll contact you in the morning.”

Alexei responds, “I am so sorry.” Both orbs shut down.

Another member of the team stands to inquire, “What went wrong, sir?”

Nealand, never the type to hide anything from his men, responds honestly for them all to hear. “I don’t know, but next time, I’m walking through that damn door myself! The sun will be rising soon. Return to your quarters.”

The men come to attention and disperse, leaving their superior staring at the orb.

As the sun peeks over the horizon, Edward places the orb into the top case of his Harley motorcycle seat with its control pad after taking out his helmet to make space for them. He dons the helmet and starts the engine of the antigravity cycle that has no wheels, but four stands to rest upon when parked.

Why didn't it work when test after test told us it would? Where is Dr. Lightner when I need him? Lightner didn't give this technology to the humans of Earth, but if anyone can help fix the bugs, it's him.

Edward speeds away, thinking of the young corporal and what to say when he breaks the sad news to his parents.

There are other parts of the world where teleportation research is being done. Edward knows that young men are being lost and that Corporal Brandt certainly won't be the last.

His thoughts drift to Behrouz. He checks the time on his shackle and decides to pay his son a visit at their training facility on the busier end of the base.

The sun will become dangerous soon. He shakes his head at the events that have transpired as he turns his bike toward Hangar 12.

***

EDF-1 is on their fourth mile leading into the obstacle course. It's the same routine as always, but depending on the captain's mood, sometimes the run is longer or shorter. It's also taking place earlier in the morning for safety against the approaching sun. Someday soon it won't matter what time of day it is; the Earth will be saturated with lethal quantities of radiation in a few short months if something isn't done. *That's why Pilas is in charge,* Folsom thinks as Sergeant Furtado calls out one of his typical sexist cadences involving a woman named Irene and how he took her out, rolled her over, rode her back, and landed her hard.

Shanti and Jen are only slightly amused but not offended, having heard this particular cadence from Alfonzo before. He finishes with; "Irene, Irene, she's the best in the land! She's an AGF-10 in the fighter command!"

Going into the obstacle course, Shanti pulls back to allow her teammates to enter it ahead of her. The monkey bars are first, and easy. Next is the swimming pool jump that Behrouz does *not* fall into this time. They've eliminated the actual swimming portion for the winter, Behrouz laments. It never really gets cold during the day in the desert, just varying degrees of hot. With spring only a few days away and the sun a hazard, none of them look forward to the heat as they normally would.

Furtado has taken the young private under his wing in the past few months. The mission to arrest Lightner was icing on the cake, solidifying the team as a cohesive unit. Under the barbed wire and over a few hurdles completes the easy parts of the course.

Then comes the pole.

Watching his lieutenant stare up the rope, Folsom shouts, “Sunrise is in a few minutes, so you best get up there!”

Furtado and Jafari stop at the sound of their captain’s command voice and return to the pole they’ve just run from to watch their frightened teammate attempt to overcome her fear.

There was some concern that Shanti’s recently mended bones might not handle the stress of an obstacle course workout. Captain Folsom disagreed, and despite a slight bending of her arms when she took the monkey bars, all is well. Her medic told him that she’d have bones with the strength and pliability of hard rubber for the rest of her life.

Wow, he said to himself at the time. *One more thing she’ll have to get used to.*

Jen has continued ahead, cognizant of her friend’s need to accomplish this task alone. “Let’s go, boys!” she calls out to them, not wanting Shanti to face further embarrassment.

Folsom, aware of the audience around the pole, leads the men back to the hangar.

They all leave Shanti staring up at the pole that, to her, towers into the sky for miles instead of the mere fifty feet she knows it is.

Private Jafari circles back, knowing he won't be missed now that they're all dismissed to shower and dress again for breakfast. He watches Shanti, unnoticed, as she gets fifteen feet into the air. *She's doing it!* he thinks, amazed. *She's ten years older than me but looks so beautiful from underneath, even in baggy fatigues.* He is silent with only the howling wind to disturb the grunts Shanti is making. *She's pretty strong, too.*

At the halfway point, he knows she can't turn back lest she fall. Then she stops. He sees her head shaking as if trying to erase a memory. *She must've glanced down.* "Need help, lieutenant?"

She looks down at him, momentarily shocked and embarrassed. "I can't move!"

Uh-oh. "I'll get the captain. Hold on!"

"Hold on? Are you trying to be funny?" she shouts, her voice quivering, betraying her fear.

"Sorry, I didn't mean it that way. I'll be right back." He thinks of the possibilities, the brownie points he'll get for doing something for her. To rescue her himself would be great, but…He pauses as he runs for the hangar. *At least she didn't throw up this time.*

The sun's rays are peeking over the horizon, turning the sky a brighter shade of blue. Shanti's hands are clenched like vices to the rope above her head. Her mind races to deal with the fear. *Down should be easy. My bones won't break again, will they? I'm practically all rubber now…but no.*

She looks in the direction of the hangar and sees Behrouz returning. He is wearing Dr. Lightner's lab coat. The few minutes he was gone felt like an hour. She watches him climb the ladder on the other side of the pole, opposite the rope. "What the hell are you doing?" she screams.

At the top of the rope, now in sunlight but well protected by the coat and other loose clothing, Behrouz climbs down the rope to meet his beautiful lieutenant face-to-face.

She cries out, more from the rope shaking than anything else. "This rope won't hold both of us!"

Behrouz chuckles at the idea that she is more afraid of the rope breaking than the sun rising. “Of course it can. You put this coat around you and let go. We’ll land together.”

“What?” Shanti says, her eyes bulging with shock and fear.

Behrouz gets behind her to wrap the coat around both of them, a complex task in that their combined size exceeds the Vorelisian doctor in *girth.*

“Let go of the rope. We’ll fall together,”

“Hell no! I told you to get the captain!”

“The sun is nearly upon us! Right now, I’m all you’ve got, lieutenant. Come on, you fell in this coat before, and this is only about thirty feet. You remember, right?”

“Of course I do, but…but…my bones…”

She hesitates longer than he’d like. The sun is upon them. Beams of light are striking their arms. He decides to take drastic action. He reaches down with his left hand and gently squeezes her right breast. She reacts with an elbow to his ribs, forcing her to release her grip on the rope.

They fall, seemingly in slow motion.

The coat provides antigravity protection as they hit the soft, thick dirt at the foot of the rope.

Shanti stands first, brushing herself off and doing a quick inventory of her body. She looks down at Behrouz for a moment before offering a hand to help him to his feet. He is smiling from ear to ear. *A little too happy*. She smiles and kisses his cheek. "That's for helping me."

He begins to blush, the smile not fading until she slaps the same cheek. "That's for *how* you helped me, *private*!"

He wonders if he went too far. *I had to do something, didn't I?* Before he can mount a defense of his actions, she smiles with a wink and leads him back to the hangar, and to safety. "Let's go."

Behrouz runs with her, anticipating the recounting of this little adventure to Alfonzo.

***

The Groom Lake Base dining hall is large enough to seat and feed a thousand troops. Several EDF teams, including numbers one, three, and seven, are seated and enjoying a well-made breakfast in the cavernous hangar. After the morning he's just had, Colonel Nealand wishes the coffee bar served alcohol. He uses his shackle to contact Behrouz upon seeing the young private enter the room and sign in for the morning meal.

A minute later, Behrouz joins him at a long bar with thirty mostly empty chairs and many types of coffee on the menu to choose from. He orders what the colonel is having—a latte.

"How are you, my friend?" Behrouz asks his father in Farsi. By all rights, the colonel should've been allowed to adopt him when he was a child instead of having to wait until he became a legal adult. *Maybe I would've had better teen years. They couldn't have been much worse than being an orphan in the most crime-ridden city in the world*, he thinks as the colonel reminds him of where they are.

"Speak English when we're together in public, private," Nealand says. "We can't be so informal. Where's your discipline?"

Behrouz's enthusiasm at seeing his father is diminished, but only slightly, although this is the second time he's gotten this treatment. *Why call me over here just to chastise me?* "Is something wrong"—he pauses before ending the question with "colonel?"

Edward gets the message but doesn't respond to it. "Plenty. I lost a man today. A man as young as you." He waits a moment to find the words. "I just felt a short visit would be in order."

"Did you not want me in the service of the Earth Defense Force?"

Edward looks up from his coffee to gaze into his young son's eyes, surprised by his own selfishness for considering such a thing earlier. *But I don't feel that way anymore, do I?* "No, I just want you to be careful. Are you getting along well with your associates?"

Behrouz's eyes light up, but he plays it cool, thinking of Shanti and the pole. "Oh, I'm getting to know them, yes."

That piece of news helps Nealand relax. He smiles as he looks past the young private at the men and women who make up Team 1. Other teams entering the hangar obscure his vision. He makes out Captain Folsom glancing in his direction. "You better get back to your meal or you will have to wait until lunch. Tell your captain I'd like to speak with him."

Not wanting to part ways with the colonel so soon, Behrouz tries to keep the conversation going. "Technically, we have two captains, you know. I heard that Lieutenant Kong was a spy for China before joining us. She was a captain for the Ministry of State Security."

The colonel responds as if deep in thought. "There's no more China, son. We're all one world now."

Behrouz watches his father finish his coffee, knowing that when the bar opens later this afternoon, he'll replace caffeine with alcohol. *The colonel carries the lives of his men in his heart. I relish having a place there.* "Well, I…OK," he says as he hesitates to get into a discussion about things he doesn't fully understand. China is no longer a country, as the United States is no longer a country, but the lands that make them up still exist, as do the people who populate them. There are people within each former country and elsewhere who would like to see globalization fail and return the borders to where they were. Then there's the argument about fewer countries creating fewer conflicts. Who would decide what countries would last and which wouldn't? Some would argue that the globalization plan that started over a hundred years ago in some minds is working outside its inevitable growing pains. *I might not last long in a debate on this subject,* Behrouz suspects. He steps away after mumbling a good-bye in Farsi.

Formalities be damned, Behrouz concludes before leaving the bar.

A minute later, Captain Folsom joins the colonel. "You wanted to speak to me, sir?"

The barista takes the captain's order of a mocha before Edward responds. "Are you still having those dreams about the"—he pauses to remember the alien name—"Zetans?"

Derrick shakes his head in dismay. "Every night, practically. When I'm around that Thimmi Captain Pilas, I think this consciousness in my head is trying to warn me about him."

"So it's not just in your mind? It's an entity inside you?"

"I really won't know that answer until I see a doctor, or a shrink."

The colonel refrains from answering until the mocha arrives and the barista is out of earshot. "I wouldn't do that. They'll have to report it to Pilas. He might see the Zetan as an enemy and want to kill it. Or you."—he adds quickly.

"What do I do, then?"

"Is it controlling your actions?"

"No, sir. Like I said, it's acting like a conscience, a little voice inside my head."

Nealand decides to change the subject since the captain seems to have this one figured out. "At least you're not seeing that Pilas character every day."

Folsom shoots a glance at the ceiling, looking for guidance, perhaps. "I may be—my team is going to be assigned protection duty when the population move gets into full swing. We're being split up to secure the domes as they're built. Construction plans are being made fast."

"No time to waste with the sun's radiation getting worse by the day."

“We’re taking refugees from the area of Belize, north of the equator, to the northern parts of Peru and Brazil, south of it. Pilas will no doubt keep an eye on things—and us.”

“When does this big move start?”

Folsom takes a long sip of his coffee before answering, “After Dr. Lightner’s brain scan today. Pilas is on his way to conduct it.”

“Keep your distance from him,” the colonel states with all the seriousness of a falling piano on an unsuspecting grandmother.

Derrick nods in agreement. “That’s unavoidable.”

Nealand looks back over Folsom’s shoulder at Behrouz and the conversation he is having with Sergeant Furtado and changes the subject again. “Keep your team around you. They’re good people.”

The captain rises from his barstool with his medium-sized mocha and sips from it. “You’re right about that. Thanks for the advice, colonel. I’ll see you soon.”

Nealand smiles and winks at the good captain. *I like this kid.* “Count on it.”

As Folsom returns to his team and a now-cold breakfast, Nealand wonders about the brain scan of Dr. Lightner he mentioned. *I can think of a few questions of my own to ask that man.*

CHAPTER TWENTY-FOUR:

Deep Space Travelers

The Vorelisian fleet moves through deep space at a velocity that outpaces their sensors. This is a somewhat dangerous position to be in under normal circumstances anywhere else in the galaxy, though First Colonel Xaix trusts his crew and computers implicitly.

Here, in Thimmi space, between two far distant systems and away from trade routes, there is literally nothing to run into unexpectedly.

Until today.

Executive Lieutenant Len Quell, reporting from the station behind his commander on the bridge of the large battle carrier, watches the instruments like a mother hen watching her eggs. “Sir, our power is at maximum. Our speed is four times light and the dark energy shield is functioning perfectly.”

Xaix senses pride in the young man’s voice. *This ship will be his in a few years.* “Very well,” he mutters from his command chair as he watches the stars move slowly across the main screen. The stars are blurred from traveling so far beyond the speed of light that they have created the illusion of blending together.

The communications station is silent for two reasons: first is that, unable to receive a message from Vorelisian space behind them at this speed, Under-Lieutenant Alice Lett is using her console to continue working on her novel. The second is that the fleet is moving through enemy space, and thus any communication sent would give away their position.

All is quiet but for the sedated hum of the engines.

Time and space complement one another in a relationship that has baffled physicists throughout the galaxy for centuries. The light-speed theory states, "The faster an object moves, the more time elapses from its origin." Therefore, despite the short time the Vorelisian fleet has been moving through Thimmi territory from Seara relative to the crew on the ships, the time that has passed for the people on the planet Seara is approaching five years.

Current science maintains that there are methods of travel that separate time from space, wormholes being the current favorite. Right now, however, the *Victory* is moving only as fast as its slowest companion via conventional means.

The fleet is a year from its target, the Thimmi planet Tanli. If it could move faster, more time would pass for those back home. The attack is a bold move by the Vorelisian government, whose troops have overcome the Thimms and their hired mercenaries, the Galestikons, on the Vorelisian planet Paal after sending ten times the amount of manpower to take the planet back. Land battles against the mercenary arm of the Galestikon military carry a high price.

The fleet will have to stop periodically to check in with headquarters to ensure that a new peace treaty hasn't been worked out before it reaches its destination.

The proximity alarm is loud enough to make a crying baby on a plane write a complaint letter when he's old enough to compose a sentence.

The ships in the fleet are preprogrammed to come to a halt at any sign of an obstruction blocking their path rather than circumnavigate any such obstruction. For the *Victory*, the operation takes just under a minute at full reverse thrust. It is a tense minute, to say the least, considering the speed the ship is traveling at. All the while, the crew doesn't know how close the obstruction is and are wondering if a collision with another ship is imminent. Stress levels rise in situations such as these.

As the thrusters are fired, the crew is pushed forward as the ship's inertial dampeners compensate for the sudden change in velocity to keep them from flying through the ship and crashing into bulkheads. Force fields are in place as a backup to the dampeners in the event of a system failure.

Central control of all ships rests with the crew of the battle carrier and its master computer. If one ship slows, they all slow, and vice versa. This is necessary to keep the fleet together in formation lest the ships hit each other or are separated by a great distance. Two ships colliding at the speed of light would leave nothing behind but dust.

Executive Lieutenant Quell, operating on standing orders in enemy territory, calls the ship to battle stations.

One klaxon stops; another starts. The call to stations klaxon is of a lower tone and slower beat, as if the ship knows when to be afraid and when to prepare to fight.

Xaix watches the screen intently, seeing nothing as the ship slows. One of his destroyers comes into view in front of the carrier, its job to protect the carrier from attack at any cost.

"Captain, the fleet has come to a halt," Quell reports. "Engine room reports thruster power is at minimum and diverting energy to defensive systems. Guns are being manned, and flight crews are scrambling to the hangar deck."

Xaix listens to the report and nods. *Just as everything should be but there is no enemy here*. He looks out into space again and whispers into First Captain Sonan's ear, "Why have we stopped?"

The tack-o points to several blips on his screen for Xaix to observe. The computer tags the blips as Thimmi vessels. "Now two…three…five…
approaching at a low light-speed on an intercept course and slowing." He checks his screen again as well as his eyes, just in case. "I count fifty now!"

Quell jumps to the tactical station to see for himself. Both lead commanders are flanking the tactical officer as he takes a breath of relief. "They seem to be colony ships mostly, sirs, judging by their ID transmitters."

Quell states the obvious. "Those can be faked."

Xaix has the same suspicion as he gets to his seat. "Shields up! Stack them forward!" Stacking refers to the layers of energy used to absorb the expected firestorm, a typical Thimmi strategy, and forward because they're approaching their enemy head-on.

"Yes, sir," Sonan responds before completing the task, and then asks, "Shall I have fighter command launch our squadrons?"

Xaix rubs his chin, thinking of his opponent's move. "Not yet. Have the pilots wait in their cockpits."

Meanwhile, Lieutenant Lett has stored her novel for a later time and is immediately receiving messages from several places at once, her computer catching up with whatever transmission waves are hitting their receivers. One of which is from the enemy ahead.

A deep and commanding voice booms over the bridge speakers. “Vorelisian ships, you are in Thimmi territory. Leave now or be destroyed.”

Quell and Xaix share a look of recognition and surprise. Their thoughts are vocalized by their tack-o, Sonan. “That’s Admiral Tolomak! I wonder why he’s not attacking. It’s not like him to give a warning first or to show mercy.”

Quell takes a moment to study the scanner and ask his navigator, “What is their heading?”

Second Captain Bowen calculates the information for the executive lieutenant. Meanwhile, the two main vessels—the Thimmi command ship and the Vorelisian battle carrier—are close enough to fit the moon between them. The two ships are unmoving, facing each other, defiant.

A few moments pass before the navigator puts the Thimmi fleet’s trajectory on the twelve-inch screen above his station as he speaks. “The Thimms are heading in the direction from where we came, sir. The planet Seara.”

Quell reacts with alarm. “They’re planning to hit us?”

"No," comes Xaix's far calmer reply, "I'd wager those transports are not loaded with troops for an invasion. They are empty. They're heading to Earth."

Sonan shakes his head. "We can't scan through their shields to determine that for sure, sir."

Tolomak, not allowing visual communication, continues with his threats. "Commander, you have one minute to alter your heading back to Vorelis."

Bowen turns to face the men still at the tactical station. He is excited to be helpful, though his statement is the most obvious to make. "Sir, he wants us to return to Vorelis, but from here, that's not the closest planet in our empire!"

Xaix rolls his eyes before raising his hand to silence him. "We know." He continues to the communications station to respond to the Thimmi directive, allowing his opponent to see him on Lieutenant Lett's screen. "Admiral Tolomak, my old friend, this is Andier Xaix. Can you see me?"

Everyone on the bridge looks at their leader with several degrees of surprise.

How does the first colonel know the Thimmi fleet commander?

Are they really old friends, or is this a deception?

After a few moments, Tolomak allows his image to be seen on Lett's monitor as he responds with a smile and in a cheery voice—for *him* anyway. "Well, First Colonel Andier Xaix. It is good to see you again." The smile drops faster than a meteor through an atmosphere as he finishes, "you now have thirty seconds to turn your ships around and head back to Vorelis. I wouldn't want this to be the last time I see you."

Quell approaches and motions for Lett to mute the transmission. "We can successfully engage them, sir."

Xaix nods in understanding. "Pride aside, I have no doubt, exec. However, by now they've transmitted our location to their headquarters, and I'm sure more ships are inbound. Fight or not, our mission has failed."

To Sonan, watching the exchange intently from his station as they all are, Xaix says, "Jay, order the cruisers into flanking positions in case our friend decides to attack anyway despite his warm attitude toward us."

"Yes, sir," comes the acknowledgement, colored with a hint of disappointment.

To Quell, Xaix says, “Len, get our engines up to speed. Connect the fleet to our computer control. Prepare to leave Thimmi space.”

Relieved not to fight from a position of defense but also ashamed at the thought of running from their enemy, he responds, “Yes, first colonel.”

Lieutenant Lett’s console beeps. She speaks up to get Xaix’s attention. “Sir! I’m receiving a message from Dr. Lightner. It’s an inner-space communication.”

Inner-space communications don’t follow the same rules as the movement of ships or standard radio waves. Inner-space technology is a carrier wave of communication that makes any message instantaneously available across tens of thousands of light-years.

With the fleet powering up, Xaix considers the fact that if he hadn’t stopped for the confrontation with Tolomak, he wouldn’t know about the message until his next scheduled stop. He has Bowen hold his position while speaking to Lett. “Do you have all of it?”

She responds quickly, “Yes, sir!”

He turns back to Bowen and lowers his hand. “Move us out.”

As the engines rumble beneath his feet, he knows he has another three seconds or so. Xaix unmutes the communications console to send his adversary a final message. "See you at Seara….old….friend."

The Vorelisian fleet disappears into the black of space before Tolomak can respond. The fleet is moving at a considerably slower speed—two times light, which is safer for space travel—which will have them in orbit of Seara in ten years.

***

On the Thimmi command ship, Tolomak laments the sudden change in the plan and the necessity to revert to plan B. Instead of a quick trip through the Searan wormhole to Earth, he and his fleet of ships are stuck with a ten-year trip to a secret base near the Vorelisian border that is a thousand light-years from Seara. It is Haros, a planet where a secret ship is being built, a ship that can create its own wormhole. *No, my friend, I won't see you at Seara, but I will see you at Earth right about the time you get there.*

Tolomak's bridge crew listens to his quiet laugh, wondering if he has lost his mind or come up with something brilliant. Both are possible. The helmsman takes a new heading from his commander and prepares a transfer request in his mind.

CHAPTER TWENTY-FIVE: Truth Be Told

EDF-1 stands at attention on the Groom Lake tarmac to welcome Captain Pilas's spacecraft, which he is free to fly now that he is running the planet. The troops are dressed in their sophisticated black uniforms with shemaghs wrapped around their heads. The shemagh is a scarf typically made from cotton and worn as protection from the sun. These, however, are made of a material designed to reflect the sun and resist its radiation.

Lieutenant Kong stands with her teammates, together watching the small spacecraft approach and land a mere fifteen yards away. While the others keep their eyes trained on the main hatch, waiting for it to open, she sees her contact, dressed as a ground serviceman, secure the struts of the small spaceship and glance in her direction. She follows him with her eyes, missing Pilas's exit from the ship.

She faces front as the Thimmi leader reviews the troops quickly. It seems obvious to her that he's in a hurry to get to the interrogation of Dr. Lightner.

Five minutes later, the team is dismissed for the day. Lieutenant Kong separates from the others to have a private conversation with the old serviceman in Mandarin behind some empty oil drums stacked near the hangar where the interrogation is to take place.

"I like to see God on Sunday," he says first, quickly and quietly.

"If only He were there to see *you*."

"He is in my memories." The old man finishes the recognition code with what can best be described as a touch of sincerity. It wasn't so much a code for him but a genuine wish for God to return to mainstream life instead of being an underground belief.

Jen, however, is irritated. "We don't need codes. You know me." *You've been in North America too long, old man*, she thinks as she continues. "You must leave this place. I will soon be forced to expose you."

"Why would you do that?" The man asks, perplexed by the idea.

"I have decided not to spy on this team, nor provide any reports on their activities. We are all one planet."

He stands straight and speaks as if he is in command of her. "Publicly, yes. But we're not ready for you to leave us."

A commanding tone, to say the least. she observes.

He continues in a low tone. “China is not willing to allow this Captain Pilas authority over us. Our deal was with Lightner and will continue to be so.”

“You have the technology Pilas gave us to survive. Most of the world believes Lightner to be a traitor. Pilas is our salvation. If we don’t do as he desires, he will allow the Earth to die, along with all of us!”

The old man looks the former captain of the MSS straight in the eyes and feels something different about her. He lingers there for a moment, then says, “Know this. The government, your government in hiding, doesn’t trust Pilas. Learn what you can from Lightner and, traitor or not, return him to China.”

That would mean surrendering my place here, which is not possible for me at this point. “If I fail?” she asks.

He chuckles. “Then I will be forced to expose your spying activities, real or imagined.”

He turns to leave, not seeing the bowie knife Jen produces from the boot sheath hidden under her pant leg. He only feels it enter his side and then his heart before he can react. She covers his mouth to muffle his dying scream as he drops to the ground. “I cannot allow that.”

She removes the knife and puts the man into one of the oil drums nearby that is not part of the stacked pyramid. Her thoughts race as to her actions and what she must do to dispose of the body. *Later tonight, I'll bury him in the desert*. She is concerned over what Folsom would say if he found out what happened here. She disregards the blood that can be barely noticed on her black uniform as she walks quickly back to the hangar where the interrogation is about to take place. *He was right about one thing; I need to learn more from Lightner. Only then can I know what path is the right one. If my people trust him, then I should as well—but what of my friends?*

***

The interrogation of Dr. Charles Lightner takes place in his cell, a six-by-eight-foot chain-linked area partitioned off from the rest of Hangar 12. The cell, or cage, has a marble slab to lie on and an aluminum pipe to use as a toilet. There are two chairs and a table that were brought into the small space just before Captain Pilas walks in, flanked by armed members of EDF-2.

"Cozy little home you have here, doctor," Pilas says with all the smugness common among jailers.

EDF-1 is gathered together on a catwalk that passes above the cell. Colonel Nealand is there, hoping to hear the right questions asked and answered; specifically, regarding the attack on the International Space Station.

Jen, wearing a new coat, joins them on the catwalk in time to hear Lightner's defiance. "I've been in worse places in my life."

Up to now, the Vorelisian scientist has been sitting upright on the marble slab near the wall. Captain Pilas motions for him to sit at the table. Reluctantly, he complies, knowing what is to come and powerless to do anything about it.

"You know that brain scanners work on the dead as well as the living, correct?" Lightner says.

"That is correct, Vorelisian, but I want you alive so I may present you to Admiral Tolomak when he gets here."

Lightner smiles, "He'll never get through the Searan wormhole. It will take him a century to get here."

"You go ahead and believe what you wish," Pilas says as he places the scanner on the table and turns it on. Its soothing hum is contradictory to its infliction of mind-invading pain. "Look into the box, please."

Charles can see the glow inside the box and averts his gaze. Instead, he turns to the audience gathered around him, both inside and outside the cell. "Hear me! You people are signing your death warrant by following this man! The Thimms created this disaster so they can save you from it! They want you to feel indebted to them!"

The scanner is a box like the hand-held one Pilas used on Dobson and McCarthy, only larger. He says, "Tell them I'm lying to them, that my people plan to kill them. Go ahead. It won't make any difference. They know that my people are their only hope of survival."

Captain Blassi and a rather large sergeant get behind Lightner and grab his head, forcing him to face the box, though his eyes are still closed. "Aren't you going to drug me? The subject is supposed to be unconscious," he pleads.

Pilas purses his lips as if about to disappoint a young child who wants a cookie. "No, ours is a slightly different technology than the Vorelisian design. You will look into the box. Once it catches your eyes, it will not release you until all the questions I ask have been answered to my satisfaction."

"Your primitive scanner can control actions? I don't believe it. I insist you drug me. I can quote the rules of organized warfare established after the Great War of—"

Unexpectedly, Pilas slaps Charles across the face. The Vorelisian doctor responds by attempting to stand. Captain Blassi and her sergeant push him down into his chair and grab his head again. This time, the glow within the box catches his eyes and holds him still.

Derrick watches from the catwalk with his team. The little voice inside his head is shouting at him. He falls to one knee from the pain that would make a migraine feel like an muscle twitch. He concentrates on his motorcycle. His team. The conversation he had with the Zetan alien Rishal. The pain subsides.

Colonel Nealand watches the two aliens and their verbal sparring. *We should intervene; this is, after all, our planet.*

Pilas asks the first question. "The scanner will now search your mind for the answer to the question 'What is the Vorelisian plan for the annexation of the planet Jexx with regard to Earth?'"

The scanner sifts through Lightner's knowledge, searching for the answer. Charles screams in agony as the machine tears through his mind. "No! Supposed…be…unconscious! Can't…pain…too…great! Please!" His attempts to turn away or even to blink are futile. The machine has control over his mind. The Vorelisian method of mind scanning is incredibly advanced and, therefore, civilized. The Thimms, however, believe that the extraction of information need not be pleasant.

Folsom continues to watch helplessly. The voice of the Zetan slave to the Thimms, Rishal, screams at him again to do something to stop this torture. Derrick is losing control. “The doctor needs a break, Pilas!” he shouts.

Pilas looks up at the EDF captain as if irritated by the interruption. “In a moment,” he replies before asking the next question.

The scanner records the answers faster, as Charles sees little else he can do but cooperate. His screams have been reduced to a whimper. After an hour of intense questioning on things from Vorelisian strategy to base locations, Pilas turns off the machine.

Charles blinks many times before dropping his head to the table. “I am a scientist, not a military expert. Why ask me things you know I know nothing about?”

Pilas leans over him so that no one else can hear. “Because it amuses me to.”

Charles looks up and is about to stand when Pilas asks the final question with the machine off. “Where is your spaceship?”

Lightner looks at the scanner, knowing it is now off but fearing the consequences of lying to this Thimmi animal. “In the Mojave, not too far from here, behind the rocks at grid location…” His head hits the table after mumbling the coordinates.

The interrogation ends with Lightner welcoming the coolness of the marble slab against his sweat-soaked clothes and the EDF teams being dismissed for the night.

Folsom passes his colleague and fellow EDF captain to ask. "Amanda, is this your secret mission? It's like you never left." He smiles, hoping she'll get the levity in his words, but she isn't laughing.

"My team and I are everywhere these days. We got dismissed from—our assignment to come here. Apparently, Pilas only trusts your team and mine to do anything." She says while motioning for her team to fall in.

"Okay. So, I guess I'll see you around." Derrick says.

She stops. "Is there something else? Something you want from me?"

He steps backward, thinking of something to say but shakes his head instead. "No. See you, captain."

***

Nealand steps outside the hangar. The sky is dark purple, as the sun's brightness is limited to the horizon. He spots Captain Folsom, Lieutenant Dae, and Sergeant Furtado listening to Pilas for a moment before the alien boards his spaceship and flies away.

Everyone who ventures outdoors wears clothing designed to protect them from the ever-present radiation of the sun, the only reprieve being after it sets, though that will change over time as the planet absorbs more and more radiation. The radiation will worsen as long as the Earth's magnetic field remains disabled. Soon, the time of day or night will be irrelevant. The entire planet will be saturated like a sponge thrown into the ocean.

As Nealand approaches the group, Behrouz runs off toward the motor pool, presumably to requisition a vehicle. As he gets to within speaking distance, he sees the team's equipment clearly in the dim light of dusk. "Going somewhere, captain?" Edward asks with all the concern of a mouse taking your last piece of cheese.

"The Mojave. Pilas gave us orders to verify the location of Lightner's spaceship," Folsom says.

Nealand looks around. "Where is your little Asian spy?"

Folsom stops himself for a second, realizing that he forgot what Lieutenant Kong's history consisted of. "Kong is feeling ill. I suggested she get to sleep early and report to sick call in the morning if she doesn't improve."

The antigravity Humvee arrives with Behrouz behind the wheel. Folsom and Nealand watch as he bounds out of the vehicle and opens the back to assist in loading the equipment. He is excited to be a part of not only this mission, but of the team as a whole.

Nealand, not taking his eyes off the young private, asks, "Mind if I tag along?"

"Jafari will love that," Folsom responds as he opens the passenger-side door of the Humvee to get in.

Nealand thinks of the espionage reports he has read that tell of computer hacking and murder and determines, "We should leave Private Jafari behind. Just in case."

"In case of what?" Derrick asks as he closes the door behind him and stands before his superior.

"In case someone tries to free Lightner."

Before Derrick can object beyond shaking his head, Jafari speaks loudly from behind them. "Why me?"

Edward puts his hands on the young man's shoulders, fully aware that he keeps disappointing his friend, and vows in his heart to make it up to him one day. "You're the only one here who I trust to guard Lightner. Your job will be the security of the Vorelisian doctor. This may be the most important job on the planet right now."

Jafari does all he can not to roll his eyes and say, *Bullshit!* Instead, he responds with a mumbled, "Yes, sir, colonel, sir" as he storms away.

Folsom walks to the rear hatch to check that his team is ready. Furtado closes the hatch and says to his captain, "I got shotgun!" After a brief pause, he adds, "sir."

Derrick smiles as he climbs into the Humvee. "I'll drive, then."

At the passenger-side door, Furtado meets Nealand, who is already occupying the front seat. "Colonel, sir, I already called…I mean. With your permission, sir, I—"

Nealand smiles while waiting for the man to finish his sentence. "Very well, sergeant. I call shotgun for the return trip."

Alfonzo smiles with genuine satisfaction and gratitude as he jumps into the seat and straps himself in next to Captain Folsom. Noticing his superior familiarizing himself with the many thruster controls, he asks, "Captain, have you ever driven an antigravity vehicle before?"

After witnessing the entertaining interaction between Alfonzo and Colonel Nealand, Derrick feels he has had enough, "Don't press your luck, sergeant. I've got this."

Furtado holds back a chuckle. "Of course, sir," he says, then mumbles to himself, "We all gotta learn sometime."

Lieutenant Dae is strapped into the rear seat. Captain Folsom checks his monitors and infrared sensor package before calling out, to the nervous one, "Dae, you've got the top turret if we need it."

Shanti responds with a nod to confirm the order as she catches the captain's eye in the rearview mirror.

The Humvee speeds away, disappearing into the desert darkness with only its lights to mark its trip to the horizon. Jafari watches it all the way there, until it is gone.

***

Meanwhile, Madeline has checked out of a motel on the outskirts of Las Vegas.

The clerk gives a cursory acknowledgement of her business and wishes her a good day.

It's eight p.m., idiot. She leaves, wondering if the young man even recognized her as his senator.

She gets into a car provided by an old crime boss with few places left to hide. He owed her a debt of gratitude for not sending him to prison years ago. *Yes, it's becoming more difficult for the criminal element to get away with things now that the shackles are improving and the world has come together. The governments of the world grow stronger when the people are at their mercy, though it is the people who allow it. Things will improve when I become first premier of the Earth.* She ponders the future as she drives toward the town of Mesquite, armed with her pistol and yearning to free the man she loves.

Will she feel the same way about shackles and free entitlements when she becomes first premier? She stores the question in the back of her mind as a smile appears on her face.

Along eastbound Highway 15, she throws her shackle out the window of the beat-up old sedan before backtracking a few miles and getting onto Highway 93 north. Because of her position in government, the FBI and MAA will swarm the wrong area looking for her.

She's "off the grid," as the saying goes. She doesn't know what will happen to her when or if she suddenly reappears. Certainly, *she* won't be sent to prison.

CHAPTER TWENTY-SIX: Choosing Sides

Skimming across the surface of the road, Derrick is getting used to this mode of travel and anticipates the day when roads will no longer be necessary. Although a paved surface is helpful for a smooth ride, even for a vehicle with no wheels, the onboard computer compensates easily for the small bumps and dips in the road's surface in this desolate part of Southern California.

It is dark. There is a quarter moon, and Derrick's headlights are blaring, but without the benefit of his low-light periscope, the available light wouldn't be enough to see the terrain ahead safely at 125 miles per hour.

From the center of Nevada to Highway 95, travel is pretty straight and level. From there, taking 190 through Death Valley and traveling south on 395, the trip is no longer than two hours to Mojave Desert National Park.

With the seats built back-to-back within the Humvee, Edward purposely positioned himself behind Derrick to question the captain on his opinions regarding globalization.

"I'm against it."

"What exactly do you find objectionable about a one-world government?" the colonel asks.

While trying to keep his full attention on the road ahead, Folsom continues to stare into the pull-down periscope-looking scanner that allows him to see beyond his headlights with light-sensitive technology. It is unlike infrared; it works to enhance the view with the light available to it, not compete for an image.

Derrick can see miles ahead. He answers without removing his eyes from the periscope. “A lack of defense, for one.”

“Defense is simple without an enemy to concern ourselves with.”

“That’s the problem. We see ourselves as good people. We’ve grown from the barbarians we were even in recent history. Some say we don’t need a military at all, that there’s no one to fight, or we don’t need police because we have shackles to restrain ourselves from committing crimes. But if you take away the soldiers, cops, and government eavesdroppers, you’re left with people as sheep who won’t see a wolf coming to their door.”

The colonel finds the analogy almost comical. “A wolf? In the form of what?”

“No direction. A government cannot maintain control over its citizens without the ability to direct their attention one way or the other.”

"Why would a government need to?" Edward asks, the confusion evident in his voice.

"Because after the soldiers and cops disappear, I'm sure some might not see the need for the existence of government. Think what would happen if a sizeable population threw away their shackles. The government, without soldiers, would be powerless."

"The government maintains control by keeping the people dependent on it. Without government to govern the people, you'd have chaos. No one wants that."

"Without government, what is left to fill the void of a governing body are corporations."

Nealand reflects on the idea of the Coca-Cola Company getting into a shooting war with Pepsi and chuckles softly to himself. "I like your insight, captain. It's scary, but I like it."

Derrick takes his eyes off the scanner for a moment as he slows the vehicle and smiles at Edward, who sees his reflection in the driver's side window. "I'm a pretty smart guy, you know."

Edward smiles back. "Was there a second reason to dislike globalization?"

"There are cultural conflicts. Some people just can't live together no matter how well intentioned. The people who blame religion as a cause of hatred are responsible for its abolition," Derrick states before pausing to check the compass on the dashboard.

"We'll get God back, I'm sure."

Derrick smiles, not as confident in Nealand's opinion as he'd like to be. "There are other factors, of course."

Edward leans forward to whisper in Derrick's ear. "Is that little voice talking to you?"

Derrick lets out a brief laugh. "My opinions are still mine, colonel."

"Would you be surprised to learn that I agree with you and that, together, we have the power to turn the world around?"

Is the colonel trying to negotiate a rebellion with me? Derrick wonders. "What can we do?" His smile disappears as he stops to check their position, which is projected on the windshield in front of him like an aircraft heads-up display (HUD) from the computer console built into the dashboard. "We're just two people."

Nealand responds quickly and quietly. "Lightner is a third. His girlfriend, Senator Verona, is a fourth. She is a shoo-in for first premier." *And there's your team*, he doesn't add.

"Not impressive enough."

"Did I mention that my team and I control teleportation technology?"

"One team—now, that's more like it," Folsom says sarcastically.

"Don't scoff, captain. There's a good portion of the world that would like to see the planet divided into the two hundred and sixty countries it was before this whole globalization thing took off. You and your team can play a major part in our struggle with your position in Washington."

He's talking treason against Pilas, Derrick thinks. *But it's not strictly treason, is it? Not if we support the Earth. That's our mission.* "I don't know," is all he can say for the moment.

Shanti has listened to the entire conversation but remained silent. *Maybe they just fear change*, she thinks as she elbows her seat to wake Furtado from his dozing. She likes the seats facing away from each other and doesn't mind riding backward, but her teammate sitting shotgun is starting to snore. "Wake up, Alfonzo."

He stirs.

***

Captain Folsom's team arrives at Mojave National Park at 10:00 p.m. With the help of Pilas's directions, they arrive at Lightner's mode of transport, hidden among the rocks. Derrick stops the vehicle and shuts it down. The resulting silence is so overwhelming that it's almost deafening as the team spreads out, never too careful in the face of the unknown.

Shanti is armed both with a handgun in its holster and an Uzi-type submachine gun slung across her back. It resembles the old Israeli guns from decades past, but is smaller, more compact, and fitted with a .22 LR fifty-round magazine. She circles the craft, looking for footprints with her headlamp pointed at the ground.

The quarter moon isn't bright enough.

Sergeant Furtado looks up at the stars, amazed at the level of darkness, which gives him the ability to see the Milky Way Galaxy stretching across the sky despite the moon's light obscuring some of it. With so many stars visible, it takes him a moment longer than usual to locate and identify the constellation of Orion.

Folsom and Nealand watch Shanti work.

Edward slaps the spaceship and asks, "We found it. Now what?"

Derrick snorts as he shakes his head. *What's with this "we" stuff?* "I'll have a flatbed crane brought in to haul it back to base. Right now, we're just here to verify its location."

“We should’ve brought the doctor here with us. He’d have gladly given us access.” Nealand predicts.

“Or he might set a trap for us.”

“You don’t really believe that, do you, captain?”

“I don’t know what to believe. I’m under orders just like you.”

“Orders from a man from another planet who is in control of the world. *Our* world.”

“Yes, Pilas is an alien, and without his help, humanity is doomed. And you want to fight him behind another alien?” Derrick says.

“We fight for the people of the Earth. What is that little voice telling you right now?”

Folsom’s sarcasm returns for a moment. “It’s late. I think it’s asleep.”

The small transport is shaped like an egg on its side and is just as smooth. Shanti shines her light on the surface to illuminate the silver-colored exterior. She marks the location of the ship with a satellite transponder so that the crane operator can find this location without having to drive.

Folsom checks his shackle, giving the controlling device more attention than usual. "What happens after we win the battle for the planet for Lightner? Assuming we can, do we then fight *his* people off?"

Nealand, walking away and caught off guard by the question for a moment, replies, "It depends on the answers I get from him."

"Answers? To what?"

In a lower tone, so as not to be heard by the others, Edward smiles and says, "His involvement in the space station attack and the magnetic field collapse. I find it odd that Pilas didn't ask any questions on those topics. Lightner may just be who he has claimed to be since the beginning—a friend."

Derrick's eyes go wide, recognizing the colonel's words as truth. The Zetan being inside his brain is screaming at him. *Use this man to help you save Lightner! Believe him!*

At just after 10:30 p.m., Folsom calls his team together. "Form up! We're heading back to base."

Furtado objects respectfully. "Sir, aren't we going to try to gain access to the interior?"

The captain shakes his head as he reiterates, “Let’s go! Our plans are changing.” He pauses before whispering to the colonel, “In more ways than one.”

Colonel Edward Nealand nods in understanding. *We just need a plan.*

Furtado, heading for the front door of the Humvee, stops at the smiling colonel and remembers. “In the rear, yes, sir.”

***

By 1:00 a.m., Madeline reaches the guard shack leading into the base from the dirt road off Highway 93. A young sergeant yawns as he greets the Nevada senator. “Good morning, ma’am. This is a restricted area. I’ll need to scan your shackle.”

She responds with annoyance in her voice. “Sergeant, I am Senator Verona. Don’t you recognize me?”

Now he does. “Yes, ma’am,” he says quickly as he stiffens his back. “I’ll just need to verify your shackle.”

“My mission requires that I not carry a shackle.” She says, pretending that she just gave up a secret.

I’ve never heard that one before, the sergeant thinks as he cocks his head, betraying his mistrust. “Who is your point of contact?" he asks as he punches keys on his shackle, creating an open channel with which to make a call.

"Colonel Nealand," she says, giving him the first name she can think of while reaching for her hidden pistol. *I don't want to have to kill this kid.*

The sergeant turns away so Madeline cannot hear him speak to, presumably, the colonel. *Got ahold of him real quick*, she thinks as she moves the safety to the red position. She thinks of her unborn child and her need to save the planet for him…her…doesn't matter. *How far does a mother go? How far does a leader go? How far should I go? Can I live with myself if I…*

The gate is up.

How long was she lost in thought? Two seconds? She looks over at the sergeant, who is waving her through with a smile. *Must be laughing his ass off inside at my expense.*

"Go ahead, you're cleared. Have a good day, ma'am," he says.

She tries not to act surprised while activating the gun's safety. She drives through the gate, careful to do so with ease. *Just like I belong here.*

***

Lieutenant Kong walks like a stealth cat in the darkness of the hangar. She startles Charles, who never heard her approach his cage. “Doctor Lightner.”

He jumps to his feet from his marble slab. He wasn’t asleep. He couldn’t sleep, as thoughts of what is to come kept him awake. “Lieutenant…” He pauses, trying to remember her name.

“Kong, sir. I want you to know that the Chinese government is still behind you.”

Unimpressed, Charles shrugs. “Pilas hasn’t persuaded China to follow him as the rest of the world seems to be doing?”

“We’re faced with death from the loss of our magnetic field. They don’t see Pilas as a better choice than you.”

Charles shakes his head. *Oh, the irony*. “What does your government propose?”

She stops, thinking she heard a noise, then continues, “Listen, we have a stable underground network through various cities in Asia and parts of Europe. Almost half the planet will be behind you in a month.”

He shakes his head slowly, allowing the worst thoughts of what may happen to the people permeate his calm demeanor. “Leaving us to fight the other half. War is coming because two alien races want to use your people to obtain a planet both claim to be theirs."

"It may not come to that. The people of the whole world will rally behind you when the truth comes out."

Lightner snorts. "Pilas asked the right questions in his interrogation, lieutenant. All he has to do is play back the answers to the people, and they will believe him. The Thimms are experts in coercion and propaganda."

We're pretty good at those things as well, she doesn't say. "If we can get ahold of that brain scanner and broadcast a live interview with you answering the *right* questions…" Her voice trails off at what she thinks is the sound of someone nearby. She looks around and sees nothing.

"Not with a Thimmi scanner. I can't go through that again," Lightner says as he holds his head in his hands. "I have one on my ship. We'll need to get it."

Jen is about to agree with him when she hears the sound of a gun's hammer being cocked. She turns to see Madeline holding a pistol on her, shaking nervously.

"Open the cell door," Madeline says with so much conviction in her voice that Jen worries what her response will be when she answers.

Jen stands up straight in defiance of being shot. “I wish I could. The door is linked to a security station in Washington. Officers will know the doctor’s cell is open and sound the alarm. My teammates will be here in seconds.”

Lightner steps forward to the edge of the chain-linked box he is trapped in, feeling a sense of hope sweep over him. “Madeline, I’m glad to see you. Please put the gun down. The lieutenant is not our enemy.”

Madeline gets closer to the cell door, forcing Jen to back away from it.

The lieutenant can see the pain in the senator’s face, the expression of someone who hasn’t thought everything through and who is about to make a rash decision. “If you do this, you can forget about becoming first premier,” Kong says matter-of-factly.

Without a word, Madeline shoots the lock off the cell with two shots. “Come on!” she shouts at her love, who quickly follows.

Madeline orders Jen to lead them into the open area of the hangar, where they find Private Jafari face down next to his rifle.

Jen moves carefully toward his body. “You didn’t kill him, did you?” she asks while checking for a pulse. *Slow but present.*

“I only knocked him over the head from behind,” Madeline says as she looks around frantically for another vehicle, feeling the pressure increasing with each passing second wasted. “We need a vehicle to escape. My car is useless now.”

Jen nearly gets a clean drop on her opponent by kicking Jafari’s rifle up from the ground and into firing position while the senator’s head is turned. “Drop it!” she says. The two are unmoving for a moment, each not wanting to shoot the other. Jen starts again in a calmer tone. “I’m on your side, Madeline. All I need to do is get Lightner to China. We can negotiate with Captain Pilas from there. You just have to trust me. Trust me! Put the gun down! I don’t want to kill you!”

Madeline begins to lower the weapon. “What happened to your alarms?”

“Oh, I lied about that,” Jen says dismissively as she, too, lowers her weapon.

The echo of their voices in the cavernous hangar subsides just before the main hangar door flies open fast and loud. The Humvee has returned, barreling in at high speed. Shanti Dae is poised atop the gun turret, holding the handle with both hands, her finger ready to pull the trigger.

Captain Folsom's voice booms over the Humvee's loudspeaker as the vehicle stops ten feet away. "Drop your weapon!"

Madeline backs up, blinded by the Humvee's lights. She is close enough to Lightner now that Shanti doesn't risk a shot, but Jen's angle is better. *I was so close to ending this*, she laments.

Charles puts a hand on Madeline's shoulder and whispers in her ear. "Madeline. Have faith in these people as I do. Think of our child."

She holds back the tears as she turns to him. "I am."

She lowers the weapon as he holds her. The team moves in. Jen takes the pistol and searches Madeline's clothing for others. She finds the scanner/transmitter that Madeline brought with her and hands it to Colonel Nealand.

Edward takes the device as he addresses Madeline. "Good idea, using my name to get onto the base, senator." He studies the scanner while turning his attention to Lightner. "Doctor, is this a brain scanner?"

"No, but I have one on my ship. It's not primitive like those of the Thimms," he says with a smile.

"Well, we wouldn't harm you for the information we need. We require some truthful answers that Pilas failed to ask. You understand."

Lightner is almost amused by the sudden shift in his interaction with these Earthers. "It's quite painless when used properly. I understand your concerns and will cooperate all I can. We have a common goal, after all."

Nealand turns to Folsom, who is walking toward them.

The captain has a stoic look on his face, as if righting a wrong long overdue. "Congratulations, doctor, on your escape." He turns to Jen and continues. "Load up some supplies, Asia is pretty far."

Jen smiles. "You knew?"

"I suspected. We're a team, aren't we?"

"Yes, sir!"

Jen passes Furtado, who remarks, "Is that a smile? Wow! I never thought I'd see one from you, lieutenant. I'm surprised."

She surprises him further by winking at him.

Folsom continues speaking to the colonel, doctor, and senator, whose eyes are spent of tears by this time. "Take the

Humvee, get to his ship, and use the scanner. Then get to China. I expect a full report on what you learn."

Colonel Nealand gives the captain a mock salute while smiling from ear to ear. "Yes, sir, captain, sir."

Derrick smiles back and shrugs. "Thank you."

"Why not take Charles's ship to Asia?" Madeline asks.

Derrick responds before Nealand can open his mouth. "Two EDF teams are on the doctor's side. The rest have yet to be convinced."

Furtado steps forward to voice his own concern. "Won't Pilas scan our minds to find out where they're going?"

Edward answers. "That's why we're not telling you. Asia is a big continent."

"But Jen will be branded a traitor for helping the doctor escape!" Furtado protests.

Folsom turns to his sergeant, seeing the deep concern for his teammate in his eyes. *Or is it something else? Attraction, maybe?* "It'll work out, Alfonzo. Sometimes you just have to have faith."

Furtado smirks, "An outdated and politically incorrect belief, sir."

With the others getting into the Humvee, Madeline overhears the conversation and adds, “Freedom isn’t free. I only hope the price we pay for it isn’t too high.”

It’s only now that Shanti has examined the bump on the back of Behrouz’s head. In a fit of rage, she sprints to the Humvee just ahead of Madeline and slaps her across the face, knocking the future leader of the planet to the floor. “You bitch!”

Folsom pulls his lieutenant away from the defenseless senator. Charles helps Madeline into the vehicle as Folsom leads Shanti in the opposite direction.

A few minutes later, the Humvee leaves, with the colonel driving the doctor, the senator, and Lieutenant Kong back to Lightner’s spaceship to get the answers he so desperately needs. From there, they will recharge their solar capacitors and head west across the Pacific Ocean to *somewhere* in Asia. Edward will return alone, hopefully unseen and not missed.

They make sure to leave their shackles behind.

***

MAA has arrived to minister to Private Jafari’s injury, with Shanti at his side. As they check on him, he regains consciousness.

Captain Folsom walks up to inquire about his private's health before turning to Shanti. "Lieutenant, I must order you to restrain yourself from similar outbursts in the future, understand?"

Shanti lowers her head in shame. "Yes, sir."

"Under normal circumstances, I would have to discipline you."

She raises her head with a big smile on her face. "I did restrain myself, sir. She's alive, isn't she?"

Folsom shakes his head and chuckles quietly as he walks away. "Carry on. I have to prepare a report on our stolen Humvee."

PART TWO: United We Fight

CHAPTER ONE: Time Passes

Ten years have passed, and the magnetic field of the Earth has faded into nonexistence. The sun's radiation has killed most of the plants and animals that have not been secured in one of seventy special farm-sized domes built primarily in North America. They are best described as ultra-advanced greenhouses.

The inhabitants of the planet are housed under similar domes that cover fifty cities on the North American continent as well as select cities in Europe. A population of five hundred million is safe, while millions more are surviving beneath other major cities in Asia, Australia, and Africa.

The peace is kept through the promise of exile from the domes. No one complains about the rationing of food, the hot air that is filtered but kept at a constant 100 degrees, or the fact that an alien is ruling the planet with an iron fist.

Captain Pilas, who now calls himself the "Great Leader of Earth," has become obsessed with his power. He toys with the emotions of the people, seeing them as something beneath pets, as pets are loved. He has run the numbers and, in order to bring fairness into the rescue, he has instituted a lottery system for their salvation.

The plan is to make the people believe that their lives have meaning, that they all have an equal chance at winning a place in one of the hundred or so colony ships he has promised are on the way. These ships will carry refugees from Earth to Jexx. Once colonized, the Galactic Council will be powerless to refuse the Thimmi Empire ownership of the planet.

The lottery is, of course, rigged to allow only the best and brightest of citizens to be selected. Only those with high IQs or impressive credentials will be saved.

In the last few years, since the lottery's inception, several hundred young women have given themselves to satisfy the alien captain's desires in the hope of being selected outside the standard lottery process. Older people and couples have paid prostitutes to work for them, and others still have given their daughters to him, some as young as twelve.

By this time, however, the number of those selected for transport has been set and will not be changed. Pilas remembers the face of the last young girl, who was whisked away about an hour ago. *These idiots will believe anything*, he thinks as he throws her ID number into a trash can in the rotunda of his palace that was once the US Capitol Building.

This morning is like the rest that have come before it since the domes were built in one remarkable and challenging year. The humans of Earth are even talking about erecting monuments on the new world to those who were most prominent in their quest for salvation. The weather under the dome is unchanging and perfect. *The dupes of this planet still haven't figured out my hand in disabling the magnetic field*, Pilas thinks.

He laughs as he exits the palace, there he sees Governor Dobson standing in front of him with a sea of people beyond. Dobson is still "leading" the United States of North America, along with 95 senators, minus the rebellious Senator Verona. The governor is standing at a podium with Director McCarthy, now security chief of the Earth, beside him. The traitorous General Childs would've held that post if he had joined Pilas as most EDF teams have. The other EDF teams have fled.

Since the collapse of the magnetic field a decade ago, the election for first premier of Earth has been held and won by Senator Madeline Lightner, who has since married the good doctor and is in exile in Asia. It's a moot point, of course, as the true and only official leader of the Earth is Great Leader Arno Pilas.

Pilas takes a moment to admire the green and white banner of the Thimmi Empire flying above him, replacing the North American standard and reflecting his power over the people.

He approaches the podium as Dobson finishes up his speech and introduces Pilas to thunderous applause.

The words Pilas has come to speak have been long awaited, yet they seem unexpected when he finally articulates them. “I have just been in contact with the Thimmi fleet approaching this planet. They’ll be here in a few days.”

The cheer of relief rising from the mass of people before him is like a breath of fresh air. The applause crescendos to the point of almost being deafening.

“Salvation at last!” someone shouts as the applause wanes, then builds again.

Even those planning to stay behind are confident that the Thimms will repair the magnetic field and desaturate the soil, as promised by Pilas.

The Thimmi captain stretches his arms wide to accept the people’s gratitude and offerings. They throw gold coins and flowers at his feet. Both are rare and precious commodities of the time.

Pilas happily accepts them. *The people love me, I am their savior, I will never give them up*, and *They will be mine forever* are just some of the thoughts racing through his deluded mind.

Checking the front of the crowd, Pilas sees a member of EDF-1, *one of the few patriotic and loyal teams at my disposal*. He doesn’t make eye contact, but feels safe knowing they are there to protect him.

***

Over the past decade, EDF teams were split up to oversee dome construction in the fifty cities controlled by the Great Leader. During that time, the members of Team One haven't seen each other in shackle communications, let alone in person, until today, when they were reunited under the dome of Washington, DC for the announcement of the coming Thimmi fleet and the commemoration of this day in history.

During their separation, the team members had progressed in their military careers. Shanti Dae is now a captain. She is surprised to see the once-shy Private Jafari has become a handsome sergeant.

Sergeant Furtado is now a master sergeant. He and Jafari meet Captain Dae while patrolling the crowd. Their good friend and teammate, Jen Kong, is still hidden out there somewhere in the world. She is still considered a fugitive and an enemy of the Thimmi Empire. To her teammates, however, she is on a mission.

Captain Folsom has refused a promotion to major until the Earth is whole again, a promise made more for his sense of self-worth than out of pride. He is dressed in his black uniform and sunglasses. On this cold December evening, he watches the crowd, content to be with his team once again.

Helping with security in the capital of the Earth are drones, fitted with antigravity generators and light-powered lasers provided by Pilas himself. Their main weapon, however, is the immobilizer, a beam of energy that attacks the nervous system of its victim, rendering them unthreatening as they become unable to move for a few minutes. Useful in crowd control, the drones typically aim for the legs to stop protestors from running. The ground police can take over from there.

The cancer that has afflicted William Childs causes Folsom to do a double take when he sees his old commander, now a civilian with long, matted hair and ragged clothes. Pilas broke Childs for questioning his motives for the world, and he was subsequently imprisoned for five years. *Certain areas will be ignored for the sake of the well connected*, Pilas decreed.

That policy is unacceptable to Childs, especially given his wife Sheila's genetics, which would essentially have left her exiled. *Pilas wants "pure" people, not enhanced ones.* William's anger grows with each step he takes closer to the edge of the stage.

He doesn't see the drones or Folsom's team closing in, as he is focused on one thing; assassination. Childs tried to get the word out on shackle media, alerting the people to the true plan, he even tried to reveal Pilas's destruction of the magnetic field and his fondness for young girls, but he was censored, labeled a madman, or just ignored for fear that Pilas would renege on saving the Earth.

Sheila knows where her husband is, but not what he is doing. She sits at home, watching events unfold on the stage, with her five children surrounding her, observing the image on the wall projected by her shackle. She thinks of William always, knowing that he is less than a month from death and that the reason for that is speaking on the stage now. The Thimmi alien doesn't deserve the accolades he gets. She wishes he were dead as she pulls her youngest closer and sees a security drone pass the camera recording the event.

"Move in on the stage by the podium! Now! Now! Now!" Folsom speaks into his shackle with urgency. "Raggedy man, long brown hair!"

Childs stares at the evil alien from the crowd with a million people behind him. He fantasizes that they are his backup as he fingers the weapon in his coat; Lightner's pistol, confiscated a decade ago. He thinks of his children and beautiful wife as he produces the weapon and points it at Pilas. "For the people!" he screams from ten yards away as he squeezes the trigger to kill the *Great* Leader.

"GUN!" Folsom shouts as Dae, five feet away at this point, pulls up her Uzi and fires ten bullets into the former general in one short burst, just beating the immobilizing beam from a nearby drone by one second. That one second would've been the end of the Great Leader if William had been able to get off a second shot.

Pity.

Childs managed to get off one burst of energy that hit Pilas's shoulder and sent him to the floor at the same time Shanti fired her weapon. He smiles at the look of pain on the Thimmi alien's face, contentment washing over his soul as he dies from his wounds. His final thoughts are not of his wife and children, but of the people of the Earth.

Shanti kicks the weapon away as she looks upon him, recognizing him immediately. "General Childs? Oh, no."

His last words are whispered, so that only Shanti hears, "I am no longer a citizen of a country or alliance, but of the planet itself. The planet Earth is my home, and by the will of her people, I will serve and defend her with my life."

She whispers back, "I understand, sir. The fight is not over."

People are running in different directions as Pilas is whisked away by members of another EDF team. At the hospital, he will no doubt have the pleasure of every nurse who hasn't been selected in the lottery.

Captain Folsom and the rest of his team join Pilas there to continue their mission of guarding the Earth's savior.

After witnessing the parade of women entering the Great Leader's room, Furtado wonders if any of them were selected in the lottery.

The local security agents will deal with General Childs's body and the frantic and distraught woman who is no doubt on her way to the capital.

CHAPTER TWO: The First Family

A mile beneath the city of Novgorod, Russia, lies another city. Novgorod no longer can sustain life, as it has no dome to protect it from the sun. The exiled and rightfully elected first premier of the planet Earth lives with her family and ten thousand people within the subways and tunnels of the once-sprawling metropolis that, at its most crowded, housed just under five hundred thousand. If someone were to venture out of the protective layers of steel and earth to the surface, they would join the hundreds of thousands of rotting corpses in the streets, some piled up at the entrances to the steel-covered tunnels in a last desperate attempt to gain entry.

Dr. Charles Lightner and Madeline were married shortly after arriving in China ten years ago and have since organized many former EDF teams to their cause, to free the planet from Thimmi control. They also made the time to have two more children after Shauna was born. She has two brothers now, not old enough to remember seeing the sun, as she does. Mark and Jake are eight and six, respectively, and they listen to stories their sister and parents tell of the Earth bathed in sunlight and are amazed. They are allowed to watch video of the small yellow star rising over the granite cliffs of Yosemite National Park and the deserts of Arabia but know that to go outside without adequate protection would mean death.

Being the protective parents they are, Charles and Madeline don't risk letting them go outside for any reason, protected or not.

Shauna leaves her ten-by-ten-foot room and rushes to her brothers' adjoining room when she hears Jake screaming in the night. Guards come running from the opposite direction, holding their pistols high, suspecting foul play. Captain Jen Kong, who keeps her weapon holstered, leads them.

Jen stops at the open steel door that appears to have been built to withstand a nuclear attack. The room is dark but for a single night-light over the boy's bed.

Mark sits, his legs dangling off the edge of his bed, watching his sister console their little brother, not knowing what to do and wondering what he would do without his sister around.

Jake is awake and sweating. His eyes are wide open in shock, but he quickly calms at the caress of Shauna's hand on his forehead. "I saw it again, Shauna!" he cries out.

"It's okay now." Shauna consoles.

"It looked like the sun! It was burning the Earth!"

"It was just a dream, Jakey. Don't worry about it."

Mark approaches Jake's bed and remarks, "Remember when he sees Indy in his dreams? Those come true, right?"

"Indy" refers to the black cat the children have named Independence, who wanders the tunnels as he pleases and returns to the Lightner home within a day of Jake seeing him in a dream. Mark continues, "His dreams become reality."

"That's just a coincidence, Mark. Go to bed," Shauna says.

Mark reluctantly complies. "If we're going to be burned by the sun, we should know when, shouldn't we?"

"They're just dreams!" Shauna shouts, not wanting to believe that any harm prophesized by a simple dream or vision could come to them.

Jen intervenes. "Hey, why don't we all go back to bed? The excitement is over."

Shauna tucks in her little brother and smiles at him as she rubs his head one last time. "The sun isn't going to kill us. Mom and Dad will save us. They'll save the whole world. You'll see."

Jake smiles back and closes his eyes. "Will you tell me the story of Kara Ester again?"

"Not tonight. Go to sleep," Shauna replies. She enjoys telling the story of the great Galestikon warrior told to her by her father. Kara was kidnapped by a vengeful pirate in the hope that her government would pay ransom to get her back. Kara not only freed herself, but the hundred slaves the pirate kept to serve him. “Maybe tomorrow night.”

Shauna joins Jen in the hallway as she closes the door behind her. Jen has dismissed the guards. “Will you report my brother’s dream to my dad?” Shauna asks.

“Of course. I’m on my way to Control right now.”

“They’re in Control a lot these days, aren’t they?”

“Yes. Soon the nightmare will be over, and we’ll be free.”

Shauna looks up at the EDF officer in her black dress uniform, admiring the patches, the rank insignia on the lapels, and the ribbons decorating the front. “Will you be going back to your team in America?”

“I hope so,” Jen says as her mind drifts to thoughts of her friends.

At Shauna’s door, the young girl goes inside. “Don’t leave without saying good-bye, okay?”

Jen smiles. “I promise.”

Shauna salutes the captain in a manner that Jen respects. Shauna admires Jen for what she has done to safeguard her and her family and what she will do to save the world. Jen salutes back, fully aware of this child's importance and her possible role in rebuilding society. *This kid might be running the planet someday.*

Jen returns to her station in Control. Her task is to hack into satellites orbiting hundreds of miles above. They keep an ear to the ground in Washington, DC and an eye on the fleet of ships orbiting the planet Neptune's moon, Triton.

After compiling information on the fleet and the attempt on Pilas's life by William Childs, Jen finds herself at the strategy room door, ready with a report. She knocks and enters without waiting for an answer.

Madeline sees her first and smiles, anticipating good news. "Yes, captain?"

Jen contemplates the digital map taking up the table in the center of the room. There are charts on the walls and computer screens embedded into consoles all around. Approaching the digital map, she recognizes the layout of the planet on the screen. It's a tactical map revealing the locations of hidden forces and their underground cities and supply lines. She reports, "There was an attempted assassination by General Childs on Captain Pilas."

Lightner looks up from his console. "Attempted?"

"Yes, sir. It was thwarted by EDF Team One."

Madeline comes closer, her face filled with concern and hope. She has aged ten years in the last three. *The end is definitely near*. "So he survived. How is your team? Any news?"

Jen responds with a certain amount of tribulation. "They're fine. I should have been with them."

Charles puts a reassuring hand on her shoulder and speaks softly, as if he were her own father. "You'll see them soon. Things will change dramatically once the Thimmi fleet gets here. It will be our time to act."

Jen snaps out of her despondent thoughts and continues with her report, "That brings me to my second report, sir. The fleet around Triton appears to be forming up."

Madeline gestures to the large monitor that is the table. "Show me."

Jen presses a few buttons on the edge of the screen to change the image from one of the map to another of deep space. The image moves, zooming in on the fleet of spacecraft milling about the Neptunian moon. The image is somewhat pixilated given the great distance involved. "I know it's hard to tell, doctor, but do you recognize these vessels?"

Lightner doesn't take long to study the live image before coming to a conclusion. "I can make out the large vessel as a battle carrier. The Thimmi variant can carry eight squadrons of fighters along with assault ships and other transports. I can't really tell what these are unless you can improve the resolution, but from my experience with ship identification, I can guess four destroyers and…" He pauses as a larger ship emerges from behind the moon, quickly joining the other ships. "That's a command ship! Right there!" Deep in thought, he steps back with a look of shock on his face.

His wife notices his reaction first, never having seen this level of fear in him before. "What does it mean, Charles?"

"Admiral Tolomak is the only fleet commander I know of who still uses a ship of this type to command from. The other Thimmi fleet commanders use the carriers. It's considered a vain luxury that their government refused to splurge on. Tolomak is the exception."

"Jexx means a lot to them, obviously." Jen observes.

Madeline nods in agreement as Charles mumbles, "They've finished loading methane and water from the moon. Wait—if they have taken the long way from their empire to get to this solar system, that means the Searan wormhole is not open to them."

"The Vorelisians must be guarding it." Madeline guesses.

"Perhaps, or someone else is." Charles replies.

Jen, still watching the Thimmi fleet, asks, "What are these tiny dots? There must be a hundred of them."

Charles peers in, straining to make sense of the pixels in front of him. "Colony ships."

Captain Kong interjects with her military intuition. "Or possibly troop carriers."

Madeline shakes her head and responds, "Doubtful. I'm sure Pilas gave Tolomak the impression that the Earth is under control. They're more likely colony ships. They want to take as many of us off the planet as they can and plant us on Jexx."

Charles nods in agreement as his wife changes the screen back to the map of the Earth.

Jen comes to attention. *This is it.* She remembers the intel on Pilas's plans. "I am ready, first premier. What are your orders?"

Madeline calls up the locations of EDF teams on her side and Colonel Nealand's teleportation team. "You will rendezvous with your team in Washington."

Charles adds, "They should be guarding Pilas during his recovery. Check that before you leave."

Madeline continues, the couple talking to Jen as one mind, one commander, united in their resolve to achieve victory. "You will take canisters of xelon gas with you. Your mission is to get the gas to your old base at Groom Lake."

"It can't be teleported there?" Jen asks.

Charles says, "No. The gas must be at the Soliquid gun based at Groom Lake before the Thimmi fleet gets here."

Jen smiles, relishing the idea of being with her friends again and fighting beside them. "I didn't know there was a gun there. We've been using hydrogen to power the Soliquid plants around the world. I've never heard of xelon."

Madeline answers for Charles, who steps aside for a moment to think of the next step. "It was built years ago under the supervision of Colonel Nealand. His teleportation team will handle the gun's use. Your team will secure the gas and complete its delivery."

Charles says, "It took a year to manufacture enough xelon gas to power the Soliquid gun. It is the most powerful element on your planet and extremely rare. It should be enough to get through the shields of the Thimmi ships." His voice trails off as he adds, "I only wish your level of technology were a little higher…"

"Any orders regarding Pilas's life?" Jen means to assassinate the Thimmi captain the first chance she gets.

Madeline presses her lips together, considering the idea and rejecting it. "We don't want his supporters after you. They still see him as their savior, and our attempts to educate them have been explained as ineffective propaganda."

"EDF teams on Pilas's side will revolt when we make our move," Charles says confidently.

"I hope so," Jen says. *The EDF is on Pilas's side because they have to be. No telling which ones will join us when the time comes.*

Charles takes Jen by the shoulders and speaks in a serious and stern tone. "You mustn't allow yourself to be captured by Pilas. You know enough for him to discover us and thwart our plans. He would easily find and kill us all if he is able to scan your mind."

"If I had a suicide pill, I wouldn't hesitate to use it," she says with all the seriousness of the moment. Everything is riding on her success in getting the xelon gas to Colonel Nealand. *The weight of the world is on my shoulders, and I accept the responsibility.*

Charles shakes his head. "No, captain. The dead can still give information to a scanner. You will have to use your gun to destroy the memory area of your brain, here." He demonstrates by taking his finger to simulate a pistol and pointing at his head behind his right ear.

Jen places her hand on the grip of her pistol, wondering for a millisecond if she would hesitate to kill herself in that fashion. She answers quickly, "Of course, sir."

Madeline, on the captain's opposite side, sees the determination in her face and admires her for it. "Colonel Garov is assembling other parts of the Soliquid weapon. He will teleport to Washington for his part of the mission. We will give him the invasion signal when the Thimms get here."

I have waited for this day for a long time. Jen thinks. Her patience is paying dividends. *We've been planning for the arrival of the Thimms for years*. "Understood," she says as she turns to leave but stops herself upon remembering another report she needs to make. "Oh, I forgot to mention that your daughter wanted me to tell you of her concern for her brother Jake. It seems that he has had another one of his dreams. She is worried about him."

Madeline's eyes go wide with shock, and she speaks with anger as she heads for the door to check on her little boy. "You should've told me that when you first came in here, captain!"

The man guarding the door closes it for her.

Charles, much calmer than his wife, who doesn't understand Vorelisian physiology, answers the unspoken question. "Our son may be gifted with insight."

"You mean like a psychic?" Jen asks, unbelievingly.

He winces at the use of that term and continues, "It's something to do with our next stage of evolution. Your people should experience the same in a thousand years or so if you continue to grow as we have."

"So would your next child have a different ability?"

"We can't have any more children—that is, I can't," he says. He's not sure if the explanation is necessary but he continues anyway. "The last sperm of a Vorelisian male is what is responsible for the evolutionary jump."

"Earth males can reproduce throughout their lifetime."

"Yes. We're different in that respect. The last thousand sperm created carry the evolution gene. Some women are impregnated with it, but many are not, I suspect."

"How many people with extra abilities are there?"

"Unknown. Not many. If Jake is suffering from visions posing as nightmares, it is something we need to take seriously and investigate. He may be seeing something we need to know. Something that can help us." Charles remembers his wife's struggle to come to terms with having children with alien characteristics, yet still be human. Simple biology demands reproduction via similar species, confirming the adage that we, as a race, are more alike than unlike throughout the galaxy.

Captain Kong puts the issue of saving the Earth back on the front burner by asking, “Where do I pick up the xelon gas?”

“Each canister can fire several sustained bursts of energy. I have a few in the armory that will be dispersed to other guns around the world. Enough, I hope, to at least destroy the Thimmi command ship. You will take two of those with you.”

“What happens after we drive away the Thimms?” *And we only have your people to worry about?* She doesn’t say.

“We will appeal to the Galactic Council for their protection on behalf of the united peoples of Earth. You will be sponsored by the Vorelisian Empire for your inclusion into the council as a full member. Once Earth is a member, the vote for proper ownership of the planet Jexx will be tipped to our favor, and you will have our thanks,” Charles explains.

“Our first vote will be to reward your empire an entire planet that you may or may not deserve?”

“A fair trade, in my opinion, given the economic benefits that await Earth when this is all over. As for whether we deserve it, I leave that answer to the diplomats.”

"It's funny to me, doctor."

"What is, captain?"

"As benevolent as the Vorelisians seem to be, how do we know that you're not just the lesser of two evils?" Jen asks.

"I understand your position and your feelings. Remember that we want Jexx for ourselves as badly as our adversary does. The difference between the Thimms and us is that we won't kill you to get it."

"And there are no elements within your own empire who would?"

He pauses for a moment to think of a satisfying answer and comes up with nothing, politics being a universal problem throughout the galaxy and something he would rather stay away from participating in. "It all comes down to trust, captain. I trusted you with my life and the lives of my wife and children. Now I'm asking you to trust me with the safety of your world and the lives of those *you* love."

Jen doesn't answer, preferring to reserve judgment for the time being. *There's a question I should've asked ten years ago when Nealand was scanning the doctor's brain in the Mojave Desert*, she thinks as she salutes him.

He returns it, reluctantly at first, but then he remembers who the captain is and her military status.

She turns on her heel and leaves.

***

A bright light passes over the cities of Novgorod, London, Sydney, Tokyo, Beijing, and many others, as if the sun had landed and is moving along the city streets looking for someone to burn, bent on killing everyone in its path.

Madeline helps her youngest boy, Jake, see the vision through. It scares him. Once he explains what he has seen to her satisfaction, and to prevent further fear in the boy, she gives him a sedative with an eyedropper that puts him out in a matter of seconds. “Pleasant dreams, sweetheart,” she says, knowing that dreams are all any of us has left.

CHAPTER THREE: Returning Home

An antigravity Hover-Ski speeds across the Atlantic Ocean from the drop-off point in Lisbon, Portugal. Jen has the canisters of xelon gas and is relieved that the sea is calm on this spring night. She cannot help but think she has forgotten something and keeps checking the cargo strapped on each side of her speeding vehicle. Going so fast, she ponders for a moment how much time the Jet Ski spends over the water as opposed to on the water. *This would be fun in Hawaii.*

As she approaches New York City, she looks back at the pink hue just touching the horizon and fears the coming sun that will kill her despite the protective clothing she wears and lotions covering her exposed skin.

Jen takes the ski beneath the water, holding her breath long enough to get under New York's protective dome. She gets to Battery Park and remembers what has been nagging her mind for the last ten hours. *I didn't say good-bye to Shauna.*

She discards the Hover-Ski and ditches her wet clothing, unseen. Safe now under the dome, she watches the sunrise and takes a moment to hope the magnetic field can be repaired soon.

In addition to the domes built over the last decade, there is also a sun-protected antigravity rail line connecting most of the domed cities on the East Coast. As Jen makes her way to the station near the Holland Tunnel, she tries to avoid contact with people. It's not easy to remain inconspicuous while at the same time avoiding people whose shackles might "see" her and report her location to Pilas's henchmen. Fortunately, as morning comes, the lines for breakfast form at the food stations set up throughout the city that she can easily avoid.

Under Pilas, everything is free. People work for themselves when something like a meal is needed. The people of New York exist to serve each other until the world returns to normal. This keeps them occupied and relatively content.

In the last decade, shackles have been updated to include a feature that scans the wearer's surrounding environment for the sights and sounds of anyone wanted by the authorities. Jen knows she is at the top of the list of fugitives next to Lightner. It was she who allowed the Vorelisian to escape and then joined him in his futile effort to alter the destiny of the Earth.

While Jen is scanning her ticket, a teenager bumps into her in his rush to leave the station. "Oh, sorry, ma'am," he mumbles as he passes.

Reflexively, she responds, "It's OK."

Too late to take it back, Jen pushes the kid away and walks quickly toward the train, hoping his shackle didn't pick up too much.

The boy's shackle, however, does pick up her reactive and regrettable response and transmits the data to Major Amanda Blassi's EDF-2 team, now stationed in New York. EDF-2 converges on the station five minutes later. Amanda orders security drones to set up a perimeter while she and two men board the train for Washington, DC.

Her senior sergeant compares the data to Captain Kong's profile. "It's her, all right. Should we search the train?"

Amanda, cognizant of the sun's position in the sky and knowing this will be a long day, takes a window seat. "Relax. We'll pick her up when we get to DC."

The sergeant takes a seat at the window on the other side of the train car and peers out the window. "Yes, ma'am," he mutters his dissatisfaction as he picks up a very old magazine to read. *They don't make magazines or books anymore.*

***

Upon arrival in Washington, DC, Jen disembarks from the train and checks the time mounted on the giant terminal clock, admiring its design for a moment. It looks as if it was made in the early 1900s. A video screen nearby shows the Great Leader being released from the hospital under the protection of EDF-1. She smiles at the sight of her friends surrounding Pilas.

Her happiness fades quickly when a gun is pressed against her back.

"Don't move."

She moves.

Surprising EDF-2's senior sergeant, she spins around fast enough to knock the gun out of his hand and put him on the ground with a quick succession of punches to his face and groin. Seeing that the man is disabled enough, Jen runs for the nearest exit, where Major Blassi is waiting for her.

Amanda smiles and speaks with conviction. "You are under arrest, captain. If you move, I will kill you."

Another sergeant and the one Jen put to the ground arrive with their weapons drawn. The man is still wincing from the pain she inflicted upon him. The smirk she makes at his continued discomfort is short-lived when he pistol-whips her for it. He hits Jen hard, rendering her unconscious despite objections from his superior.

Jen is taken not to a jail or a hospital, but to the palace where Pilas, happy to have Captain Kong in custody, makes plans for her interrogation, trial, and subsequent execution.

Inside a makeshift recovery room, Jen is stripped of her outer garments, revealing her black EDF uniform underneath. The arresting senior sergeant who beat Jen senseless leaves, passing Captain Shanti Dae and Pilas coming in.

On his way out, he remarks. “We finally got that Kong bitch!”

Shanti feigns a congratulatory tone. “Good work! We don’t need traitors.”

He agrees as he walks away, pleased with himself. She watches him go, taking note of the limp he seems to have and wishing she could kick his ass right now, but instead she catches up to Pilas, acting as his personal bodyguard for the moment.

Jen, semiconscious, is strapped to the bed, fighting to wake up.

Pilas watches her eyes open and close and gloats, “Your timing is excellent, lieutenant. The fleet is only a little over a day away. Earth’s salvation will soon be granted.” He smiles as he bends over her face with a scanner in his hand. He holds it up to her eyes and turns it on. It flickers and buzzes despite his efforts to make it work by shaking it. He retreats to the window to recharge it with the sunlight coming into the room.

Shanti leans over Jen to talk to her friend. “Hey, are you with me, Jen? Why’d you come back? Is something going to happen?”

Woozy, Jen responds in a whisper. “Shoot me in the back of my head, hurry! Behind the ear, it’s the only place!” she says as she turns her head away from Shanti. “We can’t let him scan my mind.”

“I can’t do that! I can’t kill you!” Shanti whispers back with alarm.

Jen smiles. She is weakening but manages to speak. “Get xelon gas to Nealand…Groom Lake…stop Thimmi fleet,” Jen says, and passes out just as Pilas returns.

“What did she say to you?” he demands urgently.

Hesitating, and looking at the fully charged scanner in the alien’s hand, Shanti knows she has to come up with something. “She wanted me to kill her.”

“Why?”

She shrugs. “She passed out before telling me.”

Pilas looks down at his victim. *Why is it the beautiful ones are the most untrustworthy?* “Killing her like that would be a shame.” He pauses a moment before chuckling as he glances at Shanti. “I would like that pleasure.”

Shanti doesn’t react to his words or actions. She simply stands there, dumbfounded and more than a little frightened by what is about to happen.

Pilas puts the fully charged scanner to Jen's face, motioning Shanti to assist. "Hold her eyes open. The beam needs to make contact with the brain through the eyes in order to control her movements. It's too bad she's not awake for this."

Sure, you want her awake to feel the pain of the scanner ripping into her mind before you kill her. Shanti sees no choice but to comply with Pilas's orders, lest she suffer the same fate that is to befall her friend.

A tear rolls down her cheek as a thousand thoughts race through her mind. *I can't betray her, but I don't want to die. If I could save her by sacrificing myself, I would.* She waits for the questions to come, but Pilas doesn't ask any.

He smiles as she looks at him quizzically. "The questions are preprogrammed. It sends in the questions and retrieves the answers. I've had a long time to plan for this moment."

I bet you stayed up nights working on it. She doesn't say. With the scanner's beam controlling Jen's muscles, Shanti lets go and stands back, careful to hide the satchel carrying the canisters Jen was arrested with. *Xelon gas. Edward Nealand at Groom Lake…STOP THE THIMMS!*

***

Fifteen minutes later, Pilas is aware of Lightner's plans as well as his location. Shanti sees the results of the scan when he projects them on the wall. *No mention of EDF-1's involvement.* She lets out a sigh of relief that Pilas doesn't hear. He is busy contacting Major Blassi of EDF-2 to take Captain Kong to a special prison complex in Mexico City, where she will be held pending her execution for treason against the Thimmi Empire. He finishes giving orders by telling her to get to the Soliquid gun at Groom Lake and to guard it once Kong is secured.

Shanti waits for him to finish before asking, "If there's a secret weapon at Groom Lake, don't you want to destroy it?"

"Of course not. Any weapon under my control is useful."

Shanti nods in understanding as Pilas makes another call on his shackle, this one to Captain Folsom. "You will take EDF-1 to Novgorod, Russia, and arrest Lightner and his wife. Bring his kids back with you. No sense in allowing them to witness the deaths of their parents. We can't be so cruel, can we?" he says as if he plans to cheat at chess against a grand master.

Shanti hears Folsom as he responds in the affirmative. He had no idea where the Lightners were until now.

***

Once the team is assembled near the White House, Folsom relates Pilas's orders for them to obey. "We're going to pick up the Lightners in Russia and bring them back."

Shanti objects immediately. "So we're going to let Jen die?"

Furtado, not normally one to contradict the orders of his superiors, also objects. "Yes, we have to save her from EDF-2 before they take her to Mexico!"

Jafari simply nods to both of their points of contention, agreeing that rescuing the captain is the proper course of action.

Derrick opens the door of the Humvee and gestures his team inside. "I am in command here, people! I have my orders, and now you have yours. We will rescue the Lightners and proceed from there. The Thimmi fleet should be here by that time."

The others catch the word "rescue" and not "arrest" and smile in understanding.

The captain has a plan.

Alfonzo, seated at the shotgun position, waits for his captain to climb into the driver's seat before asking, "What of Jen?" He quickly corrects himself. "Er, Captain Kong?"

Folsom responds with a note of dismay. "I'm afraid she's going to have to handle herself for the time being. Pilas is going to be watching us very closely—at least until all of our shackles mysteriously malfunction the moment we get back to this side of the Atlantic."

Shanti smiles as she holds on for the rough ride to come. *Rough in more ways than one.*

CHAPTER FOUR: Meetings and Warnings

Colonel Edward Nealand speeds along a dry lake bed toward the Soliquid plant in the Nevada desert just after sunset, when it is safest. He is northbound from the Las Vegas dome on his antigravity motorcycle. As he gets close, he can make out the structure of the solar tower climbing a thousand feet into the air.

Long abandoned as the method of Lightner's plan to destroy the Earth's magnetic field, the plant is close to looking as dilapidated as a centuries-old ghost town.

At the entrance to the facility, Edward is glad to see that the gate is secure. *No one seems to have infiltrated the place.*

He uses a key to get into the open area leading to the main door, then pulls out a teleportation orb. This one resembles a large softball rather than a baseball. The main difference between this one and the old model is that this one works. He sets it on the ground and transmits an "all-clear" message to his friend, General Garov.

While waiting for his Russian counterpart to arrive, he relishes the silence of the night and the howling wind that is whipping around the tower and through the fence with a wildness that betrays the planet's feelings about its demise. *If planets could feel, that is.*

The orb opens a holographic door that Garov walks out of. The bright door closes behind him as he takes stock of everything he is carrying as well as his own body. He has teleported all over the Internet in this fashion approximately twenty times but still isn't very comfortable with the mode of transportation, given the death of Corporal Brandt in testing. "It works!"

Edward laughs. "You say that every time you come through. It's good to see you again, old friend," he says to the man sporting a laser rifle, a duffel bag, and a big smile. "You look like an old-time revolutionary."

"Am I dressed incorrectly? This is a revolution, is it not?" the newly promoted Russian Air Force officer, who is now a part of EDF-116, replies as he reaches into his duffel bag.

Garov hands over two four-foot crystal blocks from his bag. The blocks make up the final parts of the Soliquid gun located less than a hundred miles away at the Groom Lake Base. "This is the last of the pieces to the puzzle, Edward."

"It's a shame Captain Kong couldn't teleport the gas to us," Nealand states as he examines the hardware. "That's the last piece we should be concerned with."

Garov nods in agreement. "Indeed. She should rendezvous with you at Groom Lake." He checks his shackle for the time. "In fact, she should be there tonight. Not to worry, my friend. We have other guns around the world that have received their gas canisters."

Nealand thinks of the person over the mission for a moment before changing the subject. "And your teams?"

"My invasion force is ready when I give the command. The Thimms will be here soon, and I must return to Paris to organize my people."

Nealand shakes his friend's hand. "All the cities are equipped with teleport orbs, ready for you to use. Be careful."

Garov smiles as he steps back to activate the orb for his return trip to Paris and notes how quiet it is out here in the desert. "Such peace." His face changes to one of concern, his expression saying what both men feel in their hearts. *We've been through a lot, with an end in sight. This is it.* "I hope to see you again when this is over."

"You know where I'll be. The orb will be with me. Just don't forget to call first," Nealand says with a laugh.

"Yes. When the world is whole again, we will take in a baseball game," Garov says as his holographic door opens. He is gone in an instant, as quickly as he came, thanks to the Tel-Internet Transport System. *They're going to have to rethink the acronym on that one.* Nealand thinks as he enters the Soliquid plant and starts it up. It hums like a fat bee circling one's head. *Against orders, I should be waiting for the Lightners to arrive in Vegas so I can jail them.*

When finished and satisfied that the plant is functioning properly, he gets on his bike and follows the power ducts to the gun at the base. These ducts are separate from the tubes that process the energy and will carry the powerful Soliquid to the guns at Groom Lake. Unlike light itself, this energy, in liquid form, will take the better part of an hour to arrive. It will be a steady stream of power so long as the plant is operating.

The ride to the Soliquid gun is quick and uneventful. Nealand attaches the crystal blocks to the ends of the double-barreled weapon. It is within the blocks that the xelon canisters will be installed to magnify the energy output by a million times. *Everything is proceeding according to Lightner's plan. Where are you, Kong?*

***

In the Eastern European city of Novgorod, Russia, the Lightners are picked up, though their children are left behind with the surviving citizens of the city. Hopeful good-byes and hugs are shared. Folsom watches the family and feels their love for one another. He wonders for a brief second why he never settled down but shrugs off the feeling when his team is ready to leave. *They are my family. On to the next part of the mission.*

***

Meanwhile, at a prison in Mexico City, the southernmost domed city on the planet, Jen sits in her cell with only her guard outside the bars for company. He has been staring at her for an hour, waiting for her to complain about it. She doesn't speak to him, though ignoring his gaze is proving difficult. She tunes him out by staring at the devastation outside her window, beyond the dome's edge.

Another guard arrives, a heavyset slob who wouldn't know a napkin if it slapped his face. He is sweating profusely from the heat. *It's a shame that this one delivers the meals as about half of my dinner is missing from it*, she thinks as she turns to hear him speak with the first guard, who finally looks away to acknowledge his EDF-2 teammate.

"Mealtime ain't for another hour, Billy. I think she's about to crack," the first guard says.

"Take a break. Get lost," the heavyset guard says, not taking his eyes off the beautiful woman in the cell. Jen was only sweating from the heat until just a moment ago. Her prison garb sticks to her slim build. She shuffles the light clothing to give the big man less to imagine.

The young private gets off his stool to leave. Billy takes the keys from him. "Hey, come on, Billy. That's wrong," he says, not only knowing what the man is going to do, but that he has done it before.

"You can watch if you want," Billy says while wiping away the drool on his lips. The door opens. Jen waits for the private to go through the outer door to the empty cellblock before making a move.

SLAM!

She turns quickly and recognizes the man as the senior sergeant who tried to arrest her in Washington, DC, as he walks into the light of the cell's one bulb. "How are your nuts, sergeant?" she asks, disarming him with her confidence. *I took you down before, and I'll do it again.*

"You're going to make them feel a whole lot better."

"I know Major Blassi. She won't like this," Jen says as she rises from a sitting position.

He loosens his belt and gets closer to her. "You're worth a stripe."

Come on...a little closer.

She makes a move to attack, moving faster than Rickey Henderson breaking for second base. She gets to the sergeant before he can get his zipper all the way down and kicks him hard in the groin. He doubles over and retreats backward toward the cell door.

Behind him, a security drone zaps the young captain. She is immobilized. "N—!" She tries to speak, but the numbness in her legs and arms frightens her as it spreads throughout her body.

"You know what? I won't lose anything for doing a traitorous bitch like you," Billy gloats as he regains his composure. The impact to his balls has caused him pain but has not quelled his desire for her. *Bitch needs to be taught a lesson.*

The drone's beam is deactivated. He's got a few minutes to play. He acts quickly to get her pants off. He massages her thighs to arouse himself, his fingers probing between her legs.

Jen mentally prepares herself for the violation to come. She is unable to move, and wishes Shanti had had the courage to kill her when she had the chance. *Maybe he'll be finished before I get the feeling back in my body*, she thinks.

Another guard, also wearing an EDF uniform of the camouflage variety, appears at the cell door. Billy glances over his shoulder at him, "Fuck off, sergeant! Can't you see I'm in the middle of an interrogation?"

"I wouldn't do that if I were you," the sergeant says as he levels his Uzi at Billy.

Billy rolls Jen over onto her knees, using her marble slab to balance her. "Come back in five minutes."

"I don't think so," Jafari says, wanting to shoot Billy, since he is literally half the man's build and is getting nervous that his captain isn't in the block yet.

In the dim light, the EDF-2 senior sergeant makes out the young man's face. *He looks familiar, but is not part of our team.* "I said fuck off!"

When a taller, dark-skinned man in a captain's uniform enters the cellblock, Billy recognizes them as EDF-1 members. "Captain Folsom," he says.

"Sergeant, pull your pants up and get out of here." It's Folsom's Marine Corps discipline and training that is keeping the fat slob alive for the moment.

Billy reaches for the drone control pad in his back pocket but, fortunately for the others, it is difficult to reach.

Folsom pushes the man off Jen, and she slumps to the floor, having no control over her muscles yet. "We're taking this prisoner. Get into that other cell."

Overcome with lust, the sergeant finally gets the pad out of his pocket and laughs. The drone, floating high in the corner of the cell, turns to fire on the intruders. Jafari responds to its movement by shooting it down. Pieces of burnt metal fall harmlessly to the floor.

Shanti enters the cell and puts Billy down with a few well-placed chops, blocks, and kicks when he tries to attack.

She stopped short of breaking his neck; the fool should consider himself lucky, Jafari thinks as he and Folsom watch the expert fighter take care of business with a certain level of pride. *I'm glad she's on our side.*

Shanti, satisfied that Billy won't be getting up any time soon, tends to her friend. She helps her get her pants on as the feeling returns to Jen's limbs. Shanti voices her concern at what she feared was about to happen. "That was close."

Jafari tries to allay their feelings with a quip as he stares down at the beaten and sobbing barbarian. "By the looks of him, you wouldn't have felt anything anyway."

***

Minutes later, Jen is reunited with the Lightners in the Humvee. "Madeline, I hope Jake isn't troubled by any more bad visions," She says, deflecting the concerned looks Master Sergeant Furtado is giving her.

Madeline smiles and reassures the captain that the children are safe at a location even she does not know, in the event they are captured. "He's learning to accept what he sees. I think he understands what is happening to him."

She continues to explain as the others turn to listen. Derrick has already put the vehicle in motion for the return trip. “He had a vision of me dying in an explosion in space, but we dismissed that as impossible since there’s no place to live there.”

Jen, now wearing a camouflage uniform like the rest of the team, smiles at Furtado in silent thanks for bringing it. She turns to the doctor. “Sir, I’m sorry I couldn’t end my life before Pilas got the information from me about your location and plans.”

Before Charles can respond, she lowers her head in shame. “I’ve failed you.”

Charles gives a knowing grin, anticipating her reaction to what he is about to say. “Well, captain, I’m not sorry that you’re alive. You do realize that we’re both still under arrest.”

A moment of confusion passes over Kong’s face as she looks to Shanti for confirmation.

Shanti nods and winks as she gestures to the satchel on the floor of the vehicle. “We’re under orders to deliver you and the Lightners to Pilas aboard the Thimmi command ship that entered orbit this morning.”

Derrick, glancing over his shoulder from the driver’s seat, adds, “The xelon canisters go to Nealand first. He’s waiting at the Soliquid gun for them.”

Jen's confusion mounts. "I don't understand. Why deliver me to Pilas as a prisoner to be executed?"

Alfonzo hands her a laser rifle. "We're invading the ship. The doctor feels it would help to disable their defenses when the attack begins."

Jen sits sideways in her seat to regard them all as if they've simply lost their minds. "That's suicide."

Jen stares at Shanti, who has never looked so serious. "We're going to give them Lightner's ship, too. A going-away present," she says with a nervous laugh.

Jen leans forward to tell her superior, "Captain Folsom, I don't understand!"

Derrick chuckles and responds, "Well, if you had bothered to attend the briefing, you'd know what is going on around here."

OK, he's kidding around, but..."Will someone please fill me in?"

There is laughter among them. The Humvee speeds north at over 250 miles per hour. *At over eighteen hundred miles, the trip should take almost eight hours*, Jafari estimates. "I'm taking a nap," he says.

Folsom, glancing into the rearview mirror at Captain Kong, maintains his relaxed demeanor as he explains. “Your presentation to the Thimms is a ruse to gain their confidence and trust. At the moment the battle starts, we turn on them.”

Jen nods in understanding before asking, “Then why is Shanti so nervous?”

Shanti smiles and says, “I only hope that ship doesn’t have glass decks or big windows.”

Jen pauses before joining in the laughter with the team.

Her friends.

Folsom continues his explanation. “We have a coordinated ground attack planned as well to take control of our cities.”

Jafari wakes an hour later to Captain Folsom’s repetition of the mission and each team member’s role in it. “For the people of the Earth and those we love,” Folsom says.

Jafari knows his assignment: guard the ship. *Can’t get much more boring than that*. He and Shanti share a look that says, *we’ll get through this*.

Furtado expresses concern over what may go wrong by asking, “How do we get off the ship?”

Folsom responds after a glance at Dr. Lightner, who is holding Madeline's hand and smiling like a cat on a plush new sofa. *He's obviously not worried.* "We'll use the doctor's shuttle to escape, of course. Guarding it will be Sergeant Jafari's part of the operation."

I knew it, Behrouz thinks as he shakes his head in disbelief. "Again, me as the guard? I'll never see any action at this rate."

Furtado jabs Jafari's ribs from behind while saying humorously, "Try not to get knocked over the head by a woman this time."

Sergeant Jafari catches Madeline's apologetic glance in his direction and straightens up in his seat, his smile returning.

Folsom leans toward him from the driver's seat and whispers, "Your position is the most critical. Without you, we don't get off the ship. You will see action. Count on it."

In a fleeting moment of anticipation and fear, Behrouz reminds himself that he can wait for the action—*years*, in fact.

CHAPTER FIVE: What Must Be Done

The Thimmi command ship is like a beehive with all the worker bee fighters zipping around it, providing protection. The battle carrier doesn't operate close to the command ship, for safety's sake. It is in orbit on the opposite side of the planet.

The Earth humans have nuclear weapons that are very useful against the protective energy shields of the alien ships. It is fortunate for the Thimms, however, that the missiles used to deliver those weapons move very slowly and can therefore be shot down.

"Standard deployment" is the order of the day for the Thimmi fleet. "Take no enemy for granted" is Admiral Tolomak's motto. Though he is supposed to be running this mission as a rescue, he is ready for battle. He isn't worried so much about the Earthers attacking his ship as he is about any appearance of the Vorelisians. His mind is at relative ease now that scans of the area detect no Vorelisian ships and Pilas has reported that evacuation to the planet Jexx has been agreed upon.

Captain Pilas arrived on the behemoth command ship thirty minutes ago and has just walked onto the bridge. Designed similarly to the other Thimmi ships and even some Vorelisian ships (the designs were stolen from the Vorelisians), the bridge is a flat, wide deck with the commander in the center and all his officers in front of him. Tolomak is the type of leader who enjoys pacing behind his men's backs as they follow his orders. Right now, however, he is seated.

Upon hearing the sound of the hatch opening, the crew members turn to see Pilas wearing a strange-looking outfit. Some chuckle. The admiral is not as amused by the sight. "Are velvet robes the traditional Earth uniform, captain?" he asks.

Before he can answer, the ship's XO asks, "Are you their king?"

Pilas stands tall and proud as he responds to the critique of the crew. "I am their savior. This uniform is their way of showing me their appreciation and love."

The XO responds in a mocking of Pilas's voice. "Even though I wiped out billions of lives by disabling the magnetic field of the planet."

The crew reacts with laughter. The "Great Leader of Earth" may be the savior of the people on the surface of the dying planet below, but up here, among his own people, he is no more than a messenger and low-ranking fool.

Pilas continues in his defense. "I was only following the course of action I thought best given the circumstances of the moment! How many of you could have done as I have? I alone brought this world to its knees!"

The bridge goes silent when Tolomak stands. To the crew's surprise, the admiral commends Pilas's actions. "I would have preferred plan A over plan B, but the end goal of winning Jexx for the empire is achievable because of you. You have done well, captain."

Pilas straightens up with pride as the admiral continues, "You will inform the people of Earth of our inability to restore the magnetic field. Offer our sincerest apologies."

"Yes, Admiral."

"Tell them we will relocate them to a new world. We will save as many as we can."

And allow the Earth to die after the domed cities are blown to bits. Pilas knows the plan. He knows Tolomak very well too, having been in his service his entire career. "Well, sir, you see…" Pilas starts to explain the faction supporting the Vorelisian agent, Dr. Lightner, but stops himself. *He won't be here long enough to find out about the plans Lightner put forth to the people. It will not succeed in any case.* "Will I be allowed to retain control of this planet after the evacuation?"

The helm officer speaks up, spinning around in his seat upon hearing that ridiculous idea. "You want to stay here? The planet will be dead in another few years!"

Pilas and Tolomak ignore the comment as the admiral responds, after a few moments of thought, “Once we complete the evacuation, you may do with this world whatever you like. Perhaps Earth can be an expansion of our empire after we make it a member of the council.”

Pilas sulks, hoping not to become a governor under the heel of his superiors. “I could miraculously restore the magnetic field and lead them to prosperity as an independent world…sir.”

“Ahh, you want to retire with your pets, do you? Very well; your plans are not important to me. What I do care about is the location of the Vorelisian agent on this planet. Where is he?”

Pilas, anticipating the order, lifts his shackle to send a message to a nearby Earth satellite while answering the question put to him. “Sir, his name is Dr. Charles Lightner, and I have ordered that he and the Earth traitors be brought here immediately.” He begins the process of contacting Captain Folsom to check on their progress.

“Very well. What depth of knowledge does Lightner possess?”

“Superior, sir. I will know for certain once we have him aboard.” A return signal from Folsom indicates that the doctor will be on the way shortly. “He has an Earth woman for a wife.”

Tolomak shrugs. “After twenty years on this rock, that’s understandable. Carry on, Pilas.” The captain turns to leave as the admiral raises his voice to add, “Oh, and captain, if you plan to remain on my ship, I insist you wear a proper Thimmi uniform.”

Amid the continuing snickers and murmuring of the crew, Arno bows slightly out of respect for the admiral and leaves the bridge.

Pilas’s quarters are located two decks below the bridge. It’s a short and easy walk to where he will change into his green dress uniform. As he trots the decks, he thinks about how unworthy his people see him, while the people of Earth revere him as a god. *This mission is historic, and this planet is mine! No matter what Thimmi rags I wear today, tomorrow they will be burned in favor of my robes of Earthly power! I will make my world a force to be respected throughout the galaxy.*

***

At the outskirts of Las Vegas, in the early morning hours before the sun makes its presence known in the sky, Colonel Nealand and Captain Folsom are meeting each other on their respective motorcycles.

The two men dismount and stand face-to-face in the open desert on Highway 95. Nealand is the first to speak while his eyes scan the beautiful Indian. “How’s your little Zetan friend?” he asks.

Derrick laughs. “How much time you got?”

Edward takes the satchel containing the xelon gas from Derrick and responds, “About sixty seconds.”

“It’s been quiet. I think as long as I’m against the Thimms, it will stay that way.”

“Have you been checked out?”

“Dr. Lightner assures me he’ll have a Vorelisian doctor examine my head when they get here.”

Doesn’t he mean “if” they get here? Nealand wonders. “Which won’t be soon enough.”

“First we’ve got a battle to fight. Pilas wants us up there yesterday, and I don’t want to be any later.” Derrick says, eager to get his part of the mission started.

Edward nods in agreement. “We don’t want him to become suspicious. Why don’t we trade rides? Antigravity will get you back a lot faster.”

Derrick almost laughs, thinking of all the people—none—whom he has allowed to ride in the big seat. He knows Edward's words are true, but…"You promise to bring her back to me in one piece?"

Colonel Nealand mounts the Indian and starts it up with a satisfying roar. "I'll treat her like she's mine," he says as he passes a hand over the machine's fuel tank.

Derrick becomes nervous. "No, no, fuck that, you treat her like she's *mine*!"

"I promise she'll be fine." Nealand checks his shackle for the time and continues, "Garov is starting his invasion at seven-thirty. What time shall I attack?"

"Eight a.m.," Derrick responds distractedly, unable to take his eyes off his bike. *Easy, dammit*, he thinks to himself.

Nealand looks into his eyes with a big smile, as if reading the captain's thoughts. He puts on his helmet and rides off with a wave of his hand, almost as if saying, '*So long, sucker!*'

Folsom watches his baby ride off under someone else's control for the first time since he has owned her. *I wasn't the original owner, of course, so it's not like no one has ever ridden her before.* "It's just a machine," he mumbles unconvincingly to himself as the taillight fades into the darkness with the sound of her engine.

As Derrick mounts the antigravity bike, he feels it out for comfort and weight balance. *Good resistance ratio.* He sets the distance to the ground to low—about ten inches. The hum of the electromagnetic antigravity generator fluctuates with his shifting weight on the seat.

He goes easy on the thrusters and is up to seventy in ten seconds. He continues to accelerate, coming to quickly love the Harley, as his helmet shows the information ahead coupled with the smoothness of air beneath him. "I have got to get me one of these," he says to himself wryly.

By the time he passes Needles, California, he gets a feeling of restlessness when he sees Dr. Lightner's ship coming for him from ahead. *I feel different somehow.* Normally, before a battle, he gets a feeling of anticipation, and a little nervousness passes over him. This time, however, he's feeling excited, as if looking forward to killing the enemy. *That's not like me. Must be that voice in my head again.*

***

Colonel Nealand pulls up to the Groom Lake Base, which has long been evacuated and looks run down, like a ghost town before a powerful wind buries it in desert sand. He rides through the main gate, unopposed by anyone or any*thing*, and makes his way to the Soliquid gun structure that stands as tall as a prison guard tower.

Something else is there, he thinks as he peers through the blowing sand at something moving.

He stops and turns off the powerful bike's engine, welcoming the silence but for the howl of the wind and the crunching of the ground under his boots as he swings the satchel of xelon gas over his shoulder. Taking the crystal blocks off of the bike and carrying them carefully, he walks between hangars to the gun tower.

The last thing he expected to see and hear is an antigravity aircraft hovering near the weapon and a squad of troops meandering around it. The sun's light is beginning to illuminate the horizon with a purple glow. Glancing upward, the sky is clearing and he can make out some stars lingering: Arcturus and Sirius, in addition to the planets Saturn and Jupiter.

Many of the stars appear to be moving. *Fighters*. The sun glints off the metal of the Thimmi command ship, putting a lump in Nealand's throat. He takes a deep breath and walks briskly, with purpose, to the youngest-looking among the soldiers. *The least experienced are the easiest to manipulate*. He sees the patch on the boy's sleeve before addressing him. EDF-2. *Wow, this team really does move around a lot*. He thinks before demanding. "Who's in command here?"

The boy is a corporal, a two-striper with little experience in anything, yet he has seen much of the world in his three service years. He has not, until now, met anyone with more rank than his commander. "Yes, sir. Major Blassi is in the aircraft, sir."

As the other five team members approach, Edward blurts out for all to hear, "Of course he is! Do you people realize there's a pocket of radiation approaching this location?"

"He is a *she*, sir," the corporal corrects him reluctantly, not wanting to incur the colonel's anger for being a smart-ass. *Wait, what did the colonel say about radiation?*

The senior sergeant responsible for the arrest of the traitor, Jen Kong, saunters up to the colonel. He doesn't give a crap about rank. He doesn't think highly of officers who hide behind their stars, bars, and birds, either. The sight of the EDF colonel doesn't impress him, since he doesn't know who Nealand is. Of Samoan descent, he is a large man who speaks slowly in a deep voice. "Sir, Senior Sergeant Will Banks reporting. We are well protected, colonel. What is your business here?"

Edward takes Banks's measure, assesses what kind of man he is, and responds in a sarcastic tone. "I'm here to complete the operational readiness of the weapon. of course," he says as he gestures to the giant gun behind the big man.

The young corporal is gazing at the sky as if able to see the magnetic field, or the result of a lack of one.

One of the other troops has already contacted Major Blassi via shackle, and she is now approaching from the aircraft, having hopped off the plane's wing hatch with some assistance from the antigravity bubble beneath it. Her protective clothing conforms to her full figure as she walks toward them.

Attractive, Nealand thinks as he stares at her. *Except for the highlights in her hair that make her face appear to be on fire.*

She recognizes the colonel immediately. "Good morning, Colonel Nealand. This area is off-limits to everyone. By order of the Great Leader, I'm going to have to insist you leave now."

"And my orders are to ensure this weapon is ready for firing. The enemies of the Earth may arrive soon, and we must be ready."

Amanda observes the satchel and the crystal blocks the colonel is carrying. "I have no information about this. What is in the bag?"

"Xelon gas. A gift from our Thimmi friends," he says as he points upward. "You may contact them directly if you like."

There are at least seven troops surrounding them now. Half of them train their eyes on the hundreds of fireflies in the upper atmosphere. The command ship, by comparison, is about the size of a walnut, its white keel reflecting the sun.

Amanda is unimpressed. “I’m sorry. I have orders in hand. I must insist—”

Nealand is growing impatient. “Look, I don’t want the sun or the Great Leader to kill me, so I’ll just leave these things at the gun and go peacefully, all right?”

Amanda pauses, having second thoughts, wondering if she should get confirmation of her orders as well as his.

Nealand takes advantage of her moment of confusion to really mess with her mind. “In addition, of course, I’ll need to record your order for me to leave,” he says as he activates his shackle’s “record” mode.

“Why?”

He laughs nervously, “Well, I’m not taking the fall for your mistake, major.”

The corporal, becoming more nervous by the second, sees what is only a cloud in the distance that appears to be heading toward them. He panics. “There! The empty pocket of sky!” He runs to the aircraft for cover.

Senior Sergeant Banks rolls his eyes and follows him while reassuring his commander, “I’ll take care of this,” though in his mind, being out in the open is not the best of ideas.

The rest of the squad follows him, leaving the major and colonel alone. Nealand begins to pull the guns down to the ground. *Good balance.*

"Where's the rest of your team?" Amanda asks.

"Most are dead." He lets that sink in before continuing, "I commanded the teleportation unit. It's not an exact science. That's one of the reasons Pilas assigned me here." He talks while attaching the crystal blocks and xelon gas canisters to their respective places. The liquid light from the plant miles away drips onto the ground when he disconnects the main hose to attach the xelon canisters. It is not harmful to touch it, but not advised either. The area is lit up considerably, as if someone installed a searchlight in the ground and turned it on.

Amanda admires the beauty of the light while asking, "Why would Pilas want the gun manned? The Thimms are obviously here and in control. They're our allies."

Edward answers with a nervous chuckle. "The Vorelisians want this planet, too, you know. A more accurate statement would be that they want *us*."

She smiles as she watches him complete his work. "You were bullshitting about that pocket of radiation, weren't you?"

"Could be. Why don't you check atmospheric conditions while I finish up here?"

Amanda hesitates as she pulls her shemagh tighter around her neck. "Right."

Edward, proud of himself for controlling these troops so easily, finishes up his connections and raises the guns to the sky using the control panel. He brings the targeting system online. *All I need now is for time to speed up and for the sun to take its time*. He thinks of the old howitzers of World War II. The computer beeps as it locates small targets but doesn't lock onto them.

He peers into the console screen. *Not yet.* The command ship has moved out of range in its orbit. *I hope the Thimms cooperate. How will I explain using the guns on the Thimmi ships when Amanda returns?* He doesn't look forward to explaining what he is *really* doing. "Nothing is easy," he reminds himself quietly as he turns on the pumps that draw the Soliquid into the weapon with a satisfying hum.

The mixing with the gas is proceeding. I'm ready.

***

Inside the doctor's small egg-shaped shuttle that is now approaching the Thimmi command ship, Captain Shanti Dae rides in the back to "guard" the prisoners. A solitary drone floats above her head with an immobilizing beam emitter pointed at them, just waiting for a sudden move. Any excuse to fire.

Or so it is meant to appear, Shanti thinks as she tinkers with it by spinning it around and watching it move back into position each time. Its servomotors whine in protest as she laughs, as if annoyed by her actions. She stops when she sees the nervous looks of her teammates and realizes they're close. *The time is now.*

Lightner blames her erratic behavior at the moment on her fears. *She is trying to occupy herself to not have to deal with what she is really feeling: terror.*

Captain Kong approaches her friend with concern. "It bothers me that after all the time we've spent in this unit, together and apart, you still fear heights and flying."

"I've tried to put my mind on other things, but…" Shanti trails off, not wanting to embarrass herself.

"Behrouz?"

Shanti looks up at Jen, her eyes confirming her feelings before she looks away, coincidentally at him and back. "Wh-what gave you that idea?" Her nervous laugh speaks volumes.

Jen smiles. "Oh, socking the leader of the planet to the ground because you knew she hurt him. That was my *first* clue."

"Come on, that was a decade ago!"

"So your feelings have changed, then?" Jen smiles as she hears the humming of "Ride, Captain, Ride" coming from the front of the spaceship. *Furtado must be getting anxious for the fight to come*. She changes the subject. "I have to admit I'm becoming fond of that song."

Now it is Shanti's turn to smile knowingly. "Yeah, and the guy humming it."

The two friends laugh together for a moment but are silenced by the specter of reality intruding upon them in the form of a radio transmission from the Thimmi ship ahead. Looking out the main window, Jen sees the ominous vessel ahead as they close the distance. Structural details are becoming visible on its hull.

Cannons and tractor beam emitters are trained on the small ship. The gunners at their stations no doubt recognize a Vorelisian transport when they see one.

Great Leader Pilas's voice comes through the speakers. "Vorelisian shuttle, respond or be destroyed."

The console beeps a warning, a low, warbling tone that indicates that weapons are locked onto them. One shot is all the powerful guns would need. And *poof*.

Before Captain Folsom can find the appropriate sensor to wave his hand over, the shuttle lurches forward as if they just fell off the shortest of waterfalls. A tractor beam envelopes the ship, synchronizing the ships to move in unison relative to their positions above the Earth.

Behrouz attempts to add power, but Derrick stops him. "Don't fight them," he commands as he answers the communication. "Sir, this is Captain Folsom of EDF-One. My team and I are delivering the prisoners, per your orders."

There is a short pause.

The idiot Thimmi captain is probably jumping for joy, Folsom thinks.

Pilas responds, "Very good, captain. We are bringing you aboard. You don't need to do anything. Shut down all systems upon landing in the docking bay."

"Confirmed," Folsom says before closing the channel and turning to his crew. "This is it, people. Anyone who wants to bail out, there's the hatch."

Furtado checks his weapon, sliding the power pack into position to charge the laser. "You're kidding, right, captain?"

Not really, Derrick thinks. His stare says it all. “What time do you have?”

Furtado checks his shackle, wondering why his captain doesn’t just check his own, and answers. “Oh seven hundred, sir.”

Thirty minutes of peace remain.

CHAPTER SIX: The Battle for the Earth

General Garov, back at his headquarters in Paris, has spent the last half-decade of the magnetic field crisis forming an army of soldiers, an army that has been preparing for this day of liberation in great detail, from the construction and training in the use of advanced laser weaponry to the design of the patches on their EDF uniforms.

Teams 78 through 130 comprise fifty teams of one hundred soldiers, one team for each of Pilas's cities. Over five thousand troops in all are now waiting for the clock to move.

Garov pauses to remember the twenty men and women from around the world who have disappeared into nothingness in failed tests of the Internet Teleporter. *They will not be forgotten. It is because of their sacrifice that we are able to retake our planet*. He checks his shackle for the time. *Oh seven-thirty*.

The latest test was only a year ago, and the man who survived the experience has been racked with survivor's guilt ever since. Each subsequent test has succeeded with flying colors. *Then why do I feel apprehension over this operation?* Garov asks himself quietly. *Confidence! These troops will make it to their destinations—they have to!*

He gets on his shackle to the team commanders and breathes deeply before ordering them to go through the holographic doors connected by orbs placed in each domed city ahead of the operation. "This is it! Good luck, gentlemen, and Godspeed," he says in the universal language, English, which all the European and refugee American troops understand.

Political correctness be damned. I'm not a politician. He smiles as he leads his team into the orb-created holographic door leading to Washington, DC. *We need God now more than ever,* he laments.

***

On the bridge of the Thimmi command ship, Tolomak has ordered the 100 colony transports to the surface—two ships per domed city, as per Pilas's advice—which will provide plenty of room for the long sleep the people of Earth are going to go through on their way to Jexx. It is seven thousand, two hundred light-years to a star in the Carina constellation, where the planet is located. The trip would normally take many years at speeds exceeding that of light. Tolomak knows he is without reliable access to various wormholes that would shorten the trip to hours instead of years. He has a trick up his sleeve, however, that will get him there in a day with his newfound colonists.

Each transport is a half-mile long and can comfortably hold a half million people. They will be far short of the number of people

Pilas promised to save from the planet, but then, Earthers are used to disappointment.

The communications officer speaks in an alarmed tone from his station. "Sir, Transport C-751 reports they're under attack by Earth troops armed with laser rifles. The captain has sealed his ship and is preparing for retreat!"

Tolomak turns to Pilas, now standing next to him, and simply glares while thinking of the next step…the next order…the next *death.*

Pilas feels equal to his admiral in every way; right up to the moment that the comm officer's report is complete. He feels the eyes of his superior on him and shrinks inside.

Tolomak speaks before the fool can open his mouth in defense of the indefensible. "You informed us they were united under your leadership," he says calmly.

"Yes, sir. Officially, yes. This is just a small group not affiliated with—"

"The report on Earth by a Gightian survey stated that these people wouldn't have laser weapons for another fifty years." Suddenly, the calmness in Tolomak's voice is replaced by rage. "Explain yourself!"

Pilas notes that the admiral's anger is growing with each passing second and feels the need to flee. "Sir, the Gightian report is not accurate. I can attest to that. I have been with these people for over twenty years—I know them!" He points at the telemetry on the tactical screen showing troops coming through a holographic door—pouring in like water over Yosemite Falls in June. "This faction follows Lightner. They are no match for my troops. He has given them many technologies, but we are stronger. Lightner is in our docking bay right now, ready to surrender to you, sir!"

Tolomak listens to reports from other ships in space and on the surface. Security drones are being disabled with ease. He shakes his head. *This was supposed to be a simple operation.* "Order our fighters to assist the transports. Begin loading refugees when and where possible. Any commander who brings an empty colony ship into space will be executed!"

"Yes, sir," comes Commander Angenou Logus's quick and nervous reply. He has been through several battles under Tolomak's command as his executive officer but has never seen him this angry before.

Tolomak turns back to Pilas, who has backed up toward the exit hatch. "I am placing you under arrest, captain. The charge is treason, punishable by death." He motions for his guards to take custody of the man, once the Great Leader, who is now shaking like San Francisco in 1906.

"Sir!" Pilas pleads. "I will make it up to you, I swear! This is not my fault! It's Lightner! He orchestrated this attack, but it will fail!"

The guards have him through the hatch and out of earshot a moment later.

Tolomak's anger has not diminished, however. To the XO, he says, "Let me know if there are any more surprises. I will be in the docking bay to greet our prisoners."

"Yes, Admiral."

***

It's 0750. The gun is charged; the sky is clear. The other nine guns around the globe are ready to fire as well. The Thimmi command ship will be over Colonel Nealand's position in five minutes.

Attack time.

Major Blassi approaches from the aircraft. The sun is now just behind the mountains. "Shouldn't you take cover?" she asks. "The only ships out there are friendlies, but the sun is coming."

Nealand can see the giant Thimmi ship, in a slightly higher orbit than before, approaching slowly from the opposite horizon as the sun. It's about the size of a peanut now. He thinks fast. "Major Blassi, there is something you need to know. I am not under Pilas's orders."

She moves her right hand toward the weapon on her hip as her eyes widen with surprise. "You are part of the attempted coup that is happening in Washington right now, then?"

"In all of Pilas's domed cities in fact, yes."

She pulls her weapon just as he jumps off the Soliquid gun's platform to make a grab for it. The pistol falls away when he knocks her to the ground. She scrambles away from him and activates her shackle to call her troops for help.

He is frozen as he watches EDF-2 stream out of the aircraft like a bunch of baseball players leaving the dugout in celebration of a World Series victory. *Uh-oh.*

***

In the docking bay of the Thimmi command ship, Lightner's shuttle door opens. A short ramp extends to the feet of the admiral himself. Folsom is the first one out. The sight of Tolomak is impressive. His white dress uniform reminds Derrick of the uniforms worn by the US Navy in the old days. *The good old days*. Following him, under the guard of Shanti and Furtado, are the Lightners and Jen Kong. He scans the area, noting the smug pride of the two squads of Thimmi troops in their green uniforms and the weapons held to their chests. “Where is our leader, Captain Pilas?” he asks.

Tolomak doesn’t answer the question. He simply walks up to Dr. Lightner and holds a brain scanner to his eyes. Charles knows it is useless to resist and therefore offers none. The light from the scanner bores into his mind.

The pain is greater than he expected, given his past experience. “No!” the Vorelisian screams as Folsom backs away. The Zetan in his brain is focused on Tolomak, its enemy. Derrick restrains himself by concentrating on the squads and assesses his people’s ability to overpower them. *No chance*.

Tolomak asks only one question of the doctor. “What battle forces do you have in store for me, Vorelisian?”

The scanner records the answers.

The locations of all the Soliquid guns.

The number of troops invading the domed cities and their method of teleportation.

The deception of EDF-1; Captain Folsom's team is planning to disable the ship's defenses before the guns open up, powered by xelon gas.

The admiral stands back to read the information projected on the hull of the shuttle. There is concern in his eyes. *Pilas should have warned me of this.*

Folsom walks backward into the muzzle of a laser rifle belonging to a Thimmi soldier as the admiral approaches him.

"I commend you on your effort, captain. Your weapon, please."

Derrick speaks as he hands over his pistol. "We are not a united planet. We will not be allowed to have a vote in the Galactic Council. You will not get Jexx through us."

"Your lack of unity does not surprise me, captain. The point is moot in any case. We're rescuing you from your failed magnetic field, remember?" Tolomak says.

A revelation comes to the EDF captain. "You disabled the magnetic field to create this crisis!"

"To be precise, your Great Leader is responsible for that after our original plans fell through. You can discuss it with him in your adjoining cell. Take hi—" Tolomak freezes, seeing the green glow in

Folsom's eyes and recognizing what that means instantly. "Cover his eyes! He's under the influence of a Zetan being!"

Tolomak turns away as his soldiers grab Derrick. There is a short scuffle as the second squad moves in to take weapons from the rest of Derrick's team.

Madeline approaches Tolomak as a soldier grabs her by the arm. "I am First Premier Madeline Lightner. I demand to speak to you! We can have a peaceful resolution to this action before it gets further out of hand. There are rules of war that must be followed!"

Tolomak waves her away, dismissing her like an annoying fly, as he speaks in a low tone. "The rules we adhere to do not apply to Earth, first premier. You are not part of the Galactic Council and have no representation there."

She continues shouting for the safety of the people of the world and her children. Her voice fades as she is dragged away.

The admiral watches her go as the proud smirk returns to his face. He turns to an officer in a black flight suit and hands him the brain scanner. "Use the information on the scanner to find the guns the Earthers plan to use against us and arrange an attack."

The officer is the ship's flight leader. He takes the scanner and says with regret, "I have only one squadron available for attack duty, sir. We didn't expect resistance."

"One is all you will need. This planet is no match for us."

"Yes, sir."

Confident in his actions, the admiral contacts the bridge to give his destroyers something to do. "XO, have our escorts target Earth's satellites. They're being used to teleport troops around the planet."

The answer comes without hesitation. "Yes, admiral."

***

The command ship moves to a lower orbit to remain near its escorts as they open fire on the defenseless orbiting machines, destroying them one by one. The gunners in all the vessels involved revel in the attack.

With their attention on locating, targeting, and destroying each satellite quickly and efficiently, none of the destroyers or those on the command ship notice the Vorelisian fleet now coming through Earth's wormhole behind them.

***

The EDF-1 team and the Lightners enter their cell and find that the occupant of the cell next to them is Captain Pilas, who is sitting on a metal block with his head in his hands. *Crying?* Not yet.

The partitions between the cells consist of plastic-like transparent sheets with holes for easy communication and airflow. Though not the traditional iron bars as found on Earth, these are just as firm.

Jen is the first to acknowledge the Great Leader's presence. "How the mighty have fallen," she says with genuine disgust in her voice.

The other team members chuckle for a moment. The Lightners remain silent as they sit on a metal block on their side of the partition and stare at the Thimmi captain.

Pilas looks up at the assembled gang of tormentors, feeling as though he deserves every insult they could possibly throw at him. He stands to address Madeline, whom he recognizes as the rightfully elected first premier of Earth. He approaches the plastic wall, thinking of a deal that might save his life. "Sena—first premier, if you get me out of this, I will rejuvenate the magnetic field and surrender myself to your rule of law. Your judgment will be final."

Folsom removes his blindfold, given to him by the guards to protect them from the Zetan behind the Earth captain's eyes, and approaches Pilas. "Your actions demand death, *captain*!"

The two men stare eye to eye for a moment. An idea forms in Derrick's mind that is not his. A voice assures him that everything will be okay.

Pilas agrees with Derrick's comment with a nod. "Indeed. I am ready for death at your hand, captain. I would rather die on your planet than live through what awaits me when I get back to Ti. My people see me as a traitor because I underestimated Lightner's followers."

Furtado snorts. "Imagine that!"

In an instant, the soft green glow in Folsom's eyes flashes to those of Pilas. He stumbles backward, his mind now "infected" with the Zetan entity named Rishal. "What have you done?" Pilas shouts.

Unlike the friendly addition to Folsom's mind, a mind powerful enough to resist manipulation to any great extent, the Zetan invades Pilas's mind, taking complete control. Derrick smiles at the Zetan's plan and at the relief he feels at having his mind back completely. "Our good Thimmi captain is going to get us out of here. Aren't you, *Great Leader?*"

"Yes," Pilas responds. His expression is blank, devoid of emotion.

***

The fighters swoop over the locations of the Soliquid guns around the planet and destroy them one by one. The squadron leader guides his pilots over California and into Nevada, intent on destroying the last of Earth's defenses when the executive officer contacts him. The XO's voice is full of urgency and concern. "Return at once. We are under attack by Vorelisian forces."

Alarmed, the pilot orders his wingmen to return to space and defend the fleet. "I will take care of this target," he says. They obey immediately.

Passing over the small mountains surrounding Groom Lake Base, he sees a target: not the gun, at first, but an antigravity aircraft hovering near it. Assuming it is military and without time to consult his sensors, he moves in for the kill. *The sky is mine, little people.* He waits a second for the weapons to lock onto the target. A satisfying tone confirms the lock, and he fires several bursts of energy at the aircraft.

BOOM!

***

Colonel Nealand and EDF-2 are behind the gun when the explosion occurs. He is on his knees, in handcuffs, with the entire squad surrounding him—the entire squad, save the pilot of their transport. "You see that fighter, major? That is a Thimmi fighter that just attacked us, and he's coming back around! Do you still believe they're our friends?" Nealand says.

The Thimmi fighter makes a strafing run, spitting fire at the team and killing three of the ten before Amanda curses the pilot in her heart. She sees a row of boulders the size of buses nearby and shouts at her people, "Get to cover!" while removing Nealand's handcuffs. "Colonel, I'm sorry I doubted you. We'll keep him busy; you blast his ass out of the sky!" she says.

He salutes and heads for the platform as Amanda runs for the nearest boulder, where her team is aiming their primitive but useful laser rifles at the incoming alien fighter.

Distracted by the shots that barely register against his shields, the Thimmi squadron leader misses in his second pass over the target area. "Damn!" he says as he checks his systems for damage. *They may as well be throwing rocks*. He laughs as he circles back.

Moving fast but unaffected by g-forces, he is able to maneuver his fighter in a serpentine manner. Moving in a zigzag motion toward the target, he lines up the shot from five miles out and sees a bright light from the mighty weapon ahead.

Two miles out and closing rapidly.

He ignores the warnings of his cockpit sensors telling him of the power level building in the target. He is confident that his shields will protect him long enough to get off a shot.

He is wrong.

Colonel Nealand fires the first shot of the Soliquid gun to the right of the incoming Thimmi fighter. He moves the steady beam of energy to the left until the fighter zigzags right into it. The beam is in contact with the fighter for one second before the pilot is able to turn away.

It crashes in flames beyond a nearby hill.

Major Blassi returns to the gun with her men to check on the colonel. "Are you OK?"

Nealand looks down from the platform and smiles. "Fine! You better get your people out of here. That attack won't be the last!"

The major smiles up at the colonel. "Nice shooting. We'll check for survivors of the crash."

He nods as she ushers her troops toward the hill, where smoke is billowing. He is concerned for their and his safety with the sun rising. *You only live once, and you live for a purpose.* He looks up at the silver-colored, walnut-sized spaceship coming into view again. “Here comes earthly retribution, fellas!” Edward shouts, smiling as he points the gun skyward.

***

The battle is joined in space between the Thimmi and Vorelisian fighters. The Thimms rising from Earth’s atmosphere are at a disadvantage because they have to expend energy to escape Earth’s gravity instead of using that energy for defense, as the Vorelisians are doing.

The Thimmi squadron assigned to protect the colony ships at the domed cities has been recalled to defend the fleet in orbit, thereby allowing the battles in those cities to swing toward General Garov’s troops.

Tolomak launches the remainder of his fighters. Five fresh squadrons of ten fighters each engage the Vorelisians in a matter of minutes.

***

The squad of soldiers responsible for the security of the Earth prisoners as well as their own Captain Pilas leads them all into the medical bay for brain scan, as per Tolomak’s orders. The two women under his command, followed by his men and the Lightners, flank the blindfolded Captain Folsom.

"I think your people are here," Madeline whispers into her husband's ear as she peers out a porthole at a small fighter she doesn't recognize. Her suspicions are confirmed when the Thimmi command ship fires at it. It zips away, unharmed.

Charles smiles in response. "Yes. Let's hope we get off this ship before they overwhelm its defenses and kill us."

Madeline's excitement fades quickly. She hadn't considered the fact that they're all expendable as long as the mission succeeds. "Oh God. If I die, then Dobson will be in charge."

The sergeant in charge of the squad orders them to be quiet as he removes Derrick's blindfold and warns, "Look at me and I'll kill you."

Derrick, maintaining the illusion, closes his eyes. "You don't have to worry about me," he says truthfully.

"We'll scan your brain last. First we're going to kill that Zetan parasite in your head."

Pilas interrupts to plead his case. "Sergeant, I have valuable information that may help us in this battle. I need to speak to Admiral Tolomak immediately!"

Rishal is in full control of Pilas's actions and dialogue. Pilas's mind fights futilely against the Zetan life form.

The sergeant walks up to Pilas and gets in his face. "What we need to know, traitor, we will extract before we kill you, I promise!"

The green flash of light between Pilas's eyes and the sergeant's is instant but visible, though not to his guards, who are not watching for such an event.

Rishal is becoming so good at this that the helpless man has no way to alert his men before his right arm lifts the laser rifle off his shoulder and shoots them dead before they can react.

"Oh my God!" Madeline shouts as she storms right up to the warm barrel of the rifle to complain to Rishal inside the Thimmi sergeant. "Was that really necessary?"

Rishal, in full control of the sergeant's actions, hands the rifle over to her and grabs Folsom. In another flash of emerald light, he is back inside the Earth captain's brain. The sergeant collapses to the deck, unconscious.

Derrick falls to a knee and allows the tears to fall. After a moment, he stands again. "Madam First Premier, I can't communicate with Rishal when I am awake, but he is feeling deep regret right now."

Madeline relaxes a bit now that the weapon is not under Rishal's control, knowing how much he hates the Thimms. "I understand."

Furtado quips, “His apology would’ve meant more to us if he stayed in the sergeant and said it.”

Derrick is in control but warns his team, “I will not handle a weapon for the remainder of this mission, is that clear?”

Everyone nods in compliance, knowing that he intends to allow himself to be killed rather than risk Rishal gaining further control of him. Jen is the only one to respond, “Yes, sir.”

Lightner sees an opportunity to communicate with the Zetan life form. He grabs Derrick by his shoulders to be eye to eye with him and raises his voice. “Rishal, your desire for revenge against the Thimms is pointless! The war between the Thimms and the Zetans ended a decade ago! The fact that some rogue pilot captured and used you to navigate his ship is irrelevant. We *need* the captain. Please do not interfere!”

Derrick pushes the doctor back. “He can hear you, doc. You don’t have to shout in my face.”

Derrick’s eyes go wide as if something is happening to him that he did not expect. He speaks again in a higher pitch, denoting that the words coming forth are not his. “I need to free the slaves in control of this ship before your people destroy it!”

"There are no slaves, I promise you! I don't have time to prove it to you now, but I will when this is over. Please believe me," Lightner says, more calmly this time.

Folsom's high voice continues, "I believe you. Nevertheless, I would ask to be taken before the Galactic Council to offer testimony and return to my people."

Madeline, as leader of the planet Earth, steps in to offer her own assurances. "We will arrange it, Rishal. First we have to get out of here."

Derrick, feeling relaxed and refreshed, as if a migraine had suddenly disappeared and been replaced with a feeling of euphoria, smiles. "Let's go."

In the moment of distraction caused by the Zetan, Pilas bolts from the exam room and into the corridor too fast for anyone to stop him.

Furtado, feeling responsible, as he was the closest to the captain, picks up a dead soldier's laser rifle. "Dammit!"

Shanti asks, "So are we going to sabotage the ship or escape?"

The ship rocks violently from the blast of the Soliquid gun fired from the surface of the Earth. Shanti speaks the thought racing through her head. "Never mind."

The EDF-1 team and party exit the medical bay carefully, following their previous path back to the shuttle. Klaxons blare, assaulting their ears. What few crewmen there are in the corridors have survival on their minds and pay them no attention.

CHAPTER SEVEN: Winners and Losers

On the bridge of the Thimmi command ship, Admiral Tolomak is watching his crew follow his orders. The tactical officer has completed targeting all of Earth's domed cities. The admiral turns to his communications officer with a smile just before another burst of energy rocks his mighty ship. *No time to waste.* "Contact my good friend Xaix. Tell him that I will destroy all the protected cities of Earth if he does not withdraw immediately." *If we cannot persuade the people here, the Vorelisians certainly will not.*

"Yes, sir," is the quick reply as Pilas squeezes through the main hatch before it is completely open. He jumps into the center circle where Tolomak and his executive officer are, weapon in hand and breathing heavily.

Logus is a tall man and a loyal one. He gets between the captain and his admiral quickly while regarding the weapon. "What is this, Pilas?"

Pilas, trying to see past the large XO, lowers the laser rifle and reports, "Admiral! The prisoners have freed themselves. Allow me to lead a squad to recapture them!"

Logus, his voice commanding and firm, steps toward the panting captain and asks in a whisper, holding back his irritation, "How did they escape?"

Not wanting to admit that he was used by Folsom's Zetan intruder, Pilas hands the rifle to Logus and jumps to the side to lie, "I am not sure, sir. The Zetan somehow got into the squad leader's mind and killed the squad."

The admiral is neither amused nor impressed with this fool. "Why is a doomed man so willing to assist me? If you were smart, you would steal an escape pod and run to the Vorelisians, begging for mercy."

The bridge crew laughs at the insult to Pilas's bravery. He continues, trying to prove himself worthy of a second chance. "I wish to redeem myself to you, sir. You have but to command me, and I will take my own life." He says the words quite convincingly while hoping beyond hope that the admiral doesn't take him up on it.

Logus, meanwhile, is studying the weapon. *Fully charged, that figures. Pilas didn't fight the escaping Earthers, he simply ran.*

Tolomak, however, buys the sales pitch and relents. "Very well. Recapture the prisoners, and I will reinstate your rank and position as leader of the Earth."

Arno is overjoyed, though he fights to conceal it. "I won't let you down, sir."

Logus assigns a squad to the captain and hands his rifle back. One squad is all they can spare as the soldiers join the maintenance crews in managing battle and damage control.

The point is driven home by another barrage of laser fire from the Vorelisians and the Soliquid gun on Earth.

The shields are weakening.

Tolomak's attention is distracted by the beam of light emanating from the Soliquid gun on Earth that strikes the battle carrier hovering over the Arctic Circle. He witnesses the mighty carrier listing toward the planet. From this distance, it is not immediately apparent that it is falling. After a few seconds, it becomes obvious. "Tell them to abandon ship!"

The communications officer tries contacting the vessel while the officer at the sensors delivers somber news. "Their comm is down, sir."

"No! This is not possible. I want that weapon destroyed at once!" Tolomak commands.

The crew moves to comply. The destroyers are flanking the command ship to protect it. The fighters are defending against the Vorelisian fighters.

Escape pods are being jettisoned from the carrier as it falls.

Logus pauses to reflect on the thousands of people on the carrier who will burn up along with their ship as it continues downward.

A moment wasted.

***

Colonel Nealand, putting his own safety aside, waits in the sunlight for the Soliquid gun to recharge. *I only have a few shots left*. He aims at the command ship. *It's farther away than the carrier was, but still in my sights*. His computer-assisted targeting system allows him to zoom-in on the target. *30% Charge*.

He watches and waits, though he's getting impatient. Then he sees a puff of light and what looks like a missile exit the big Thimmi ship. *Uh-oh.*

He fires the weak charge that probably won't amount to much and jumps off the platform and onto Folsom's motorcycle. He starts it up quickly and speeds away, using every ounce of power the bike can deliver to get as much distance as possible from the gun.

He is a mile and a half away when he hears, then feels, the missile detonate behind him, destroying the Soliquid gun in a mighty explosion. The shockwave from the blast throws him off the bike at a hundred miles per hour. He and the Indian slide along the desert floor and come to a stop against a mountain of sand. Barely conscious, he witnesses small figures dressed in black coming over the hill to assist him. His shackle is beeping wildly, as if detecting each broken bone, each scrape. It is trying to notify the MAA, but its satellite is no longer in space.

Just prior to passing out, Edward looks up to see the battle carrier burning up in the atmosphere and estimates its remains will crash near Great Basin National Park, a few hundred miles away.

***

With the exodus of the Thimmi fighters that sped off to defend Tolomak's command ship, General Garov and his team of nine men and women are making headway against the token defense of the Thimms at their colony ship just outside the dome in Washington, DC.

At the main hatch of the giant transport ship, Garov leads the charge himself. "Attack!" he shouts before laying into the enemy with his laser rifle on full auto. The shots come faster in this mode, but are weaker. The strategy is to distract them while the rest of the team gets in close for a kill shot.

As they make their way up the main ramp and into the ship, the first thing Garov notices are Thimmi personnel, dressed like medical orderlies, acting as caretakers of the Earthers they are helping into the stasis chambers. They are preparing the people for the long sleep to come. There are hundreds being loaded on the opposite side of the ship. *Not even a battle keeps these aliens from their duties.*

Continuing into the ship, Garov and his team meet little resistance as they arrive at the bridge, where Captain Kon Dirn is barking orders nervously. “Find them! Where are they?” he shouts.

The XO shakes his head, unable to answer that question.

Frustrated, Dirn throws up his hands and continues shouting. “Close the ramps! Get us off the ground. We’re leaving for Jexx immediately.”

The helmsman objects, “Tolomak will be angry if we leave now.”

Garov interrupts. “I won’t be very happy either. I like this planet.”

The captain surrenders without argument.

The engines are powered down.

Success!

Garov gets into the captain’s chair. It will take some time to free the Earthers, who will no doubt wonder what is happening.

Some will resist having to stay on this planet. Garov contemplates what to tell them when they are freed from their stasis chambers.

For the people still streaming into the ship, Alexei gets on the intercom to inform them of the most important news of the century. “Citizens, this is General Garov of Earth Defense Force Team Seventy-Three. You must be made aware that the Thimmi Empire’s plans are being halted. The Vorelisians are here to help us. Please remain calm. There is nothing to fear. Please return to the safety of the Washington dome immediately.”

Suddenly, there is an earsplitting noise, as if every piece of china were dropped from an airplane at once and allowed to crash simultaneously onto solid rock. People who are in the process of leaving the transport quickly turn back, having witnessed the indestructible dome that covers the city of Washington, DC, shatter like cheap glass and crash onto the streets below.

Garov, stopped by the flash of light immediatcly preceding the crash of the dome, continues speaking to the people. “Remain in the ship until we have assessed what is happening.”

Captain Dirn, while being handcuffed by one of Garov’s soldiers, says with a smug attitude, “Your planet is going to die. That is what is happening. This battle is not over!”

The Thimmi captain is taken out the hatch as Garov turns to look at the great city through the ship's view screen. *We've overcome worse odds. Good thing the city was evacuated. If only we had satellite communication, I would know how the other teams are faring.*

What Garov doesn't know is both good and bad. His fifty-two teams were only somewhat successful in capturing the colony transports. Some were destroyed under self-destruct orders; a few got away into space and are on their way to Jexx.

The final count of those who escaped may not be known for some time.

***

On the bridge of the Vorelisian battle carrier, First Colonel Xaix considers the options available to him as Executive Lieutenant Len Quell approaches with a report.

"True to his word, Admiral Tolomak has destroyed the dome over Earth's capital city, sir," Quell reports.

Xaix looks at the various tactical screens around him, watching his forces retreat to his position near the wormhole. *So close. We can all go home right now and leave these Earth people to becomes slaves to the Thimmi Empire, or do something foolish and try to save them.* In his heart, he doesn't even consider the implications of obtaining Jexx for the Vorelisian government. *Lives are at stake*.

The choice is easy.

"Have First Captain Cammos ready his assault force. They will launch at a moment's notice," he orders.

Confused, Quell says, "But, sir, we can't board the Thimmi command ship with their shields up. They must be disabled first…"

On the main screen, Tolomak's forces are lining themselves up in front of his command ship like an offensive line protecting the quarterback.

Coward. Xaix chuckles quietly as he explains to his exec, "We wait for a break. By now, I'm sure the admiral has taken my friend prisoner."

Quell nods in agreement. "That sounds like something he would do; stop the Vorelisian influence on the planet. But wouldn't he use Lightner as a bargaining chip to force us to retreat into the wormhole?"

Xaix looks up at Quell from his command chair with a shit-eating grin on his face. "That's why we're launching Cammos's assault force."

Quell has served with this man for years and has yet to completely understand his methods. He sounds out what he thinks is the plan. “We’re hoping for an opening in their defenses by Lightner, who is most likely locked up in that ship.”

Turning back to the tactical screens mounted above the helm and at his feet, Xaix’s expression becomes stoic. “I’m not hoping for it. I’m counting on it.”

***

Master Sergeant Furtado is on point, leading the group of Earthers back to the docking bay. Dr. Lightner is right behind him, so close, in fact, that Madeline keeps pulling him back. “Charlie, stay with me!”

He smiles at her as he speaks to Captain Folsom, who is walking next to Madeline to protect her, wishing *she* was moving at a slower pace. “Captain, do you hear that?”

Derrick calls the group to a halt to listen to what the good doctor is talking about.

There are no sounds of footsteps. No laser fire hitting the ship. It’s as if the whole crew went to sleep when, in fact, they are anxiously waiting for something to happen. Right at this moment, though, there is no *battle*.

"The fighting has stopped," Folsom says.

"Impossible!" Madeline objects forcefully but quietly. "Your people wouldn't give up so easily, would they? We're still here!"

Shanti, behind her captain with Jen, speaks out of turn, but voices what they are all secretly thinking. "Did we lose?"

***

Captain Pilas turns a corner in the corridor ahead of the Earth group, leading his seven troops behind him. He spots the Earthers and Lightner standing there—*just waiting to be killed.*

"There they are! Fire!" he commands.

His squad fills the corridor, exposed but with the element of surprise.

Master Sergeant Furtado takes the first shot in the chest and goes down to his knees. He cannot return fire, though he fights to remain still in order to cover his friends behind him. He manages to protect the team and the Lightners long enough for them to get to cover safely by using his body as a shield that takes shot after shot.

Jen, whose priority is also protecting the team, has gotten them all around the corner and into a small room. It is fortunate for her that the lights are off, lest they see her face wrought with sadness and despair at the loss of a good teammate, a friend…a *love*.

Lightner listens for Pilas's team that passes by, not checking the locked door. After a moment of silence, he turns the lights on. "They'll start checking all the rooms on this deck once they realize we're still on it."

Jen, clutching her weapon and itching for revenge, stutters in her speech. "W-what now?"

Shanti observes her friend. Jen is not afraid of combat; she is pissed beyond consolation. "We have to get Alfonzo."

Folsom raises his hand to get their attention and prevent rash decisions. "The plan is the same. We have to get off this ship." His tone changes, reflecting the opinion of the Zetan in his head. "He died for us. We must then live for him."

Madeline, in her concern for the captain, wonders if Rishal is somehow gaining more control over him.

During the discussion, Dr. Lightner has found an exit in the form of a ladder leading to the deck below.

Captain Pilas and his men have also arrived at the door.

BLAST! ZZZT! The door is being fired upon and is slowly melting. In a few seconds they'll gain entry. The Earthers escape to the deck below.

Getting back into the corridor and to the portholes, Madeline looks out at the planet Earth and the line of large dots above it representing the Vorelisian fleet. Her view changes as the command ship turns. “What is happening? Are we leaving?”

Lightner dismisses the idea. “The Earth is hostage right now. Tolomak won’t give up his position until Xaix retreats.”

Jen and Shanti become tense at the sound of footsteps. Pilas is not as dumb as they gave him credit for, it seems.

Behrouz, silent up to now, trying to come to grips with the death of his friend but also bent on self-preservation, approaches Derrick with news of a discovery. “Sir, the room over here is loaded with electronics. Could be a radio room. Maybe we can call for help.”

In another context, that last statement would be laughable, Jen considers as she shakes her head.

Lightner steps in. “I wouldn’t count on help at the moment, but we should make my friend Xaix aware of our situation.”

Charles pulls Derrick toward the room in question. “It’s worth a shot!”

Jen’s objections go unheard. She wants to fight to avenge Alfonzo’s death, not continue running and hiding.

Inside the room with the door locked behind them, they realize that Behrouz's report was an understatement. Inside the expansive room is enough electronic equipment to open a Radio Shack store. The parts and devices are not radios, however, nor can they be made into radios.

Charles recognizes some of the devices as explosive triggers. They are used in sabotage, and each contains a small amount of powder that can be set off using a special frequency, similar to radio-controlled detonators. As a safety factor, they are not put directly into bombs. The powder in question is referred to as PE-110. Each trigger contains enough of the explosive to burn one's hand.

Charles opens one and takes out a teaspoon of the powder. He finds a small box about the size of a paperback novel and puts the powder in it. "Help me get these devices emptied. Put the powder in the box. Quickly!"

Madeline starts opening triggers and taking out the powder without question.

Shanti, however, does have a question. "What are we doing?"

Charles smiles at her as he works. "We're making a small but powerful bomb."

Jen, Derrick, and Behrouz like the sound of that. They tear into the devices as if their lives depended on it. The team works quickly, getting the box filled and sealed in five minutes.

Charles looks up the frequency required to set off the PE-110 on a nearby computer. “Four thousand, one hundred and ten quertz,” he mumbles. “Excellent.”

Derrick queries as he watches the doctor attach the detonator to the box with tape. “OK, so we have a bomb. How are we going to use it?”

Lightner stops working, giving thought to his role on Earth, to his wife and family. He decides in the here and now that his place is in the battle. He knows Thimmi ship designs and where to place the bomb for maximum effect. “I am going to the engineering section to blow up the main engine,” he says. “I’m sure my friend Xaix out there is watching and will attack once the ship is devoid of main power.”

Folsom smiles and shakes his head slowly. “Doctor, you’re too valuable to risk. I can’t allow it.”

Behrouz steps forward. “I’ll do it!”

“NO!” Shanti objects, then quickly tries to conceal her feelings. “I mean, I’ll go with him, sir.”

Madeline, as if making her own opinion heard loud and clear, grabs the bomb from her husband and hands it to Behrouz. “Good luck, sergeant,” she says as she listens to the sound of Pilas’s troops returning to the area. Their boots are reverberating on the metal deck somewhere in the corridor—but close.

Folsom reluctantly agrees. *You wanted action, kid. This is it.* “Very well. But make sure you get to the docking bay as quickly as possible after you plant it. We’ll set it off from there.” He turns to the doctor. “You can set it off from your ship, right?”

“Yes,” is his short and simple answer.

At the door, Jen darts into the corridor. Seeing no one, she motions for the others to follow her. They split up. The Lightners, under the protection of Folsom and Kong, run off into the heart of the ship, intending to draw Pilas and his men away from Jafari and Dae.

Right now, the success or failure of the battle rests with the Vorelisians and the EDF team’s ability to improve the odds by disabling this giant ship.

Behrouz leads Shanti toward the rear of the ship, walking through an outer corridor with a full view of the battle outside, which remains in a lull. *Weird*, he thinks, *how all the destroyers, capital ships, transports, and fighters can just sit across from their counterparts without firing a shot.* It's an eerie sight.

***

A colony transport leaves Earth. Upon reaching space, it is intercepted by a Vorelisian fighter. The pilot, acting on his own, tries to force the transport toward the Vorelisian fleet. When a missile leaves the command ship, he retreats, allowing the transport to continue into space.

The city of Chicago is destroyed.

***

Assuming that the standoff will probably last for hours, Tolomak decides to assign more squads to search for and kill the Earth intruders on his ship. "And have them kill Pilas while they're at it," he commands.

Logus agrees with the command as well as Tolomak's opinion of Earth's Great Leader, whom he assigned to this planet in the first place. "Yes, sir. Right away."

***

A short time later, one of Tolomak's squads has come upon Behrouz and Shanti as they are entering the engineering wing. The Earthers manage to evade them and reach the engine room.

Unsure of where to place the bomb in such a large, cavernous place that resembles a blimp hangar, the sergeant laments, “We should’ve brought the doctor with us.”

At the opposite side of the room, there are many generators that complement the main engines. There are also controls on that side of the room manned by personnel in chairs and on their feet. A fire maintenance crew is standing by in the event of another attack. Behrouz and Shanti make their way closer, using ducts, columns, and boxes for cover. *They have no idea we’re here.*

Shanti smiles at their good fortune, until the squad looking for them returns. An additional squad joins them on the floor and above, on the catwalks lining the walls of the cavernous space. *Twenty troops in all, how the hell are we supposed to—.* Shanti doesn’t finish the unspoken question, as her thoughts are interrupted by a voice from above.

“YOU TWO, HALT!”

Behrouz, acting on impulse as well as instinct, flashes back to his childhood days in Teheran when the police would come after him and his friends. He watches Shanti expertly pick off the catwalk soldiers one by one before he throws the box toward the squad near the generators as if it is a fat, square rock.

Not knowing what the object is at first, the squad runs for cover.

"What the fuck did you do that for?" Shanti screams while finishing off the last of the catwalkers. She levels her weapon at the new threat straight ahead.

"You shoot them! I'll shoot the bomb!" Behrouz says.

The troops, also using objects for cover, are slowly advancing.

"We don't know if an energy weapon can set it off!" Shanti shouts above the din of laser shots.

Behrouz stops. *It's always worked in the movies. It makes sense for it to work now.* "I got this!" He fires and misses.

Shanti picks off another soldier.

Behrouz misses again.

The Thimms are getting closer. Pretty soon, they'll be on top of the Earthers. Shanti takes control. "Retreat to the wall!"

They move together, laying down suppressing fire to cover their retreat. At the entrance from where they came, they stop behind a column.

Behrouz can barely see the target now. "I—"

Before he can finish, Shanti takes aim and fires a shot at the box that, from this distance, is the size of a penny. Her first shot misses. She fires four more in quick succession while screaming, "Come on!"

BOOM!

The deck beneath their feet drops away. Enemy bodies fly.

Jafari falls with the Thimms at first, but manages to grab onto a broken conduit. Shanti, her back stuck to the wall, is relieved that he didn't continue to the hull of the ship below them; that would've meant his death.

Shanti relaxes a bit, forcing herself to overcome the fear gripping her and taking control of her body. *I cannot stay here. Behrouz needs me!* She goes down to all fours to crawl closer to him.

The power goes out along with the hum of the generators. *We've done it!*

Behrouz manages to turn the power level of his rifle to minimum. The light at the end of the weapon's scope provides enough illumination for Shanti to see where he is. "Any rope up there?"

Shanti crawls to a control panel on the wall that she uses to quell her fears. *I cannot be afraid.* "If you can swing over to me, I can grab you."

"You'll fall! You can't hold me up. I'll take you down with me! What about your fear of heights?"

She smiles at the memory of their little adventure on the pole. "I'm all you got, sergeant! Now get your ass over here!"

He obeys, forcing himself closer to the captain with each swing of his body. She reaches for his hand and takes it just as her grip on the wall slips. *Damn my rubber arms!*

They begin to fall together. The gravity fails. They embrace while tumbling in the weightless environment until they reach a column, which Jafari pushes off of to propel them toward the hatch from where they entered.

Into the main corridor and still in flight from the lack of gravity, he comments with a laugh. "I hope the gravity doesn't come *on* that fast!"

Using the walls for guidance and leverage, they continue quickly down the corridor, this time with the sun shining through the portholes, providing light with which to see.

The ship begins to list, a sign of good things to come.

If they survive.

***

First Captain Cammos has served with different assault teams in his career as a follower. A follower is a citizen of Vorelis who serves the empire. Today he leads Vorelisian Assault Force Three against the Thimms. His pulse picks up quickly as the order comes from the executive officer: “Invade the Thimmi command ship. They are vulnerable.”

From their hiding place behind Earth’s moon, the team flies into harm’s way in a burst of speed that will have them on target in one minute. Cammos puts a reassuring hand on his pilot’s shoulder, secure in the knowledge that he will get them through enemy fire safely, though he’s not completely sure if he is reassuring the pilot or himself with his action.

Warning sounds indicate that a Thimmi destroyer has already targeted them. Countermeasures are activated. “Break off!” Cammos commands urgently. “Bring us around the planet’s south pole. We’ll attack them from the northern side.”

“Right,” is the pilot’s short response as he accelerates even more while agreeing with the course of action. “I trust another minute won’t affect the mission.”

The tight quarters of the small vessel give one of Cammos's men the opportunity to whisper in his ear, "Gives Tolomak more time to destroy another city."

Cammos nods. "We can't help them if we die trying," he whispers back. As the ship approaches the South Pole of Earth, away from the battle temporarily, he looks over the faces of his men. Most have the stoic expressions of those who have made peace with the stars. Two in particular are from the planet Paal. This battle will be of special significance to them. *They will have the chance to enact revenge on their Thimmi counterparts for the decimation of their home world.*

He shouts for them all to hear over the sound of the engines that are firing, pushing the small craft around Earth while the planet's gravity assists. *The sound of superiority.* "Add a little more time! We're going to surprise them from the north without engines!"

The pilot raises an eyebrow as he glances in his first captain's direction. The stealth maneuver Cammos is planning is a typical Vorelisian strategy, one the Thimms know well. They couldn't possibly employ it were the command ship still active, but with the Thimmi ship listing and obviously disabled, the odds favor the invaders.

***

Inside the docking bay of the Thimmi command ship, Dr. Lightner's group has returned to the shuttle. Gravity has also returned, making getting into the small shuttle that much easier. Jen gets to the hatch first and lets Madeline and the doctor in. She stops Captain Folsom as he approaches. He doesn't have to be psychic to know what she is about to ask him. *A blind man could see this one coming from the orbit of Saturn.* "Sir, I'd like to request I be allowed to search for Shanti and Beh—, er, Captain Dae and Sergeant Jafari."

"We're not leaving without them, but we have to secure our location. I need you here," Folsom says like a father giving bad news to his child, news the child will handle with professionalism.

She nods in understanding and lifts her weapon at the sound of boots on metal approaching fast. A Thimmi squad appears at the opposite end of the docking bay and opens fire on the shuttle. Derrick and Jen take cover and return fire.

Derrick catches Jen's concerned look. His earlier order about not holding a weapon for the duration of this mission is revoked when he says, "Rishal wants to live too."

Some of the laser impacts have disabled the shuttle. Lightner learns this fact quickly after the engines fail to start. "We have to find another way off this ship!"

Joining the others outside the shuttle, Charles gives the captain the bad news.

The docking bay is square-shaped with several access points, the one leading to space being the most prominent, as it lies at the center of the bay. A ship would have to go straight down through that hole to exit. A force field covers the hole to keep the air inside.

As the doctor and captain discuss strategy and means of escape, the Thimmi squad is advancing on their position. Jen is picking them off one by one as they do, though they are inching closer with each metal crate they take cover behind.

The battle is going well until a second Thimmi squad enters from another direction, effectively pinning the Earthers down.

Lightner, protecting his wife as best he can, shoves her back into his useless shuttle. *It's only good as cover at this point.*

Matters get worse when a third squad enters behind the first and opens up on the Earthers as well. Folsom and Jen are about to join the Lightners in the shuttle as a means of retreat until Folsom sees Behrouz and Shanti entering the bay from behind the second Thimmi squad and surprising them with bursts of laser fire that force the Thimms into taking cover with the first squad that is nearly depleted.

Using the walls and ships for cover, Behrouz and Dae fight their way to their comrades. Outnumbered and outgunned, Jen is pleased to have the good fortune to die with her friends. *Though that's not the desired course of action.*

Lightner points to the three Galestikon fighters nearby. “If we can get to those fighters, we may have a chance!” he shouts over the noise the laser blasts produce. The shots are so frequent that the metal crate they're covering behind is becoming hot to the touch.

Folsom agrees, but not with confidence. “They look like two-seaters. Can you fly one?”

“I can. We'd have a better chance at survival if we split up.”

“How do you mean?”

“You take my wife. I'll take one of your people—Captain Kong, I guess. The sergeant here is a fast learner. I can talk him through the basics in moments. These Galestikon fighters practically fly themselves.”

Folsom mulls quietly. *Three fighters, three groups. Now if we can just get to them.* “We need some kind of diversion.”

As if granting his wish, First Captain Cammos's assault ship enters the docking bay through the center hole.

Shocked is the understatement of the year as the Thimmi troops redirect their fire at their newest and more familiar enemy. The Vorelisian assault ship is blocking the Earthers from danger. Captain Folsom leads them to the three fighters unopposed.

From the lower gun turret of the Vorelisian assault ship floating over the exit of the docking bay like a harbinger of death, Cammos looks out the small porthole at the retreating Earthers and recognizes Doctor Lightner among them. They make eye contact. Charles points to the fighters and makes an 'X' with his left hand while pointing at the Thimms with his right. Cammos nods, noting the frown on the doctor's face.

The group reaches the first fighter, where they take cover briefly. The Thimms still don't have a direct shot at them and are so concerned with the Vorelisian ship that they aren't paying attention to them anyway. Lightner huddles with the group and apologizes. "I'm sorry for the noise, but we're covered!"

Shanti, puzzled at the statement, cocks her head to one side and asks, "What noise?"

They all look over in time to see the mighty cannon on the Vorelisian ship's lower turret open up with ferocity on the Thimmi troops, cutting them down easily. The troops behind cover that doesn't include a bulkhead have no chance, as the gun is many times more powerful than the rifles the Thimms are using to fight with. It's like going up against a machine gun with a six-shooter, and the machine gun is protected.

Captain Arno Pilas, late to the party but just in time to make a difference, pulls survivors back to the corridor he was surveying the battle from and closes the hatch, trapping the Earthers inside the docking bay for a few minutes at least. The only way out is through the deck; just what he wants. *I can still get Lightner!*

He takes a moment to consider the batteries powering the dim lighting, the artificial gravity, and the force field holding the air inside the ship. He searches for the controls. *I can end this battle myself!*

The Vorelisians stop firing.

First Captain Cammos exits the assault ship via an extended ramp to the deck. The ship itself is still hovering over the hole, ready to depart. Cammos greets Lightner with a handshake. “Doctor, it is a privilege to meet you, sir.”

Folsom, nervously checking his surroundings for new threats, didn’t realize the doctor was so well known. “We don’t have time for pleasantries. Pilas isn’t going to give up so easily,” he says.

Cammos, perhaps overly confident, smiles as he greets the captain. “Our fighters are moving in for the kill. They should be here at any time. We'll have cover when we leave. I don't foresee any problems."

Just then, the force field holding back the vacuum of space fails, causing the air to escape rapidly. They only have a few moments of oxygen remaining, and the temperature is falling faster than a rock off a cliff.

Derrick's remark goes unheard over the din of the rushing air past his ears. "I see a problem now."

Cammos grabs Madeline, who is being pulled toward the hole in the deck, and puts her on the assault ship's ramp. "Get on the ship! Get on the ship! We only have seconds!"

Jafari, already in a fighter, closes the hatch and starts the engines. The small craft resembles a sports car compared to the Vorelisian and Thimmi fighters mixing it up in space. Part of the start-up procedure includes an automatic pressurizing of the cockpit. Feeling safe for the moment, he motions to Shanti to get to the assault ship, as she is closer to it than to him. She reaches out her hand, letting him know that she'd rather leave with him, but relents when Captain Folsom pulls her onto the assault ship's ramp. At the hatch of the Vorelisian craft, she looks back to see her love giving her a thumbs-up and returns it with a smile. *I'll see you on Earth.*

Seeing that his wife is safely on board the assault ship, Dr. Lightner struggles to climb into the second Galestikon fighter's cockpit due to the pressure of the air against him, attempting to pull him toward his doom. The lowering of the oxygen level coupled with the dropping temperature doesn't help matters. He sees Behrouz in the first fighter watching him with deep concern, ready to assist at the first sign the doctor can't make it.

Charles gives Behrouz a wave and points to the assault ship now exiting the docking bay. It drops through the hole in the deck and is gone instantly. Behrouz nods once and follows it just as Charles starts to close the bubble-topped canopy of the Galestikon fighter that resembles the kind found on US Air Force F-16s. It is normally heavy, but with the artificial gravity weakened, it is not a problem. *No time to wait for the fighter to close it for me.*

***

On the bridge of the Thimmi command ship, Tolomak gives the order to abandon ship. It is an order he has never given and is reluctant to now, despite the listing of his pride toward the planet's atmosphere. His crew obeys quickly and without question.

The disciplined crew does not panic in this situation. The escape pods are ejected and captured by the Vorelisian destroyers closing in on the command ship, relieving the fighters of their duty to destroy it. Vorelisians are nothing if not merciful, even to a ruthless enemy. Also, if the command ship is about to self-destruct, the destroyers will fare better than the lesser-shielded fighters.

Tolomak gets a final computer report that all the crew has evacuated but for Pilas in the docking bay. Not willing to go down with the ship to save the foolish captain, he assumes Pilas will make his escape before the ship enters the atmosphere.

The ship shakes violently as it begins to fall apart due to the pull of Earth's gravity and the damage already sustained. Tolomak gets to a private escape pod and ejects away from the ship and planet. Spotting an escaping colony ship, he radios it to pick him up. He manages to get clear of the battle and on his way to Neptune to make his escape before his old friend Xaix can figure out where he went.

***

Unwilling to wait an hour for the docking bay to pressurize, Pilas gets into a space suit and enters through an airlock in time to see Lightner leaving through the hole in the deck. With no air in the bay to impede him and with the help of Earth's gravity, Pilas has no problem getting to the third Galestikon fighter. He manages to power it up and pursue his enemy out of the large ship moments before it burns up in the atmosphere.

CHAPTER EIGHT: The Chase

Pilas flies away from the battle and assumes Lightner will do the same so as not to be mistaken for an enemy. His jammers are on to prevent the Vorelisian doctor from calling for help.

After scanning the area three times, Pilas becomes frustrated. "Where are you!" he cries out maniacally. His heart rate picks up when he finally catches a glint of the sun on metal heading toward the moon. "There you are!" The Thimmi captain laughs as he increases speed to catch up.

***

Upon leaving the Thimmi command ship, Charles turns away from the planet, knowing Pilas will be pursuing him shortly. He looks back at the Vorelisian fighters attacking the command ship at will. Smoke billows from the hull breeches until there is no more air to fuel the fires.

The empty hulk burns up in the atmosphere like a giant meteor. It streaks across the night sky over Japan, and what is left of it crashes harmlessly into the Pacific Ocean.

It takes the Vorelisian doctor a few moments to figure out the communications system. He keeps trying to reach the Vorelisian fleet commander as the fighter sets a course toward the moon at his request. "First Colonel Xaix, come in, please. Vorelisian command, this is Doctor Charles Lightner aboard a Galestikon fighter. Is anyone receiving me?"

Under-Lieutenant Lett responds in her usual professional tone. "Good to hear from you, doctor."

Charles sits back in his seat, finally able to relax. It's nice to see the friendly face of one of his own people. She's Vorelisian, not Pallayian as he is, but the difference is only skin deep. She has a green tint to her complexion compared to his orange.

Charles is about to explain why he is flying a Galestikon fighter when his old friend pops his face into the image projected onto the canopy in front of him. "Charles! It's good to see you again!"

"Andier, thank you. It's good to see you as well. Any word from your assault force? They have my wife aboard."

Andier's grin would give a Cheshire cat a run for its money. "They checked in five minutes ago. They're safe on the planet's surface. Somewhere called San Francisco. Where are you?"

"I'm on my way to—" A buzz sound follows. Lieutenant Lett tries to regain contact but gives up. "Someone is jamming him, sir."

Xaix fumes. "Track the source. I want to know where he is."

At the tactical station, First Captain Sonan has a quick answer. “Sir, it’s a Galestikon jamming signal. It is in motion toward Earth’s moon.”

Xaix returns to his seat as he commands, “Send a squadron to search for and protect Lightner!”

“Yes, sir,” Sonan replies as he contacts one of the squadron leaders nearby.

Executive Officer Quell approaches his superior. “Still no idea on the whereabouts of Tolomak. He most likely went down with his ship.”

Xaix speaks slowly and succinctly. “No. He wouldn’t go down with his ship. I’ll wager he has escaped and is already thinking up a new plan for the annexation of Jexx for the Thimms.”

Under-Lieutenant Lett turns to inquire, “Sir, why would Lightner go to the moon? He’d be much safer to fly to us, wouldn’t he?”

Quell jumps to a scanning station for the answer to that question. In a moment, he has it. “I’m reading negative energy from a ship on the moon that may be responsible for the collapse of the planet’s magnetic field. He must want to take it out himself.”

Xaix turns to Sonan. “Warn our squadron to be aware of that ship and send a destroyer to assist.”

“Yes, sir.”

***

A laser blast has permanently knocked out Lightner’s radio with a ZZZT sound.

Charles looks back to see the third Galestikon fighter turning away and circling around for another pass. *Pilas seems like a good pilot. I’m just a scientist.*

Pilas takes another shot at him, this time missing as Charles picks up speed and zigzags away. In his cockpit, Pilas screams as if Charles can hear him across space. “I should’ve killed you when I had the chance!”

Pilas chastises himself for shooting Lightner’s antennae instead of his engines. He wanted this to be torturous for his adversary, a slow death. *You took the Earth from me! Now you will die!* Pilas is sweating profusely despite the cool temperature inside his cockpit. Flying straight at his zigzagging enemy, he knows he will catch him. *One more minute and you will be mine!*

Over the lunar coordinates of the Thimmi transport, Lightner activates the weapons control system and targets the large craft. He is surprised by both the ferocity and accuracy of the defensive weapons the transport is using against his shields as it opens up on his fighter. *They should hold me for one pass at least*. He wishes this old fighter had a Keral stone, a rare mineral that absorbs energy. The Galestikons have upgraded their modern fighters with them. Some soldiers even put them on their ceremonial swords for added protection in certain missions, thus turning them into useful weapons once again.

Laser blasts strike Lightner's fighter again and again, making targeting difficult but not impossible as he turns to dive straight down at his target. His pirouette maneuver confuses the enemy transport for a moment before it starts firing again, at both his and Pilas's fighters.

"Nice try, but you won't get away from me that easily!" Pilas shouts as he follows his prey into the firestorm of energy. His shields are now being assaulted. Blinded by the light of blasts hitting his canopy, he tries to read his instruments that show his target is fairly close, but altitude information is obscured by the constant flashing. He fires again and again, not knowing for sure if he is even hitting Lightner's fighter or not. Pilas is unaware of the speed at which he is gaining on the Vorelisian doctor, assisted by the gravity of the moon.

Lightner approaches the transport with his six missiles armed. He fires the first two, hoping the transport doesn't target them.

He fires two more as his engines fail from Pilas's laser fire. *This looks like a one-way trip now*, Charles laments.

He fires his last two missiles and secures his space helmet for ejection. *Better to have one shot to live than none at all.* He pulls the ejection handle just as the first two missiles strike the Thimmi transport.

The shooting from the surface stops.

Charles ejects out and back from his fighter before decelerating. Pilas passes him a second later.

Pilas watches Lightner zip past his cockpit window and curses him. "I've got you now, you—" He turns back to look ahead at the explosions occurring in front of him. He activates his reverse thrusters to slow down but it is too late. His turning thrusters are useless at the high speed he is going.

"No! No! No! I cannot lose the Earth! I can't!" he cries out hopelessly just before his fighter slams into the remains of the Thimmi transport, adding one last explosion to finish it off in a mighty fireball.

The Vorelisian squadron arrives a moment later, attracted by the explosion on the lunar surface. They find Lightner floating in space, shaken and broken in places, but alive. The destroyer picks him up.

It is not long before Charles is reunited with his wife and children on Earth.

EPILOGUE: A New Beginning

In the months following the destruction of the Thimmi transport on the moon, the Earth's magnetic field has returned to full strength around the entire planet.

The Vorelisians have remained to assist in the cleanup and rebuilding effort in addition to relocating citizens back to their homes around the world. Part of the cleanup involves the use of purifiers that beam nutrients into the soil while extracting and eliminating radiation.

Charles and his children travel the world with Madeline as she makes speeches in heavily populated regions in order to lay out her plan for the future. During a stop in Japan, Charles's youngest son, Jake, sees a purifier up close as it operates over a farm and recognizes it immediately. "Dad, it's the sun from my dream!"

Jakes brother and sister laugh at hearing this. Shauna remarks, "All this time you thought the sun was burning up the planet when it was just one of these things?"

Charles smiles and takes his son by the hand as they walk along a rural road near Kyoto. *I had a hunch.*

***

In addition to rebuilding the cities destroyed by the sun and the Thimms, the Earthers launch dozens of satellites to rebuild the Internet. Worldwide communication is key to speeding the process of making Earth at least as advanced as it was before the Thimms and Vorelisians arrived.

Upon coding new operating systems to function with the Internet teleporters around the world, a mystery is solved. Corporal Lewis Brandt appears from a holographic door in Moscow. He is confused, to say the least, and hasn't aged since the accident that supposedly cost him his life.

As the Internet regains a footing in society and expands once again, Brandt comes to realize that he has a special ability. He can read the inputs of information from users all over the world. His mind is a server, interconnected with computers everywhere. This frightens him to the point of seeking out the Vorelisians for answers.

The North American government learns of this miracle and seeks ways to use it, including forming a special intelligence team known as the Internetters with the newly promoted Captain Brandt leading the twenty other test subjects who also supposedly died but who are now reappearing.

Dissatisfied with the lack of knowledge the Vorelisians have on the subject of minds being computerized, Lewis accepts the new assignment and considers how best to put this new ability to good use.

***

The news of Brandt's survival and transformation reaches the ears of Colonels Nealand and Garov, now dressed in the baseball jerseys of their favorite teams. They wander the parks of the Cactus League in Arizona as spring training begins. The Grapefruit, Kangaroo, and Mediterranean Leagues are also in full swing. March 21 is fast approaching, and with its arrival, the calendar will be altered to make the first day of spring the first day of the year.

March 21 will become January 1, New Year's Day, year one. The event has been lauded as a major daylight saving day by comedians around the world but is made to mark the most important event in Earth's history: the day when the people announced in one voice, "We are one world, and we are not afraid!"

Garov chooses a game between the Mariners and Giants to tell his friend of his pending retirement. "We have our freedom back. It's about time I start enjoying it," he says.

Nealand asks his friend to reconsider. "I thought of you as commander of the new space station. It will be finished in five years."

Alexei thinks for half an inning before commenting, “I suppose I could come out of retirement at that time.”

Watching the game intently, Nealand only smiles in response.

***

The Galestikons, the enforcers of the Galactic Council’s resolutions, arrive on Earth after learning that the Thimms were in possession of three of their fighters. The leader of the Galestikon delegation, Joran Castor, agrees to allow Earth possession of the last remaining fighter for defensive purposes. He also delivers a gift to the fledgling member of the Galactic Community: a transport that resembles a large ballistic missile submarine. It is called the *Kenma*. It is a long and cylindrical craft intended to get the Earth’s ambassador to the capital of the Milky Way in time for the votes on Earth’s membership and, subsequently, Jexx.

EDF-1, under the command of the newly promoted Lieutenant Colonel Folsom, will escort the ambassador to Galactico under Vorelisian escort whilst in their territory.

The Zetan life form within Derrick’s brain is especially relieved at this news, though it is also afraid. Rishal and Derrick have another conversation in the large meadow where they first met.

"I won't live forever, Derrick. We need to move quickly lest I die before denouncing the Thimms in open session," Rishal says.

"I will get you to Galactico. It looks as though I will be able to keep that promise after all," Folsom says confidently.

Rishal, resembling Alfonzo Furtado this time, hops to the ground from his perch in the elm tree and shakes Derrick's hand. "Thank you."

***

Year two on the new calendar begins with the release of new shackles for the entire population over the age of thirteen.

Madeline, doubling as the governor of the United States of North America, works with her fellow leaders to bring about the beginnings of a new world order, a new collective human society that can and will work together intergalactically and well as locally. The Earth is both united and divided to share what the galaxy has to offer while its people embrace cultural differences among themselves.

To assist in this effort, it is mandated that there will be one currency, the dollar, earned through work and service and spent on luxury items only; one language, English; and one belief in God.

There is peace throughout the world, a world with few borders, but with similar customs and traditions. The people are content—for now.

***

Derrick Folsom's crew is in training with representatives from the planet Gight. Gightian scientists and engineers have come to Earth to teach Folsom's people their respective roles in the mission to come.

Another year of training passes before the Galestikon transport *Kenma* is ready for launch. During that time, the ship has been upgraded with a Soliquid gun for defense and various attachments to assist in gravity manipulation, probing, scanning, and power control.

The ship goes from looking like a sleek submarine to one that looks like it has a severe case of mumps and some serious birthmarks. Its engines are upgraded by the Galestikons themselves to run on dark matter, an abundant source of energy in space that has only recently been tapped into.

Major Kong arrives at the ship looking nervous. She breathes deeply as she greets the crew, including Major Amanda Blassi, who is still leading EDF-2, though her men and women have transferred out and have been replaced with fresh faces and eager minds and hearts that yearn for exploration of the unknown.

Jen arrives on the bridge of the *Kenma* and is relieved to be alone. The ship's electronics and life support systems are running on external power provided by the launch station here at the Washington Spaceport, which was once Andrews Air Force Base. She buries her head in her hands at her console for a moment, thinking of what she has done to get to this point. She brushes herself off mentally and goes to work. She looks forward to her duties as tactical officer and second in command to Folsom.

***

The ambassador's party is the next group to arrive on the *Kenma*. The ambassador is former President Richard Dobson. Pardoned for his acts of treason by Madeline upon starting her second term as first premier, he was selected for this position to appease the millions of supporters he still has. The upside is that he will be off the Earth and out of her hair for a long time.

Dobson claims to have turned over a new leaf while entering a new chapter in his life; surely, he doesn't want to end up committing suicide like McCarthy did. The fewer questions asked, the fewer lies need to be told.

***

Admiral Shan Tolomak has returned to Thimmi space. He and his fleet of ships have been assigned the task of protecting the farthest planets in the empire from nonexistent danger. He considers his exile while pondering ways of obtaining Jexx for the empire, both legally and otherwise. He takes comfort in the fact that he is not being punished for his failures by his leader, but rather, has been put into hiding to prevent the Galactic Council from arresting him.

The Thimms have had sanctions put on them for their actions toward Earth, economic sanctions that will no doubt hurt them in the short term.

The Galactic Council hasn't completed its investigation of the battles between Ti and Vorelis, but since the shooting has stopped and both sides have returned to a peaceful posture, there is apparently no rush to do so.

In a blow to Vorelis's plans for the annexation of Jexx, the council has decreed that Earth will not have a vote on the ownership of the disputed world, whether the young planet is voted into the community or not.

The Vorelisians, however, true to their word to assist Earth after the battle with the Thimms, are living up to their promises.

***

The *Kenma* launches on June 17, Year 3. The transport lifts off from the Washington spaceport, its antigravity generators functioning perfectly. The ship may be an old relic of over a hundred years, but with the modifications, she's like a young lady again.

The ship reaches space in minutes, the crew watching where they are able. The Earth falls beneath them. Home recedes but is never gone.

In its current orbit, the moon is in line with Earth's "tail."

Derrick, sitting in his command chair, orders Master Sergeant Jafari, his helmsman, to use Earth's natural satellite as a guide. The bridge crew is still in full dress uniform after the ceremonies and Madeline's dedication of this great mission of hope that took place prior to the launch. Derrick keeps in mind the discussion he had with Rishal and the one he had with Dr. Lightner just before boarding. *Yes, I have missions to accomplish that are more than just dropping off an ambassador.* He smiles at the challenge ahead and relishes it.

Behrouz activates the wormhole sensor, and a small monitor comes to life on the helm console. It shows waves of energy falling away from the Earth as it moves through space. As the *Kenma* heads toward the moon, the waves of energy come together to form a rift and, eventually, a dark hole appears ahead of the moon. Pulses quicken as the ship gets closer to it.

Shanti reports from her scanning station, "No NEOs in sight, sir," referring to near-Earth objects.

Folsom, strapped into his seat, turns to the newest member of his crew behind him, a Gightian engineer who is taking the spot Alfonzo would have had. He is a civilian whose name is Varos Glinn. "How are the engines doing, Glinn?"

Varos, with his grayish complexion and buzz-cut black hair, looks and feels out of place, though he expects the trust between him and the Earthers to grow with experience. "We can enter the wormhole at any time." His response is in English with a slight English accent, much to the crew's surprise.

"Thank you," Derrick replies and faces front. He watches the wormhole on Behrouz's monitor grow larger as they close in on it. The space outside the main window gives no indication that anything is in front of them but the moon.

The ship begins to buffet a little. Varos attempts to allay their nervousness. "A little turbulence is expected. Once inside, we'll have a short, smooth ride to the planet Seara."

Derrick relaxes, maintaining his composure to help calm his crew. *They're fine.* He turns to Jen, seeing the sadness in her face. She hasn't spoken much since reporting from training. "Are you okay, major?"

Jen forces a brief smile. “Yes, sir,” she says with a nod.

For a moment, Folsom feels as if the ship is indeed on the water as it moves laterally in an undulating motion to enter the wormhole.

To conceal his nervousness, Jafari begins humming “Ride, Captain, Ride.”

After a few moments of increasing turbulence, Shanti joins in. Varos, who doesn’t know the song, remains silent.

Derrick, while watching Jen’s eyes tear up, thinks of saying something to comfort her until she joins in with the lyrics. Her voice cracks just a bit, though she is in no way embarrassed.

End of Volume One.

www.ingramcontent.com/pod-product-compliance
Lightning Source LLC
Chambersburg PA
CBHW020246030726
47499CB00001B/80

* 9 7 8 0 9 9 7 3 2 3 8 0 1 *